continued on next page . . .

MEAN STREAK
Nominated for the Edgar Award

"[Carolyn Wheat] has an extraordinary ear for how people talk. I'm always jealous of the way she can create the sense of a person . . . with a few lines of dialogue."

—Sara Paretsky

"Her knowledge of the court, the law, and the dirty tricks and conspiracies of the ambitious lends enormous flavor to the narrative."

—*Newsday*

"Wheat draws these characters with no-nonsense reality and a lot of heart. She's terrific, too, on the hard-bitten judges, lawyers and court personnel who slave under an imperfect legal system that would turn Bambi into a cynic."

—*New York Post*

FRESH KILLS

"Cass Jameson is back! Carolyn Wheat writes of New York's outer boroughs with the familiarity of an insider . . . *Fresh Kills* is a heartbreaking tale as ancient as the Old Testament and as up-to-date as tomorrow morning's newscast."

—Margaret Maron

"Mounting emotional tension . . . a canny whodunit."

—*Kirkus Reviews*

"She does a remarkably thorough and sensitive job of dealing with the emotionally charged issue of adoption."

—*New York Times Book Review*

Berkley Prime Crime Books by Carolyn Wheat

FRESH KILLS
DEAD MAN'S THOUGHTS
MEAN STREAK
WHERE NOBODY DIES
TROUBLED WATERS
SWORN TO DEFEND

SWORN TO DEFEND

Carolyn Wheat

BERKLEY PRIME CRIME, NEW YORK

for Judy,
sister
cheerleader
safe house
but most of all,
friend

SWORN TO DEFEND

A Berkley Prime Crime Book / published by arrangement with
the author

PRINTING HISTORY
Berkley Prime Crime hardcover edition / August 1998
Berkley Prime Crime edition / August 1999

All rights reserved.
Copyright © 1998 by Carolyn Wheat.
This book may not be reproduced in whole or in part,
by mimeograph of any other means, without permission.
For information address: The Berkley Publishing Group,
a division of Penguin Putnam Inc.,
375 Hudson Street, New York, New York 10014.

The Penguin Putnam Inc. World Wide Web site address is
http://www.penguinputnam.com

ISBN: 0-425-16932-4

Berkley Prime Crime Books are published
by The Berkley Publishing Group,
a division of Penguin Putnam Inc.,
375 Hudson Street, New York, New York 10014.
The Name BERKLEY PRIME CRIME and the BERKLEY PRIME CRIME
design are trademarks belonging to Penguin Putnam Inc.

PRINTED IN THE UNITED STATES OF AMERICA

10 9 8 7 6 5 4 3 2 1

The Reading

❦

"It's not as bad as it looks." Dorinda's voice carried absolutely no conviction, but she said the words with stubborn insistence. I surveyed the three brightly colored pasteboards on the table in front of me. Complex pictures, with heavily religious overtones in spite of their pagan origin. Angels and devils and Death on a black horse, carrying a banner emblazoned with a lush white flower. Even the flower looked sinister, like a deathcap mushroom disguised as an innocent bloom.

"Not so bad?" I looked into the guileless blue eyes of my second-oldest friend. "Hey, I'm no Tarot expert, but even I know the Death card isn't exactly good news."

"It might not mean actual physical death," she pointed out. "It could mean the death of hopes and dreams."

It was a good day for hopes and dreams to die. A dripping-wet September day, with soggy leaves underfoot and huge puddles in the gutters, as if nature itself needed a damned good cry.

Dorinda and I sat in the window table in the Morning Glory, the smells of her hanging baskets of herbs in our nostrils—sweet basil and thyme and rosemary for remembrance and—

"Do you have rue?"

"You mean, do I regret things? Like maybe the Death card stands for regrets?"

"No, I mean up there. In the pots. The herb."

"No. It's not good for cooking. I only cook with them, Cass, I don't use them to cast spells or anything."

I gave my friend a wry smile. Even with her straw-blond hair and her farm girl's build and her cornflower eyes, she looked as much at home with a Tarot deck as any gypsy. I had no doubt at all that if she'd wanted to cast a spell, she could do it. With or without rue.

"The death of hopes and dreams," I repeated in a slow, sleepy voice. On a day like this, even a double espresso didn't necessarily produce actual wakefulness.

"That makes me feel so much better." I touched the Death card, pulling it ever so slightly toward me. Trying, I suppose, to control it. "I get to live, but my hopes and dreams don't. Could be worse, I guess."

Actually, the reading couldn't have been much worse. First, the Lovers—a card I firmly denied had any relevance to my life after Matt Riordan. Then the Devil—a card I was all too familiar with, since it probably represented my entire criminal clientele. And now Death. What next?

The fourth card was the Tower Struck by Lightning.

"Oh, good. Now I know how I'm going to die. I'm going to fall out of a tower during a thunderstorm. I'm glad that's settled. I'll just stay out of skyscrapers the minute it starts to rain."

"It's a powerful card," Dorinda said in a thoughtful tone, as if the card were a pure abstraction, with no impact upon the life of someone she professed to love. "In fact, the combination of Death and the Tower really sends a message."

"Message received," I replied. "Now tell me what I have to do to prevent the message from coming true. I don't want to be struck by lightning, and I don't care whether we're talking real or metaphoric bolts from the blue. All I want is a quiet life."

"A quiet life." She raised her eyes to her painted tin ceiling. Artist friends had recently retouched it, adding shades of mauve and lavender to the embossed design. "I've known you how many years?"

We both gave the question some thought and said at the same time: "Twenty-six."

Twenty-six *years*? Twenty-six years since I first walked across the quad at Kent State with a long-haired hippie chick from the Upper Peninsula of Michigan? She was trying to interest me in a new coffeehouse downtown, with improvised autoharp music and bad poetry; I countered by inviting her to protest ROTC on campus. We took one another up on our respective invitations—once. Then I left her to the flower children and she left the protests to me. But we continued to be friends.

"I have never," she pronounced, now completely into Oracle Mode, "known you to have the slightest interest in a quiet life. Why start now? The Cassie J. I know and love would say, 'Hey, a tower struck by lightning. Fantastic. When?' "

"In old age begins wisdom. Start the lightning without me. And turn the next card before this reading gets any more terrifying."

But the last card was the most terrifying of all.

It was Justice.

And sometimes Justice is the worst thing that can happen.

CHAPTER ONE

Innocence is a bitch. Innocent clients haunt you till the day you die. No matter that you've done your best; your guy's serving time for something he didn't do, and it's all your fault. If you were half the lawyer you think you are, you'd have convinced the jury to let him go.

Fortunately, I hadn't had all that many innocent clients in the course of my practice.

Keith Jernigan was one of them.

I was on my way to the Appellate Division to argue for his freedom, scuffing my feet in golden-brown sycamore leaves and gazing at the pure blue sky through feathery Japanese maple leaves against neat brick town houses. It was a perfect fall day, crisp and bright as a fresh-picked apple, but I didn't care about the play of sunlight on the brownstones or the bronze chrysanthemums in ornate planters next to intricate wrought-iron gates. All I cared about was whether I could convince a majority of the appellate judges that a gross miscarriage of justice had taken place.

Because if I couldn't—

Because if I couldn't, a guy who called me the Trojan princess, who sent me letters with my first name spelled out in Greek, who sent me cards at Christmas and on my birthday, who had the sharpest wit and the sweetest smile I'd ever seen, a guy who had absolutely completely totally not committed the crime for which he was serving time—that guy was going to rot in jail for seven more years and I'd lose whatever tiny shred of faith I had left in the criminal justice system.

But that thought didn't bear thinking. I couldn't lose this case. I just couldn't.

I heard Kate's voice before I saw her. I lifted my eyes from the fallen leaves to see a large, solidly built woman walking toward me, a smile softening her strong features.

" 'Oh, there once was a union maid,' " she sang, her deep voice booming the words all over Henry Street. She wore a trenchcoat with a teal-and-rust scarf around her throat, slacks, and comfortable shoes.

I took up the next line of the song, " 'who never was afraid.' " My voice was an octave higher than hers; we both struggled through the next words of the song. It had been a while since we'd sung it.

We belted out the chorus together: " 'Oh, you can't scare me, I'm sticking to the union. I'm sticking to the union, till the day I die.' "

Kate Avelard and I had met during a Legal Aid strike. New York's Legal Aid Society, essentially the biggest law firm in the world, was a union shop. We'd voted to strike twice in my time; our slogan the second time out was "Manhattan talks, Brooklyn walks." And walk we did; I must have covered twenty miles a day just marching in front of the Brooklyn courthouses, a huge hand-lettered cardboard sign around my neck.

But we hadn't stuck to the union; we hadn't stayed with Legal Aid. We'd both left to form our own private practices. I still specialized in criminal law, while Kate had become one of the leading divorce experts in Brooklyn Heights, where spouses were inclined to fight to the death for the right to stay in the brownstone both had renovated with a great deal of sweat and tears.

"Kate," I said, letting myself be swept into her embrace and giving her the almost-kiss of two women who had once been close and were now something more than acquaintances but less than friends. "How are you doing?"

As I headed toward the close of my first half-century, this was no longer a rhetorical question. It meant various things, from "Did they find a lump?" to "Have you scheduled your hip replacement yet?" to "You mean Benjamin didn't get into Yale?" In this case, it meant "Are you getting through the day without Marc? Is it possible to lose a husband like him to a horrible disease and still find life remotely worth living?"

"I'm okay," she said shortly. "So are the kids, believe it or not. Zachary just started middle school at St. Ann's and Hilary's on the honor roll at Packer. If it weren't for my goddamn clients," she went on with a bitterness I hadn't heard from her even in the darkest days of Marc's illness, "I'd be fine."

"Been there, done that," I said, trying to keep it light. "I'm on my way to AD2 even as we speak." I didn't bother keeping the brag out of my tone.

"The Appellate Division?" She raised an eloquent eyebrow. "Does that mean you're going respectable? Cass Jameson, fighter for truth and justice, putting on a three-piece suit and groveling before the madams?"

The reference was to legendary Legal Aid lawyer Martin Erdmann, who once said in *Life* magazine that appeals judges were nothing more than whores who had become madams.

"So," Kate went on, in what struck me as a forced version of her old blunt humor, "are you on a winner or a loser?"

"I have to win," I said. "My client is innocent."

"You have my sympathy," Kate replied with a wry twist of her mouth. "So is this your first appeal, or what?"

"It is not," I replied indignantly.

Kate knew me too well. The humor lines around her generous mouth twitched as she put her next question to the witness: "Is it your third?"

"Well, no, now that you mention it. I did one appeal in a previous life, when I was pissed as hell at Judge Anselm for the way he treated me during the trial. My client ran out of money the minute the handcuffs clicked on his wrist, so I did it for free. And lost it for free."

"But did it make you feel better?"

"Hell, no. The appellate judges gave me a hard time for saying bad things about their old pal Noah Anselm and affirmed without opinion." Enough years had passed that I could smile as I told the rest of the story. "And then my ungrateful bastard of a client proceeded to bring a pro se writ of habeas corpus on the grounds that his appellate lawyer was not only incompetent but sleeping with the prosecution. To this day that turkey owes me five hundred bucks for the transcript I had made for him."

"Yeah," Kate said with a sympathetic shake of her head, "this would be a great job if it weren't for the clients." It was an old Legal Aid mantra, and I gave it the perfunctory smile she seemed to expect.

I was about to go into the obligatory we-must-have-lunch noises when Kate grabbed my arm with a grip so tight it hurt.

"Speaking of crazy clients," she began in a tone that tried for lightness and sounded frantic instead, "There's this ex-wife I represented who thinks I'm responsible for her husband's being a vindictive bastard. She thinks I should have been able to get her a fortune even though she signed away her rights in a prenup you couldn't break with a blowtorch. She's filed a complaint against me with the disciplinary committee."

"Gee, that's—" I had to run. I had to get to court. But this wasn't the kind of thing you could blow off; a lawyer's entire right to practice was governed by the disciplinary committee of the state bar. No wonder Kate seemed agitated.

Her grip grew even tighter and she closed her eyes. "Those last few months with Marc were just so hard," she said in a low voice. "He couldn't sleep. He couldn't move. He couldn't talk. It was really important to him that I sit with him for as long as I could every night. But that meant I was running on two, three hours' sleep. I made a few mistakes."

Words were beyond inadequate, but I made a stab at it anyway. "It sounds horrible."

The scene was all too easy to picture. The back parlor of Kate and Marc's very Victorian house on Willow Place; Marc lying on the overstuffed chaise longue they'd bought on Atlantic Avenue. He'd been one of the most passionate and articulate lawyers I'd ever seen work a courtroom, pacing back and forth on long, restless legs as he challenged the jury to do the right thing. By the end, he lay on that couch day and night, unable to move or form words or eat more than baby food. His mind was still active, but none of his muscles would obey his brain's commands. He was like a log, stiff and unmoving. A log with eyes; a log who could dream.

"So maybe I didn't do as much hand-holding as I usually do with my divorce clients," Kate went on. "Maybe I didn't answer every phone call or explain every clause in the settlement agreement. Maybe I sent my associate to court on my behalf once too often. But I swear to God, Cass, I did not neglect a legal matter to the point where I deserve to be disbarred."

A cold chill traveled down my back. "It's that serious?"

She nodded and let go of my arm. The blood rushed back

in, causing a tingling sensation. "The hearing is next week. Do you think you could—that is, I need—could you come in and say a few words for me?"

"Of course," I answered warmly. I gave her a hug. "I'll do whatever I can."

Which wasn't much. Kate and I had lunch maybe four times a year, went to the occasional play or movie together, and saw one another at the rare Women's Bar Association meetings we both chose to attend. What concrete evidence I could give regarding her competence as a lawyer would take all of five minutes and do her very little good. That she had asked me at all spoke to her desperation.

As I said my belated good-bye, I reflected on the terrible turn Kate's seemingly charmed life had taken. First Marc, now this. What would she do if the committee barred her from the practice of law? How would she support herself and her children?

I banished the thought from my mind; I had enough to worry about. And I was worried; I hastened my steps toward the courthouse, dashing across the street just in time to beat a car racing toward the corner. I was a bundle of nerves by the time I reached Pierrepont Street.

That alone was exciting. When was the last time I'd been nervous about a court appearance? Even a full-blown criminal trial no longer had the power to knot my stomach. I might lose sleep working on the summation, but it wasn't sheer fear that kept me awake, the way it had the first fifty times I'd stood before a jury.

But this would be different. This wasn't a street fight disguised as a legal proceeding. This was an argument in which differing interpretations of law would be presented.

If the Appellate Division, First Department, courthouse in Manhattan, where I'd taken my oath as a lawyer, was a Gothic cathedral of the law, then the Second Department was a Protestant meetinghouse. Its austere lines and jewel-box proportions were in sharp contrast to the ornate, overblown style of its Manhattan counterpart, with its stained-glass dome and overpowering wood-and-brass ornamentation. This courthouse was equally dignified, but without the florid Gilded Age excess. The cloakroom didn't boast long brass pegs on which nineteenth-century lawyers once placed their beaver hats while addressing the court.

You walked in through tall brass doors, into a lobby bounded by four black marble columns. They flanked twin entrances, one to the clerk's office and the other to the single courtroom. Straight ahead was the lawyers' waiting room, carpeted in crimson, with long polished tables of dark wood and wine-colored leather chairs. It was like a men's club, with pictures of long-dead judges on the wall in place of hunting prints.

I announced myself and my case to the clerk at the lobby desk. I tried to keep the pride out of my voice, but there was something about arguing an appeal that made me feel truly lawyerly. The courthouse itself was so clean, so quiet, so unlike the criminal court where I spent so much of my time. The appellate process was so far above the dirt and grime and sorrow of my usual work in the bowels of the criminal justice system. Like that "Star Trek" episode where some people lived in the clouds and the rest worked the mines underneath the surface of the planet.

How had I gotten stuck in the mines when the clouds were only as far away as Monroe Place?

The clerk announced that the judges were taking the bench. My heart leapt, and I had to reassure myself that I was more than ready for action. Only the action wasn't ready for me. The judges took their time in coming out and there were five arguments ahead of mine. I tried my best to listen, figuring I could learn something, but my mind wouldn't stay focused. How could I listen to a civil case about a subcontractor in a cement deal when I had to marshal my thoughts about Keith Jernigan?

If it please the court, I would begin, *this is an appeal from a conviction of the Supreme Court, Kings County—*

Did it have to be that wordy? What if I forgot to say Kings County? Should I say *a conviction for robbery in the first degree* then or later? What had the Legal Aid lawyer standing before the bench just said in her opening?

My palms were wet. Not damp. Wet. And it wasn't hot, either outside or in. This I knew from the fact that my feet were cold.

If only Keith were guilty.

If he'd really committed the crime, this would all be an intellectual exercise, a game with no downside to losing. But it wasn't. It was Keith's life. He either walked free or did seven more years for a crime I was totally convinced he hadn't—

I couldn't let myself think about that. Not and do the job I'd come to do.

Back to the issues. *This conviction should be reversed for three reasons: one—*

No. *This conviction* must *be reversed.* Much stronger.

The Legal Aid lawyer who'd been arguing sat down, smoothing her skirt and perching on the chair like a cat. The district attorney, a pale young man in a brown corduroy jacket, stood and poured himself a glass of water.

Rule Number One of appellate argument: never drink the water.

The D.A. had one eye on the presiding judge and the other on his shoes. Which left no eye for the pitcher or the glass. The water missed the glass by two inches; the poor guy was pouring water directly onto the floor. When it splashed his pants leg, he jumped. The pitcher dropped from his hand and hit the carpet. Water was everywhere. He turned red. He mumbled. He dropped to his knees as if he could mop up the spill with his bare hands.

Then he keeled over. He'd been kneeling and he just went

over, stiff as a dead dog, his face landing in the wet spot next to the pitcher.

Heart attack? I wasn't the only one with my own heart in my mouth. All the lawyers rose and craned their necks. The court officers ran to the guy and turned him over. One loosened a tie. The other picked up the pitcher. A third opened the D.A.'s mouth.

"He just fainted, Your Honor," one of the officers called to the presiding judge.

"Then get him out of here. Let's get on with the docket." Louis Hochheiser waved his hand as if to spirit the hapless D.A. into another world. The court officers helped the man to his feet and walked him outside.

I sat back and let out a long breath. What if that happened to me? What if I got up to the bench and forgot every word I was going to say? What if my eyes rolled up in my head and I hit the ground in a dead faint?

I'd have to leave town and change my name.

Too much money for new stationery. I squared my shoulders and reminded myself I'd been in practice for as long as I'd been an adult. I'd faced hundreds of lower court judges, and appellate judges were, as Kate had reminded me, members of the oldest profession.

I pictured Presiding Justice Lieberman in a low-cut dress, sitting in a red-wallpapered parlor, honky-tonk music playing in the background. Oddly enough, it helped. By the time the clerk called "People of the State of New York versus Jernigan," I was calm.

You have to own the courthouse. Words of wisdom from my first Legal Aid mentor. I hadn't thought about Nathan for a long time. I owed him a lot. He'd died a long time ago, but he was still with me in so many ways.

I stepped up to the appellant's table and laid out my file, taking my time. I owned the courthouse. I, not the men and women on the high bench, set the pace. I stepped to the podium, adjusted the microphone to my height, and said the opening words I'd rehearsed a hundred times. My voice sounded too loud in my ears; I wasn't used to a microphone. I backed up an inch and continued telling the court why I was here, why the conviction of Keith Jernigan had to be reversed.

Madigan and Rizzo looked bored. Bored is not good in a judge. Neither is impatience, which was what emanated like a malevolent aura from Hochheiser and Lieberman. Only Doolan gave me the minimal attention basic politeness called for.

I raised my chin and looked straight into his twinkly blue eyes. The eyes of an Irish charmer. The eyes of a loving uncle. The eyes of a man who hated me and my client and everyone on the planet like us. If I managed to get him on our side, I'd win. If I didn't—well, there were still four others to work on. But it didn't hurt to go for the hardest nut first.

"Your Honor, my client was wrongly convicted of robbery in the first degree because the identification procedure to which he was subjected was fatally flawed."

Presiding Justice Aaron Lieberman woke from what had seemed a trance and leaned into his microphone. "We *can* read, Counselor. Please don't quote your own brief."

Blood rushed to my face. Did Lieberman think I was talking like that because I wanted to? I figured that was the way you were supposed to address the appellate court. You were supposed to sound formal and stiff and bloodless.

Well, hell, if he wanted me to be myself—

"Keith Jernigan served two years and five months in prison for something he didn't do." I stopped and raked the bench with my eyes.

"Yes, a jury found him guilty," I went on, answering what I'd expected would be the first objection. "And, yes, three witnesses identified a photograph and then picked him out of a lineup. But the photo array was completely tainted by the arresting officer's showing the photographs to the witnesses at the same time, instead of separately. He should have—"

"Counselor," Justice Hochheiser cut in, his old man's voice a weak instrument, "even if the photo array was less fair than it should have been, didn't the subsequent lineup serve to purge the taint?"

Judges get to interrupt. That's one of the basic rules of appellate argument. The lawyer is there to answer questions. In fact, to be a successful advocate, you have to love the questions. You have to embrace them as an opportunity, not view them as an interruption.

So I embraced the question. "Far from it, Your Honor," I replied. "In fact, one of the witnesses actually admitted on the stand that he picked my client out of the lineup not because he actually recalled him from the incident, but because he'd seen my client's photograph."

I tapped my forefinger on the podium for emphasis and the microphone magnified the sound so that it resembled a galloping horse on an old radio show. I clasped my hands behind my back to keep them from touching anything else, and plowed ahead.

"This is what happened with all the witnesses, Your Honor. They picked Keith Jernigan out of the lineup because he was the only one whose face they were familiar with, and they were familiar with it because his was the only photo Officer Bentley showed them."

"Counselor, are you accusing this officer of framing your client?"

Deep breath time. Because the appellate judges weren't there to make new findings of fact, and this question was designed to pull me into a discussion of fact instead of law. If I let them do that, they had the perfect out as far as reversing Keith's conviction was concerned: the jury heard the facts, the jury decided the case, and they weren't going to interfere with that.

"No, Your Honor," I said. "I am not speculating as to how

the photo ended up being shown to the witnesses. All I'm saying is that the showing tainted identification procedures and resulted in my client's conviction for a crime he did not commit."

There were two little button-lights on the podium. The first one, the white light, went on at the two-minute warning mark. I'd missed that light completely; now the red one lit up. It was over. My time was up. I'd said everything I'd be allowed to say.

I hoped to God it would be enough.

I sat down, my knees shaking and my body bathed in sweat. I felt as if I'd run five miles and then been doused with a bucketful of ice-cold water.

Water. I picked up the pitcher and poured some into the paper cup on the table. My hand shook; the water spilled on the shiny surface. I was only half- listening to the D.A.'s argument. I felt faint; if I didn't get some water, I might fold up.

I lifted the cup. Some joker had punched holes in the bottom with a pencil. Water streamed out of the holes as if from a fountain, splashing on my skirt. I put it down and smiled weakly at the bench.

I had violated the first rule of appellate argument; I'd tried to drink the water.

CHAPTER
TWO

I was wet from head to toe, wearing a shroud of clammy sweat and water from the leaky glass.

Why call it a glass when it was made of waxed cardboard?

And why think about cardboard glasses when the district attorney was trying to convince the judges to let Keith rot in jail?

Mainly because there was nothing I could do about it. I had no right to rebut the D.A.'s argument, and I knew what he was saying based on the brief he'd submitted. According to him, the identification procedure was perfectly fine, and even if it wasn't, no defendant was entitled to a perfect trial, just a fair one.

I tuned in to the fact that Lieberman was hammering the guy, hitting him hard on the issue of the single photograph.

Hope leapt in my breast. Was there a chance I hadn't

blown it with what I was sure the judges would see as an emotional rather than a legal argument?

When it was over, the D.A. picked up his file and I followed suit, making my way on wobbly legs down the long aisle to the doors in the rear of the courtroom. I felt wired to the gills and exhausted at the same time; I had a quick fantasy of going into the men's club lawyers' room and sacking out on one of the red leather couches.

Outside, the long low light of late afternoon filtered through the autumn leaves, creating a scene any painter would have loved. The Gothic church across the street added a sinister note, an Edgar Allan Poe heaviness to the Brooklyn Heights street scene. The cold wind went through my light jacket; my sweat-soaked clothes felt like an icy blanket as I walked the mile or so to the brownstone that contained my office and my home.

A yellow cab pulled up in front of the building just as I reached the corner. Nellis Cartwright stepped out and paid the driver. She started up the stairs, but stopped and waved when she saw me.

She was a new divorcée, subletting the apartment above mine. Dorinda's restaurant, the Morning Glory, occupied the ground floor, my office spanned the parlor floor, I lived on the third, and rented out the fourth. My prime tenant, Jerry Laboda, who taught at Brooklyn Law School, was doing a stint as a visiting professor in Indiana. So for the balance of the term, he'd sublet to this woman, who'd moved in three weeks earlier.

"Cass," she said, drawing out the name as if to add warmth to the single syllable. She was tall and slender with short platinum hair cut in an asymmetric style that only a truly beautiful face could carry off. I felt unusually clumsy and drab whenever I caught a glimpse of her.

"Can I buy you a cup of coffee?" She even stood like a model, leaning on one hip with the other leg thrust forward in a stance that should have looked artificial but somehow worked for her. She was a moving sculpture instead of a flesh-and-blood woman, and the long, smoke-gray Donna Karan dress emphasized her angles.

"Can you ever," I replied. "I have never in my life stood more in need of the healing brew than I do at this moment." I pushed sopping wet hair off my brow and tried not to feel envious of her impeccable grooming; I suspected that blond, slender Nellis had never broken a sweat in her life.

"If I know Dorinda," I said, gesturing toward the Morning Glory, "she's got a cup with my name on it ready and waiting."

This was the literal truth, although the cup said CASSIE, since Cassandra isn't a name you can always find on coffee mugs.

"Actually," Nellis said, dropping her eyes in a shy gesture I recognized at once as the sign of an acquaintance about to become a client, "there's something I need to talk to you about. Do you think we could take the coffee upstairs to your office?"

A private practitioner never turns down the chance to acquire a new client. A lawyer whose entire income depends upon what she can earn by the sweat of her own brow is always ready to listen, always open to new business.

But I was tired and drained and hyper and preoccupied with Keith Jernigan and it was late and I was in no mood to start a new case.

"Listen," I said, "ordinarily I'd say yes, but it's been a long day. Do you think you could make an appointment and see me during office—"

"Oh, God, yes, of course, I didn't think." She turned away, her face flaming. "I'll go up and see your secretary right—" Nervous fingers twisted the ring on her left hand.

A wedding ring. A divorcée still wearing her wedding ring.

I sighed. Only one thing, in my considerable experience, had the power to transform a poised, mature woman like

Nellis Cartwright into a basket case of self-conscious embarrassment.

I was willing to lay odds that her ex-husband had been emotionally if not physically abusive.

"Hey, no problem," I said with forced cheerfulness. "I'll get that coffee from Dorinda and be right up. You can tell Marvella—that's my secretary—that we have an appointment. Do you want plain or flavored?"

It took a good three minutes to convince her I was sincere. She finally agreed to decaf but insisted on waiting for me instead of going inside by herself.

Dorinda wanted a blow-by-blow account of the oral argument, but I said it would have to wait and took two cups of coffee upstairs.

My waiting room reflects my interest in photography. Posters from museum shows mingle with old political posters; a Louis Hines black-and-white shot of an immigrant boy in a cap three sizes too large is next to Shirley Chisolm's Unbought and Unbossed poster from her presidential campaign. My Mailer-for-mayor poster faces the newest addition: press photogs with huge bulky flash cameras and oversized press passes in the bands of their jaunty fedoras.

And then there were one or two little things of my own. Pictures of which I was inordinately proud, even if they did look amateurish next to the masters.

As we stepped into the waiting room, Nellis pointed to a photograph I'd had mounted on wallboard. It showed a little girl swinging in the park; the swing chain had become a blur, as had her outstretched, sneakered feet, but her bright eyes in her dark face grabbed the camera and wouldn't let go. I'd liked the picture a lot, and decided it cheered the place up to see a happy child on the wall.

"Did you take this?" She walked over to it and stood before it in her model-stance.

"Yes. I'm something of an amateur photographer."

"Me too," she said. Then she looked at the carpeted floor and murmured, "Only I guess I'm not exactly an amateur."

"I'd like to see your work," I said, and meant it. For one thing, I love photographs, and for another, it might help relax this tightly strung woman to talk about something other than her unhappy marriage before getting down to business.

"I have a few things upstairs if you'd like to see them sometime." Her voice was soft, tentative. As if there was a possibility I might decline, might decide seeing her photographs wasn't worth the climb up one set of stairs.

"How's now?" I handed her the decaf, still with the cover on the Styrofoam cup. "We can talk just as well in your apartment as we can here."

Her smile wiped the tentative look from her face. She visibly relaxed, as if my ready acceptance of her offer dissolved a great fear. We climbed the stairs to the top floor apartment in silence.

The place looked about the same as it did when Jerry Laboda occupied it. He'd left his mismatched furniture and oversized stereo, but he'd taken his books with him to Indiana. The main difference was the wall space. Nellis had taken down Jerry's Miró and Kandinsky prints and replaced them with her own framed photographs.

The first one hit me between the eyes. A skull. A skull hidden behind a model's face. The skull beneath the skin. The face was perfectly made-up, vacant, a doll's face. Only upon closer inspection could the shadows be seen as hollow spaces where the eyes used to be. Only at a certain angle did the sharply curved lips cover skeleton teeth.

It hit me then. What she meant by saying she wasn't exactly an amateur.

"Oh, my God. I saw your show at the Witkin." The Witkin Gallery was the most prestigious photography gallery in New York City, which made it the best in the world.

I clapped my hand to my mouth. "I can't believe this. I really loved your stuff. You want to know the truth, I had a pretty bad case of photo envy for a while. I kept thinking, Why am I even bothering to take pictures anymore? I'll never do anything that good."

She didn't simper. She didn't even say thank you. She frowned a little and asked, "You don't think it owes too much to Jerry Uelsmann?"

I laughed. "The mark of a true artist. Never think your work is good enough. There's always room for criticism."

"Yes, but you haven't answered the question."

"Well, he does double exposure too, so I guess there's a connection. But you added color to some of yours, which he never does. You also pushed the envelope of the grotesque. I liked that clown series a lot. Nothing more sinister than a clown."

Now she inclined her head in a gracious gesture and said, "Thank you. It means a lot when people who know what they're talking about like my work."

People who know what they're talking about. Nellis Cartwright had just called me "people who know what they're talking about." I felt a hot rush of pleasure and pride.

"You really like double exposure."

"Yes. I've been experimenting with multiple exposures. Sometimes double, sometimes triple."

"How do you do a triple exposure?" My eyes traveled back to the skull-face. I wondered if the model had seen the finished image. If she had, she'd never view her profession the same way again; she'd always be aware that her beauty masked the bony truth of death.

One more layer, one more detail, emerged upon that closer look. Out of one of the hollow eyes, a snake's head peered with beady eyes.

Creepy. Seriously creepy.

"You double-expose in the camera," she explained, the tiny smile at the corner of her mouth telling me she'd noticed that I'd noticed. "That gives you a double image on the negative. Then you expose a different negative on the paper, and before you print it, you expose the double negative over that. Triple exposure."

Now I turned toward her. "That must take an enormous amount of control. Preplanning. It doesn't just happen by accident."

She smiled, revealing tiny, perfect teeth like grains of rice. "It did the first time," she admitted. "But I found the result so provocative that I decided to play with it a little bit."

She pointed to a photo on the other side of the room, above one of Jerry's giant speakers. I walked toward it, seeing only a marvelously intricate tree, all twisted and misshapen, the grain revealed by a bleaching wind. As I grew closer, I saw the naked female body in the tree's trunk. What had seemed to be a knot was a breast; what had appeared to be a knothole was the woman's vagina. Her arms were outstretched, merged with bare branches.

It was a disturbing image. Was the woman one with the tree, a wood nymph dancing in the wind, her arm-branches swaying in ecstasy? Or was she trapped inside the wood, screaming for release?

Then I reached the photo itself. The woman's hair was on fire. Flames peered from the tangled branches, rising upward from the woman's forehead, mingling with the long wavy hair that billowed upward into the tree.

Now the truth was clear. Her undulating body was not writhing with pleasure, but with pain. Or did ecstasy and agony coexist, two sides of the same coin?

The tree and the woman were in black-and-white, printed on soft, almost sepia-toned paper, but the fire was almost yellow, almost in color.

"It's a platinum print," Nellis said. "On handmade Japanese paper. And the flames are hand-colored."

"What do you call it?"

"I don't know yet. Maybe something neutral, like *Tree: Number Four.*"

"I always liked those surrealist names. You know, the ones that have nothing to do with the picture itself. The ones that raise more questions than they answer."

"I haven't shown it yet. Maybe I never will."

"Too personal?"

"Too self-indulgent. Work should be more disciplined. Less—oh, I don't know." Nellis ran her hands through her white-blond hair. "Less embarrassing, I suppose. I can just imagine what the critics would say if they saw this."

"You shouldn't worry about critics. Just do what—"

"That's easy for you to say." Her tentative tone was gone; she was shrill in her indignant protest. "You don't know what it's like to pour your whole soul into your work and have someone come along and dismiss it with a few patronizing words. And don't tell me that doesn't matter, because it does. It means the next gallery isn't going to be as welcoming. It means the next time I apply for a grant, I might not get it. It means I can't support myself without taking some other job that takes me away from my work. So don't tell me to forget about the critics. They're the people who make the difference between my being a working photographer and a—"

"Look, I'm sorry." I raised my hands in a gesture of concession. "You're right. I don't know anything about being a professional artist. It was the kind of cliché people say all the time, and I just didn't think."

"Oh, God, I can't believe I lashed out at you like that." Her lower lip trembled. She raised a shaking hand to her mouth and covered her lips. She drew a ragged breath and said, "God, I can't believe what's happening to me. I'm so on edge all the time. So crazy."

"That didn't sound crazy. It sounded like perfect sense. I just didn't understand." It seemed vital to reassure this fragile woman, who was so easily convinced she'd done something wrong.

"What did you want to talk to me about?" I asked, although I had a pretty good idea of what was coming. "I warn you, I know nothing about copyrights or gallery contracts."

"It's about my divorce."

Her words confirmed my suspicions. A divorcée taking the first, few, tentative steps toward a separate life outside the marriage. Living in a student-style sublet until she was able to establish herself. Still fragile and uncertain of her own creative abilities after years of put-downs by a supposedly loving spouse.

I'd seen it all before.

I'd seen it, but I'd done my level best not to represent it. In the past, I'd have slipped Nellis Cartwright one of Kate Avelard's business cards.

After talking to Kate in the Heights, that no longer seemed like a good idea.

"Give me a general idea," I said. I pulled out one of the director's chair barstools and sat down.

She took the other one, but she perched instead of sitting. As if she couldn't let herself relax even in this space she considered home. "First of all, you have to know who my husband is. Was."

Something vague tickled the corner of my brain. I did know who Nellis Cartwright of the Witkin Gallery had been married to; I just couldn't—

"Grant Eddington." She said the name as though it alone would tell me everything I needed to know.

And it did.

Grant Eddington was a critic. No—Grant Eddington was *the* critic. The one whose thumb up or down meant that multi-million-dollar musicals either ran for five years or closed in five days. The one whose scathing reviews sent seasoned actors running back to Hollywood in tears. The one who'd stated in print that his wife's artistic ambitions were as pathetic as Zelda Fitzgerald's.

No wonder Nellis didn't take praise easily. She wasn't used to it.

"You know how he is," the cool blond said. "He either loves or hates—and he's so much better at hating."

"So when he decided the marriage was over, it was over with a capital—"

"Oh, yes. I came home one afternoon and found a note asking me to move out by midnight. And when I tried to talk about it, he refused and said if I wasn't gone by then, I'd lose the right to any possible settlement."

Her perfect lips curled. "When I tried to pay for my room at the Plaza with a credit card, I found that none of them worked anymore. Grant made a preemptive strike against all our assets, leaving me with nothing. I had to go to court every month to beg for enough to live on. I—" Her voice choked. She raised a shaking hand to her mouth and said, "Oh, God, I'm sorry. I'll try to pull myself—"

"Hey, don't worry about it. But I have to ask—if the divorce is final, what do you think a lawyer can do for you at this stage?"

"He screwed me out of what I should have had," Nellis said, her tone hardening like nail polish. It hadn't occurred to me that a woman who knew how to apply lip-liner could also swear.

"But you did agree to some kind of settlement, right? I mean, this divorce is a done deal, not something that's still pending in court, right?"

She nodded. "But now I find out all kinds of things I didn't know before. He's got money he kept hidden from me."

"So you're alleging fraud?"

"I guess so," she said, the uncertainty returning to her tone.

"It's a long shot," I said. "You have to understand that courts don't like overturning decrees they've already made.

But," I went on, "I could at least read the settlement decree, talk to an accountant, check the figures. Then we could talk some more about maybe reopening the settlement—if it looks as though you have a case."

Her thanks were far more profuse than my actual commitment warranted.

I took my leave and went back down to the Morning Glory.

"What I need," I said, slipping into the stool nearest the old-fashioned cash register, "is a forensic accountant."

"What you need," Dorinda said with her maddening cheerfulness, "is a nice glass of chilled tamarind juice." She pushed burnt-orange liquid at me. I gave it a tentative sip, grimaced at the sour taste, and put my coffee mug on the counter for a refill.

"Spider," she said firmly.

"Where?" I jumped off the stool and looked around, then remembered.

"You mean your new boyfriend Spider?" I was annoyed at myself for overreacting and convinced that this time Dorinda had gone around the bend. "I said I needed an accountant, not a musician."

"You're in luck, Cass. He's both." She pushed keys on the cash register and the door flew open with a clang. She reached into the drawer, lifting the heavy money clip, and fished out a card, which she handed across the counter.

It was plain white pasteboard and proclaimed in dark, raised letters: SPIDER TANNENBAUM, BLUES ACCOUNTANT.

"You *are* kidding. I mean, this can't be—"

"He's an accountant by day and a bluesman at night."

"Then I'd better call him during the day."

Card One: The Lovers

❧

NELLIS CARTWRIGHT STEPPED DAINTILY INTO THE STREET AND RAISED TWO IMPERIOUS FINGERS. THE CAB SQUEALED TO a stop. "Just don't be goin' to Brooklyn, lady," the black man behind the wheel said. "I don't do no Brooklyn this time of night."

"I," she replied, scooting into the backseat along shiny plastic seat covers, "never do Brooklyn." She was afraid the seat covers would rip her Victoria's Secret hose, which were real silk held in place by a real black-lace garter belt. Just the way Grant liked her to wear. She wasn't crazy about the feel of the little metal hooks in her thighs, and the bare space between her legs struck her as impossibly dangerous in a city of rapists and thugs, but she did love the way Grant's eyes made their way up her legs and lit with a carnal gleam when he realized she was wearing old-fashioned stockings.

And then there was the way he slid his hand up her skirt, riding her thigh until he came to the button-hook. He'd pretend to grope, as if trying to figure out this intricate appliance, but he was really reveling in the fact that his fingers touched her softest, most sensitive skin.

An old blues song wafted its way into her memory.

Don't you feel my leg.
Don't you feel my leg.
Cause if you feel my leg, you're gonna feel my thigh.
And if you feel my thigh, you're gonna go too high.
So don't you feel my leg.

She leaned back into the seat and visualized herself singing the words, low and sexy, into Grant's surprised ear. Give him a nice big bulge in those Brooks Brothers pants of his.

The cab slowed; the driver said over his shoulder, "This it, lady? This where you want to be let off?"

She couldn't blame the skepticism in his tone. This wasn't the kind of place you'd expect a woman wearing a Betsey Johnson dress and Maud Frizon shoes to walk into voluntarily. But Manhattan fund-raisers were always on the lookout for the new, and a cocktail party on a barge in the Hudson was someone's idea of cutting-edge chic. And Grant Eddington was nothing if not chic. Down to his perfectly pedicured toenails.

Tonight she'd let him feel her leg. All the way up. Tonight she'd drop the mask of indifference and give him what he so clearly wanted from her.

But she'd been right to hold back all these weeks. Grant wasn't a man who valued what came easily. She'd made him wait for her, made him desire her even more by doling herself out to him like sugar cubes in a cut-glass bowl, served by tiny silver tongs.

The thought of later, of what would come after they'd made the rounds, worked the room, brought a delicious wetness to the place between her legs. No panties absorbed the flood; it coated her thighs like honey, made her slippery and open. Any man who knew could sidle up behind her, lift her skirt, thrust his rough hand into her and bring her to glorious, anonymous climax.

The hand that barely touched her shoulder made her

shiver; her nipples contracted into tiny hard points underneath the pewter silk dress. She looked up into the bluest eyes she'd ever seen.

"Grant," she half-whispered, "I was just thinking about you. I'll bet you can't guess what I'm wearing under this—"

The blue eyes were hard. "Oh, I think I can, darling."

Darling wasn't good. Darling was always, with Grant, used sarcastically.

"I think every man in this room knows exactly what you have on under that dress. Precisely nothing."

The warmth between Nellis's legs turned cold and clammy. "But, Grant, I thought you liked—"

"What I enjoy in private and what I desire in public are two different things," he replied. His hand gripped her arm tightly; there would be a bruise in the morning. But not tonight. Tonight no one would know how badly he'd hurt her.

"I would have thought a woman of taste would understand that."

He squeezed her arm a little tighter and then walked away without a backward glance.

Nellis didn't know how she made it to the ladies room without being stopped. Surely someone noticed a woman with tears streaming down her face, groping in her thousand-dollar hand-beaded evening bag for a Kleenex.

Don't you feel my leg.

Grant wasn't going to feel her leg or any other part of her anatomy. She was going to throw cold water on her face and go straight home, cry for a week, and then forget Grant Eddington existed on this or any other planet.

But when she stepped out of the powder room, face back in place, he was waiting for her, a smile on his lips. "Mr. Mayor," he said to the tall man standing next to him, "I'd like you to meet a very special friend of mine."

That night they made long, sweet, tender love on her new

satin sheets. He was so gentle, and he lingered so lovingly over every inch of her skin, that she sobbed uncontrollably when she reached climax. She had never in her entire life felt so wanted.

CHAPTER
THREE

"Now we turn on the safe-light," I said, then realized my companion wouldn't know what that meant. "You can't expose photographs in regular light, so this is a special bulb that lets us see what we're doing without ruining the prints."

Three long days had passed since I'd argued Keith's appeal; I was hoping the court would come down with a decision before the Jewish New Year, which always managed to close the courts for at least a week.

I needed something to take my mind off the obsessive thoughts I kept having about the decision. It had been too long since I'd put up my blackout curtain, donned my acid-stained "Photographers Do It in the Dark" T-shirt, and turned my kitchen into a darkroom. Today I was doing it in the dark with Marvella's fourteen-year-old son, Oliver, who wore a Buju Banton T-shirt and pants five times too big for him. He also wore an expression of boredom I hoped to change into one of intense interest. He usually spent his after-school time playing Dungeons and Dragons on the computer, but I'd lured him into the darkroom today.

Oliver nodded, although I wasn't sure he really remembered what I was talking about. I'd given him a crash course in photo processing before we set up the darkroom, but I'd been so busy filling the trays with solution, setting out the tongs, and putting the enlarger together that I hadn't reviewed the procedures.

I pulled the chain on the antique wrought-iron floor lamp with the oversized red bulb that served as my darkroom illumination. When I switched off the overhead lights, the room flooded with a low-level amber glow, not unlike the streetlamps of the gaslight era. It took a moment for my eyes to adjust, and then I felt the peace that always enveloped me when I committed myself to a couple of hours in the darkroom. I was safe in the glow of the bulb, safe from needy clients and angry judges, from pending motions and briefs to be written and court appearances that couldn't be adjourned. All that mattered was the negative in the enlarger and the photographic paper going through its cycle of chemical baths. All that mattered was focus and exposure and timing and keeping the dust off the negative.

Nobody was going to jail if my picture turned out badly. Nobody was going to do time for something he didn't do if my photograph came out fuzzy or overexposed. In the darkroom, unlike the courtroom, I was free to fail.

"Let's try this at thirty seconds," I said. I'd already shown Oliver how to place the negative in the metal holder inside the enlarger. I'd placed unexposed paper into the easel and positioned it beneath the enlarger lamp. I handed Oliver the oversized clock and let him adjust the timer. Then I turned on the enlarger and watched the picture appear on the paper.

"Hey, it's like backwards," Oliver exclaimed. "All the shit that supposed to be dark is light."

Oliver's mother would have told him not to say *shit*. I contented myself with remarking, "Good observation.

That's because this is still the negative. When we put the picture into the developer bath, it will come up positive." I suited action to words, taking the paper out of the easel and slipping it into the first tray along the counter.

Usually when I print, I watch the picture come up. I love the way a blank piece of paper becomes a photograph. Sometimes I love it so much I let the paper stay in too long and end up with a too-dark print. But today my eyes were on Oliver's face. Would he get the same thrill I did? Would he see the magic of an image forming where only a minute earlier there had been nothing?

"Here it come," he said, a note of triumph in his voice. He gave me a white-toothed grin. "Here come the skull."

Then he lowered his voice and did a perfect imitation of the old Here-come-the-judge routine, substituting the word *skull* for *judge*.

The kid was a born comic. He already spoke several languages, in that he could switch from a street argot so arcane I couldn't understand a word to perfectly grammatical English; he could imitate his parents' Jamaican accent so well you'd think he just got off the plane from Kingston; or he could do a Southern drawl that had you believing he'd been born in Alabama.

"It's coming up nicely," I agreed. "I'd suggest we leave it in for another minute. If it's too light it won't have impact."

"Yeah," he agreed. "Skull like that gotta jump off the picture. Like it's gonna *bite* somebody." If you closed your eyes, you could hear Jim Carrey's over-the-top delivery of the word *bite*.

He reached for the tongs. "Can I take it out when it's done?"

"Sure," I said. "But what did I tell you about the tongs?"

"They gotta stay in they own tray. Can't go mixing up the chemicals or the picture be ruined."

"Right. So you can pick up the picture with those tongs,

but don't let the tongs get into the second bath. Just toss the picture into the tray when we're ready."

"I forgot what the second bath do."

"It's called the stop bath. It stops the developer from working, so the picture doesn't go all black."

"That the one smell like my old sweat socks?" He put thumb and finger over his broad nose and said, "Whooeee, that stuff shore do stink, maw. I think the outhouse done got turned over again."

"Let me guess," I said. "You've been watching 'The Beverly Hillbillies' on Nick at Nite."

"Nah," he said with a contemptuous shake of his head. "This one called 'The Real McCoys' and there's this old dude talks cracker."

"Walter Brennan," I murmured, wondering at television's amazing ability to recycle itself and infect new generations with the same useless information my mind was filled with. But that wasn't helping my student learn the information I was trying to put in his head.

"No, that one is the fixer. It's called hypo." I pointed to the first tray and nodded. "Okay, move it now."

Oliver reached in with the tongs and picked up the picture. I knew what would happen before he did; he didn't have a firm grip and the paper floated away from him, landing half in and half out of the tray.

"I'm sorry, Ms. J." His voice rose anxiously. "I musta lost hold of it."

"That's okay, Oliver. Pick it up and move it."

"But it's gonna be all screwed up." He pointed to the picture. "See, the one part still in the tub gonna be darker than—"

"Hey, don't worry about it. This was a test print anyway. Just for practice."

Time is vital in photography. The extra seconds we'd spent discussing the matter had brought the picture to the point of ruin. I picked it up with the tips of my fingers and tossed it into the trash bin. "We'll try another one," I said lightly.

This time Oliver moved the picture from developer to stop bath to fixer without a hitch. When the picture was ready I dropped it into an empty tray and said, "Let's go outside and see how it looks."

I pushed the heavy black curtain away from the door and opened it. Oliver followed as I stepped into my living room.

"Lookin' good, Ms. J.," he said. "I like how them hollow eyes be starin' out the skull." He widened his own eyes in imitation.

"Do you think they ought to be darker?"

"Like black holes in space?" He considered the matter. "Yeah. Like you could look into 'em and see your own death."

Marvella will kill me. I wanted to show the kid what it was like to create something. I wanted to help him see that there was life beyond Crown Heights, Brooklyn. The last thing I wanted was to remind him that in his fourteen years of life he'd buried two friends and seen three others permanently maimed by gunshot wounds.

"Where you take this picture at, anyway? Where you go to find a skull like this?"

"It was at a street fair. A long time ago. I don't even remember where it was. There was a table with a lot of stuff for sale on it, and one of the things for sale was a skull."

"Man, I wish I'd seen that. I'd of bought it. Take it home and—"

"Take it home and watch your mother skin you alive."

He laughed. His unstraightened teeth shone in his dark face. "Yeah," he agreed. "I wouldn't need nobody else's skull. I be a skeleton myself when Mama finish with me."

Oliver lifted his head and tilted it slightly to one side, thrust his chin out, placed his hands on his hips and said in a falsetto, "What you mean, boy, bringin' home de skull of de dead to dis house? You t'ink you Rasta-man, gonna smear you face wit' chicken blood? Noooo, you good Met'odist boy and we Met'odists don't have no skulls in our house. Don't try me, boy."

I laughed in spite of myself. "You'd better not let Marvella catch you at that."

I pointed at the picture. "Think I should zoom in on the skull itself? Cut out all that stuff in the background?"

"Yeah." His finger, ebony-dark with a pink underside, pointed at the picture. "You don't need this other shit, you hear what I'm sayin'? Whole point of the picture is the skull. Say you chop off this part over here and then down there."

"You've got a good eye, Oliver. That's exactly what I think we should do."

So we did. We printed the skull picture another eight times before we had a print we both liked. I put it into the dryer and hunted for a mat. When I found one, I slipped the picture inside and handed it to Oliver.

"Congratulations," I said. "You've just produced your first professional photographic print. I was thirty years old before I did that."

He looked at the picture and smiled, a deep satisfied smile. "Yeah. It look real good, Ms. J. Good enough to be in a art museum."

Now was the time. Now came the moment I'd really been working toward. Marvella had decided it was time for Oliver to hear The Talk, to learn the facts of life all kids like him had to learn if they wanted to stay alive.

The Talk wasn't about sex or drugs or gangs. It wasn't about AIDS or going to college or getting a girl pregnant or any of the things that occupied the worried thoughts of suburban parents. The Talk was about how not to die in a jail cell as a victim of police brutality.

I was backing up The Talk by giving Oliver a copy of a pamphlet I'd bought in front of the courthouse. Written by a woman named Carol Taylor, it was called *The Little Black Book* and it contained thirty rules for dealing with cops and other authority figures as well as savvy tips for surviving on the streets.

"Oliver," I began, keeping my tone conversational, "what would you do if the police stopped you on the street?"

"You mean like they push me up against a car, like that?"

"It could be up against a car, I suppose."

"Yeah, that's how they do. They shout, 'You, spread 'em' and like you better go upside that car and open your legs or you get hit with the stick. I seen 'em hit one dude didn't go fast enough and he had a limp and shit, couldn't go as fast as they wanted, but they hit him anyway. We was all yellin' at 'em, sayin' the man walking as fast he can, don't hit him, but they kept on hitting him."

"Is this something you saw, or did it ever happen to you?"

He shrugged. "Happen to me a couple times. I seen it happen a lot to other dudes, though. Like they be walkin' down the street, not doin' nothin', and the cops roll up on 'em and make 'em spread they legs. Search 'em for drugs and shit. Find some, don't find some, it don't matter, 'cause they be back next week do the same damn thing."

"So you know that if the cops tell you to do something, you'd better do it and not try to be a hero, right?"

"Yeah." His tone said he didn't like giving this answer one little bit.

"Oliver, this is important. If a cop feels like you might do something to hurt him, or if he thought you had a gun, he could shoot you. It's important not to mouth off at them. Just let them search and when they don't find anything, they'll move on to someone else."

"What if they find something I ain't got?"

"I'm not following—" But then I was following, and I swallowed hard. It was a hell of a question from a fourteen-year-old. But then most fourteen-year-olds of my acquaintance had never been asked to spread them.

"You mean you're afraid the police might plant evidence on you? 'Find' drugs or a gun that you didn't really have?"

He nodded, his dark, round face solemn.

"Look, most cops really aren't like that." His face registered an impassive skepticism; I decided I'd better not argue the point.

"For one thing, you say nothing. You have the right to remain silent, so use it. I'll give you my card, and the minute they give you a phone call from the precinct, which they have to do by law, you call me. Don't answer any questions or make any statements. Call me. Got that?"

He nodded, his round, boyish face looking younger than his fourteen years, although his body was growing into manhood. He was big, if plump, and his skin was very, very dark.

This was what worried Marvella—that when people who didn't know him saw her son, they didn't see a funny, sweet kid with a pleasant disposition and a great sense of humor. They didn't see an A student who liked computer games and reggae music.

They saw a young urban black male. They saw a potential threat. They saw someone who might be carrying a gun in his waistband.

That was precisely what the Korean lady in the fruit store down the block had seen when Oliver walked in to buy a bottle of juice. She'd screamed and chased him out of the store with a broom, even after he showed her the money for the drink.

What worried Marvella was that some day, some time, the person behind the counter or in the patrol car might have a gun and use it because they saw, not Oliver Jackman, but a predator with a hulking body and coal-black skin.

I hoped The Talk had done even a tiny particle of good. I wasn't at all sure it had.

The knock on the door was loud and insistent. "Ms. J., you got a phone call out here," Marvella shouted.

"Can't you take a message?" I called back.

"It's the clerk from the Appellate Division," she replied. "He says he got news about that Keith."

I raced to the phone, heart pounding.

"Yes?" I said, hardly bothering to catch my breath. "Is there a decision?"

"Ms. Jameson, the court has come down with its ruling. I thought you should know at once because—"

"Oh, God, I won! Really? I mean, you're sure?" The only reason to call was so I could get a jump on the order that would release Keith from prison; if the court had affirmed the conviction, he wouldn't be going anywhere, so there would be no hurry.

"The court reversed the conviction in a four-to-one decision," the clerk said. "The case has been remanded to Brooklyn Supreme Court for a new trial, but I thought you'd want to make a bail application in the meantime."

"Yes. I mean, thank you. How soon can I get a copy of the papers?"

"The decision is ready and this office is open until five o'clock," the bland voice replied. "And, Counselor?"

"Yes?"

"Congratulations. Nice win."

I felt light-headed and lighter-hearted. I was a hot-air balloon about to sail over the rooftops of Brooklyn. I was high as a flag on the Fourth of July. I hugged Marvella and thanked her profusely for typing and retyping my brief; I ran back to the darkroom and hugged Oliver. I ran downstairs to the Morning Glory and hugged Dorinda. I would have run out onto the street and started hugging people walking by except that I had work to do.

Reversed and remanded. Those were the words the clerk had used, the ones that would be on the order. Which meant that the case against Keith hadn't gone away entirely. He was no longer a convicted felon, but he was facing the old charges just as if he'd never had a trial. The district attorney would have to decide whether or not to retry him, and until that time, he was entitled to bail.

But was he entitled to bail he could make?

It was up to me to convince a court to set bail in a reasonable amount, and one way I could do that was to convince the trial judge that we had a good chance of winning the case.

There was one slight problem: Judge Lucius Tolliver was no fan of mine, and he'd leaned heavily in favor of the prosecution the first time around. I'd have to pull out all the stops to get Keith out of jail pending trial, and then I'd have to work on the D.A.'s office to consider dismissing the charges instead of trying for a second bite at the conviction apple.

I opened my top desk drawer and pulled out the last letter Keith had sent me from prison. I smiled as I read it for what was probably the fourth time. *From your mouth*, I had thought, *to God's ear*. For once, God was listening.

> Dear κασανδρα,
>
> I thought of you today when I caught a glimpse of a PBS program about the Greeks. Of course the stupid Neanderthals in the TV room changed the channel immediately so they could watch two overgrown bullies yank each others' hair out and bellow like apes. I think they call it professional wrestling.
>
> Anyway, the program mentioned Cassandra, the Princess of Troy, King Priam's daughter. I got intrigued, so I went to the prison library and looked her up in the encyclopedia. What a woman—no wonder you were named for her. Not only did she blow off Apollo—hey, if a god isn't good enough for you, maybe you're a little too picky—but she continued to diss him even after he threatened to punish her. My kind of woman.

You probably know the rest of the story. Apollo cursed Cassandra, gave her the gift of prophecy, and then made it so that nobody would believe her even when she predicted the truth. Even at the end of her life, she kept screaming that Clytemnestra was going to kill her, and all the people who heard her laughed and jeered and then Clytie stabbed her, just like she predicted.

Is that a riot or what? Here's this poor woman yelling about someone's going to kill her, and all the stupid townspeople are saying to each other, "Hey, isn't that Cassandra, the one who always predicts the truth but nobody listens?" And then they stand around and watch while Clytie hacks her from stem to stern. Of course, Clytie gets hers from the Furies, but by then it's too late for poor Cassie.

That would never happen to you, though. You'd be smart enough to figure out a way to grab the knife and stab Clytie instead. Then you'd wipe the blood on your dress and walk out of that house like a princess. And if the Furies didn't like it, well, too bad for them.

I can see you now, walking out of the courthouse like a Trojan princess, after winning my case.

Sincerely,

Keith

As I drafted the papers that would order the prison to release Keith Jernigan, I remembered Dorinda's Tarot reading. She'd predicted that the outcome would be Justice; I smiled to myself as I realized how right she'd been. I'd tilted against the windmills of injustice and, for once in my professional life, I'd come out the winner.

This was why I'd gone to law school in the first place.

This was why I got up every morning and slogged to work in the dingy, dark, dirty, ugly pits of the criminal courts.

I could count the number of truly bet-the-farm innocent clients I'd ever represented on the fingers of one hand.

Now I could also use the thumb.

It felt wonderful.

CHAPTER FOUR

"Why did you stay with him?" I sipped the mulled cider Nellis Cartwright had set in front of me. It was redolent with spices, sharp with cloves and cinnamon and all the tastes of autumn.

It was Sunday afternoon; I'd looked over the documents Nellis had given me regarding her divorce, and I'd assigned Spider Tannenbaum, Blues Accountant, the task of looking into the financial aspects of the settlement. But the emotional angle was important to me, and not as a matter of mere curiosity. If I was going to take the case, I had to have some idea of what my client really wanted—and I suspected Nellis wanted more than just money.

"Do you read his reviews?" She set her huge earthenware mug on Jerry Laboda's scarred coffee table.

I admitted I did, even though I seldom bought Broadway theater tickets anymore. Too expensive. But Grant Eddington's reviews were to be savored for their bitchy wit even if you never saw the play in question. It was easy to understand why a famous actress had once thrown a drink in his face at Sardi's.

"Then you understand. He's the same way with people as he is with plays. He loves as extravagantly as he hates."

She ran her tongue over her thin lips and added, "Grant could treat me so wonderfully sometimes. Not just flowers and lingerie, romantic cliché kinds of things, but—oh, he could say something tender that showed he'd been listening to every nuance. He could create a romantic evening like I'd always dreamed about, everything perfect, and it would be mine alone. My favorite music, my flowers, my special dinner—"

She broke off and gazed at me with intense gray eyes. "God, I sound as if all I'm talking about is *things*. It really wasn't just that; it was the whole way I felt when I was with him. I felt—bigger, somehow. More beautiful, more talented. And then when he'd snatch all that away, when he'd turn on me and say something positively cruel, something humiliating, I'd feel like the most worthless person on earth. Like I deserved to be told I was nothing but a slob who had no real talent but was living off him and playing at photography."

"He said that?"

"Oh, yes, that and more. He could be so unbelievably warm and then he'd turn it off like a faucet and the ice would form and everything good between us would freeze. The worst of it was that every time the thaw set in, I was ready for spring. I waited through a lot of emotional winters with him, and always the spring came and we were fine again. Until this last one. Until he threw me out, quite literally."

She reached for a large portfolio on the coffee table and opened it. "I guess this was another reason I stayed," she said. "We worked on this together for over three years."

I took the portfolio and set it on my lap. She pointed to the first photograph.

"They're called *netsuke*," she said, pronouncing the word with a two-syllable guttural sound that was nothing like my idea of how to say the word. I knew only that they were Japanese carved figures about three inches high, usually made from ivory.

Instead of the usual head-on view of a carved object, these close-up color pictures were beautifully lit so as to reveal the curve of line, the delicate features, the sheen of wood or ivory. And the *netsuke* were displayed, not merely standing on a tiny pedestal, but in a setting that complemented the carving.

A swan, her neck bent gracefully over her delicately feathered back, sat on a bed of blue-green velvet arranged to resemble the surface of a pond. A yellowed ivory figure of a bearded sage riding on a giant fish was pictured against a backdrop of water flowing over decorative stones. A tiny mouse with big ears peeked out from a burlap sack; artfully arranged grains of pearly rice made it appear that he was about to have lunch.

"These are fabulous." I was having a hard time thinking up superlatives for this woman's work. The pictures were perfect as representations of the *netsuke* and also as works of art by themselves.

"It's a fabulous collection," she said, her tone dry. "I ought to know. I helped Grant build it. He only owned four pieces when we met; his passions were furniture and brushwork scrolls. I taught him about *sagemono*."

She responded to my raised eyebrow by explaining, "*Sagemono* is a collective term; *netsuke* are part of a *sagemono* collection."

She turned the page. "I advised him on all his purchases, introduced him to the best dealers in Japan, went with him to countless auctions. Of course, I thought I was helping him put together a collection for both of us."

"You signed the prenuptial agreement," I pointed out. That much I'd gathered from my still rather cursory skimming of the documents she'd given me. "He made it clear when you married that—"

"No, it wasn't clear," she cut in, her tone sharp. "I'm getting sick and tired of people treating me like the village idiot. I thought the words meant exactly what they said: that Grant wanted to keep everything he owned *before* we got married. It never occurred to me that it covered things we acquired during the marriage. That part of it came as a complete shock, let me tell you."

"I see your point," I said carefully. "The word *prenuptial* could be a bit misleading. It means the agreement is entered into before marriage, not that it only covers property owned before the marriage."

"Well, I know that now, but at the time I honestly believed that Grant had an interest in being fair. I guess I thought I was entitled to share in what we achieved as a couple."

"The money he put into the collection was his, though, wasn't it?"

"For the most part," she conceded. "But I did what he wanted me to do, which was put my own career on the back burner so I could nurture his. I managed the house, entertained, kept in touch with dealers all over the world. I was the one who made the how-are-you phone calls, sent the birthday cards and anniversary presents, went to the gallery openings, and kept my ears open for news of a private sale or exclusive auction. There isn't a piece in that collection I didn't see before Grant did. There's more to creating a world-class art collection than money, and I have a right to at least some of what we built together."

I turned the page and another photograph stared up at me. An ivory skull with a perfectly carved snake winding through the eye-holes, its head looking up with blank reptilian eyes. It was photographed against a background of dull black fabric, which brought out the creamy ivory patina.

The picture looked vaguely familiar; it was only when I

glanced up that I recalled the skull beneath the skin in Nellis's photograph of the model. She smiled when I asked and said that, yes, she'd used the *netsuke* as one of the images for the picture.

"How much would a piece like this be worth?"

"We paid eighteen-fifty," she said. "But Grant could sell it for twenty-four."

"Thousand?"

She laughed. "No, hundred. This isn't a particularly spectacular *netsuke*, in spite of the grisly subject matter. It's a nice piece, but it isn't by a name carver or anything."

"So if this is only worth twenty-four hundred dollars," I began, treading carefully around what I sensed was this woman's obsession, "is it really worth fighting over? I mean," I added hastily, "I'm not saying that's chump change, but it's not exactly the price of an original Picasso either."

Nellis lifted her hand and ticked off her answer on her French-manicured fingers. "One, he owns over sixty *netsuke*. Two, some of them are worth a lot more than this; I think the most expensive piece in the collection is valued at forty thousand dollars. Three, this is only one portion of the collection. The furniture, the artwork, the snuff bottles—it all adds up to a very valuable collection, and I want my share of it."

"Let me ask another question. Didn't I see in the settlement papers that you did receive some Japanese antiques?"

"Garbage. He used the divorce to dump the least important pieces on me, take a tax loss, and turn the money into truly fine specimens. The collection only got stronger after the divorce. He took the cream and left me with skim milk."

Cross-examining one's own client is a part of the job no lawyer really enjoys. But sometimes it's vital to help a client see the weaknesses in her own case before too much time, money, and energy are committed to a losing cause. The trouble was that Nellis Cartwright Eddington had already expended time, money, and energy and I suspected no force on earth was going to stop her throwing more into the cause, losing or not. She was obsessed—as obsessed with her wrongs as her husband was with his collection.

"Who did the appraisal?"

"A snake named Richard Matsumoto."

Involuntarily, I glanced down at the photograph of the snake wending its twisted way through the skull.

"One appraiser?"

My Herculean effort to keep my voice neutral was a failure.

"You don't understand!" Nellis stood up and walked toward the breakfast bar she'd made out of a long white Parsons table flanked by tall director's chair barstools in primary colors. She hit the table with her fist; the hollow thud was unsatisfactory if she wanted a powerful sound.

"He was a friend! He and that dumpy, uninteresting little wife of his came to our house for dinner at least once a month. I sent his children birthday cards and graduation presents. I lunched with Hanae at the Palm Court on the second Tuesday of every month; I drove her to Paterson so she could shop at the mall. I never expected Richard to shaft me in the appraisal."

"But he did business with your husband. Grant was the one who paid the bills. Didn't you suspect he wouldn't be evenhanded?"

"Obviously not. Obviously, I thought he was a man of honor. A man who'd at least tell the plain truth about every piece in the collection and not fudge."

I leaned forward and opened my notebook. "Give me three ways to fudge an appraisal of Japanese antiques."

I looked up and elaborated. "Not necessarily three things you think he actually did, just three things—well, I guess three things you'd have done if you were in collusion with a crooked appraiser."

For the first time, the look she gave me was one of grudging respect. She turned the closest barstool and leaned into it until she was in a sitting position, then hoisted herself up.

"For one thing, many *netsuke* are representations of the same or similar subjects."

"One mouse looks a lot like another?"

"Exactly. So the appraiser writes: 'Mouse, artist unknown' when the truth is that the piece was carved by Kaigyosukai."

"He's a biggie, I take it."

She smiled and nodded. "One of the best—and most valuable. Nothing carved by him goes for under fifty thousand in today's market."

I turned the album back to the mouse in the rice sack. "Whereas this little guy is worth—what?"

"Somewhere in the neighborhood of two thousand."

"Okay, that's one. Fake attribution. Give me another." Then a thought struck me. "Hold on a minute. Didn't these guys sign their work? Wouldn't a phony 'artist unknown' attribution get this Richard in trouble? Appraisers are licensed."

"It isn't easy to read Japanese signatures, for one thing. And for another, some carvers had apprentices who copied their styles. So not every piece with a certain signature on it really qualifies as that artist's work. It's complex, but believe me, it's a fertile ground for fudging."

"Okay. I'll take your word for it. On to number two."

Nellis drew in a breath and let it out in a long, slow sigh. "I think the snuff bottles are a possibility. They're also quite variable as to value, with some in the five hundred range and others going for ten times that much. And they can look very similar; I remember an eight-color bottle that was painted on the inside. Very difficult and beautiful and it went for something in the high thirties. But I've seen bottles I couldn't tell apart from that one go for under a thousand."

"So why? How could one be worth so much more than the other?"

"It's like everything else. Rarity. A certain artist, a certain period, a certain material—it doesn't matter, so long as there are fewer of one kind than another. Anything you can pick up too easily is cheap compared to something that doesn't come along every day."

She nodded and drummed her fingers on the wooden armrest of her chair. "I can see Richard doing that. Entering a valuable snuff bottle as a cheap copy to fool me into thinking Grant and I were both getting the same quality when the truth was that Grant took the good ones and left me with the dreck."

"Want to try for number three?"

She leaned forward, a conspirator's smile on her face. "I thought of this one a long time ago, but I could never prove it. Now maybe I have a chance. Do you know anything about *tansu*?"

I shook my head. "Are they like *netsuke*?"

She laughed. "No. *Tansu* are wooden chests. They were used for all kinds of things in the Japanese household. Some were specially constructed to hold kimonos, like a modern chest of drawers, while others held the ceremonial swords. There are chests used in shops and others made especially to hold the items for the tea ceremony."

She stood up and motioned toward the bedroom. "Here, I'll show you."

I followed her into the room, and went straight to what looked like a large wooden crate. It was beautiful. Simple and classic, yet with a modernity that stemmed from its complete and utter functionality. There were little drawers and big drawers, cubbyholes and sliding doors, and one locked safe on the bottom. The wood was dark and lustrous and the metalwork was chased with an intricate pattern.

"You think he faked the chests, too? Had modern ones made to look like antiques?"

"The *choba dansu* were known to have secret compartments," she said, with an air of conspiratorial triumph.

"Ah. Secret compartments just big enough to hold a few *netsuke* or snuff bottles, you mean."

"That's it exactly. He bought several chests in the months before the separation. What's to say they didn't come here from Japan with a few extra items inside?"

"You think he'd screw around with Customs? There are bound to be records."

"Maybe Richard added the goodies after the chests came to the auction house. I don't know. All I know is that Grant told me once he was finished with *tansu*. He was going to concentrate on snuff bottles and *netsuke*. And then all of a sudden these new chests started arriving. I can't help but wonder if he wasn't planning the divorce and filling the cubbyholes with little items I'd never realize he owned."

Hidden compartments inside antique chests. This case was beginning to sound like a job for Judy Bolton.

"This is really gorgeous," I said, running my hand along the wood. "I'm surprised Grant let you have this one."

"Oh, I had to fight hard for this little beauty," she said with a smile, "but every time I think of how much he wanted to keep it, I get a warm glow inside."

Back in the office, there was a message on my answering machine. Grant Eddington's personal assistant wanted me to call on her employer at precisely eight o'clock this evening. There were, she said in her crisp British voice, matters of mutual concern to be discussed.

I considered not going. I considered calling back and explaining in some detail that discussing a client's legal matters with the enemy wasn't a good idea. But when I called Nellis and told her about the call, she urged me to go.

"I want you to see for yourself what he's like," she said. "I want you to tell me exactly what he says about me."

At precisely five minutes to eight, I was in the elevator of a Fifth Avenue apartment building, being wafted to the penthouse in perfect silence. Nellis had told me the elevator used to play classical music until Grant accused the co-op board of turning a masterpiece of pre-war architecture into a nouveau riche Kmart.

The elevator door opened and deposited me in a tiny wood-paneled foyer. The only decoration was a tall lacquered table with a Japanese flower arrangement lit from above with a floodlight. The flowers, Nellis said, were redone every day, so the blooms were always at their peak. She'd once suggested the addition of a small brush painting above the *ikebana*, but Grant had given her a look of such disdain that she'd never mentioned it again.

The door of the Fifth Avenue apartment opened and a man in a charcoal suit with a faint chalk stripe motioned me into a foyer and then into a large living room. In one hand, he held a brandy snifter; I accepted warily when he asked if I'd join him. Much as I considered drinking on the job to be a bad idea, I wanted to taste whatever cognac this perfectionist thought worthy.

It was heaven. Smooth and light, yet with depths of fire. I gave a genuine expression of appreciation and swirled the liquid in the hand-blown glass, sniffing the bouquet once more before getting down to business.

"You have some extraordinary pieces," I said, glancing around the room at an array of Asian antiques that would make any museum salivate.

There was a screen with what I was certain were genuine inlaid ivory and jade flowers; a huge Japanese chest on wheels and another made of rising steps, each filled with drawers and cubbyholes. Displays of colorful snuff bottles in glass cases filled every wall. The effect was a decidedly non-Japanese overabundance, as if Grant couldn't bear not to have every one of his favorites available at all times.

My host broke into my thoughts. "And which of my things does my dear former wife feel herself entitled to this time?"

"This time?"

"Surely you don't imagine you're the first lawyer she's inveigled into championing her ridiculous cause?"

"Inveigled," I repeated, drawing out the word respectfully. "Most guys would say 'conned,' but you—"

"Why do I have the feeling," he said, raising his voice only slightly to overtake mine, "that if you were speaking to one of your less affluent clients, you wouldn't refer to him as a 'guy.'"

He was right; I was deliberately trying to cut through his civilized manner, bring him down to a level I could deal with.

"Look," I said, "let's stop playing games. You called me. Why?"

"I take it you've reviewed the terms of the settlement," he said.

I nodded. Reviewed wasn't exactly the word; skimmed would have been closer to the mark. "And I've read the prenuptial agreement."

"Of which you don't approve," he amended.

"I didn't say that." I had, in fact, tried damned hard not to let him see that, but the man was perceptive.

"Most lawyers disapprove of it," he explained.

Then he smiled, an unexpectedly warm smile that gave me the tiniest hint of what had made Nellis stay with him. "And all women disapprove of it."

"Can you blame them? You ask your future wife to renounce all claims to anything you own or will own. You expect her to leave the marriage with exactly what she brought into it and not a penny more."

"Why is that unreasonable?" Grant's eyes widened, changing before my eyes from sea-gray to blue. "I earn my living. Nellis earned hers. Why is she entitled to a portion of mine?"

"Why get married?"

Now the smile showed teeth. "You'll have to ask Ms. Cartwright that question," he replied smoothly. "It was her idea. I was perfectly content to live in what our society so delightfully calls sin."

"Could I possibly," I began, my tone tentative, "have a closer look at those *netsuke*?" I took care to pronounce the word the way Nellis had, as a two-syllable guttural sound.

The effort wasn't lost on Grant. "Of course," he said, turning on the charming smile I'd seen before I started talking finance. "All collectors delight in showing off their treasures."

He stood up and walked toward the nearest glass case. I followed, noting the thickness of the carpet beneath my feet as I walked across the room.

If he'd intended to shock by leading me to this display case first, he succeeded. Nellis hadn't told me there were X-rated *netsuke*.

I stared in fascination at the tiny figures, which showed couples, both hetero and otherwise, engaged in a variety of sex acts. One woman caressed the ivory breasts of her female partner; a man mounted a woman from behind; another man opened his kimono and a woman knelt to receive his ivory penis.

Grant reached in and picked up the carving. "This one in particular," he said, handing it to me, "reminds me of one of my former wife's lesser talents."

CHAPTER FIVE

Nothing on earth was going to induce me to reply. But the damage Grant had undoubtedly intended had been done; a mental image formed that I had a hard time pushing out of my mind. I glanced down at the naughty *netsuke* and I noticed one I'd missed before. A naked woman, smooth in her ivory purity, lay on her back. Over her face and genitals squatted twin octopi, their tentacles embracing her, their voracious mouths pleasuring her.

Another mental image it was going to be difficult to shake.

Grant placed the piece back in the case and motioned me toward a second one. This was PG; animals and figures engaged in nonsexual activities. He plucked one from the center of the display and said, "Open your hand."

I did; he placed the object in the center of my palm and said, "Now close your fingers slowly and gently."

The smoothness spoke to me first. Hard as I knew ivory

to be, this was like holding silk. The coolness of the surface turned to warmth as the object absorbed my body heat. My fingers traced the pattern; the carving was a tiger and her cub, and I could feel the stripes cut into the ivory. I let my fingers roam, finding the bared teeth, the bulging eyes, the curled tails of the two beasts. There was a hole in the carving, where the cord would go when the *netsuke* was worn as it was meant to be.

"That is how one must first come to *netsuke*," Grant explained. "Through touch. The visual is extremely important, I assure you, but what sets them apart from statuary is that element of touch. They must be pleasant on the hand, something to be fingered and stroked. Too many contemporary *netsuke* are rough-edged, sharp. Not user-friendly, in the egregious phrasing of our age."

"This feels wonderful," I said.

Grant reached over and opened my hand. "It should. It is one hundred and fifty years old. That means it has been touched by many hands."

I looked down at the tiny object. A mother tiger, looking far more like a Chinese dog than an actual tiger, stared up with an expression of fierce protectiveness on her animal face. Her cub crouched under her body, looking up at her with a child's loving trust. Both bodies were sinuously cat-like, with tails that swirled around them like snakes.

"It's exquisite," I said, using a word I hadn't known was in my vocabulary.

"It's by a carver named Okakoto," Grant said. "And, just in case you think I'm concealing its true worth, it would fetch at least sixty thousand dollars at auction. Not, of course, that I would ever sell it. But I do admit that I have some pieces that are worth a great deal. How my former wife arrives at the conclusion that I'm concealing assets from her, I have no idea. My collection is catalogued and the provenance of everything in it is established. I do not buy gray-market antiques, much less black-market ones."

I turned the *netsuke* over in my hand and focused on the paws.

"Looking for the signature?"

"I'll admit I won't recognize it," I said. "But you did say the name of the carver, so I assume there's a signature or a chop."

Grant lifted the little animals from my palm, which felt strangely bereft. He turned it over; as I'd guessed, there were tiny carved characters on the mother's rear paw. "The signature was authenticated by an expert."

"Are all your things this valuable?"

He wasn't gullible enough to answer in the affirmative. He smiled and added, "I have eighty-nine *netsuke*, forty-two snuff bottles, and a collection of Asian furniture that's the envy of every Orientalist I know, not to mention the brush paintings, the pottery, and the woodblock prints. I am a collector, Ms. Jameson. I collect, therefore I am. And my collection isn't a secret to anyone who knows me. My wife married my collection when she married me; but that doesn't entitle her to break it up and take portions of it. She knew that when she walked down the aisle. I am beginning to resent her continual suspicion that I've cheated her in any way. She received a perfectly fair settlement, and I will not give her another penny. Is that understood?"

"Didn't Nellis give you a great deal of advice about what to buy? Isn't she really the architect of the *sagemono* portion of your collection?"

"I doubt those are words you've ever used before, Ms. Jameson," he said in a pleasant but mocking tone. "I seriously doubt that your usual clientele are in the habit of referring to the architecture of a collection, are they?"

I felt my face flush. Before I could respond, he went on, "I detect the fine hand of my former wife even in your choice of words. I would tread carefully if I were you, Ms. Jameson, truly I would. If she puts words in your mouth, don't let her convince you to say those words in open court.

I won't hesitate to ask for punitive sanctions against a lawyer I feel is bringing frivolous motions."

I knew better than to ask whether his words were a threat. Of course they were. And he hadn't shown me the carving of the tiger and her cub by accident, either. His message was clear: I will protect this collection like a mother tiger protects her young.

It wasn't until I stepped out of the Bergen Street subway station that I realized Grant Eddington had not once referred to Nellis by her first name.

The next day was a frantic whirl of court appearances and motions to be filed and general all-around craziness. The clock said 4:40 when I stood in front of my ancient and weary copying machine waiting for the Birnbaum divorce papers to emerge onto the tray. I had less than twenty minutes to staple them together and make a mad dash to the courthouse to get them filed so that Lissa Birnbaum could stop having her daily nervous breakdown.

"You'd better hurry, you're gonna get there before they close," Marvella said. She sat at the typewriter she insisted on keeping on her desk in spite of the thousand-dollar computer I'd bought for the office.

The computer was in use, however. Oliver sat in a swivel chair, his mouse clicking on images of dragons and swords. Role-playing, it was called. The kid lived in Crown Heights, Brooklyn, but his soul occupied a seat at the Round Table.

Marvella and her husband, Covington, weren't crazy about Oliver's taste in computer games, but they both admitted they'd rather see him sitting at a computer than out on the street, so they let him play for two hours after school so long as he also did his homework. I was happy to donate my computer to the cause.

"Yo, Ms. J.," he said without looking at me.

"Yo, Oliver." I peered at the grisly image on the screen. "So what are you today, a dwarf or a mage?"

"Both. Only dwarves can't really be mages, so I'm only a half-dwarf."

"Does that mean you're only half a mage? And why can't you say 'magician' like everyone else? What's this 'mage' thing?"

He turned and fixed me with his dark eyes. "A magician ain't no mage. A magician be a dude with a hat and a rabbit and shit. A mage got the power."

"Oliver, what I tell you about talking that street talk?" Marvella's tone was sharp. "You know better than to say 'ain't' and 'he be.' You want to grow up with a good job, or you want to end up like street trash?"

"Mom, I know more about computers than any other kid in school. I'm not gonna be trash. But sometimes you gotta talk like the homeys, get down a little. It don't mean nothin'."

As the kid's lawyer, I could have advised him that the last remark was one too many. Marvella sat up straighter in her chair, adjusted her bulk, and gave her son a look that could melt paint. "You are not no homey. You don't have to 'get down' with people who are never gonna make something of themselves, people who are lazy, welfare people. Your father and I came from Jamaica to work, not to take money and sit on our butts all day and—"

Oliver held up a pudgy hand, very dark on one side, very pink on the other. "Okay, Ma. I've heard this before. I don't like it when you dump on my friends just 'cause some of them been on welfare."

"I just don't want you making the kind of mistakes that have Ms. Jameson in criminal court all day. Too many boys ruin their lives with stealing and drugs."

Oliver turned his attention back to the screen. The dragon had vanished, replaced by flying toasters. He hit the mouse and the screen saver dissolved. He muttered, "Stealing. The only stealing I do is when I'm a full dwarf. Everybody knows dwarves make the best thieves."

I declined comment on the political incorrectness of this remark, knowing full well that Oliver had never seen a real dwarf. He was back in Dungeons and Dragons land, where dwarves and elves and mages replaced gangs and guns in his imagination. I hoped that this kid never fully stepped into the real world. His only hope was to live in a cocoon until he could be safely gotten into college. Preferably outside New York City.

I opened the door, preparing to step out into the late fall afternoon, but my way was blocked by a good-looking young man wearing a blue work shirt and clean jeans.

I almost didn't recognize him. I'd only seen him twice, both times when I had him brought down from his upstate prison so I could talk to him in person about his appeal.

"Keith!" I said, enthusiastically enough, I hoped, to cover the slight delay between seeing the young man on my doorstep and welcoming him inside. I stepped back to let him into the front parlor, which served as my office waiting area, but instead of walking in, he grabbed me around the waist and gave me a big hug.

"I didn't know you were out," I said. "Raul filed the order yesterday but—"

He squeezed me so tight my breath caught in my chest.

"You don't know how good it feels," he said in a low voice, his breath tickling my neck, "to be a free man again. And I owe it all to you, my Trojan princess."

Marvella, standing in the doorway of her office, gave me a quizzical look. I gently extricated myself from Keith's embrace and said, "It's my name. Cassandra was the daughter of Priam, the king of Troy."

"Which makes her the Trojan princess," Keith finished. He stepped toward the center of the room. "And you must be the marvelous Marvella."

This nickname she liked. Her dark face relaxed into a tiny concession of a smile and she welcomed Keith with a dignified handshake before returning to the typewriter.

"Listen, it's great to see you," I said, slightly out of breath, "but I have to get to court. Do you want to wait here till I get back, or would you rather—"

"Oh, I don't mind waiting," Keith said. He stepped into Marvella's office and stood over Oliver's shoulder, looking at the computer screen.

"Ah, I perceive that you're a dwarf. Small and cunning," he said with a wink in my direction, "but wise in the ways of the ancients."

Oliver looked at him with something like respect.

"Although when I was Dungeon Master, I liked to run a Red Messenger."

"What's that?" Oliver asked. "I never heard of a Red Messenger before."

"It's a different game. In fact," Keith said as he pulled a chair close to Oliver's and sat down, "it's one of the characters in a live-action adventure game I used to play."

"Live action?" Oliver's voice rose to a boyish treble I didn't often hear from him anymore. "You mean like dudes dressed up and shit?"

"Oliver!" The click of keys didn't even slow down as Marvella issued her warning.

"Oh, it's much more than just costumes," Keith said, his own voice carrying a wealth of enthusiasm. "You take on the attributes of the character and act out all the situations."

"What does the Red Messenger do?" I asked, intrigued in spite of myself.

"The Red Messenger is a warrior-priest," Keith replied. "He wears the red sash of his office and he carries the double-edged sword of the assassin."

"Cool," Oliver proclaimed.

I glanced over at Marvella to see how she felt about her son learning how to play the role of assassin, but she was engrossed in the motion papers I'd left for her to type.

"Mind if I get in the game?" Keith asked, pointing to the screen. "I'm a pretty fair traveling mage, if I do say so."

He turned and gave me another wink. "Spells 'R' Us," he said jauntily.

I decided I might as well leave Keith with his new play-mate and walked back toward the door. The last words I heard as I closed the door behind me were, "Roll your damage."

I knew just enough to be able to visualize a seventeen-sided die rolling around the screen in a three-dimensional simulation. Whatever appeared on the final face would dictate the next move.

As to live role-playing, I decided that upon my return, I'd inform Keith that Oliver's entire life was a live-action adventure and he didn't need to be running around in the park wearing a red sash and carrying a double-edged sword in order to feel the thrill of combat. He could get that just by walking home from school down the wrong block.

When I'd filed my court papers, I put the receipt for the filing fee in the Birnbaum folder and walked quickly back to the office. On the way, I stopped in to the Morning Glory, where Dorinda stood behind the counter, her thick, wheat-colored hair in a Mom Walton bun.

"Did you see Keith?" I tried to make it sound casual, but the note of pride in my voice was hard to suppress. What I really meant was, Did you see the living embodiment of my tremendous talent as a lawyer and my brilliant ability to assess the human character?

"I did more than see him," she replied with a sweet, smug smile on her un-made-up features.

"It was really cosmic," she went on. She took a cup from the shelf and, without waiting to be asked, poured coffee into it and handed it to me.

"You mean you fed him. Good."

"I mean I hired him."

"Hired him to do what? Can he cook?"

"I don't know."

"Then what—" I caught up at last; it often takes me a

minute to unravel the workings of Dorinda's mind, even after all the years we've known each other.

"Ah, the delivery business. You finally decided to go through with it and you hired Keith to make the deliveries."

"Right. Remember how Ezra used to say I ought to add delivery service?"

"Ezra was six boyfriends ago. You're just getting around to it now?"

"Fast is not my best thing. Besides," she added with disarming clarity, "if I'd done it before, I'd already have a delivery boy and I wouldn't need Keith and then it wouldn't be so cosmic."

"Being cosmic is everything," I murmured into my cup. Sometimes I think Dorinda had too much fun back in the sixties.

Upstairs, the office was quiet. Marvella had put the covers on both computer and typewriter; she and Oliver would have taken the Court Street bus and then transferred to one that got them to Crown Heights. Keith lay on the waiting room couch, his shoes off, his arm covering his ears in a protective gesture he might have learned in prison, where the need to muffle noise had to be great.

"Hey," he said in a low, lazy drawl as I tiptoed past him on my way to my office. "Did you and Dorinda really go to Kent State?"

"Yeah," I replied.

"Cool," Keith said, echoing Oliver Jackman. "I heard about Kent State in my history class."

"Oh, no," I protested. "I refuse to allow events in which I participated to be considered part of history. History, by definition, is all the stuff that happened before I got to the planet. Everything after that is current events."

"It wasn't current to me," he pointed out with a crooked smile. "I was born in nineteen—"

"I do not want to know." I held up a hand and put a mock-disapproving look on my face. "I don't need more reminders of the passing years, thank you very much."

"In that case, what are you doing for dinner?"

Dinner? Hadn't I just had lunch? Where had the afternoon disappeared to?

"I thought maybe the River Café," he said airily. I would have accused him of doing a David Niven imitation, but I was afraid he'd ask who David Niven was.

When I didn't answer, he said, "Or maybe you'd prefer Gage and Tollner?"

The restaurants he named were among the best Brooklyn had to offer, and they charged accordingly. This from a man who'd only just been hired as a delivery boy.

"We could get a giant burrito from the place on Bergen Street," I countered. "Or there's Atlantic Avenue. The best hummus and baba ganoush in—"

"I want us to celebrate," he said. The look on his face was a near-pout.

It occurred to me for the first time that by offering to eat something less expensive, I'd tacitly agreed to eat dinner with him in the first place, something I seldom if ever did with clients. But then Keith was a special client.

"Compromise," I said. "The Japanese place downstairs, and I promise to order the extra-fancy bento box. Okay?"

He opened his mouth to protest, but I'd already planned my next move. "And we'll have a party here tomorrow night. After all," I said in my most persuasive tone, "I wasn't the only person who helped win this case. Don't you want to celebrate with Marvella and Raul and the rest of my office family?"

The clear answer to that was a resounding "no," but Keith didn't say it. Instead he waited while I changed into jeans and a flannel shirt and we went downstairs to the Sakura, home of the best sushi in Brooklyn.

As we dipped our sushi into tiny bowls of soy sauce mixed with wasabe, Keith told me how he'd survived in prison. He'd become a "writer," a jailhouse lawyer who helped inmates draft writs that might get them out of prison. Because of this skill, he commanded enough respect that he was left alone; some of the toughest guys on the cell block were his "clients" and they made it very clear what would happen to anyone who interfered with Keith's ability to write.

"So, hey, you've got any jobs you need doing around the office," he said with that disarming grin I liked so much, "you just let me know. I wrote the best habes in Dannemora and don't you forget it."

"I'm sure you did," I replied. I was filled with good food and the lingering tastes of ginger and miso and soy rolled around my tongue. I sipped green tea and relaxed into the calm of the Japanese surroundings.

"I mean it," Keith said, suddenly very serious. He picked up my hand and held it in his. "Anything you need, ever, you just ask. You were the only person who understood. The only one I could count on. You mean a lot to me, and—"

"And it's time to turn into a pumpkin and get some rest for tomorrow," I said. I slipped my hand out from under his and prepared to stand up.

He took the abrupt change of mood in good humor, pulling out his wallet and tossing a couple of bills on the table, then motioning the waitress for the bill. He walked me to my doorstep and then turned toward the subway station on Bergen Street.

It occurred to me, too late, to wonder if he had a place to stay.

The phone was ringing when I got inside the apartment on the third floor of my building. I picked it up and heard the slightly Southern-flavored accent of my friend and colleague Mickey Dechter. Mickey was a social worker who sometimes saw clients in the spare office downstairs; we had occasional clients in common, but since lawyers are strictly forbidden to go into partnership with nonlawyers, our relationship was informal.

"Have you talked to Lissa Birnbaum yet?"

"I filed the papers at precisely four fifty-nine," I replied, hoping I didn't sound too defensive.

"Yes, but did you tell Lissa you'd filed them? She's called me five times in the last hour, Cass. The poor woman is tearing her hair out. She needs reassurance."

"I'm sure you reassured her," I said. "You with your social worker bedside manner."

"She needs reassurance from her lawyer," Mickey said, her honeyed tones taking on a tartness I was all too familiar with. "She's one of those who can't make a decision without second-guessing it ten times and by the eleventh time, she'll be asking you to withdraw the divorce petition. So if I were you, I'd get on the phone before she gets to the eleventh reconsideration. Where were you, anyway?"

"Celebrating my victory over the forces of injustice," I said lightly.

"Who with?"

"With Keith, if it's any of your business. We had Japanese downstairs."

"You had dinner with a client?"

"Yeah. Dinner. A meal, eaten in a public place, by two adult human beings, one of whom happens to be a lawyer and the other of whom happens to be a client. If there's anything wrong with—"

"You know what's wrong with it."

"He just wanted to celebrate. Hell," I added, trying to lighten things up, "his first suggestion was the River Café, so—"

"So it's all right to have dinner with a client as long as the bill is under twenty dollars?"

The next sound I heard was a long, exasperated sigh. "It's blurring the lines, Cass. It's sending him the wrong message.

It's a potential problem, and my advice is to leave it at one meal. Don't let yourself get too friendly with this guy."

"Yes, Mother," I said as I prepared to hang up the phone. But I said it under my breath, just loudly enough to be heard but not loudly enough to be called on it.

And if Keith wanted to have lunch tomorrow, I'd be happy to buy the burrito.

So there.

CHAPTER SIX

It wasn't as big or as noisy as the old Legal Aid parties I'd once known. One downside to having my own practice was that it limited the number of people I could celebrate with. But winning Keith Jernigan's case definitely warranted a blowout, and the parlor floor of my Cobble Hill brownstone was jumping with reggae music and shouted conversation.

Marvella was doing a hot island dance with her husband, Covington, who'd dropped in after finishing his shift at the Transit Authority. They were both over forty, and she carried a few more pounds than most white women found attractive, but she radiated a sexuality those starved models never came close to.

I swayed to the music, a plastic champagne glass in my hand, while Oliver tried to match hip-hop moves to the rhythms of his parents' native land. He was dressed in the ubiquitous teenage uniform of incredibly oversized pants, huge moon-boot athletic shoes, and a T-shirt with a medieval dragon on the front. He was a cross between street tough and geek—and he was smart enough to know that the only thing that would save him from oblivion was that geek side.

The door opened and a slight Puerto Rican woman stepped in with a wave and a smile. I waved back and gave a quick, knowing nod as she raised her eyebrows to the ceiling and rolled her eyes. Any minute now, the music would change from reggae to salsa; the Latin influence had arrived in the person of Angie, my investigator, and her cousin.

Raul was a former corrections officer who helped me out with prison visits; he'd spent more time with Keith up in Dannemora than I had. Angie was leaving the next day for an extended trip to Puerto Rico to see her family, so Raul was stepping in as my primary process-server and investigator for the next month or two.

Raul poured drinks for himself and Angie, then took over the sound equipment. I continued swaying, changing my movements only slightly to accommodate the new, more sinuous, rhythms.

A hand grasped mine. It was a cool, strong hand and its firmness indicated its owner would not take no for an answer. I responded to the wry smile with one of my own, and let the hand draw me closer to the wiry body.

"Having a good time?" I called out over the music.

"How could I not be?" His voice cracked slightly as he raised it over the din. "They don't have too many parties where I used to live."

Where he used to live was, of course, jail. Keith Jernigan, the guest of honor at this celebratory bash, said the words with his characteristic self-deprecating humor. He'd never whined about his situation; in fact, he complained a lot less than many of my clients who'd actually committed the crimes that had them behind bars. One of the many reasons I liked him. He was smart and funny and innocent. A huge change from my usual run of criminal clients, most of whom were near-illiterate and angry as hell and guilty, guilty, guilty.

Keith pulled me closer and rocked me with the music, doing a passable marengue. I followed, holding my champagne glass aloft so as not to spill any on my blouse. He cocked an eyebrow, then took it deftly from my hand and set it on a table without missing a beat.

"I like the girl I'm dancing with to concentrate on me, not her drink," he said, with just a hint of real pique beneath the bantering tone.

"I wasn't concentrating on it, I was just—"

"Hey, joke," he cut in. He gave me a push and spun me around like a flamenco dancer. The skirt I was wearing was one of my long ones; it widened like a bell as I whirled and then fell back into his arms.

It was fun. The music, the champagne, the heady victory combined to produce a giddiness I hadn't felt in a long time. Not since my early days as a lawyer, when I worked sixty-hour weeks for the Legal Aid Society and then partied hard on Friday night at Capulet's, a bar on—where else?—Montague Street.

What brought Legal Aid and the old days into my mind so often lately? Was it running into Kate Avelard on Henry Street? Or was it just a general feeling that I was getting older and that a lot of good times in my life were in a distant past?

I glanced around the room. The party filled the working office as well as the waiting area; drinks stood melting on tables and bowls half-filled with chip crumbs were everywhere. Dorinda was drinking a cranberry juice and nodding at something Raul was saying to her. The Jackmans were still dancing; the switch to Latin music had brought out even more of the earth mother in Marvella, who slid her body alongside her husband's in a way I wasn't sure their teenaged son ought to see.

Keith's warm breath smelled of rye whisky and potato

chips. The fact that I could smell it at all meant he was too close. I danced away lightly, not wanting to insult him, but determined to maintain a lawyer-client distance between us.

"Hey, where you going?" He reached out a hand to grab mine.

"Bathroom," I called back. "Sorry."

In the bathroom, I splashed cold water on my sweating face and let it drip down my neck, soaking my blouse. I buried my face in a towel and let the moisture sink into the thick terry cloth.

I wanted to go back outside and dance till my feet hurt and drink to my victory and believe in my heart of hearts that for once in my legal life I'd really truly been on the side of the angels.

But some tiny part of Mickey's warning had lodged in my brain like a shard of ice, keeping me from letting go completely with Keith.

When I stepped back into the parlor, Raul took my hand and led me onto the makeshift dance floor. The music lent itself to the cha-cha, the only Latin dance I had any real ability to do. And even then I had to count. *One, two three. One, two three. Turn, two three. Back, two three.*

I hoped I didn't look too hopelessly Midwestern-Anglo-stiff—and then I decided that I looked however I looked and to hell with it. I let the music tell me how to move and I let Raul answer my movements with his and I got hot and sweaty and loose.

About forty minutes later, the party began breaking up. First the Jackmans headed home to Crown Heights, taking a reluctant Oliver (who'd already made a play date with Keith to resume their game). Then Angie shoved the last of the paper plates into a garbage bag and said she and Raul had plans to see the latest kung fu movie in Chinatown. Dorinda had salads to make for tomorrow's lunch, and Keith—

Keith wasn't going anywhere. Keith wanted to take me to dinner again.

"Keith, look at me," I protested. "I'm covered with sweat, I'm tired. Tonight's just not—"

"How about tomorrow?"

I was framing an answer when a voice called through the open door, "Hey, is everything all right in here?"

I turned. Nellis Cartwright stood in the doorway, a concerned look on her face. I glanced down at my sweat-soaked blouse, which was no longer tucked into my skirt, and at my bare legs (I'd slipped off the pantyhose and started dancing barefoot early on in the party). She, on the other hand, looked like a page out of a magazine, every champagne-blond hair in place, wearing a designer suit and carrying a large, thin portfolio along with an expensive handbag.

"Sure," I said, breaking away from Keith and walking toward her. "Why do you ask?"

"It looked like you had a break-in," she replied.

Keith broke into laughter and stepped over to join us. "It *was* a pretty good party," he said. "And there's not much difference between the aftermath of a burglary and a good party."

When was the last time I'd had a client who used the word *aftermath*?

"Tomorrow's fine," I said to Keith. "I've really had a taste for one of those giant burritos."

"Seven okay?" His face was radiant. "I should be finished with the deliveries by then." He gave my hand a quick squeeze, then turned and took the steps to the sidewalk two at a time.

"New boyfriend?" Nellis asked.

"No, a client," I replied. I pushed sopping wet hair off my brow. I didn't know this woman well enough to discuss my private life.

Instead, I brought her up to date on my meeting with Grant, omitting any reference to the X-rated *netsuke*. I did tell her about another piece Grant had shown me. It was a long-faced woman with her hands folded in front of her and her mouth open as if she was groaning. Flames carved in ivory licked at her feet.

She was called the Lantern Ghost; Grant said she was the spirit of a woman who'd killed her husband.

Nellis capped the story with a lifted eyebrow. "Did my former husband tell you the Lantern Ghost killed her husband because he was unfaithful?"

I admitted that he'd omitted that part of the story; Nellis said she wasn't surprised.

Then I asked a question I very quickly realized I should have asked a long time ago. A question destined to change our entire relationship. "Hey, before I forget—did you have your own attorney during your divorce, or did you and Grant have the same lawyer?"

"Did I have a 'lawyer'?" Nellis put sarcastic quotes around the word. "That depends on how you define your terms. I had a person who stood next to me in court—when she bothered to show up. Half the time she sent a law student who had to beg the court's permission to open his mouth. Even when she showed, she was late and didn't remember the first thing about the case. She'd start talking about a beach house in the Hamptons when Grant and I had a ski house on Hunter Mountain, that kind of thing. Like she couldn't be bothered to keep things straight. By the end, I felt as if I was totally alone. I had no faith in her anymore. But I had no money to hire someone else."

"I'm sorry to hear your lawyer was female," I remarked. "I guess I still hope we're better than the guys when it comes to representing other women."

Nellis twisted the sapphire ring on her hand. "That's exactly what I thought when I hired her," she said. "I didn't want some cigar-chomping old fart who thought women should stay in the kitchen. I asked around, got some names. She actually came highly recommended, believe it or not. A couple of women I know said she was the best thing that happened to them during their divorces, that she was always there for them. All I know is, she never seemed to be there for me."

"Not having a bedside manner isn't a breach of the Canon of Ethics," I said, as gently as I could. "This lawyer may not have been a hand-holder, but that doesn't mean she didn't do a good job on the substantive matters."

It was more honest than I'd intended to be. More honest than I should have been with a civilian. Nellis did exactly what I'd have done if someone had said those words to me. She bristled. "I didn't need my hand held, for God's sake. I needed someone to investigate all of Grant's holdings, to get me a truly equitable distribution. She took everything he said at face value. She never looked for hidden assets, even though I kept telling her there had to be more. She went through the motions, that's all. Just went through the motions."

Since I'd entered the fray as an appellate lawyer, I'd heard a great many variations on the theme of My Lawyer Sold Me Out. It was never my favorite argument; I knew too much about how hard the average lawyer worked for her clients to enjoy hearing my fellow attorneys trashed by their lowlife former clients. And you didn't have to be serving time to be a lowlife. Too many people who'd gotten into deep trouble under their own steam wanted to blame their lawyers when they couldn't get out of their self-created messes. I wasn't about to help Nellis dump on her previous counsel unless that lawyer really deserved it.

"Look, whatever went on between you and your lawyer, I have to tell you that the only way you'll have a chance to change the court order is to prove that this lawyer was incompetent. Not just careless or uncaring, but outright incompetent. That's the only thing the court will listen to at this stage."

"I already have a complaint before the bar association," Nellis countered. "If it's the last thing I do, I'm going to see Kate Avelard disbarred."

The breath rushed out of my lungs. "Kate Avelard?"

"You know her?" Surprise was quickly replaced by a cynical smile. "Of course you do. All you lawyers know each other and I'll bet you all stick together. You won't take my case now that you know who my last lawyer was. You're just like all the rest of them."

"Kate Avelard's a good lawyer." I said the words, but even as they left my mouth I realized I didn't know the truth of that statement. Not anymore. Kate had been a good lawyer once, but was she still? Could Kate have grown negligent while Marc lay on the daybed, slowly ebbing away?

It was possible.

And if she had dropped the ball in Nellis Eddington's case, then not only had Nellis been cheated of proper legal representation, but Kate was going to be punished for putting her dying husband ahead of her clients.

And there was nothing on God's earth I could do about it.

I invited Nellis inside and spent the next forty minutes explaining to her why I couldn't take her case. I even resorted to reading her the appropriate passages from the Canon of Ethics, the rules that regulate the professional lives of attorneys. But all "conflict of interest" meant to her was that I was on Kate's side and not hers and everyone was against her and how could anyone expect justice in a system like this and—

And finally I just said that's how it is. I told her I'd asked Spider to look into her finances and said he could still work for her if she wanted him, but that I was off the case and would be happy to return the files she'd given me.

The files that, interestingly enough, never had mentioned the name of her former counsel.

Had Nellis been keeping that information from me because she knew damned well it would mean the end of our professional relationship?

I had to talk to Kate. Since I wasn't taking the case, there was no ethical reason I couldn't. So I showered and changed, then walked the long, cool, refreshing blocks to the Heights, savoring the smells of fall as I kicked piles of dry leaves with my sneakered feet.

The tree-lined streets and spacious, well-preserved brownstones of an earlier age came into view as I turned from Henry Street toward the Promenade. Brooklyn Heights was a natural stage set for an Edith Wharton movie; its leaded glass windows and crystal chandeliers winked at me through huge tall windows with delicate lace curtains. The railings were black lacquered wrought iron in intricate patterns, with boot-scrapers on the second step so that visitors could clean the mud from their shoes before entering the parlor.

Willow Place is as quaint as it gets in the Heights. Tall, carved oak doors and beveled glass windows. Shiny brass knockers and discreet bronze plaques proclaiming the year the brownstones were built. The one on Kate Avelard's house said 1841.

I lifted the knocker and realized it was in the shape of a gavel. Since neither Kate nor Marc had been elevated to the bench, I had to see it as a token of hope. I shook my head; if Nellis had her way, there was no chance of Kate's seeing a black robe in her future. She'd be damned lucky to keep her license to practice law.

I rapped three times. Authoritative but not obnoxious. I peered through the oval window as I waited. There were huge vases with fresh flowers in the tiny foyer.

I stepped back when a figure came toward the door. She called out, "Who is it?" and opened the door with a broad smile when I replied.

"Cass. What a nice surprise. Come on in." She beckoned me into the hallway, where the smell of the exotic blooms was almost overpowering.

I followed her through the huge sliding door into the front parlor. It was decorated much as it would have been in 1841, with the obvious addition of electricity instead of gas. Kate was one of those Victoriana buffs who went for the real thing. A red velvet sofa with truly ugly woodwork, two claw-footed end tables, pictures hung on long ribbons from the molding under the ceiling. Antimacassars on every chair. Knickknacks on every surface. An embroidered fire screen in front of the fireplace. The effect was overwhelming, ornate, and oppressive, yet somehow homey.

I sat in a wine-velvet chair and felt myself engulfed by atmosphere. Sherlock Holmes could have stepped in from the rear parlor and I wouldn't have blinked an eye.

"Tell me there's nothing in this room that was made from human hair."

Kate laughed. "Can't." She pointed toward the corner. "See that mourning piece?"

"The droopy willow with the tombstones? Cheerful little thing."

"On the table underneath I have a collection of miniatures. Four of them have locks of hair inside."

"Oh, well, locks."

"The hair embroidery is upstairs in my office." Laughter lay below the surface of her voice.

"God, the Victorians and death. What was that about?" Even before I finished, I remembered Marc.

"Oh, hell, Kate, I'm sorry. I didn't mean that the way it—"

She waved my apology away with a hand draped in bracelets. "Don't be. I was a collector long before Marc got sick. All this morbidity has nothing to do with reality. Maybe that's why I love it. Victorian death is so neat, so ethereal. Not nearly as messy as it is in real life."

"He was a good guy."

She nodded. "Yes, he was. I miss him every day. And the funny thing is, I don't just miss him the way he was before he got sick. I miss him lying on the chaise longue upstairs, when he couldn't talk anymore. I miss him just being there, watching the kids and me go about our lives. Listening to whoever sat next to him in that wicker chair. We'd all do that, Zack and Hilary and I. Sit in that chair and tell him all about our day, what we were doing. He'd listen and blink once in a while to let us know he was focusing on what we were saying."

Her eyes teared. "At least I think he was focusing. Because if not, we were probably boring the poor man to death." What could have been a sob became a laugh instead. Which said it all for me about Kate and Marc and their marriage.

"So what brings you here, Cass?"

"One of your former clients wanted to hire me." I didn't add that she was living in my brownstone.

"Oh, God. Another dissatisfied customer." Kate's face fell, all traces of amusement gone. "Just how badly did this one trash me?"

"This has happened before?"

She nodded. "Unfortunately. I was a bit distracted while Marc was ill. I didn't do all the little things you have to do to keep clients happy. I didn't always return calls, and I sent David to cover some of my court appearances."

"David?"

"My assistant, David Leventhal. He was a law graduate when I hired him, but he passed the bar last November. He was perfectly capable, but some clients resent it when you can't make it yourself."

"I think Nellis is upset by more than—"

"Nellis Eddington?"

I nodded. "Yeah, a divorce case. She—"

Kate's lips tightened. "I remember her all too well. Let me warn you, Cass, that woman's obsessed. She's convinced her husband is some secret Rockefeller, with money hidden somewhere. I investigated Grant Eddington thoroughly and there just aren't any hidden assets. I got Nellis as good a deal as she was ever going to get. She's a reasonably young woman with a profession; judges just don't give alimony in cases like hers anymore. Her trouble is, she wants to be an artist and she expects her husband to subsidize her. She doesn't want to do what it takes to make a living in her profession. That's the whole case in a nutshell. Take my advice, Cass. Stay away from that woman at all costs."

"She's filing charges against you with the bar association."

The words were muttered, but I heard them all too clearly. "She'll have to get in line."

"That bad?"

"That bad. I swear, Cass, I wasn't totally out to lunch. I took care of things. But somehow all my unhappy clients—and you know from experience, there are always some unhappy clients—have gotten together to make my life a living hell."

We sat in silence for a moment. Then I said, trying to keep my voice neutral and not accusing, "I suppose you did all the standard things, credit history, real property check, stocks, bonds, whatever."

She nodded. "Of course. But it's not as if he has massive sums of money hidden away. He writes, for God's sake. His drama critic job pays a salary, he's got a few investments, he lectures and writes, and he's got those Japanese antiques that the entire city knows about. His assets are pretty much out there for everyone to see."

"So why is Nellis convinced there's more?"

Kate puffed out her cheeks and gave a loud sigh. "Because she's a trophy wife who can't stand being downsized. It's that simple. Bitchy, but true. Grant married her because he wanted someone pretty and talented on his arm, and now he's traded her in for a younger model. It's nasty, but it's not fraud."

"You're saying she's making up this fraud charge in order to—"

"I don't know if she's making it up," Kate said. Her fingers moved nervously along the edge of her clawfoot chair.

"She may well believe it. All I know is, my accountants vetted the settlement and said it was fair. I still have no reason to doubt that opinion."

"God, this must be awful. All this second-guessing. I told Nellis I couldn't take her case, but—"

This time the long sigh was ragged, as if tears were just below the surface. "Did you ever have that nightmare where you're in court, about to sum up to the jury, and you suddenly realize you have no earthly idea what the case is about? And then you look down and realize you're naked? Ever have that one?"

I nodded; we've all had that one.

"Well, that dream is now my life. Every mistake I ever made is under a microscope. Every client who ever left my office unsatisfied is giving the bar committee an earful. I lie awake at night trying to remember all the things I've ever done in my practice that might raise a question. And there are some. There are always some."

I gave her another nod as she continued her sad litany. "The affidavits that weren't exactly signed on the day they were dated, the complaint I drew up before my investigator came back with all the facts, the money that went into my safe for a week before it was deposited."

I tried for a lighter atmosphere. "Cheer up, Kate. It could be worse. Your malpractice insurance might have lapsed."

The dead silence that followed told me I'd made anything but a joke.

Which meant that Kate not only had her career and her livelihood at stake, she stood to lose every single thing she owned if Nellis proved negligence and damages.

And there was nothing I could do about it.

CHAPTER SEVEN

In the two weeks that followed, September turned to October, the temperature dropped, and more leaves littered the streets. The gaiety of Rosh Hashanah, the Jewish New Year, gave way to the solemnity of Yom Kippur, the Day of Atonement. Gorgeous blue skies alternated with blustery, damp reminders of the winter to come.

I spent a good part of the time in a state of euphoria over my victory; whatever setbacks I suffered in other cases could always be assuaged by recalling Keith Jernigan's reversed conviction. I even had a brief interview with a reporter from the *New York Law Journal* about the case. At one point, he asked if Keith might sue the city for wrongful arrest; I said we were a long way from that, since he was still facing trial on the charges, but that we couldn't rule it out.

Our half-hour interview became three paragraphs on page eight, but I clipped it and stuck it on the bulletin board anyway.

And the fax attacks began.

At first, I thought they were some sort of public service announcement. I'd go to the fax machine tray and there would be a decision of the grievance committee regarding some hapless lawyer who'd screwed up. Or an appellate court opinion affirming the poor sap's disbarment. I thought perhaps I'd gotten on some mailing list or other.

They didn't seem threatening. At first.

But then, just in case I wasn't getting the point, they began arriving with little notes in the margins. Notes that said things like "Watch out, this could be you."

The fax of the day was an opinion by the New York State Bar Association regarding a lawyer's participation in a divorce mediation service. It was a very clear statement that a lawyer could not participate in any kind of partnership with a nonlawyer.

The block-printed note of the day read: "Don't you think you and Ms. Dechter are in violation of this ruling? I'm willing to bet the bar association will see it that way."

I'd thrown away the first three or four of the faxes, thinking they were just junk mail for the nineties, but I'd started a file after the notes began. I put this one into the folder, but it nagged at me all the same.

The answer was no. Mickey Dechter and I were not in violation of the Canon of Ethics because we were not partners. She rented office space from me and a few of my clients went to her for counseling, just as a few of hers sought legal advice from me. We were most definitely not in the divorce mediation business, because I wasn't a damned fool and I'd seen that opinion when it first came out in January 1996.

But there's another rule in the Canon of Ethics that deals with "the appearance of impropriety"—and that one just might hit the mark if anyone filed a complaint about our arrangement.

Who wanted me on edge thinking about possible ethics violations?

A certain collector of Japanese antiquities came to mind. But could I prove it?

The faxes had all been sent from a 212 exchange, which meant Manhattan. I'd given Raul the task of tracking the phone number, but with no results so far. There was no central listing of fax numbers, no reverse directory that automatically included them. And there were fax machines in every private mailbox storefront, offering anonymity at three bucks a throw.

The other important development during that period was the Brooklyn D.A.'s decision to retry Keith Jernigan on the robbery charge.

Keith, meanwhile, had become a fixture around the place. He was there when I came down for coffee in the morning, and when I stopped in for lunch, and he was there again when I picked up my takeout dinner.

When he wasn't delivering Dorinda's meals, he was upstairs in my office, sitting at the computer with Oliver or collating and stapling motion papers for Marvella, or helping Raul write his investigation reports. Sometimes he was at the computer by himself, programming it to do something faster and more efficiently than it had before. Sometimes he was on Lexis, printing out court decisions he was sure I'd need for one of my cases.

It was like having a law student working for me. A law student who worked for free.

I liked having Keith around. It made me feel good to look at him and Oliver role-playing together. But I knew it couldn't—and, more to the point—shouldn't last. He had to make his own new life, find a better-paying full-time job, maybe go back to school and get an advanced degree.

When I said something along those lines, about four days after he came out of jail, his face fell. "You're not trying to get rid of me, are you?"

He said it in a tone that tried for kidding but came out as

adolescent-defensive. It occurred to me for the first time just how important my approval was to him.

I hastened to explain. "No, no, of course not. I enjoy having you around. But, let's face it, delivering Dorinda's black bean soup with jalapeño cornbread isn't much of a career path. You can do a lot better for yourself, Keith."

"Like someone's going to hire a guy who just came out of the joint," he said, with a twisted smile.

"I can give you a reference," I said lightly, "and so can Dorinda. Why not," I went on, trying to sound as if the thought had just come to me, "go back to the job you had before you got arrested? Where was that, anyway?"

"Met Life," he said. "But I don't think I'd want to go back there. Too many bad vibes."

"Well, maybe another insurance company would—"

"No," he said, cutting me off with a chopping hand motion. "I'm finished with that. I'll find something else, if you really think I should."

And he did. The next day, Keith announced that he'd taken a second job at an electronics store on Hudson Street in Manhattan. He worked the weekend shift, so he'd still be able to deliver for Dorinda during the week, which was her busiest time thanks to the two-career families who lived in Cobble Hill.

The Monday after he started the job, he brought a hand-held scanner, a cellular phone, and a pocket-sized tape recorder and set them all on my desk. He stood back and waited for my reaction, a look of anticipation on his face.

"Keith, what is all this?"

"Presents," he replied. "Presents from me to you. I get a twenty percent discount as an employee at the store."

"Keith, this stuff must have cost twice what you made this weekend, even with a twenty percent discount."

"Don't you like it?"

"Well, sure, but—"

"Then don't worry about what it cost. Besides, it's all

stuff they were going to get rid of anyway. There are new upgrades coming out on those models, and the boss couldn't wait to get rid of them."

"Well, thank you. I certainly can put these to good use."

It did strike me as a coincidence—to say the least—that the very model of cellular phone I'd been wanting to buy was about to go on sale at Keith's store. And as for the hand-held scanner, I knew for a fact that the one he'd brought me was state-of-the-art and very expensive.

But the look on Keith's face when he laid them on my desk said he'd be mortified if I turned them down.

I only hoped he had enough money to pay his living expenses.

The second, and more troubling, thought didn't come to me until late in the day.

I hoped to hell he hadn't stolen the stuff from his new employer.

Why had that thought crossed my mind at all? Didn't I believe in my heart of hearts that Keith was innocent?

Well, yes, but—

But what?

But there was something weird in the way he hung around. Didn't he have a life of his own to go back to now that he was free?

On the afternoon of the ethics fax, I was just entering the office after a long court day, when the doorbell rang. Marvella had gone home, so I opened the door myself.

I hadn't seen so many red roses since my great-aunt Bridget's funeral. At first I figured the delivery boy had the wrong address; I stood in the doorway and tried to muster the wits to give correct directions. But the enormous bouquet was for me, and the delivery boy was Keith Jernigan.

I blurted the first thing that came into my head. "How the hell many of those *are* there?"

"Four dozen," he replied cheerfully. "I wanted more, but these were all the red ones the guy had." He inclined his head in the direction of the Korean grocery store up the block. "I remembered you liked red. Deep ruby red. These reminded me of you, so I—"

"Keith, you don't have a full-time job." I was in blurting mode, a side effect of caffeine deprivation. "You can't afford to buy roses and expensive electronics."

His face fell. I had the distinct impression that if I said one more word, he'd throw the immense bouquet into the gutter. And that would be even more of a waste. They might as well grace my office.

I opened the door and coaxed him inside. "Thank you," I said, trying for the right amount of effusiveness to make up for my earlier remarks. "I can't remember the last time anyone brought me flowers." I leaned into the bouquet and sniffed. "God, these are gorgeous."

"I hope you have a big enough vase." Keith strode past me and headed up the stairs to my apartment.

"I thought I'd put them in the office," I protested. I wasn't exactly sure why, but I didn't want Keith in my private space.

"Oh, no," he answered, taking the steps at a fast clip. "I pictured them in your boudoir."

"My what?" I mobilized myself and trotted up the stairs in his wake. The door was still open; he stepped inside before I could call him back.

"Vases in the kitchen or what?" By the time I reached the kitchen, he had cabinets open. The roses lay on the countertop, swaddled in green tissue paper. He moved from one set of shelves to the other, methodically intent upon his hunt.

"I'll get one," I said, speaking loudly, as if unsure of making myself heard. I knelt and opened the cabinet just underneath the cutting board. The biggest vases were in back, so I had to take out the electric wok and the fondue set before I pulled out a huge cylindrical vase, cobalt blue with a heavy glass bottom.

It was coated with dust fixed in place by years of cooking grease in the air. So much for the last time I had flowers; it had to have been before I moved to Brooklyn. I needed either a better class of client or a boyfriend.

I stood up, the blood rushing to my head. Keith pried the vase out of my hands and ran water in the sink. He picked up a dishcloth and squeezed dish soap on it, then set to work scrubbing off the grime.

Sometimes one's consciousness is high, and other times it hits the basement. "You'd make some lucky girl a great husband." Even as the words left my mouth, they reminded me of my uncle Lester, Great-Aunt Bridget's loutish second husband, a man so full of clichés that conversation with him had an oddly soothing quality. No surprises.

Why was I standing in my own kitchen sounding like Uncle Lester?

Maybe because the last time a man had stood at my sink and washed a dish in my presence was twelve years ago.

Maybe because the last time a client had been in my kitchen was never.

I turned toward the coffee machine and lifted the basket out. "Want some? I've got a nice estate Java I could grind."

"I knew you weren't the Tasters' Choice type," he said with that wry tone of voice I liked so much.

"Shall I take that as a yes?"

Was this flirting?

His answering smile told me he thought it was. I busied myself with the coffee, grateful for the whine of the grinder, which prevented conversation for a moment. By the time I had the coffee ready, he'd arranged the roses in a symmetrical if oversized grouping.

"Wouldn't it be better to take some out for a second vase? I could put one in the living room here and the other downstairs."

The smile froze. He stiffened and his voice sounded strained. "I bought them for your bedroom. That's where they belong."

But you don't.

Once I'd said the words, even if only to myself, I relaxed. I was overprotecting my privacy. What did I expect Keith to do—take one look at the unmade bed, throw me on it, rip off my clothes, and have his way with me?

Just letting him walk into the bedroom, put the vase on the bed table, and then walk out again wasn't such a big deal. Was it?

I followed him into the room as if he required supervision. After he placed the roses just so on the table next to the bed, moving my Mickey Mouse alarm clock and half-read Anne Perry novel to one side, he stood and surveyed the room.

"I like it," he said. It was a line from a romantic movie, delivered exactly the way Tom Cruise or maybe Hugh Grant would have said it. Dragging the words out, as if paying a high compliment. Acting as if his appreciation of my taste meant we were soul mates on some deep level the rest of the world couldn't appreciate.

Or was I reading too much into his words? On the theory that I was, I said, "Coffee should be ready. Thanks again for the roses. They look wonderful."

I waited in the doorway for him to exit the room. As he passed me, his hand brushed, ever so lightly, ever so accidentally, against my breast.

Mickey was right. God, I hated it when my friends were right and I was wrong and in some tiny part of my brain I'd always known they were right but I didn't listen because they sounded like my parents, like the people I'd grown up with in Ohio, like all the sensible, white-bread, bland, never-take-a-chance types I'd left home to get away from. I hated the fact that sometimes the conventional wisdom actually contained wisdom and not just convention.

Mickey had said from the beginning that Keith wanted to be more than just a client, and here was the blood-red living proof in the form of a roomful of roses, their rich, sweet scent filling my nostrils even as I wished them somewhere else.

That, I decided, could be arranged. As soon as Keith took off on the delivery bike, conveying Dorinda's pad Thai noodles to an address on President Street, I called a car service, bundled the roses into a huge but manageable bunch, and sped off toward Long Island College Hospital.

The woman at the desk peered at me over her reading glasses. "Broke up with the boyfriend, hon?" She answered her own question in a gravelly, New York voice. "I see it all the time. The boyfriend thinks a bunch of flowers is all it takes to get his girl back. She thinks different, and the patients get the benefits."

She picked up the white phone on her desk and within minutes a candy striper appeared with a wheeled cart. "You want these should go to as many patients as possible, right?"

It hadn't occurred to me that what I was doing was routine; that they would have seen roses delivered like this before.

"I guess so," I said. "Especially if they haven't already got flowers in their rooms."

"Oh, yeah," the desk lady agreed, "that goes without saying. There's a lot of people here without families, or their families haven't got the money to pony up for a bouquet. They'll appreciate these, hon, even if the boyfriend's a first-class rat."

"He's not exactly a—"

"Oh, don't start defending him, hon. A guy sends a bunch of roses like that, he probably broke a rib, at least. We see it all the time down here. Just don't let him think he can buy you off with flowers. You get him into some kind of treatment or it's no go. Don't let him walk all over you."

The candy striper pulled the roses from the bouquet and set them, one by one, into bud vases. Keith's gift, it seemed, would brighten the rooms of forty-eight patients. I thanked the desk lady, she thanked me back, and I stepped back outside feeling good about what I'd done.

Meanwhile, back at the office, Lissa Birnbaum had decided she and Craig really needed to get into marriage counseling. She was certain that with a few sessions of soul-baring, their love could be rekindled. I gently reminded her that Craig was presently living with a younger associate in his real estate firm and that counseling was not an option.

As she dissolved in tears on the phone, I found myself wishing for one-tenth of Mickey's bedside manner. She'd have been able, I was sure, to calm Lissa down, whereas every word out of my mouth only served to bring on more sobs.

"He's a rat, Lissa," I said at last. "Get over him. He treated you like dirt, he ran around on you, he even said he wasn't sure your kids were really his—do you really want him back?"

"You don't understand," she wailed. "I love him."

"No, I don't understand," I said, exasperation getting the better of me. "I don't understand one little bit. But that doesn't matter. You filed for divorce and you were right. Let the law take its course. Get child support for Melanie and Jason. Move on with your life."

I held the phone away from my ear and waited for the inevitable. "I can't move on," Lissa moaned. "I still love him in spite of everything."

I wasn't proud of the words I said next. Mickey would never have said them.

"He doesn't love you. I know that hurts like hell, but it's the truth, Lissa, and the sooner you deal with that, the better off you'll be."

"You don't understand," she said again.

That brought us back to square one. I suggested she make an appointment with Mickey, her therapist, and got off the line.

I was drenched in sweat. Four hours in the criminal court pens had nothing on ten minutes with Lissa Birnbaum.

The fax machine made its "incoming call" noise. I stepped over to it, expecting to see Craig Birnbaum's answering papers or perhaps a request for an adjournment from opposing counsel.

What I didn't expect was a picture. Grainy, black-and-white, almost a mugshot.

It was a woman.

Maybe.

It was hard to tell; the face seemed blurred, somehow. Unfinished. Like a Halloween mask.

The next piece of paper to come out of the fax was block-printed in big black capital letters.

THIS IS WHAT KEITH JERNIGAN DID TO TOBIE DAVID.
THIS IS THE GUY YOU GOT A WALK FOR.

I studied the picture more closely.

The face was a woman's. At least I thought it was a woman. Hard to tell. Her face was—

—gone. Melted. Like one of those Hiroshima maidens after the A-bomb fell on their city.

What did the writer mean, Keith did this?

As if the fax machine itself could hear my thoughts, another piece of paper came slowly out onto the tray.

It was a clipping from an old newspaper, a tabloid, although I couldn't tell which one. The headline read: WOMAN FIGHTS FOR LIFE IN ACID ATTACK

Her name was Tobie David. She worked for the Metropolitan Life Insurance Company in Manhattan. She was walking to work from her apartment on East 25th Street when a man ran up to her and flung the contents of a bottle in her face.

The bottle contained lye, a corrosive substance that, in

essence, melted her face. She was rushed to the hospital where, it was said, doctors were working to save her sight, since the acid had affected her eyes as well as her skin.

Her former boyfriend was wanted for questioning in connection with the incident.

His name was Keith Jernigan.

I looked back down at the photograph of the woman with the ruined face. Had Keith really done this to her?

He hadn't committed the liquor store robbery. That I was still sure of. He was innocent on that charge.

But was he guilty of something worse?

As if this wasn't enough to absorb, one more hand-lettered piece of paper rolled onto the tray of my fax machine.

I read the words with growing horror.

WHERE'S TOBIE NOW?
KEITH ISN'T FINISHED WITH HER.
BELIEVE THIS.

Card Two: The Devil

LIKE ALL GOOD STORIES, THIS ONE STARTED WITH "ONCE UPON A TIME."

Once upon a time there was a girl named Linda and she worked in an office in the Bronx. One day she went walking in a park and met a man named Burt. He was everything she'd ever wanted in a man. He was sophisticated, romantic, mature, very much in love with her, and—

And married.

They became lovers anyway. He sent her flowers and took her to nightclubs. There were nightclubs back then, places like the Copacabana, where worldly men knew how to show a girl a good time.

But Linda wanted more. She wanted to be Burt's wife.

He couldn't bring himself to leave his wife, and so Linda ended it. Told him she never wanted to see him again.

Burt couldn't stand it. He went a little bit crazy with grief and despair.

One day there was a knock at Linda's door. When she opened it, a man she'd never seen before told her he had a present for her. He was carrying a bottle of soda. He shook it till it fizzed and aimed the fizz at her face.

The bottle contained more than soda. It contained lye.

Linda's face was so scarred she lost one eye and had trouble with the other. Her face was ruined.

Burt was arrested, convicted, and sent to jail for fourteen long years.

He wrote her letters. He sent her money. He thought about her night and day and promised he'd take care of her when he was released from prison.

On the day he got out, he was interviewed by a local reporter. He sat on a park bench and answered questions, looking straight into the camera and speaking from his heart. He said, "Linda, I know you're out there. I love you and I want to marry you."

Linda was out there. She saw, with what was left of her vision, and the love in Burt's eyes poured into her very soul.

They were married the next day. The absolute next day.

Now twenty years had passed, and Burt was once again on television. He sat with Linda, patting her knee and gazing at her with total love in his eyes, in spite of the scars on her cheek. She was totally blind now, but she smiled as he talked about their twenty years of marriage.

Keith Jernigan thought it was the most romantic story he'd ever heard.

CHAPTER EIGHT

"Go ahead and say it. I deserve it. You were right and I was—"

"Oh, cut it out," Mickey said. "I hate it when you try to act humble. It doesn't suit you one bit. And don't think I enjoy being right about a thing like this. Just look at that poor girl."

The photo lay on the coffee table in my tiny living room. I sat on the futon while Mickey occupied the mission-style rocker I'd been given by my antique dealer clients.

"I don't have to look at her," I replied. "Believe me, that face has haunted me from the minute I first saw that picture."

"Well, if you don't want to end up looking like her," Mickey pronounced, "you'd better tell Keith Jernigan to go away and stay away."

"This is a social worker talking? Whatever happened to compassion, to understanding, to 'nothing human is alien to me'?"

"I didn't say it was alien, I said it was dangerous. Leaving yourself open to attack is not an act of compassion. It's an act of stupidity."

"Thank you, Doctor Laura." I stood up and walked into the kitchen—a mere five steps away—for the coffeepot. Neither of us really needed a refill; I just wanted a chance to regroup.

"He *is* my client," I pointed out as I lifted the glass pot from the hot plate.

"You won his case," came the reply. "Doesn't that make him an ex-client?"

"Not if there's a retrial. I'm on the case until a judge relieves me."

"So get relieved." She placed a hand over her cup and shook her head. I poured coffee into my own cup, even though I didn't really want it either.

"It's not that easy," I said. "You have to have grounds."

"This," she said, picking up the photo and waving it under my nose, "doesn't look to you like grounds for getting off this case?"

"Mick, we don't know the whole story. We don't know—"

"So find out." She held the photo steady, making certain I couldn't turn away from the grotesque image. "Find out before you look like her. Please."

The thing is, lawyers have ethics. Hard to believe, but true. It wasn't really up to me to decide whether or not to represent Keith Jernigan. A court had assigned me to the case and only a court could relieve me of that assignment.

I pulled my pamphlet-sized copy of the *Code of Professional Responsibility* from the shelf and opened it to Disciplinary Rule 2-110. It spelled out in detail exactly what constituted grounds for withdrawal from legal employment; one clause said I could withdraw if my client "persists in a course of action involving the lawyer's services that the lawyer reasonably believes is criminal or fraudulent."

Keith's crime against Tobie, if any, had occurred long before I'd ever met him.

Although the fax message said he was going to pay her back for framing him on the robbery charge. If true, that was a threat of future criminal activity which I ought to report to the police and which might constitute grounds for being relieved.

But it was only an anonymous threat with absolutely no physical evidence to connect it with Keith. Anyone could have sent the fax.

So at this point in time, I decided, I had no grounds to withdraw from the case of the man I'd sworn to defend. But that didn't mean I had to stick my head in the sand either.

I had a package ready by the time Raul came in to work the next morning. I handed it over and said in crisp, businesslike tones, as if I wasn't asking him to dig dirt on our own client, "I want you to find out everything you can about Keith's past life before his arrest."

I opened the file and pointed to his one prior brush with the law. The charges had been dismissed, and the incident had happened almost seven years earlier, but now it was no longer a matter of ancient history. "Find out exactly what this old beef was about."

"It happened, like, what, upstate?" Raul pointed to the unfamiliar county name on the rap sheet.

"Yeah. I'm not sure where exactly, but he did say he went to Cornell. So I'd guess this is Ithaca. It's still in the NYSIIS system, though," I added, referring to the state criminal records division.

Then I showed him the picture. "This girl may be involved," I went on. "Although the charges that were dismissed are for malicious mischief, which is only property. Someone wanted me to know that Keith was responsible for this. I need to know exactly what that means."

"Man, this girl's messed up bad," Raul said, shaking his

head. "Somebody has to feel a powerful hate to do a thing like that."

I left Raul working the computer and went to court. When I came back for a quick lunch and an update, he filled me in on what he'd found out.

"So like it wasn't about throwing acid on nobody," he said through a mouthful of Dorinda's cheese and avocado sandwich on olive bread, "but it did *involve* acid. So it's like more than a coincidence but less than a—"

"Raul, what are you talking about?" My own sandwich lay untouched as I reflected, not for the first time, that teaching Raul to speak and write understandable reports was going to be a major challenge.

"The beef," he said, as if that explained everything. He took a swallow of iced Orange Zinger and prepared to wrap his mouth around another large hunk of sandwich.

"Raul, do me a favor and stop eating for a minute," I said. He raised his eyebrows as if this were the most unreasonable request he'd ever heard, but he closed his mouth.

"Back up. You say the prior arrest had something to do with acid, but it wasn't about throwing acid at this girl?"

"Right. See, that's what I'm saying. It was like about acid, but it wasn't—"

"Raul. Exactly what did Keith do?"

"He threw acid on some dude's car. A real expensive car, like a collector's item. An old car. From England or someplace. Ruined the finish, the dude was furious, but he couldn't prove nothin' so the charges was squashed."

"Who was this dude?"

Raul shrugged. "Some teacher."

"Okay, you can eat now," I said. "I guess that's a dead end."

Acid thrown on the finish of a vintage car; acid thrown into the face of a young woman.

My laserlike brain was detecting a pattern here. An escalating pattern.

I reached for the Green Book, which contained the addresses and phone numbers of every official in New York City. I found the number for the 19th Precinct and dialed, then asked to speak to a detective. When a husky female voice said, "PDU, Mazzanti," I identified myself and said I wanted to talk to someone about an old case.

"How old? Are we talking last month or Judge Crater?"

"In between," I replied.

I peered at the fax of the newspaper article and said, "Three years, give or take."

"I was here. Shoot." In the background, there were sounds of talking and keys clicking, general office noises.

"Tobie David. Girl with acid thrown—"

"Oh, Jesus. That one. You better believe I remember that case. Like it was yesterday. To this day, I swear, I have nightmares about some prick with a ski mask throwing acid in my face."

"Could you tell me about it?"

"Who are you? Why do you want to know?" Cop caution and New York paranoia took over; Mazzanti's antennae were up.

"I'm Keith Jernigan's lawyer, Cassandra Jameson. I just won his appeal on a robbery conviction."

"Oh, Jesus. You got that piece of shit off and now you want to know all about Tobie David? Why? So that little prick can—"

I raised my voice. "Nothing you say to me will get to him. I'm an officer of the court, and I—"

"Oh, yeah," she replied. "I've heard that one before. You defense lawyers are all alike."

"That's as may be," I said, "but I still need to know about Tobie David. Was Keith arrested for the attack? What happened to the charges? Nothing about this appears on his yellow sheet."

"That's because the poor little fool was too scared to make an ID," the detective answered. "We brought Jernigan in so many times we could have charged him rent, but she kept saying she couldn't be sure, it might have been him, she knew it was him, but she didn't see a face, she couldn't tell if it was his voice. Bottom line, she folded and he walked."

Mazzanti exhaled in that long, slow way that tells you someone's taking a drag on a cigarette. "Made me sick," she went on. "Made all of us sick. Especially since the prick had a history of harassment."

I treaded carefully. "A history of harassment without an arrest record? How exactly did that happen?"

"Ah, shit, you remember the way it was, right?" Another long exhale. "Back in those days, and it wasn't really so long ago, but in some ways, it might as well have been a century, cops blew off stuff like that. Called it boyfriend-girlfriend, or if you were in the Sixth, boyfriend-boyfriend, and basically left it to the parties to work it out themselves. We didn't really think in terms of stalking back then, just looked at each incident as a separate thing, and if it wasn't a crime, that was that. So the little petty stuff Tobie David complained about didn't really get anyone's attention. Until the fucker hit her with the acid, and then we all felt like crap because we didn't take her seriously enough."

I contemplated the last portion of the fax warning. "Where is she now?"

Before Mazzanti could respond, I added, "I know you won't give me an address or anything, but do you know where she is, and if she's all right?"

"No idea, Counselor. She left her job and her apartment after the attack."

To report or not to report.

I had to report. Just in case.

"I've had an anonymous fax telling me that Tobie David is in danger from my client. I have no idea who sent it or whether there's any truth in it, but I think someone in authority should know about it."

"So you picked me."

"You got lucky when you answered the phone."

"Fax it over, I'll talk to my lieutenant about it."

As I slid the papers into the sending tray, I noticed that this particular set of faxes had been sent, not from the 212 exchange, but from a 718 number, which meant Queens or Brooklyn.

It felt very strange turning my own client in to the police, but the Canon of Ethics was clear: I had a duty to report future crimes, even if I was ethically obligated to conceal past ones.

At five-thirty Keith walked into my office, a big smile on his face and a mug of Dorinda's coffee in his hand. It was a mug I hadn't seen before, hand-thrown and edged with blue paint. He turned it toward me as he placed it into my hand. My name in Greek—κασανδρα—jumped out at me.

My thanks were perfunctory at best. How could I enjoy a gift from a man who'd ruined a young girl's life?

I handed him first the photo and then the faxed article and watched while he read in silence. I noticed that his face was bruised, his jaw swollen, his knuckles cut.

"Been in a fight, Keith?"

He shook his head and gave me a pale imitation of his old smile. "Some guy tried to rip me off in the Village," he said. "He hit me, I hit him, and he ran off without my wallet."

"I'm sorry," I said, although I had the strong feeling I'd just been lied to. Probably not for the first time. "But what do you have to say about this girl?"

"The cops thought I did it," Keith admitted. "They didn't believe me when I told them I loved her; I couldn't do anything to hurt her."

"The newspapers said you'd broken up."

"Oh, that was just a temporary thing, believe me. Tobie and I were meant for each other. She was just going through a stage. She was young, you know, she needed time to think. So I moved out and let her date other guys for a while. I knew she'd come back to me eventually. And then this awful thing happened."

Tears started in his eyes. "I couldn't believe it when the police came and told me. I couldn't believe it when they started thinking I did it. I just hoped Tobie didn't see it that way. I wanted to visit her in the hospital, but they wouldn't let me. They had a cop by her bed all the time."

"Did you ever see her again?"

He shook his head. "I waited by the door when I heard she was going to be released," he said sadly, "but then they took her out another door. All I know is that she told the cops she couldn't say for sure that I was the one. She didn't get enough of a good look, she said."

The newspaper had already said as much. It had been a frigid January morning and the assailant had worn a ski mask, which obscured his features without looking particularly suspicious in view of the wind chill.

"What happened to the two of you after she came home from the hospital?"

"She never came home," Keith replied. "I went to her apartment and the super said some lady came and moved all her stuff out the day after it happened. She never went back there, and she never came back to work either."

"Came back to work?" I echoed. "You mean she worked at Met Life, too?"

"Sure, that's where we met."

"You met at work, went out a few times, and then she dumped you?" The flippant tone was on purpose. I wanted to prod and poke and jab at him until I got a response I felt I could trust, a genuine emotion that would, somehow, tell me the truth of the situation. "And then you flipped out and threw acid at her. As if any girl who didn't want to see you anymore didn't deserve to have a face."

"I didn't do it!" Keith jumped from his chair and lifted his arms in the air. "I don't know what I have to do to convince you. I'm innocent. Those cops thought I was guilty and that's why they set me up for the robbery, but I swear to you, I could never hurt Tobie."

It took a minute for the subordinate clause to catch my attention. "What do you mean, that's why the cops set you up for the robbery? Are you saying you think they framed you on purpose?"

"I know that's what every loser behind bars tells his lawyer," he replied with a ghost of his old ironic tone, "so I didn't bring it up before. I knew we'd have a better chance on appeal if I didn't try to convince the court that it was a frame job."

"Well, you were right about that," I muttered. I remembered Detective Mazzanti saying that the entire precinct "felt like crap" when Tobie David was attacked and no arrest could be made. Was it possible that someone had decided to make Keith pay for his crime by setting him up on another charge? And how easy was that going to be to prove in a court of law?

"Whoever wrote this note seems to think you might hold Tobie responsible for having you set up," I said. "That is, if there was a setup in the first place. But you seem to think there was," I continued in a conversational tone, "so do you blame her for your conviction on the robbery charge?"

"Of course not," he replied, his eyes widening with indignation. "I know Tobie better than that. The cops didn't like me, so they showed my picture to that liquor store guy to get me in trouble. This one cop even said he wished he could put me away for a long time. Well, he got his wish, didn't he?"

"What about Tobie?"

"What about her?" The tone was the sullen, I-ain't-did-nothin' grunt I'd heard so often from so many criminal clients. A tone I'd never expected to hear from Keith.

"Is she in any danger from you?"

"I don't even know where she is."

"But if you did know?"

"I'd ask her to marry me. No matter what she looks like on the outside, she's a beautiful person on the inside and that's what counts."

Had Keith destroyed Tobie's outer beauty in order to convince her that he and he alone could appreciate her inner qualities?

With absolutely no evidence beyond the look on his face when we talked about it, I concluded that he had.

The only question was what I was going to do about it.

"Listen, Keith," I began, steepling my fingers and speaking slowly and deliberately, "I've been giving this a lot of thought and I—"

"And you're going to blame me just like all the rest of them."

Was that what I was doing?

Probably.

Did it bother me?

Yes.

Was I going to let my passion for the underdog, my lawyer's commitment to due process, endanger my employees and friends?

No.

I finished the sentence.

"I've decided it would be for the best if you didn't spend so much time around here. I'll still represent you, if that's what you want, but I'd rather you didn't—"

"I suppose that means Dorinda's about to tell me she can't use me anymore," he said, the bitterness in his tone palpable. "And then comes the part where Marvella says she doesn't want Oliver talking to me. You all want me to go away and never come back, right?"

I hardened my heart against the look on his face, the look of a kid trying his absolute best to get into the game in spite of all the other kids telling him he's not wanted. The look of a kid so desperate for friends that he'll say or do anything to gain admittance into what he sees as a golden circle.

I sighed. "Doing a thing like this is bad enough," I said, glancing at the picture of the girl with the ruined face. "But lying about it is—"

"You mean if I confess you won't get off my case?"

"I didn't say that."

"I was afraid to tell you the truth. I was afraid you'd hate me. I couldn't stand it if you hated me."

"I— Are you saying you threw the acid? Are you telling me—"

I'd known the truth from the minute I'd seen the picture. I had no idea exactly why; maybe because no one would send a message like that unless it were true, or maybe because I'd glimpsed something passionate and obsessive in Keith. And yet hearing his confession sent a chill of fear along my spine.

"I didn't mean it," he said. "I didn't realize how strong the acid was. I just wanted her to know how much I loved her. How bad I felt that she cut me off. It was like that song. Like the sun going down on me, and living the whole rest of my life in dark night. It—it made me go crazy. I really didn't feel like myself when I did it. I felt as if someone else took over my body and made me go after her with that bottle."

"But you denied it when the police came to ask you questions. Your guilt wasn't strong enough for you to admit what you did, was it?"

If he'd shown the slightest hint of sarcasm, I'd have been outraged. But his answer was so pure, so innocently said, that I had no choice but to yield to the irony it represented.

"Don't I have the right to remain silent?"

I had to allow that he did. I had to admit that my entire practice as a criminal defense lawyer was based on the fact that the prosecution had to prove guilt beyond a reasonable doubt without the help of the defendant, who couldn't be forced to help his accusers send him to jail.

Even if he'd done the unforgivable, he had his rights. And

I'd taken an oath to preserve and protect those rights. I was sworn to defend him unless and until such time as a court relieved me of the obligation. And no matter how appalled I was by Keith's treatment of Tobie, that alone didn't constitute grounds under the Code of Professional Responsibility.

"You have to understand how badly I feel about this," Keith said. His tone was one of frank pleading. "I know I did a terrible thing. I lost my head, I went crazy. I didn't think. But I could never do a thing like that again. I know better now. I know I have to be careful of letting my emotions get the better of me. I promise, this is in the past and—"

I held up a hand. "Let me think about this," I said. "Let me get some more information about Tobie David and let me talk it over with my staff. It's as much their decision as mine whether we stay on the case. We'll call a meeting and talk it over, and then I'll let you know. Meanwhile," I said, hardening my heart against the look of terror on his face, "I want you to stay away from this building. Don't call, don't come by. Stop working for Dorinda. Give us all time to absorb this information and decide what to do. Okay?"

He nodded but made no answer. His lip trembled and I was afraid he was going to cry. He got up and walked, then ran toward the door, slamming it on the way out and taking the stone steps two at a time. The last I saw of him, he was racing down Bergen Street toward the subway.

It was only later that I realized he'd punched out one of the glass windows in the front door with his bare hand. Droplets of blood lay congealing on the stoop amid shards of glass.

CHAPTER
NINE

There was no Tobie David. Not anymore. At least not according to the report Raul placed on my desk the next morning.

A Tobie David had worked for the Metropolitan Life Insurance Company in its Madison Square headquarters in Manhattan for nine months. She'd lived on East 26th—an easy walk to work.

No person named Tobie David could be found in any New York telephone book, nor did she have an unlisted number, nor was she registered to vote. She didn't own a car, didn't pay taxes, and hadn't died. Or at least, she hadn't died in a way that left a record. I had a morbid vision of the young woman's body being lowered into a pauper's common grave on Hart Island up in the Bronx. Unidentified and unmourned, victim of a lonely suicide.

I sat behind my desk and reread the investigation report. She'd listed her high school as Girls High in Brooklyn, but a call to the Board of Education produced a flat-out denial that a Tobie David had ever attended school there. Six Davids had been confirmed, from Andrea to Sylvia, but none of them were the right age.

She had to have some family. She couldn't have just appeared out of the blue and then disappeared back into it. Family—why did that thought nag at me so tantalizingly?

Then I remembered. It had been a long time since I'd worked for someone else. But in the days when I punched a clock for the Legal Aid Society, I'd filled out a number of forms on which I'd had to list a beneficiary in case of death, an emergency notification number in case of accident. What name had the elusive Ms. David put on her employment application?

I picked up the phone and called Met Life; Tobie's emergency number and her beneficiary were one and the same: Sylvia Franken, who lived at 324 East 81st Street, apartment 2F. Relationship to applicant: aunt. In all probability, the former Sylvia David of Girls High School.

But why an aunt instead of a mother or father? Was Tobie an orphan?

I picked up the phone again and then put it down without calling the number. Sylvia Franken would have every reason in the world to shield her niece from strangers.

I endured the usual subway madness of crowded cars and beggars and intercoms that spat incomprehensible instructions at me. The tedium was relieved only by a ragged black man with a saxophone, who played the Twilight Zone theme. I gave him a quarter for trenchant social commentary.

"I rang the bell marked S&L FRANKEN and stood next to the intercom, ready to identify myself. But as what? As a lawyer prying into Tobie's life? As someone warning her about a potential threat? How was I going to get all this into a sound-bite-length message through an intercom?

I didn't have to. The buzzer sounded; I quickly stepped to the door, grabbed the handle, and pushed as hard as I could.

I all but fell into the tiny foyer, which was littered with pink menus from a local Chinese restaurant.

The menus explained why I'd been buzzed in without being asked to talk into the intercom.

"You don't look like you're delivering kung pao chicken," the short woman with the nasal New York accent said when she opened the door.

"I'm not. I'm here about Tobie."

Her mascaraed eyes narrowed. "What about her?"

"You're her aunt?"

"You wouldn't be here if you didn't know that already. What is this, one of those 'Whatever Happened To?' segments for local TV or something?"

Sylvia Franken was one of those five-feet-nothing New York women who dominate people far taller by sheer force of personality. She was edging toward sixty, but she'd probably been just this tough when she was twenty.

"No," I replied. "I'm a lawyer. I represent Keith Jernigan. I wanted Tobie to know he's out of jail and might try to hurt her again."

"Ha. Let him try. Believe me, the way they've got that girl locked up, he'll have one he'll of a time getting close to her."

Whatever reaction I'd expected, this wasn't it. "Could I come in and talk to you about all this?"

"Sure, what the hell. Stay and eat Chinese when it comes. If it ever comes; those kids, I swear, take the long way through Welfare Island on their way over here."

"What do you mean, those people have her locked up? Is she in a hospital?"

"Ha. Might as well be, poor kid." Sylvia motioned me inside; I followed her into a vest-pocket kitchen with a half-stove and tiny refrigerator. The cabinets were bright red with white handles; a dish towel with an embroidered red apple and a matching potholder in the shape of an apple hung on hooks next to the stove.

"I used to be a teacher," Sylvia said, ushering me to a small table in the kitchen. "That's how come there's all this apple stuff in here. Kids want to give you a present, they don't know what to get, they give you something with an apple. You know, like an apple for the teacher."

"Nice," I said.

"Ah, it's okay if you like apples. Here, take a seat."

I pulled out the chair closest to me and sat at a two-person table against the wall. It had a red-checked tablecloth with—yes—apples in the white squares and it was flush against the window that faced the airshaft. Tenements had airshafts by law, so tenants in the rear apartments received at least a modicum of light and air. Before the law, they lived like moles, in near-total darkness save for gas lamps most of them couldn't afford to keep lit.

While Sylvia poured me a diet soda, I reflected on the improbability of every single item in the apartment being a present from a child. Sylvia either liked apples a lot better than she'd claimed, or she was very proud of her career as a teacher.

"You went to Girls' High School," I said, after taking the tall glass with thanks. It did not have an apple on it; the glass was instead dedicated to the proposition that the New York Mets were and always would be Number One.

"Yeah, I figured you knew that. You probably also know I helped Tobie fake her job application. I figured Met Life wouldn't bother to check, and if they did, I could come up with a cover story. I work at the Board of Ed; I could have told them the records got screwed up. Everybody believes the worst about the Board of Ed and they aren't wrong, either."

She sat down and settled herself in. She wore a forest green turtleneck with a sweater-vest, jeans, and hiking boots, yet her ears sported chunky gold earrings and her fingernails were painted bright red.

"But why? She wasn't hiding from Keith then. What did she have to lie about?"

"I did the same thing when I was her age. Exact same thing, believe me. Changed my name first, though. When you talked to Girls' High, they said I was Sylvia David, right?"

"Right."

"Well, I'm not. Not on my birth certificate, anyway. I was born Zivyah Davidoff. When I was sixteen, I decided I'd had enough of living like a *shayne maidel* from Minsk. I wanted to be American. I wanted to be modern."

She took a sip of soda and then struck herself on the forehead. "Do I sound like a letter from the *Daily Forward*, or what? Just like a little greenhorn, straight off the boat. My grandmother could have said the same exact words in 1911, and probably did."

I was beginning to get this. "You were Orthodox in those days?"

"Orthodox. Sweetie, we were way beyond Orthodox. We were positively primitive. My father had a great conversion when I was twelve. We left our nice apartment in Stuyvesant Town and moved to a kosher slum in Brooklyn. I had to go to a religious school at first, but I finally succeeded in getting him to let me go to Girls' High. I promised him I'd get married right after graduation, and then I took off as soon as I had my diploma. Of course, what I did meant that they refused to let Tobah go to a public school. So she graduated from this rinky-dink religious academy that just barely taught girls to read in English."

"You called her Tobah. Is that her real name?"

"Tobah Davidoff, yeah. She decided to go by Tobie David when she got out, imitating me and my Sylvia. Ha, that's a good one, actually. I left home in 1972. If I'd really wanted to sound American, I should've called myself Harmony or Heather or some damn name like that. I was so sheltered I didn't realize only women over sixty were called Sylvia, and they all had big hair and bigger boobs."

Sylvia's hair was cropped short, a salt-and-pepper pixie cut. She caught me looking and ran her fingers through it. "Just growing back. Wiped out by chemo. Maybe that's why I made that crack about the boobs, since I only got one myself."

It took effort to restrain myself from cupping my hand protectively over my own breasts.

"I'm sorry," I said, feeling the full force of the inadequacy of the words.

"Ah, don't be. Whatever doesn't kill ya makes ya stronger."

"Is that how Tobie feels?"

"I hope so. Jesus God, I hope so." She stood up abruptly and walked toward the refrigerator. "Want more soda? And where in hell is that Chinese?"

As if on cue, the doorbell rang. Sylvia buzzed the visitor in, and in a minute she opened the door to a young Asian boy holding a brown paper bag filled with delicious smells.

"Let me get this," I said, reaching for my bag. Sylvia nodded agreement and I handed the kid a twenty. I got six back and handed him two for a tip.

Sylvia put plates on the table. Red plates.

"Hey, is that Depression glass?"

"Ha. Depression glass, they call it now. My mother got them at the movies, back in 1934. Paid a whole eight bucks for the set, twelve place settings. I only got six; my sister Mimmi got the rest. Uses them for Pesach, just like Mama did. I use mine every day. They go nice with the tablecloth, don't they?"

I agreed that they did. Sylvia handed me a set of wooden chopsticks and used another to push huge mounds of food from the cardboard containers onto my plate. The food smelled wonderful, and I realized I hadn't eaten for some time. Very unlike me.

She gave me three dumplings and put three on her own plate. "I was gonna save some of these for tomorrow, but they're so much better fresh. Let's eat them now, and if there's gonna be leftovers, it'll be the chicken."

"I still don't quite understand where Tobie is now," I said, after swallowing the first little pillow of a dumpling in its soy-vinegar sauce.

"She's back home with her parents," Sylvia replied. She held her chopsticks aloft. "Back in the dark ages in the Crown Heights *shtetl*. I'm surprised they don't have gates to keep the Jews in at night, like in the old country."

"And you think she's safe there? That Keith couldn't get to her if he wanted to?"

"Why should he want to?" Sylvia's generous mouth thinned to a bitter line. "He already fucked the poor kid up. Excuse my French, but she left home so she could have a life, live like a person and not a brood mare—and that bastard took it all away from her just because she didn't want to see him anymore."

"I had a fax that said he might want revenge for what he thinks she did to him."

"What *she* did to *him*? What kind of crazy talk is that? She's the one with the scars."

"He served time in jail for something he didn't do. He might think Tobah had him framed."

"He was in jail? Good. He deserved it. But Tobah didn't put him there, believe me. All she wants is to figure out a way to go on living."

"Has she? Figured out a way?"

"Yeah, I think she has. I think she's going to be okay. Not okay like I was, but okay in her own way. She's engaged to a man who needs a mother for his kids. The first wife died," Sylvia confided in a low voice. "Ovarian cancer. So Tobah gets a ready-made family, but at least she has a place in the community. She isn't stared at and made fun of whenever she leaves the house, the way she was in Manhattan after the attack."

I could picture it all too clearly. Riding the bus, children pointing and calling out. Teenagers making remarks about taking ugly pills, grown women sliding away from her as if facial scars were contagious. And a sheltered young woman with little dating experience—how would she ever learn to trust another man after one who said he loved her took away her face?

"I still feel like shit when I think about it," Sylvia went on. Her food, forgotten, congealed on the plate. "If I hadn't helped her get away, she might have stayed in Crown Heights and none of this would've happened. But I saw myself in her; I knew what it felt like to want to go to college, to do more with your life than make kreplach and raise kids. So I helped her—and it turned out, I helped ruin her life."

"You didn't know what would happen."

"No, I didn't know. But I should have known one thing; for a kid like Tobah, a guy like Keith was bad news. He wasn't religious, he wasn't Jewish, he didn't respect her traditions. Which she, by the way, never stopped observing even if she was looking for a broader horizon. I know for a fact," she said, waving her chopsticks in spite of dangling bean sprouts, "that she lit the *shabbos* candles every Friday night, even if she did go out to a movie on Saturday with him once in a while. She'd break some rules, but never all the rules."

I opened my mouth to try for one more soothing cliché, but Sylvia was on a roll and wasn't to be stopped. "But me, I thought, what the hell, I went out with non-Jewish guys before I married Lou Franken. I even dated a couple of black guys. I thought, hey, she's a kid. Let her experiment before she settles down with some nice Conservative guy from Long Island, sets up a kosher house in Great Neck. Ha. Was I wrong. And because I was wrong, that poor kid is walking around with half a face."

She dropped her chopsticks onto her plate and reached inside her sleeve for a hankie. "I can't eat, thinking about all this."

"You said you thought she'd be all right, living in Crown Heights," I repeated. "You said they had her locked up."

"Figure of speech. It's not like she never leaves the house or anything. But she doesn't ride the subway, never leaves the neighborhood where everybody knows her and her story. Nobody there is going to let Keith get within ten feet of her."

"Well, that's good. But I'd still like to see her and tell her about this in person. Warn her to be extra-careful."

"I don't know. It could stir everything up again. She's made her peace with it."

"But if something else happened?" I was falling into Sylvia's speech rhythms; any second now, I'd claim to be *verklempt*.

"If something else happened to that kid, I'd rip this Keith's balls off with my bare hands."

"Not if I get there first," I said firmly. "I didn't get him out of jail so he could go after her."

The grim look on Sylvia's pleasant face said I'd finally won her heart. I pushed my luck. "Tell me everything you remember about Keith."

Sylvia ran her tongue across her top teeth, then pursed her lips. She raised her bottom lip and thrust it forward, then followed with a smacking noise that might have been made by an exasperated chimpanzee.

It was with great effort that I sat in silence, letting her convince herself to tell me what I had to know.

"He was—" She sighed; her right hand waved in the air, as if trying to find a sign language that would convey her meaning more precisely than mere words. "He was quiet, kind of shy. But he had a good sense of humor. I liked that about him. And he wasn't always trying to get some girl into bed. He was after a serious relationship."

I traced a pattern of my own onto the vinyl kitchen tablecloth with my finger. "But he wasn't Jewish."

"I noticed." Sylvia's tone was dry as matzoh. "That's another one of the things I liked."

"You wanted Tobah to go out with a guy who wasn't Jewish?"

"Don't sound so shocked. It's not like she'd be the first."

True. Over half the married couples I knew owned menorahs and Christmas trees. But for Tobah?

"I wanted her to have fun." She stopped and heard her own words, and her eyes turned bleak. "Yeah, listen to me. Fun. She had a lot of fun all right, with that crazy lunatic. First he tried to own her, told her what to do every minute, kept her from making any new friends. And when she finally told him where to go, he threw acid in her face. Some fun, huh?"

"You didn't know."

She let out a long breath and said, "No, I didn't know. Not at first, and by the time I did, Tobie wouldn't listen to a thing I said. But I was the one who tried to play God. I was the one who thought Tobie should do what I did, date a lot of different kinds of men and then settle down—outside of the *shtetl*. I didn't stop to think that she wasn't me and Keith wasn't like the men I went out with."

"Where did Keith live?"

"Where did he live?" She repeated the words slowly, raised her eyes to the ceiling, and said after a pause, "I think he was staying with a friend. Or he had his friend's place for a while."

"He didn't have his own place?" I tried to keep the disappointment out of my voice. This explained why Raul had come up empty; the guy was a professional roommate. No name on the lease, no traceable history. Almost as if he'd planned to become a stalker.

"I remember it was outside the city," Sylvia went on. "Long Island, maybe." She closed her eyes and sat in Buddha silence for a moment. Then she opened her eyes suddenly, like a baby startled into wakefulness. "Yeah, that was it. The North Shore of Long Island. I remember he used to get fussed if they had to stay even a minute late. He had the train schedules in his head and he'd always carry on about how if he missed his train, he was stuck in the city until nine. Why he couldn't just take the next train, I don't know, but he had this elaborate explanation about changing trains and which ones ran express, it was enough to make you crazy."

"Do you remember the name of the town?"

"They all sound alike, those towns. Pishegoss, Mishegoss, that kind of name."

I made my own translation. "You mean like Patchogue?"

"Could be. Something like that. I guess they're Indian names, right?"

"I guess you've never been to the North Shore."

"Ha. From my neighborhood, you got as far as Coney Island, you were already at the end of the known world. Now, you go to Coney, you get mugged for your hot-dog money. You go to Brighton, you got the crazy Russians to worry about. Better you should stay home and take a cold bath."

There was a tiny gleam in Sylvia's eye that told me she was well aware that she was doing a Molly Goldberg imitation. She was enjoying her role as native guide to the arcane world of the ultra-Orthodox, and she was playing down her own sophistication and assimilation into the larger world in order to enhance her value to me. But she was doing it for Tobah, and besides, it was fun. Fun to listen to her and fun to picture her playing Auntie Mame to her shy, newly emerging butterfly of a niece.

If only their fun hadn't ended in tragedy.

When I returned home, I took the mail out of the box and sat down at my desk. A pink envelope caught my eye, and I opened it first.

It was a standard "thinking of you" message with a soft-focus vase of daisies on a table, a telephone in the background. Inside, the card begged me to call and talk, "the way we used to. I miss you."

The word *miss* was underlined eight times. I counted. And after the printed words came the block printing.

I HAVE TO TALK TO YOU.
PLEASE.

Have was also underlined, ten times. *Please* was underlined thirteen times, in heavy strokes that gouged the card paper.

There was no signature, but I didn't need one. I placed the card inside the folder that already held five earlier cards, beginning with the birthday card Keith had sent me from prison and the congratulations card I'd kept for my scrapbook.

I gave a bitter laugh. These cards weren't going in a scrapbook; they were becoming part of a dossier. A file on Keith Jernigan that I could use as soon as he did something that rose to the level of a crime.

I had no doubt that this was the direction in which he was heading.

As if I hadn't collected enough incriminating information on my client, a fax came through that said, in the same block letters:

ASK TOBAH'S NEIGHBORS HOW KEITH GOT THOSE BRUISES.
HE TRIED TO ATTACK HER, BUT THEY PROTECTED HER.

WHO WILL PROTECT YOU?

CHAPTER
TEN

The Union Street bus takes the rider on a journey through several different Brooklyns. For me, it started with the walk down Court Street, which transported me from my neighborhood of yuppies and Arabs to Italy. I passed D'Amico's, with its old-fashioned coffee roaster in the window. A man turning shiny brown beans with a big wooden paddle looked up and smiled as I walked by.

Could I bring Tobah a pound of coffee? Was coffee kosher?

I was on my way to meet the woman whose life Keith had ruined. I'd called Sylvia Franken about the fax. She agreed it was time Tobah knew what was going on. So she told me how and where I could meet her elusive niece.

Further along Court Street, I passed a shop with huge pale yellow cheeses in the window, long salamis, and huge jars with artistically arranged olives and peppers. The store could have been transported to Brooklyn directly from downtown Sicily, except for one little thing: it was owned by Russian immigrants.

They might know what was kosher. Maybe I could bring Tobah a cheese.

By the time I reached the bus stop at Union Street, I realized what I was doing. I was pretending this was a social situation; that I wasn't meeting Tobah Davidoff to tell her that her life was in danger.

I had copies of the faxes in my tote bag. Raul had checked the sending number and discovered they'd been sent from one of the many mailbox–copy shop–fax places in downtown Brooklyn. They were very busy and very anonymous. But I sent Raul to see if he could get a description of the person who'd sent them; there was a chance someone might remember Keith's black eye and bruised chin.

I boarded the bus and dropped a subway token into the slot, then took a front seat. The empty bus bounced and jogged its way along the bumpy street, passing brownstones owned by Italians and then Puerto Ricans before crossing into Park Slope, the more upscale neighborhood which boasted brownstones trimmed with gargoyles.

The sycamores were bare, but leaves of gold still clung to the ginkgoes, and the maples were in high color. Flowers were still in bloom, but tended toward the deep yellows and reds of fall instead of the pinks and purples of spring. It was a beautiful day, crisp and fresh and bright, and the bus ride was a tranquil rest from my increasingly paranoid thoughts.

We turned at the park and headed straight into Grand Army Plaza, a huge overblown monument to the Union dead in the Civil War. A great arch, better suited to Paris than Brooklyn, dominated the plaza; a fountain behind it spun water into the air for the autumn breeze to blow into swirling sculpture. The plaza was in the center of a circle, from which major Brooklyn avenues spun out like spokes from a wheel. Prospect Park opened its gates on one side of the wheel, while the gold-trimmed art deco Brooklyn Public Library dominated the adjacent corner. Large apartment houses claimed the other vantage points.

I got off the bus as close to the library as I could. I had a fleeting moment's desire to stop and do more research on the Chasidic community, but dismissed the idea as sheer cowardice.

I wasn't just traversing geography. I was about to go several hundred years into the past.

The Chasidim used electricity, except on the Sabbath. They drove cars, they had a Web site on the Internet. But they dressed and in many ways lived as if they were still in a Polish *shtetl*. The men wore black suits with long coats, white shirts, and broad-brimmed hats. The more extreme sects favored huge fur-trimmed hats. The women wore skirts that fell below the knee and the married ones covered their hair when they went out in public.

I had the feeling that the minute I crossed into their territory, I would be marked with a huge red letter—not *A* for Adultery, but *S* for Shiksa. *U* for Unbeliever. *U* for Unclean. *G* for Get Out of Here and Leave Us Alone.

But if Tobah Davidoff's life was in danger, she needed to know about it. And I didn't feel this was a message I could relay by telephone. She deserved to hear it in person, to talk to someone who knew Keith and understood the danger.

I strode past the edge of the park, then passed the Brooklyn Botanic Garden entrance next to the Brooklyn Museum. Part of my knowledge of Orthodox Jews came from seeing families out for a Sunday outing in the garden; the little boys tucking their side-curls behind their ears, beautifully embroidered yarmulkes pinned to their fine hair with bobby pins. The little girls dressed like their mothers, in long, modest skirts. Fathers wearing the black uniform, like crows amid the brighter birds.

I stayed on Eastern Parkway and walked into another Brooklyn. Crown Heights, where Marvella Jackman lived, was predominately West Indian. On the corner of Bedford

Avenue, a grocery advertised hot roti and Red Stripe beer. A sign on the side of a huge brick apartment building proclaimed Tuesday as Reggae Night at the Dance-o-drome on Empire Boulevard. It was hard to imagine a Jewish enclave in this very Caribbean setting, but I had it on good authority that if I kept going, I'd find myself in the center of the Lubavitch Chasidic community, named for the small town in Poland where they originated.

Kingston Avenue, ironically enough—since Kingston is the capital of Jamaica—was the main street of the Lubavitcher settlement.

The apartments and storefronts looked exactly the same as they had in the block just before Kingston, but instead of touting Jamaican meat patties and mauby, the signs said "Moshiach is coming!" Storefronts were crammed with silver candlesticks and prayer shawls instead of reggae tapes and Ziggy Marley posters. The men who gathered in small knots in the recessed doorways of storefronts wore white shirts and black trousers instead of bright tropical prints and chinos. Some stores had signs entirely in Hebrew, and there were Hebrew bumper stickers on the parked cars.

I'd traveled, not necessarily into the past, but definitely to another country.

I saw the sign halfway down the block. Tel Aviv Pizza, conveniently located next to the store selling Jewish books. Food for the body and the spirit. Both storefronts had huge color pictures of the late Rebbe Menachem Schneerson in the window. He was an old man with a full, almost preternaturally white beard and an air of playful solemnity. His photograph adorned books, postcards, framed pictures, and even a clock with Hebrew letters.

Up the next block, parked near the corner, stood the Mitzva Tank, a bus from which members of the community—males—exhorted worldly Jews to return to the fold. I'd seen it in Manhattan several times; the black-suited Chasidim asked passersby if they were Jewish and handed pamphlets to those who replied in the affirmative.

I opened the door to the pizza parlor and was met by the sound of twenty or so six-year-olds. All boys, they wore the long-sleeved white shirts and black pants that were the uniform of the Chasidic male. They all wore yarmulkes, some of which were elaborately embroidered with Jewish symbols and letters. Three older men wearing black coats and hats seemed to be supervising them, handing out pizza slices and shepherding the stragglers into the booths.

I felt conspicuous in the extreme. I'd worn pants instead of a skirt; I knew better but I also knew I wasn't really going to pass as one of them, so why not be myself?

The boys were an interesting combination of regular boyness and Chasidic strangeness. They dressed like old men, but their faces were the same ones you'd see on any school bus. They laughed and poked one another and shared jokes, but their speech was as foreign as if they'd been born in Poland instead of Brooklyn. One boy scolded another for doing something he didn't like, but he did it by shaking his finger in the other boy's face and chanting loudly, as if repeating his yeshiva lesson.

They were noisy but controlled, clearly enjoying their treat, but when one of the teachers asked a question in loud Hebrew, they all chanted the proper response with enthusiasm.

Meanwhile, the man at the counter wanted me to order something, so I asked for a mushroom pizza and a diet soda. I stepped over to the only free booth and took a seat. On the wall above the table was a framed piece of paper in Hebrew and English.

It was a detailed discourse regarding the proper premeal prayer to be recited before eating pizza. It turned out you treated the pizza like a "beigel" as far as saying prayers was concerned.

The boys broke into song. It took me a minute to realize

they were singing "Happy Birthday" to one of their friends—in Hebrew. Then they sang another song, an exuberant melody with words I couldn't understand. They cleaned up the paper plates and the men threw them into the wastebasket and led them outside, two by two, into the sunshine.

The place became eerily quiet once they left. Two young men with very new beards came in and ordered pizza, and then the door opened to admit a woman with a stroller and two small children.

It was Tobah. Her face was half-obscured by a scarf wound around her head, but I could see that her face wasn't quite right. When she saw me, the part of her mouth that could manage a smile did. I smiled back; I was halfway out of the booth, ready to help her with the door, but the little girl, who wore white tights and a long skirt, took the stroller and maneuvered it next to the booth, while Tobah led the toddler.

Tobah slid into the seat across from me; the little boy snuggled close to her, hiding his face in her scarf.

She was young, which I'd expected. She was also fresh and bright-looking and softly pretty, with thick black hair that cascaded around her face and dark eyes with long lashes—correction, one eye had lashes; one eye was large and luminous. The other was glass.

She wore a heavy brown knit sweater over a long skirt with blue flowers on a dark brown background; the challis scarf around her head picked up those shades and added gold.

"Yakov, don't be shy. The lady won't hurt you," Tobah said. She ruffled the boy's blond curls and he giggled, but kept his face hidden.

"Oh, you're just being a funny boy. You can't eat pizza with your head in my lap, you know. You're going to have to come out of there sometime."

Another giggle. Tobah raised her eyes and indicated the

little girl, who sat on her other side. "This is Miryam, and she's my very best helper."

Miryam inclined her head with grave dignity and said, "I'm very pleased to meet you."

She couldn't have been more than six, the same age as the little yeshiva boys, but she wasn't in Hebrew school. She didn't wear a yarmulke or recite lessons. Instead, she wore a long skirt and learned how to be a proper Chasidic wife.

"And this is Yakov, who doesn't want to come out and say shalom," Tobah went on, "and the little one in the stroller is Armin."

Yakov peeked. His eyes were a startling blue and his smile was one you couldn't see without smiling back. I smiled back. He giggled and buried his face deeper in Tobah's flowered scarf.

"Yakov's still a baby," Miryam said. "I'm a big girl. I helped decorate the *succah*, didn't I, Mama Tobah?"

Mama Tobah. Somehow the relationship of Tobah to these children hadn't been clear to me before. But hadn't Sylvia said that Tobah was going to marry a widower with children? Were all these little ones about to become her responsibility?

A muffled voice shouted, "I did too. I helped, didn't I, Tobah? I made the clouds."

"You made the clouds," Tobah said. "And they were wonderful clouds."

"They were just cotton balls stuck on with glue," Miryam confided. "They were baby clouds. I made clouds like that when I was a baby, but this time I made a poster of the *Ushpizim*."

I'd done my homework. I knew the *Ushpizim* were the invisible guests at the *Succoth* suppers, which were eaten in tents in the open autumn air. I'd glimpsed a few of them on my walk; hidden in backyards or on fire escapes, they were leaf-covered bowers with tables inside, waiting for the faithful to come and dine under the stars.

"A very good poster," Tobah agreed. "So many colors."

A plump man whose white stomach poked out through the gaps in his too-small shirt brought over the pizza. I added more soft drinks to the order, and offered pizza slices all around. I waited while Tobah and Miryam obeyed the piece of paper above the table and said the proper prayer in silence.

Yakov raised his head and gave the pizza a dazzling smile. He reached for a slice and dragged it across the waxed paper. His little hands were plump and pink. He wore a sky blue yarmulke with embroidered silver letters all around it. Bobby pins held it in place on his fine curls.

He would go to the yeshiva. In a few short years, he'd be one of the boys reciting lessons, and a few years after that he'd have his bar mitzvah and take his place as an adult, with duties and privileges his older sister would never know, no matter how long she lived.

Even little Armin, asleep in the stroller, his royal blue yarmulke slipping down his forehead, was considered his sister's superior simply by being a male.

I was looking at Armin and Yakov in part so I wouldn't stare at Tobah.

Eating wasn't easy for her. Eating pizza was even more difficult than eating with a fork. She lifted the slice to her mouth and inserted the end, slowly, into the side of her mouth that wasn't scarred. She bit off a small chunk and chewed on her good side. The scarred part of her mouth scarcely moved as she ate.

I ate in silence, contemplating Tobah's journey. She'd left this protected enclave to see and participate in the larger world. And the larger world had hurt her beyond imagining. One wrong move, one wrong date, and she'd been scarred for life. Now she was back where she started, back in the closed world she'd tried to escape.

Home is the place that when you have to go there, they have to take you in.

And the wife replies, *I should have called it something you somehow haven't to deserve.*

But isn't that the same thing?

When you have to go there, they have to take you in. Because you don't have to deserve it. Because where you're going is home, and the people who have to take you in are family.

No, the real problem with the quote was the part about "when you *have* to go there." Going home is one thing; having to go home is quite another.

Tobah Davidoff had to go home. She might have gone anyway, if she'd been given a choice. But Keith Jernigan didn't give her a choice.

And that was his greatest crime.

I was so wrapped up in my own thoughts that I didn't hear Tobah at first. Her voice was low, as if she feared being overheard. And considering that this neighborhood gave new meaning to the term "tight-knit community," she probably wasn't wrong.

"I got a card from him," she said again. She held the half-eaten pizza slice near her mouth, making it hard to see her lips moving.

I nodded to show I understood. "What kind of card?"

"For the New Year," she replied. I gave another nod. Everyone in New York City is aware of the Jewish New Year, Rosh Hashanah, whether or not we celebrate it. Courts are closed down, businesses keep shorter hours, and on Yom Kippur the city grinds to a halt and takes inventory of its many sins.

Sending New Year's cards to one's Jewish friends is surely not unusual. But for Keith to send one to Tobah seemed a particularly obscene gesture.

"It's a time for *T'shuvah*," she explained. "A time to forgive and to ask for forgiveness."

"And Keith was asking you to forgive him?"

She nodded. "He wanted me to forgive him, and he said he forgave me."

"He said he thought you were behind his arrest for the robbery?"

"Not in the card itself," she explained. She dropped her eyes and seemed to realize for the first time that she still held the pizza slice in her hand. She lowered it onto the wax paper.

It took a minute for the implication to sink in. "You mean the card wasn't the only communication you had?"

She nodded so vigorously the scarf slid from her head and fell to her shoulder. She didn't bother replacing it; I could see the scars it covered up.

It wasn't just the face. The hair on that side of Tobah's head seemed stuck on like a doll's. There were clumps of hair and other blank spaces, red and blotchy, where no hair would grow. She only had half an ear, the lower part having melted into a large globelike lump. Her mouth was pulled tight and her nose melted into her cheek and the glass eye stared unmoving out of a deeply scarred socket with no eyebrow above it and no lashes on the heavy, reptilian lid.

"He came to see me," she whispered in an urgent tone. "Twice. Once my brothers saw him and beat him up."

Had I misjudged Keith? Was he really trying to make amends for his terrible deeds?

"He came back a second time."

Another thought struck me. "How? How in the world could you two meet without the whole community knowing about it?"

I glanced around the pizza parlor. There were four others in the place, and two of them worked there. But I had no doubt that by sundown everyone in Crown Heights would know that Tobah Davidoff had talked to a shiksa at the Tel Aviv. So how had she and Keith managed to have a meeting no one seemed to—

"I went to buy fruit," she said simply.

"Fruit."

"Tropical fruit."

The penny dropped. "You went to a Jamaican fruit stand?"

"It's only around the corner, two blocks away. But no one else from here goes there, so I knew I wouldn't see anyone I knew. And they wouldn't see me. And besides," she added with a smile, "I'd end up with the best fruit centerpiece on the block. No one else had mangoes and pomegranates on their table for the *Succoth* supper."

"I like mangoes," Yakov confided. He also liked pizza; he'd put away three slices.

"They're too slippery," Miryam proclaimed. "I like apples better."

"Apples are good," Yakov agreed. "I like apple pancakes."

He turned the full force of his blue eyes on me and said, "Mama Tobah makes the best apple pancakes in the world. She puts on cimmanon."

"That's *cinnamon*, baby."

"Miryam, please don't call your brother a baby."

Tears threatened to overwhelm Yakov; Miryam, too, looked ready to cry. And Armin showed signs of waking up from his nap.

It was time to finish this conversation and get out of here.

"Okay. You met at the fruit market. And said what exactly?"

"He said he forgave me. I said what for. He said he knew I made the police put him in jail. I said I didn't, but that I forgave him."

My eyes refused to leave her scarred face. "You believed him when he said he wanted forgiveness?"

"I believed him. For one thing, he showed me his scar."

"*His* scar?"

"When he was in prison, he worked in the kitchen for a while. He started thinking about what he'd done to me, and he decided he had to pay a price. So he deliberately spilled hot fat on himself. He has a burn scar on his stomach about the size of a melon."

"On his stomach. I notice he left his face alone."

"There's only so much you can ask in the name of atonement. Hashem guided him to do what he did. And maybe it's not enough, but it does mean he's not trying to hurt me. The only person in danger from Keith is Keith."

The real question, of course, was *How?* How is it possible for any human being to reach a level of enlightenment that would permit her to forgive a thing like this?

That was the real question, but I didn't have time for it. I needed hard facts instead.

So even before Tobah answered, I interrupted myself. "Did you get any information about where he was living?"

She bit her lower lip, the part without scars. "He said something about taking two buses and changing on Flatbush Avenue. So I think he must be in Brooklyn somewhere or he'd have taken the subway."

"That makes sense," I said. When you live in Brooklyn, you live on your subway line and the only places you can get to without a hassle are places on that line. Buses are a lot easier for getting to the rest of Brooklyn.

"And he told me the name of the neighborhood, but I don't remember what he said," Tobah added with an apologetic air. "I remember it sounded funny, and he said it was made out of initials."

Armin had woken and was making fussing noises that threatened to become tears. Yakov and Miryam were growing restless, tugging at Tobah's arms and shifting in their seats. The interview was over.

"Listen, thanks for talking to me," I said.

"I did forgive him," she said again as she gathered her things and wrapped the scarf around her head, concealing the worst of the scars. "I asked Hashem for strength and I forgave him for what he did to me. It was a mitzvah in disguise," she added, looking at Yakov with a face that radiated joy.

"I wouldn't be happy today if I hadn't suffered that pain in the past. My marriage to Mordechai was *beshert*. Meant to be. And it wouldn't have happened if I'd stayed out there with Keith. So, yes, I forgave. Keith knows I forgave him, so he has no reason to want to hurt me now. I believe that, and I hope you do too."

I wasn't sure. I only knew one thing as I made my way to the bus stop on St. John's Place, and that was that I could never, in my wildest imagination, conceive of looking into the mirror and seeing a face like Tobah's and forgiving the man who had done that to me.

By the time I got home, laden down with bags of home-made pumpkin fettucine and plastic containers of pesto sauce and artichoke hearts, a pound of fresh-roasted coffee and a block of imported chocolate, the sun was below the rooftops.

At first I decided they must be at the Korean grocery. Had the woman's nightmare come true and she'd been robbed and killed in her own store?

But as I drew closer, the truth dawned. The police, uniformed and plainclothes, were standing on my stoop, ringing my doorbell.

CHAPTER
ELEVEN

Keith! My heart bounced in my chest and I started to run. Had he broken into my office and shot himself on the floor? Had he threatened Marvella? Had he stolen those electronic gifts he'd given me?

I decided it was encouraging that I was thinking in a descending order of awfulness. Now that I'd learned the truth about his attempt to see Tobah, I feared him less. And I had new doubts about the anonymous faxer. Or faxers, given the two different exchanges.

But when I reached my house, too out of breath to formulate a question, one of the cops asked, "Are you Nellis Cartwright? Also known as Nellis Eddington?"

I shook my head. Bent double, my shopping bags scraping the stone steps, I could only wait for composure to return.

Two plainclothesmen, one in a drab brown suit, the other in a sport jacket and chinos, flashed badges at me and identified themselves as Ackerman and Gallagher.

"Nellis Cartwright, also known as Nellis Eddington, lives at this address?" The older one, Ackerman, put his ID back in his pocket and blocked my way with what was meant to be a casual stance.

I chose not to challenge his right to keep me from entering my own house. For the moment.

"She does."

"May we come in, ma'am?" Ackerman, whose steel-gray hair and mustache marked him as a man on the verge of retirement, did all the talking.

"I'll tell her you're here." I fished my keys out of my bag, picked up my shopping bags, and made for the door.

"You're the landlady, right?"

"Yes, but—"

"Then you could let us in," he said. "You have the authority."

"I have a fair idea of my rights," I said, tilting my head in the direction of my parlor-floor office window, the one proclaiming my name and profession in gold letters.

"Ah, shit, she's a lawyer," Gallagher said. He gave me a sour look. "I guess you'll do this your way."

"Yes, I will." My tone remained cheerful, but I raised my voice just loud enough, I hoped, to send it through the open window. "My tenant has the complete authority to decide whether or not to let you into her apartment. I have no legal right to admit you past her locked door. So even if I let you in, you'll have to ask her consent before you search."

"Not exactly," the older cop said. He reached into his jacket pocket and pulled out a legal document folded in thirds. "I have a search warrant signed by Judge Bugowsky."

"The voice of the Bug is heard in the land," I murmured as I reached for the document.

I wasn't actually representing Nellis, and if the detective had asked point-blank, I'd have admitted the fact. But he dïdn't ask and I didn't tell. He handed me the search warrant and I gave it a quick read.

Nellis had accused Grant of hiding treasures from her, and now Grant was returning the favor. In legalese, he'd told the judge that he "had probable cause to believe that certain items of value, namely, seven Japanese carved objects herein described, had been taken from him by means of fraud and would be found in the possession of Nellis Cartwright Eddington, former wife of the deponent."

The probable cause came from a "reliable informant." I raised an eyebrow at this; clearly Grant had been spying on Nellis in some way.

I followed the cops upstairs. Even if I wasn't her lawyer, I couldn't abandon Nellis with the cops literally on her doorstep. And since it was my doorstep, too, I decided I had every right to monitor the situation.

The cops weren't happy with my hovering over them, but they knew better than to pick a fight with a lawyer who owned the building. At least, it was only the two detectives who came upstairs; the uniforms waited on the stoop.

The search was thorough but not nasty. The kind of search they do when the subject of the warrant is white and middle-class instead of dark and poor. No food spilled on the kitchen floor, no ripping open of cushions. Pretty much an eyeball search, but with everything in the apartment meticulously turned over and scrutinized.

The *netsuke* in the cherrywood cabinet were discussed at length. Nellis produced a listing from the divorce settlement describing each one.

"This looks like it checks out," Ackerman said, "but I'm no expert. Maybe we ought to take it in and have someone look at it."

"Not without a phone call to the judge," I countered. "These items are clearly not the same as the ones you're looking for."

"How can you be so sure?"

"For one thing," I began, enjoying the chance to show off my newfound knowledge, "you're looking for an *inro* as well as the *netsuke*. Well, all these are *netsuke*. Ms. Cartwright never owned one of the *inro*."

Nellis caught the drift and added, "And then there are the *ojime*. What about the *ojime*?"

"What the hell's—what's an *ojime*?" The older cop's face was turning red; he was suppressing, not very successfully, a rather large amount of frustration.

"It's a bead. A carved bead."

"This is kinda beadlike," the younger detective said, pointing to a tiny mouse *netsuke*.

"It's not a bead, though. It's not what you're looking for."

We spent another ten minutes arguing about whether they could take Nellis's *netsuke* for comparison. Finally, I said, "Look, I know the Department has a legal bureau. Why not call them and ask one of your own lawyers what to do?"

The next thing I knew, I was engaged in an extremely technical discussion of Japanese *sagemono* with a young woman at the other end of a telephone. I read the detailed list Grant Eddington had given to the police indicating the items he'd said were stolen from him, and I explained that the objects the cop wanted to take were nothing like the ones described as missing.

"Why not let the judge decide?" the young woman asked for the third time.

"Because I've seen the Property Clerk's office," I replied in a sweet tone, "and I know if this stuff ends up in there it'll come back damaged, and neither one of us wants that. Grant Eddington doesn't want that. These carvings simply aren't the ones described in the warrant, and if the police take them anyway, it will be a—"

"What about in here?" Detective Gallagher stood in the

doorway to the bedroom and pointed toward the *choba dansu* Nellis had shown me.

"Didn't the guy tell the judge these things had secret compartments or something?"

"Good thinking," the older cop said. His florid face broke into a smile of triumph.

"I have to go now," I said into the phone. I hung up and strode toward the bedroom just as the detectives reached the chest.

The irony of the situation wasn't lost on either Nellis or me. She'd accused her husband of cheating her by hiding *netsuke* in a secret compartment in one of his chests, and now he'd told the police that she'd done exactly the same thing.

Nellis walked straight into the bedroom and began removing drawers from the merchant's chest. One by one, she eased them out of their holes and laid them on the floor.

They contained pantyhose and lacy underthings, bras and panties and teddies and satin lingerie cases tied with huge pastel ribbons. Extremely feminine and very much at odds with the heavy, masculine simplicity of the chest itself.

The *choba dansu* had one locked safe on its right side. Nellis took a heavy iron key and placed it into the lock, turned it, and swung open the safe door. Inside were three tiny horizontal drawers and two that went deep into the chest like safety deposit boxes in the bank.

She was kneeling; she looked up at the cops and gave a smirky smile as she carefully pulled out the first drawer.

"Crotchless panties," she said in a matter-of-fact tone as she set the first of the horizontal drawers onto her bed.

The second drawer contained what she demurely referred to as "bedroom toys." Detective Ackerman's face was bright red, while Gallagher seemed more curious than embarrassed.

The third drawer was slightly shorter than the other two, a fact not lost on Ackerman.

"Hey," he said, pointing. "Why is that one—"

"I'll show you," Nellis said, her smile even broader. She reached into the well of the safe and pulled out a tiny box, just large enough to fit in the space behind the short drawer.

"Here's your so-called secret hiding place," she said with palpable contempt. "As you can see, it's about the size of an eyeglass case. Not exactly huge. And, as you can also see, it contains tit clamps. Can we perhaps bring this ridiculous scene to a close, now that you've uncovered all my deepest secrets?"

Ackerman wasn't a quitter. He was obviously uncomfortable but he wasn't giving up yet. "What about those other two drawers?"

They were about three inches square, too small for a handle. Instead there were little metal buttons on each; Nellis put her long fingernails between the button and the drawer and gently eased them out of their holes. They were identical in length and they were empty.

"I haven't found anything I'd like to put in these as yet," she said. "But then my dear husband hasn't been giving me presents lately."

The cops, especially Ackerman, blustered a bit about maybe coming back with another warrant once they obtained more evidence, but they were routed and they knew it. If Nellis Cartwright had somehow managed to steal Japanese antiques from her ex, they weren't in her apartment.

Once the heavy footsteps of the cops were no longer heard on the stairwell, Nellis turned and said, "Thanks for being there with me. I don't know what they'd have done if you hadn't been there."

"Actually, I don't think it made much difference," I said. "But I really think you ought to consider getting a lawyer with some criminal experience, if this is the kind of thing Grant's going to do from now on."

"Well, as you can see, it's not easy to get a lawyer when you're busy accusing one of them of malpractice."

"Hey, that's not why I can't represent you. If you were bringing those charges against someone I didn't know, I might—"

"You *might*. Yes," she said with a bitter edge, "a lot of people say they 'might' help me out. But I need a little bit more than that."

"I'm sorry," I said, although as I walked down the stairs to my own apartment, I wondered why I'd said it. I wasn't sorry, not one little bit, to be off the hook as far as Nellis was concerned. It wasn't just that Kate and I went back too far for me to turn on her and accuse her of malpractice; it was something about Nellis herself and her love-hate relationship with Grant that made me all too glad not to be her lawyer.

I needed a break. All this craziness was getting to me. I went into my closet darkroom and lifted the heavy brown plastic jugs from the lower shelf to the counter. I opened first one, then the next and poured solution into my marked trays. As always, the sharp tang of fixer soothed my nostrils.

I had some snow shots I wanted to print. Every winter, snow transforms my chosen borough into a Currier and Ives print. Snow blankets the sidewalk and outlines the brownstone windows and etches patterns on the wrought-iron railings. Bare trees with snow-laden branches droop over the sidewalk like the Victorian mourning picture in Kate Avelard's parlor.

After one especially picturesque snowfall, I'd stepped into my hiking boots, wrapped several scarves around my neck, and taken my camera out for a stroll. I'd come back with three rolls shot on three different speeds of film. All black and white. All eagerly awaiting the artistic hand of the master printer.

I'd marked up my contact sheets with a grease pencil, picking out the shots I liked best. I went for a classic church-seen-through-snow-flurries shot, the kind of thing that could grace the cover of the *New York Times Magazine* (at least in my dreams).

I set up the enlarger and put the negative in the holder. I stuck my hand in the cardboard box with my standard paper and pulled out a sheet. I anchored it in the easel and turned on the light, exposing the church picture. I gave it a lot of light, compensating for the swirl of flurries I knew would obscure the church.

I popped the picture into the developing bath and waited impatiently for the image to come up.

First the steeple, then the outline of the church itself took form. But there was something else—something that didn't belong. I studied the picture, but couldn't make it out. It looked as though there were holes in the church. Big dark holes that—

It couldn't be. I rescued the print from the developer bath before it blacked out completely and slid it into the stop bath. My suspicions were confirmed. I moved the paper to the fixer and let it sit while I considered the implications.

The image that had superimposed itself over my church shot was the skull I'd printed with Oliver.

But how? How had I put one negative into the enlarger and gotten a double exposure?

There was only one explanation. The paper I'd used had been preexposed. Someone had taken a sheet from the box, exposed the skull negative on it, and then replaced the paper in the box. Without the developer bath, the image would remain latent, unseen. Ready to emerge on the paper as soon as it hit the developer, even if another image had been exposed on top of it.

The resulting double exposure was actually quite interesting. The juxtaposition of church and skull was something I would never have tried on my own, but it was worth pursuing.

Except for one thing. Who in hell had gotten into my darkroom and played around with my images? Who had—

Oliver?

I'd shown him how to use the equipment. I'd shown him the skull negatives. Had he decided to play a trick on me, deliberately leaving the exposed paper in the box so I'd be surprised when I next came in to print?

I'd have to talk to him about respect for other people's things. For other people's images. I picked up the next sheet in the box and dropped it directly into the developer bath. The skull emerged slowly but menacingly from the seemingly blank paper.

A third, fourth, and fifth sheet likewise produced the skull image. The sixth and seventh sheets came out black, no image.

I went back to printing my church pictures, which seemed surprisingly flat without the grisly addition of the skull.

The next day, when Oliver came to my office after school, I took him aside.

"You know, I really like having you here," I began.

"I like it too, Ms. J. I showed some of my homies at school that skull picture, and they thought it was funky."

"Yeah, well, about that skull picture. I went to print some other stuff, and this is what happened." I reached into my portfolio and pulled out the double exposure. I handed it to Oliver and carefully studied his face.

He lit up. "Hey, this is major def. How'd you do this, Ms. J.? How'd you put that skull over the church like that?"

Okay, so he hadn't done it on purpose. "What happened was," I began, trying to keep my tone stern in the face of the kid's obvious delight, "someone exposed the skull picture onto a blank piece of paper and then put the paper back in the box. When I went to get fresh paper for the church picture, I took one with the skull already on it. When I put the paper in the bath, both pictures came up together. It's called a double exposure."

"I think it be better if the skull be darker and the church be like real light. Like there's a funeral goin on inside so the people be thinkin' about death."

"Oliver, I'm not showing you this so we can talk about aesthetics. I don't want you messing around with my darkroom when I'm not here. I don't want you leaving undeveloped pictures in my clean paper box."

"You think I done this?" Oliver's voice rose in the I-ain't-did-nothin' protest I'd spent so many work days hearing in the pens behind the courtrooms of Brooklyn. "You think I put that skull on the paper? I don't even know how to do all that, and besides, I never went in there without you bein' there. That be the God's honest truth." I heard Marvella in that last phrase.

I wasn't sure whether to believe him, but I was certain that if I didn't accept his word, I'd lose him as a photography student. I nodded and said, "Good. I like having you here, but I have to know I can trust you. My pictures mean a lot to me, and I don't want to have to worry that they'll be ruined."

We stepped behind the black curtain into the world of darkness, but the darkest thought of all didn't strike me until he went home with Marvella: if Oliver hadn't exposed the skull pictures and left them in my paper box, who had?

Keith. Keith Jernigan had been in my darkroom, without my knowledge. He'd used my resin-coated paper to send a message.

I said as much to Mickey when she finished with her clients.

"Cass, someone broke in," she said. "You can't just let that go."

"How do I know someone broke in?" I waved the picture

under Mickey's nose and said, "How do I know for sure I didn't expose the skull picture on some paper and put it back in the folder by mistake? How do I know Oliver didn't do it?"

"He says he didn't." Mickey sat in the client chair directly across from my desk, but my position of authority in the big chair didn't help one bit.

"Maybe he did it by mistake."

"He says he wasn't in your darkroom by himself. I believe him."

"Then maybe someone else did it by mistake."

"Ah, we're getting somewhere." She leaned back and clasped her hands behind her head, then swiveled in the chair like a teenager on the soda shoppe stool.

"God, I hate it when you do that. It's worse than Dorinda and her damned Tarot cards."

"Do what?"

"That oh-so-superior Social-Worker-Knows-All tone of voice. Just what do you mean by 'Ah, we're getting—' "

"You know what I mean. You think Keith could have done it, and you don't want to think it was him. But if he did do it, you want it to have been a mistake and not a break-in."

"All that actually makes sense to you?"

"You're the one it makes sense to, Cass. Otherwise, you'd call the police and tell them you had a break-in."

"A break-in with nothing stolen, nothing ransacked, nothing destroyed—just a picture exposed on several sheets of resin-coated photographic paper. Oh, they'll put a special task force on that one. Double exposure in the first degree."

"Now I *know* you're scared it was Keith. Sarcasm is always your last refuge."

"I'll call the police if and when there's an actual crime for them to investigate."

That night when I went upstairs to bed, there was a white cotton nightgown laid out on my bed. It was the fancy Saks

Fifth Avenue Victorian-style gown, with ribbons and lace, that I'd bought for a special weekend with Matt in Cape May. A weekend we never had, since I'd been moved to trial and had to spend my time preparing my cross-examination.

It was a lovely nightgown, and I'd always liked the way it looked spread across the quilt that covered my bed.

The only trouble was, I hadn't put it there.

CHAPTER
TWELVE

"Could I speak to Detective Button, please." I deliberately made it a statement instead of raising my inflection at the end. I didn't want to sound needy.

Which was pretty stupid, because the minute Button heard my name, he'd know I was needy. He'd know because I'd never called him before unless I was neck-deep in the big muddy and needed some serious cop help.

Calling Button, the detective I'd first met back when Nathan was murdered and who had become an almost-friend, was my compromise between listening to Mickey and officially reporting the incidents to the police and my own preferred alternative, sweeping the whole mess under a nice big rug of denial. Button I could talk to off the record, get a little advice from without pressing charges against my own client.

"There's no one here by that name," the voice on the phone said.

"Are you sure? Is this the Eight-Four precinct?"

"Of course I'm sure. And this is the Eight-Four, but we don't have no Detective Button here. Not since I came to the house, anyways."

"And how long ago was that?"

"I been here five months already. I know all the detectives, and none of them is named Button."

"Well, maybe he got promoted, or transferred or something. Could I talk to one of the other detectives? Preferably the one who's been there the longest."

"That would be Smitty. I mean Detective Schmidt. I'll transfer the call."

After the usual clicks, a deep voice said, "PDU. Schmidt."

"Detective Schmidt?" This time I let my inflection rise; Smitty sounded like an old-time cop who'd be happier talking to an old-time deferential female. "Do you know where I can find Detective Leroy Button?"

"You want to find Lee-Roy?" the voice boomed.

That said it all. Button hated the name Leroy. He used to say, "You can call me Lee or you can call me Roy. But nobody calls me Leroy and gets away with it since my grandmother passed. Nobody." And here was this loud man calling him Lee-Roy. Not a close friend.

"Well, he might be a little hard to find, seeing as how he's retired."

"Retired? Button?"

"Last I heard, Lee-Roy was gone fishin' for the rest of his life," the man said with a nasty chuckle.

I considered asking for Ackerman, then decided against it. He hadn't struck me as sympathetic to Nellis or to me; he'd probably blow me off or, worse, treat me like a scared old maid who sees rapists under the bed.

Gallagher, the younger cop, had seemed at least human. I left a half-hearted message for him to call me when he came on duty, although I didn't know what he could tell me that I didn't already know.

I was keeping a file of all the mystery faxes, including the one I'd received this morning about the Queens lawyer disbarred for using his position as executor of an estate to milk extra fees out of the beneficiary, holding the estate hostage to his own greed. It had no relevance that I could see to my own practice, but it was clearly meant to tell me something, so I shoved it into the folder with the others.

As soon as I put the phone back in its cradle, it rang. I picked it up and was asked by a crisp British voice if I'd please wait for Mr. Eddington.

"I assume you know why I'm calling," he said without preamble.

I went for the same detached, slightly wry tone he was using. "I assume it has something to do with that ridiculous search warrant."

"We are talking about six extremely rare signed *netsuke*, four ivory and two wood, plus one *inro* and four *ojime*," he said. "Total value almost eighty thousand dollars. Hardly ridiculous, Ms. Jameson."

"I didn't say your antiques were ridiculous," I countered sweetly, "I said the search warrant was ridiculous."

"I lent those pieces to a museum in Orange County, California." His tone was excessively patient; he'd clearly expected the cops to unearth the stolen items and couldn't quite wrap his mind around the fact that they hadn't.

"Upon their return, I examined them, and discovered that I was in possession of markedly inferior representations of similar objects. I know what I sent, Ms. Jameson—and they were not the same items that were returned to me."

"And how do you think Nellis managed to accomplish this?"

God help me, I sounded like her defense counsel. An instinctive reaction, but one I wasn't prepared to turn into a career move.

"As a hypothetical question, of course," I added hastily.

"I assume complicity with someone in the shipping company," he said, "or perhaps a bribe offered to a gallery employee. I do know that this is exactly the sort of thing my wife would consider a fitting punishment for what she sees as my sins."

Grant Eddington talked like an annual report. But underneath the precise voice with the perfect diction, I could hear rage. Animal, primitive rage like one of his carved ivory tigers.

I hoped in all sincerity that Nellis hadn't been the one who stole his treasures.

But I wasn't about to place bets on it.

Nor was I about to get into this mess any deeper than I already was.

"Look," I said firmly, "I am not now and never have been your ex-wife's lawyer. I don't care if she has your property, it's nothing to do with me. So why don't you—"

"Perhaps you'd care to know," Grant said, overriding me with his strong voice, "that Nellis is going around all over town saying that you *are* her lawyer. It doesn't, of course, surprise me that she's lying about it, but you might want to put a stop to it if you really are on the sidelines."

Anger swept through me. I'd tried to help Nellis as much as I could under the circumstances, and I'd told her honestly why I couldn't represent her. How dare she take advantage by using my name in unauthorized ways?

"There's something else you should know," Grant went on. "Nellis is the one who told me to call you and discuss the return of the *sagemono*. She seemed to think you were the right person to act as go-between."

"What? You mean she admitted she had them all the time? And she said I'd—" Fury choked me. "Just what exactly is it she said I'd do, anyway?"

"Arrange payment for their return, of course. She wants

money. She knows I'll give her money in return for those pieces. They're very special to me."

"That would be blackmail." Not my brightest response, but the fact that his suggestion was all too plausible hit me hard. Everything I knew about Nellis Cartwright Eddington said she was totally capable of holding her ex-husband's precious artwork hostage until she got what she believed she deserved.

"Of course it would. But I want my property, and if I have to pay off a lying bitch to get it, well, then consider her paid off."

I opened my mouth to say that I absolutely, positively, was not involved in this mess and that he'd have to talk to Nellis directly. But Grant hung up the phone before the words left my mouth.

I dialed his number and got the British secretary. She told me Grant had just stepped out and couldn't be reached. I started to leave a message, but chickened out. *No, I won't help your former wife blackmail you* wasn't something I wanted to convey through a third party.

At least, I thought with satisfaction, the rampant paranoia I was starting to feel had its up side: I slid the cassette out of the tape recorder I'd hooked up to the phone and put it aside for safekeeping. If anyone challenged my version of the conversation with Grant, I'd have a way to prove my own—

Or would I? I played it back, and the silence at the end sounded louder than all the words that had gone before. Grant had told me to pay off Nellis, and he'd hung up before my indignant, resounding, innocent *"No"* could be heard.

Anyone listening to the tape might conclude that I'd agreed to act as go-between, that I had no ethical problem helping a woman extort money from her ex-husband by means of theft.

I had to see Grant and convince him I was out of this whole mess. Forever. I wouldn't talk to Nellis, I wouldn't talk to him, I'd call the cops if either one of them came within ten feet of me. I'd refuse to answer the phone, I'd—

Marvella brought in the mail. I picked up the carved African letter opener she'd given me and slit open the first envelope. Then I noticed a pastel card envelope with all-too-familiar block printing on the front—and no postmark.

Hand delivered.

I slit open the peach-colored envelope and pulled out the card. It showed a kitten and a puppy, almost unbearably cute with their silly grins and matching neck-bows. Each animal occupied one side of the card, and they had their backs to one another in what appeared to be a mutual pout. The card read, "Let's kiss and make up. I hate it when we fight."

I opened it up. Now the kitten and puppy were kissing; tiny pink hearts floated around the happy couple.

Nice. Cute and nice and sappy and harmless—

Except for the hand-lettered note underneath the animals.

LOOK BEHIND YOU WHEN YOU COME HOME TONIGHT.

I'LL BE WAITING FOR YOU AT THE BERGEN STREET SUBWAY STATION.

The joke was on him, I thought as I shoved the card into the folder. I wasn't going out tonight, so he could wait till dawn for all I cared. I'd be home in my apartment catching up on some serious television watching.

But I was going out tomorrow night. So perhaps he'd just mistaken the day. And how had he known I was—

And then I remembered. I *was* going out tonight. I'd promised to meet Dorinda and go with her to hear Spider Tannenbaum, Blues Accountant, perform at a cafe in Brooklyn Heights. It was unlikely that I'd take the subway home; it was walking distance. But that wasn't the question.

How in hell had Keith Jernigan known I was supposed to go out at all?

You walk along the Promenade, the Brooklyn Bridge glittering in the twilight distance like a cheap rhinestone choker. Behind it Manhattan tries and fails to augment its grandeur. You smell river air and cigarettes smoked by fellow strollers. You hear foghorns and cars speeding below your feet on the Brooklyn-Queens Expressway, which runs directly underneath. The air cools as darkness descends.

Where the Promenade comes to an end, you take a right and then walk along the street until you reach the hill by the Jehovah's Witnesses printing plant. You go down the hill and find yourself walking on cobblestone, the bridge a huge presence looming over the river-level street. There's a tiny lighthouse building and a barge tied up at the pier, and another, larger barge whose twinkling lights proclaim it as the River Café, a fancy restaurant right in the river. There's the Eagle Warehouse, now transformed into luxury apartments. The whine of traffic from the bridge has you wondering how much the developers had to spend on soundproofing in order to turn the warehouse into living space worth half a mil for a one-bedroom.

The place you're going is far less upscale. It's a blocky, nondescript five-story almost directly under the bridge itself. It once housed ferry offices and whorehouses. It's now home to a motley group of tenants who won it in a rent strike. In the last window on the end, third floor, lives Dorinda Blalock. You yell up to her when you reach the building, and within minutes, she's at the window throwing down a velvet bag with the front door key inside. You pick it up, fish out the key, open the door, and climb the stairs to the most spectacular Brooklyn Bridge view in the entire city. And it's rent-free.

"So what time is the first set?" I asked, once I was settled into the hammock chair with an iced herbal tea at my elbow.

It tasted sour; Dorinda said it was hibiscus. I thought perhaps a little sugar would help, but I should have known better. Dorinda brought out a honey pot with a wooden stick. I was supposed to swizzle and drizzle, which I did—but more on the pants than in the tea.

"He starts about nine, nine-thirty. They wait till they check out the crowd. Spider says playing for just a few people is a real bummer. He likes the place to jump a little before he gets going."

"Okay, so we should be there—"

"Will you stop planning ahead? You're like this serious control freak. Why not just go when we feel like it? We'll get there when we get there."

"I don't want to miss him. I'm not going to this place to buy two overpriced drinks and listen to a jukebox. I want to hear Spider."

"Relax, Cass. We won't miss him." She reached into a carved Indonesian box on the table and pulled out a pre-rolled joint. "Let's get mellow before we go over there," she invited.

I was seriously tempted, but declined. My life was surreal enough already without adding to the unreality level.

Spider was playing at a little place on Henry Street called Le Chat Noir. It was decorated with the predictable copy of Toulouse-Lautrec's black cat and the name was spelled out in large red art nouveau letters. The smoky atmosphere near the bar, the tiny round tables on the sidewalk, the jazz permeating Henry Street all spoke of illicit nights in a New Orleans black-and-tan. I had an impulse to order absinthe and smoke a Turkish cigarette in an ivory holder.

Around us, the staid brownstones kept their quiet vigil. Dorinda and I walked in and found a table as far away from the bar smoke as possible. She ordered a mango daiquiri; I wrinkled my nose and opted for a Cuba Libre made with dark rum.

There were more Lautrec imitations on the walls. Can-

can dancers with skirts hiked up and black stockings. It took me a moment to realize all the dancers had cat faces, and tails curling from underneath their petticoated skirts. The patrons at the little round tables in the pictures were all cats, too. Their faces wore expressions ranging from frankly curious to disgusted to openly salacious. It was as if Georg Grosz had taken over where Lautrec left off, adding his trenchant social commentary to what should have been a purely decorative art.

"These murals are weird," I shouted to Dorinda. Shouting was required because an old Louis Armstrong number filled the tiny room.

"Yeah, aren't they cool?" Dorinda lifted her glass in a wordless toast. "The guy who painted them used to live in my building. He went back to Guam, though, last I heard."

"The guy was from Guam?"

This was the difference between Dorinda and me: she knew people from Guam. I wasn't even sure there really was a Guam. Maybe they made it up.

"Well, maybe not Guam. Maybe Bosnia or someplace like that."

"Dorinda, there's a big difference between Guam and Bosnia."

Why was I bothering? Didn't I know I'd just get an eye-rolling, what-are-you-on-about-now response? And, in a way, she was right. I'd never meet this guy, so who really cared where he was from?

We were well into our second drinks and had run out of topics of conversation worth shouting in order to discuss when the music died down and the lights went even dimmer than they already were, a feat I hadn't thought possible. One spot hit a corner of the room where a tall stool sat behind a microphone.

I hadn't seen Spider come in. But suddenly he was there, stepping from the last seat at the end of the bar over to the stool, guitar in one hand and drink in the other. His tall, geeky body lowered itself onto the stool and he settled the guitar on his lap. The spot hit his face at an angle that turned the planes of his face into something sinister and interesting. He strummed a few chords and adjusted the strings; his guitar was one of those flat electric ones that look more like modern sculpture than a musical instrument.

When he had it tuned the way he wanted it, he looked up and gave Dorinda a nod and a smile. He saw me and included me in his greeting. "I'm going to sing this first song," he said, placing his mouth too close to the microphone, "for a special guest in the back of the room. She's not a judge yet, but she could be someday, so seeing her puts me in mind of this old tune."

The accent was a cross between Brooklyn and the very deep South. He lifted his right hand and began a twangy rhythm. " 'Judge,' " he sang, " 'Judge, good kind judge, send me to the 'lectric chair.' "

His voice wasn't strong, but it had shadings that went from growl to purr to yelps of surprise or outrage as he told the tale of a man who "sliced up his sweet patootie" and therefore deserved the 'lectric chair. He modernized the tune by singing, "Judge Ito, please, send me to the 'lectric chair." That line alone brought the house down; by the time he finished, there was enthusiastic applause coupled with a few whistles and shouts.

He was a Brooklyn Jewish bluesman with the voice and attitude of a segregated black man. He wrung piteous sounds out of both the guitar and his voice, pleading for some woman to take him back or forgive him. Then he'd switch gears and sing about the road or the whiskey. The last song in the set was a quiet but funky version of "Mr. Blue." I was singing along under my breath, wholly inside the music and my own high, when I realized I was falling in love with Dorinda's man.

When he set down the guitar and strode over to our table, I realized it wasn't him I was in love with; it was the music and, more than that, the idea of the music. The freedom it represented, the pain transcended by art. The wonderful way Spider himself took a limited voice and turned it into an instrument that expressed every single emotion, every nuance.

If my fairy godmother had shown up with three wishes, I would have used one to get myself a guitar just like Spider's.

"What's your real name?" I said as Spider pulled a chair from the next table and straddled it. I was just high enough to think this was a terrific opening line.

"What difference does that make?" he shouted. The juke was on again; this time Ella sang about love for sale.

I nodded. "You're right. It doesn't."

"It's Craig," Dorinda replied.

Craig Tannenbaum. No, Spider had been right. It didn't matter except to bring him, somehow, down to an ordinary level. Spider Tannenbaum, Blues Accountant, was an adventurer, a magician with a guitar, a roving bluesman. Craig Tannenbaum was just another CPA.

I put Craig into a mental file drawer and ordered another drink.

I stayed for the next set and the one after that. By the time I left Le Chat Noir, I was a little wobbly on my feet and more than a little drunk with music and alcohol. My head ached from the cigarette smoke; I'd have to send all my clothes to the cleaners. But it had been worth it. I felt exalted by the music, taken to another plane of existence.

"Come home with me," Dorinda begged. "You can sleep on the futon."

"That futon ought to be outlawed by the Geneva Convention as an instrument of torture."

"Then you take the bed and I'll sleep on the futon. I don't want you walking home at this time of night."

"It's not night, it's morning." This struck me as an irrefutable argument. "It must be, what, one a.m.?"

"It's two-thirty and at least come home and we'll call a car service."

Spider had an accounting gig up in Westchester in the morning; he'd gone home alone to get what was left of a good night's sleep. I had a court appearance at nine-thirty before a judge who was likely to start talking contempt if you weren't in the courtroom by nine-thirty-two.

The most sensible thing would have been to go home with Dorinda.

I was in no mood to be sensible.

We discussed the matter for another ten minutes, with me getting more stubborn by the second. I finally turned and walked away in the direction of my brownstone, the heels of my half-boots clicking on the sidewalk. Dorinda sighed and walked the other way.

About halfway home, I heard footsteps behind me. I wheeled, ready to confront her with a really strong statement about my ability to take care of myself, thank you very much, and my complete non-need for a baby-sitter.

But Dorinda wasn't there.

Neither was anyone else.

The same thing happened three more times. I'd hear footsteps and turn, only to see an empty street with sinister shadows thrown up by street lamps and lights from shuttered businesses. But there was nobody following me—or so I'd think until the next time I heard the noise behind me.

It wasn't just the noise. It was that creepy feeling you get when you're sure someone is watching or following. It was the growing sense that I wasn't safe out here, not really, despite my smart-alecky attitude with Dorinda.

This was her fault. She made me jumpy, with her talk of futons and car services. Hell, this was Brooklyn. Nothing could happen to me in Brooklyn. I lived here, I owned property here, and I was goddamned if I was going to stop walking to my own goddamn house just because some other people were scared of their own—

There it was again. Right behind me.

I whirled around, ready to confront.

The empty street laughed at me.

I mean that literally. I saw nobody, but I heard a maniacal giggle from somewhere to the left. I jumped, startled and alarmed by the sudden confirmation of the suspicion that I was being followed. Yet there was still nobody there. I peered into the darkness at the storefronts along Court Street. Where was he? In the stairwell leading to the subway? The hollow echo of the laugh said that might be a possibility.

The laugh came again, high-pitched and forced. I stood on the pavement, torn between running home as fast as I could and going down the steps to find whoever was laughing at me.

It sounded strange, but my thought was that the laughter didn't strike me as menacing. Just weird. I began my descent into the bowels of the subway, one gingerly step at a time.

The laugh came again just as I rounded the corner to the second set of steps. When I reached the bottom, I looked toward the teller's cage. A pile of dirty clothes with a face attached sat huddled under the graffiti-splotched subway map, a wine bottle in his lap. He gave me a half-toothless grin and did the laugh again.

"Give me some cash money, girlie," he said when he saw me looking at him.

He looked like Spider Tannenbaum sang.

"No," I said, and turned to hike back up the stairs. Then I stopped, the incongruity hitting me. I'd been more than willing to enter Spider's fantasy world of the down-and-out, but I was repelled by this smelly example of the reality. I forced myself to walk back and give the bum a buck. He thanked me with another high-pitched giggle. He hadn't been following me. He was too drunk to stand, by the look of him.

And yet I still felt wary as I trudged the rest of the way

home along Court Street. I still felt someone was dogging my every step.

I turned around several times, hoping to catch a glimpse of Keith's leather bomber jacket, but every time I whirled and stared, the street was empty.

There was a message on my answering machine to call a police precinct in Manhattan. At first I thought it must be Detective Button; he'd finally gotten the message that I wanted to talk to him. But when I gave my name, someone tossed the phone onto a table and yelled for Palmieri.

I introduced myself a second time to the gravelly voice that picked up the phone. "Oh, yeah," he said, "you're the kid's lawyer."

"What kid?" It was late and I was tired; a trip to Manhattan night court didn't sound like fun. "Most of my clients get busted in Brooklyn. And they wait till their first court date to bring me in."

"All I know is, this one had your card on him. You want to come down here, fine. You want to blow the kid off, fine too. We're taking him to Family Court for intake in about an hour."

I sighed. Maybe it was the way the cop said "blow the kid off" that got me. "What's his name?"

"Oliver Jackman."

CHAPTER
THIRTEEN

"**H**e's a good kid," I told Detective Palmieri as I walked into the Nineteenth Precinct Detective Unit. "I know you hear that all the time, but in this case it's true. Believe me, Oliver's never been in trouble before."

"I believe you," Palmieri said. Then he smiled and raised his palms upward. "Of course, the reason I believe you is that I ran his prints and he's clean. And I've been around long enough to know that a kid his age from his neighborhood without a sheet has to be a good kid. So tell me," he went on, "what your 'good kid' was doing climbing up some lady's fire escape?"

"That's what Oliver did? Burglary?" I sat down on the hard chair nearest the desk Detective Palmieri sat behind. "I can't believe it. He wouldn't do a thing like that; he's a—"

"I know, I heard that part already." Palmieri waved me to silence. "If I may ask, what's your relationship to this kid?"

"His mother is my legal secretary," I said. "He hangs out

in my office after school sometimes. I've gotten to know him, and—" I broke off before I could say one more time that Oliver was a good kid.

"I happen to think you're right about Oliver Jackman," the detective said. "I think he's one of the few who might learn his lesson the first time out. I'm willing to recommend ROR when we get to Family Court."

I thanked him profusely as he walked me through a hallway into a dirty, windowless room with a cage in the corner. Oliver wasn't in it. Instead, he sat on a straight chair next to a battered table. He slumped in his seat like a kid ready to fall asleep in math class. It was only when you looked more closely that you noticed his wrist wore an iron bracelet and that the other half of the handcuff was secured to the table leg.

When he saw me, he sat up a little straighter. He squared his jaw and tried to look like a street kid who'd been here twenty times before. But the slight redness around his eyes told me he'd already shed tears and the quaver in his voice threatened to bring them on again.

"You tell my moms I'm in here?"

I shook my head. "Not yet. But she'll have to know sometime. Where does she think you are, anyway? It's after three a.m., for God's sake."

"I told her I be stayin' with my cousin James. He say he stay with me some nights and he be out doin' all kinds of shit and whatnot, so I just tell my folks I be over there."

"Oliver, cut that macho street shit and get real." I gave my voice all the edge I was sure Marvella would have put into it. "I don't know a damn thing about your cousin James, but I do know you're not half as tough as you're trying to sound. Now, believe it or not, this detective doesn't want to bang you away for the rest of your natural life. He'd like to help me find a way out for you. But you have to tell me what this is all about."

Detective Palmieri cleared his throat. "Take your time,"

he said. "I'll be at my desk when you're finished." He stepped toward the door and closed it behind him. I gave him full marks for tact; Oliver wasn't about to drop his gangsta act with a cop watching.

I walked toward a chair and pulled it toward Oliver. I lowered myself into it and stared at my client. He wore the ubiquitous B-boy uniform of baggy pants, a collarless shirt, and a rugby-style loose shirt over it. The rugby shirt had the slash W that stood for Wu-Tang Clan. I wondered for the first time whether the fashion of oversized clothes was meant to make kids look bigger and more dangerous than they really were. His legs were sprawled in front of him and his feet seemed huge in black and white athletic shoes.

He pulled at the handcuff on his wrist. "Why he have to lock me up like this?" His voice cracked. "Like a animal."

I glanced at the cage. "Because he can't put you in there," I said, keeping my tone flat. The thought of Oliver in the cage sent a jolt of pure fury through me.

"You're a juvenile, and that means you have to be handled a certain way. You aren't as 'locked up' as you think you are. You won't go to jail. You'll be taken to Family Court. No matter how it all comes out, you won't have a criminal record. In fact," I said, letting my voice brighten, "you're damn lucky, getting busted at fourteen. If you were eighteen, you'd be looking at two-to-six minimum for this. If you were sixteen, they might try to move you to adult court and send you upstate. But you're a kid, so you'll catch a break."

Oliver's big brown eyes stared into mine for a moment, and then he looked away. "I won't be catching any breaks from my moms," he muttered.

"No, you won't. She'll cut off your balls and cook them for breakfast." I got a wan smile for this remark. "With plantains."

"Word up," he said with feeling. Now the smile got a little larger. "Ripe plantains. She doesn't like those green ones."

"So, Oliver—what were you thinking? What the hell were you doing on someone's roof?"

He shrugged. I'd seen that shrug before, from hundreds of street kids caught in hundreds of petty, stupid crimes that would consign them to a lifetime of lawbreaking and punishment. It was a shrug that said not only "I don't know" but "I don't care." The message was: my life is shit and it doesn't matter whether I throw it away.

But it did matter. It mattered so much that I wanted to take my open palm and hit Oliver across the mouth. How dare he throw his life away, and how dare he act as if his life belonged only to himself? What about Marvella and Covington, who lived their whole lives for their only son?

I settled for hitting him with sarcasm. "What, you were taking a stroll? Out for a little air?"

He looked away furtively and I realized he was holding something back. "You weren't alone, were you?"

The kid was one of the worst liars I'd ever seen. He shook his head quickly and said, "It ain't *like* that. . . . Check it out. It was just me." He widened his eyes and gazed at me with a look of perfect innocence.

"No," I said, letting myself think out loud. "That's the only thing that makes sense. Somebody else got you into this and left you holding the bag. But who?" I gave him a shrewd glance. "This cousin James, where was he when all this was going on?"

"James be out with his crew. I ain't down with them."

The disgust in his tone sold me. Whether the disgust was for James and his crew or for himself for not being down with them didn't matter. It was a genuine emotion and it took James off the hook.

"Okay, not James. Then who? Oliver, listen to me. You've got one chance of surviving this thing, and that's to tell the truth. If someone else was involved, I can try to talk

Detective Palmieri into letting you go in return for your help. Don't take the fall for someone else." I leaned forward on the chair, putting my face close to his, willing him to understand.

"You want me to jam up my homey just to save my black ass?"

"Goddamn right I do!" I slammed my fist on the table; the sound reverberated through the bare room in a thoroughly satisfying way.

"I don't know who this other dude is, but I do know your black ass is a pretty valuable commodity. Oliver, you've got to get beyond this schoolyard idea that you never rat on a friend. Sometimes you do. Sometimes the friend's done something he ought to pay for. And you'd be a fool to take the rap for something he did."

He mumbled something I didn't get. When I asked him to repeat it, he said, "I *said* I ain't no fool. But I ain't no rat neither."

"Then you're between a rock and a hard place." The look he gave me said a translation was in order. "See, a rock *is* a hard place, right?"

A nod. "So if you're between a rock and a hard place, then you're between two rocks. Which means whichever way you go, you're going to run into a rock. So it doesn't matter which one you pick. It's a hard choice, but there's a downside either way."

"No," he said, shaking his head decisively. "A rat be a thousand times worse than a fool. You a fool, you just stupid. You don't know what's up. But you a rat, you be dead. Ain't nobody trust you, ain't nobody give you no respect. See what I'm sayin'?"

He strained against the handcuffs; spittle collected at the sides of his mouth. If Oliver Jackman had a philosophy of life, I was hearing it now. "You like a nothing, got nobody behind you. You—"

"You are gonna sit there and tell me you've got nobody

behind you?" I let my voice go as loud as it wanted to. "You have got the best people in the world behind you, and don't you forget it. Your mother and father are—"

Some tiny corner of my mind flashed back to a moment of my own lily-white suburban adolescence. I was sitting in the principal's office in Chagrin Falls High School and the assistant principal was giving me pretty much the same speech. I was staring straight ahead, refusing to look her in the eye, refusing to let the words penetrate my shell of cool.

I blew her off.

Just like Oliver was bound to blow me off.

He was a kid. A normal kid who wanted desperately to belong. To be part of what sociologists would call his peer group. Just as I had decided it was much cooler to ditch school and smoke marijuana than to make the honor roll. The difference was that Oliver's peer group were felons-in-training—and the penalties faced by a young urban black male were far more severe than anything that could have happened to me.

"Ah, shit," I said under my breath, and settled for a new tack.

"I get the picture. So what was this, Oliver, a gang thing? You went out with a bunch of guys, some kind of initiation, is that it?"

"Gang. Ain't no gangs out there no more. Don't you know nothin', Ms. J.?" This time the shrug spoke of contempt, not indifference. "We got crews, homeys that chill together, that's all. Ain't no gangs, just dudes gettin' down. Runnin' together. Doin' shit together."

"Okay. So you were with a crew. Who exactly—"

"I didn't *say* nothin' about no crew. It ain't *like* that."

My patience, never my strong suit, evaporated like the misty rain on my sweatshirt. "So what the bloody hell was it *like*? If it wasn't a crew, who was it? Who was with you on that roof? Tell me right now or I'm walking out of here and calling your mother."

"I *told* you. Nobody with me."

"Oliver—" I stood up and fished in my pocket. I pulled out a quarter and held it up. "I'm going to take this downstairs and put it into the pay phone and I'm going to dial—"

"It wasn't his fault!" Oliver's voice rose to a treble and he jerked in his chair. "I must have got the wrong window!"

I sat back down. "What do you mean?"

"He said she be in the game."

"On the game? You mean you thought this woman in the apartment was a whore?"

"I don't *know* if she a ho'. I thought she playin' the game. She supposed to be a woman warrior-mage."

Mage. The name given to magic users in Dungeons and Dragons.

"In the game. You mean this is all part of a role-playing game?"

Oliver nodded. He swallowed a lump in his throat and explained, "The DM told me to go to this lady apartment and cast a level-three spell. See," he went on, excitement bubbling underneath the surface, "if I do this correct, I get to be a Red Messenger."

Oh, no.

I raised my eyes to the water-stained ceiling and prayed to the patron saint of defense lawyers that the Dungeon Master wasn't Keith Jernigan.

"So I climb up the fire escape and open her window," Oliver said. His hands strained against the cuffs; he found it hard to talk without accompanying gestures. "So I can get inside and lay my spell. Only she seen me and start screamin' and shit. I don't know what's up with that, but I figure when she know it's just the game, she'll tell the cops and let me go. But she didn't."

A chill went through me. I knew the answer deep in my bones, but I had to ask the question, hoping against hope I'd hear something other than what I knew to be the truth.

"Who's the Dungeon Master, Oliver? Who sent you there?"

Another mumbled response, but this time I didn't need it repeated. The name was clear enough: "Keith."

Which meant that Oliver hadn't been casting a spell, he'd been an accomplice to stalking.

Manhattan Family Court was one of the most forbidding buildings ever constructed; it's a shiny black marble cube with few windows and no mercy. It was staffed by a skeleton crew at this time of night, but the intake part was jumping. Cops from all over the borough were bringing underage felons in for processing. The place was a sea of hooded sweatshirts; I felt right at home in mine. I pulled it over my head and shook out the droplets of rain. Underneath, I was dressed in an all-purpose night court outfit of turtleneck and blazer over jeans.

In one corner of the lobby, a bail bondsman balanced papers on his briefcase so a thirtyish woman could sign for her son's release. In another corner, five kids in hooded sweats and baggy pants clapped their homey on the back as they bopped out of the building. In the center of the lobby, where the circular information stand—which was never actually manned by anyone dispensing information—dominated, a teenager with a baby strapped to her stomach harangued a young man for getting himself jammed up one more time.

I felt strangely at home, in a way I hadn't in the Appellate Division. This was my world, the place where I knew my way around and knew how to get things done.

I walked into the intake part, conveniently located on the first floor. I made my way to the front, past more bleary-eyed family members and a handful of private attorneys marking time in the front row. I nodded at one guy I vaguely recognized but didn't know why; five minutes later I realized the reason I hadn't known him was that the last time we'd met, he'd had hair.

I told the desk clerk who I was and why I was there.

The judge frowned at me over his half-glasses. "Keep it down over there," he said. "This may be the lobster shift, but it's not the Fulton Fish Market."

"Sorry, Your Honor," I said loudly enough to be heard at the bench.

It wouldn't go on his record. That was the thought that took possession of me as I made my way to the front row, where the lawyers sat. This was juvenile court, and whatever happened to Oliver here wouldn't stay with him for the rest of his life.

I closed my eyes and let that thought take root in my overheated brain. God, if I couldn't make this go away, Oliver was as good as dead. Dead because a black kid with a rap sheet was never getting out of Crown Heights. Dead because with nothing to look forward to, he had no reason on God's earth to resist the gangs and the drugs. Dead because he'd always had a marginal chance at best to stay alive, and this meant the end of that chance.

It could be worse. At least I had a chance to get Oliver out of jail before Marvella found out where he was.

Or so I thought. There was a stirring in the pew behind me; I turned and stared into the implacable face of my secretary.

"I need to talk to you right now, Ms. Jameson," she said, loudly enough to draw a glare from a tall, thin court officer standing in the aisle.

I nodded and rose, then followed her into the hall. It was a short walk, but it felt like a long journey. This wasn't going to be pleasant.

"Marvella, I want you to know I'm going to do everything I can to—"

"No, you are not." Her normally pleasant face was closed and angry. "You've done enough, you and that Keith. I raised my boy to be a good man, and now he's in jail like a common thief."

The rage was apparent, in the cold voice and hard eyes. But there was a bewildered pain underneath. "He listened to that Keith instead of to his mother and father."

"Did Covington come with you?"

Now the tight mouth opened into a smile of malicious triumph. "My husband is with our lawyer."

"But I'm your—"

I drew in a deep breath and let it out. "You have to do what you think is best for Oliver," I said with effort. A lot of effort; Marvella had been part of my little office family for eight years. Her hiring another lawyer for her son was nothing less than a slap in the face.

And yet, she was right. She was right because for the moment anyway, Keith Jernigan was my client as well. And it was a gross conflict of interest to trade one client's freedom for that of another, a fact I'd conveniently pushed aside in my zeal to get Oliver released.

"And if you think I'm going to be coming in to work tomorrow, you'd better think again. I can't work for nobody who puts my son in jail, Ms. Jameson. No job is worth that."

I'd been surprised and hurt; now my own anger kicked in. "You think I put Oliver in jail? You think I told him to go climbing up some woman's fire escape?"

"He was only doing what that Keith tell him to do. Detective Palmieri told me that."

"Well, I'm not responsible for Keith. I'm his lawyer, not his keeper."

"You got him out of jail. If he'd stayed there, Oliver would be home in his own bed tonight."

"Marvella, if I'd had any idea that this could happen, I'd never have let Keith in the door. You have to believe that."

Covington Jackman walked up to his wife and touched her on the shoulder. The dapper black man with him had a lean and hungry look. He extended a long-fingered hand and said, in a soft velvet voice, "I'm Councilman Henry Toulouse. Mr. Covington here has asked me to step in and represent his son. If you have any papers I ought to see, I would be most grateful if you turned them over to me."

I turned them over; I would have liked to inform the councilman that his client's name was Mr. Jackman and not Mr. Covington, but I had no time. The minute the contents of my file entered his shapely hands, Toulouse turned and walked into the courtroom, followed by Marvella and her husband.

I'd lost a secretary and I'd lost a friend.

No, make that two friends. Covington I knew only slightly, but Oliver had become my computer guru and dark-room buddy. I'd miss his incessant mouse-clicks and talk of dwarves and mages, his wide-eyed wonder and street-smart wit.

I walked over to the nearest drinking fountain, ignored the used bubble gum, and swallowed enough water to shrink the lump in my throat.

One thing was clear: I was no longer going to represent Keith Jernigan. It was time to get off his case. At the moment, I hated him as much as I'd ever hated anyone. I hated him for putting Oliver's very life in jeopardy; I hated him for being less innocent than I'd needed him to be; and I hated him for making me hate him.

CHAPTER FOURTEEN

There was no point in my sticking around, but I couldn't leave until I knew Oliver was going to be all right. Even if I wasn't his lawyer, there had to be something I could do.

One of the elevators opened to reveal two women, one short and dressed in a skirt and jacket, the other taller and wearing wool pants with a fisherman's sweater. I stepped toward them. "Are you the corp counsel on the Jackman case?"

The tall woman jumped and backed away. "Get away from me. You have no right to come—"

"It's okay, Fran," the skirted woman said, resting her hand lightly on her companion's arm. "I'm sure this lady doesn't mean any harm."

"She was at the police station. She knows that boy. She wants me to drop the charges."

I was beginning to think this hadn't been one of my better ideas.

The skirted woman said, "I'm Ann Petroniak."

"I do know Oliver Jackman," I said, including the tall woman in my glance, "and he's a good kid. A really good kid."

"Oh, sure." The tall woman stepped forward, anger distorting her features. "Good kids always hang out on someone else's fire escape and stare into windows and look at you while you're taking a shower." The tall woman's voice was high-pitched, her words coming fast. She clutched her purse to her chest as though I'd tried to steal it.

"I was just getting back to normal," she went on, tears filling her eyes. One dropped down her cheek, and another followed.

"You don't know what it's like, living in constant fear. I knew he'd come back. I always knew he wouldn't let me go, even if it was five years ago. I knew." She stabbed herself in the chest with an angry finger.

"Nobody believed me, they said I was crazy, paranoid." Her voice rose; people at the other end of the hallway turned to stare at us. "They said I was making it up, or seeing things that weren't there. But that boy was there. That boy was there. I didn't make that up."

She was sobbing now, her hands wiping her cheeks with an obsessive frenzy, as though by wiping away the tears she could blot out her memories.

The corp counsel gave me a steady look. "I don't think this is the time or the place to talk," she said. "We'll see you in court."

I followed the two women into the courtroom, where Petroniak would discover in short order that I wasn't Oliver's lawyer. She gave me a raised-eyebrow look when Councilman Toulouse stood up next to Oliver, but then she turned to the business at hand. Palmieri was as good as his word; Oliver was released into Marvella's custody and told to return for a hearing in three weeks.

When the arraignment was over, Marvella refused to look

at me, much less listen to any apologies. At least Oliver was free, I told myself as I strode to the door.

Outside, I came face to face with the tall woman in the fisherman's sweater, the woman I'd heard Petroniak call Fran. She was weeping into a Kleenex and asking a uniformed court officer to please, please call her a cab.

"Ma'am, I don't have the authority to do that," he said. "There are some phone numbers of cab companies in the clerk's office, but it wouldn't be right for me to—"

"I can't believe this! They let that boy go, and he might follow me home, and here you are refusing to—"

I couldn't help myself. "He's not going to follow you anywhere," I said loudly. "His parents are here and they're going to take him—"

"You don't know that!" She wheeled on me and her face twisted with fury. "That animal would do anything to—"

"He's not an animal! He's a good kid. He got into—"

"I don't mean him. I mean Keith." She was shouting now, her voice verging on hysterics. "I know he used that boy. I know that much. But how can I go home alone, knowing Keith might be there? Maybe the boy will go home, I don't know, I don't care. All I know is I can't make one move without seeing his eyes. His eyes are watching me. All the time. All the time."

Oh, boy. The court officer gave me a look that said if she kept on like this, she wouldn't get a cab ride home, she'd get an all-expense-paid trip to Bellevue.

"Um—you said something about you and Keith knowing each other five years ago?"

"We met in college," she said. Oddly enough, being asked to share her experience seemed to calm her instead of fanning the flames. The court officer melted away, apparently relieved to be let off the hook.

"Cornell?" I asked.

"How do you know that?" Suspicion was back with a

vengeance. She took one step backward and clutched her purse tightly.

Honesty was the only possible course if I wasn't going to lose my connection to this frightened woman. "Because I represent Keith on another case."

"So you know what he did to me and to that poor Jewish girl."

"I know about Tobah," I said. "But I didn't know about you until Oliver's arrest. I'd be grateful for anything you could tell me about him."

I suddenly remembered what Raul had found out about Keith's past. "I heard something," I said tentatively, "about Keith damaging a professor's car with acid. Do you know anything—"

"That should have told me," she said with grim bitterness. "That alone should have been a major warning signal. But me, stupid little me, I thought he was getting even for something and that made it—well, not exactly right; even if I was in love with him, I knew it wasn't right—but that professor was so cruel to people in class, he treated everyone like garbage, and it seemed almost like poetic justice for Keith to ruin his car. It was a Rolls-Royce," she explained with a wry twist of her mouth, "and he treated it like his baby. I heard he cried when he saw what the lye did to his silver finish."

"But they never proved it was him," I went on. "So I guess he got away with it."

"Oh, Keith's very good at getting away with things. After all, he never paid the price for what he did to me."

"What exactly did he do to you?"

It occurred to me that I was once again digging up dirt on my own client. But I reasoned that the truth would make me free—free of Keith and his troubles, free to go on to other cases without fear of what he might do to me or to people I loved.

I realized in that moment that I'd decided, at last, to make a concerted effort to get relieved as counsel for Keith Jernigan.

"We met when I was a sophomore," Fran said. "Have you been to Cornell?"

I shook my head.

"It's huge. I mean, it's so big it's overwhelming. Especially to a girl from Delphi. The whole town is just about the size of the liberal arts college at Cornell. I felt—oh, I cried myself to sleep that whole freshman year. I didn't know anybody, and I felt like everyone in school knew more than I did and dressed better and had more friends and—that first year was sheer hell."

"And then you met Keith," I prompted. I wanted to offer Fran a cup of coffee and a place to sit, but I was afraid she'd realize she was speaking openly to someone she had no real reason to trust.

"He was so smart," she said. "Smarter and funnier and just—well, I don't know, more alive than anyone else I'd met. And he loved me. Right from the beginning, he knew we had something special. We moved in together the first week we met and we were together for another five years."

"Five? Didn't you graduate?"

"I graduated and started on my master's," she said. "By that time, things weren't so good between Keith and me. He'd dropped out, for one thing."

"So he was jealous of your success?"

"I think so. Of course, at the time, I still thought he was the smart one and I was just a plodder. That, of course, was what Keith made me think. That he was some kind of genius who was above doing Mickey Mouse stuff like homework, whereas I was the 'good little girl' who was nothing more than a good test-taker."

"Boy," I said with a sympathetic shake of my head. "That definitely reminds me of a couple of my college boyfriends. The ones who thought ending the war in Vietnam was more important than grades. And, yeah, I remember thinking they were right. Only I ended up with a law degree and I imagine some of them are still working at minimum wage jobs."

"Then you do understand. You understand why I can never forgive him."

"Why? What did he do that was so—"

"He destroyed my master's thesis. I don't just mean he ruined the actual pages, either. He got to the computer and crashed the hard disk, then burned the floppies with some kind of acid. All my research materials disappeared too. I begged for an extension, and the college gave it to me, but I never could get it together after that. For one thing, he still followed me and called my house day and night and made my life a living hell. So I left Ithaca and I still don't have my degree and I'm a total basket case who jumps every time someone looks at me sideways, and it's all because of Keith."

"God, that's terrible," I said. I was about to go for the follow-up—why punish Oliver for the sins of Keith—when Ms. Petroniak stormed through the revolving doors.

"You have no right to talk to this woman," she said, placing her hand on Fran's arm.

"It's all right, Ann," Fran replied. "She's not hurting me. I was just telling her—"

"You shouldn't be telling her anything," the corporation counsel said. "And you—" The loathing on her face was plain as she turned her attention to me. "You should be ashamed of yourself, interfering in this case. You have no business standing here, and you should know better than to harass a complaining witness."

"I wasn't harassing her," I said, hoping I didn't sound as defensive as I felt. "I was just trying to—"

"I don't care what you were trying to do. Stay away from this witness. I'm warning you, Ms. Jameson."

She took the taller woman by the elbow and shepherded her back inside the courthouse. "We'll get a police officer to take you home," she said in a soothing tone.

Fran took out her Kleenex and began to sob.

As I rode the subway back to Brooklyn, I wondered where the hell Keith Jernigan was. Could Fran's paranoia be nothing more than the literal truth?

Would the Red Messenger on her fire escape this time be, not Oliver Jackman, dwarf-mage, but Keith Jernigan, Dungeon Master?

I climbed out of the subway station at about 4:30 a.m. and turned toward Bergen Street, pushing my way through a small crowd of guys hanging out, smoking, talking Spanish. I walked at a brisk clip along the street, passing the Italian Iron Work company, with its painted flag of Italy on the concrete wall and decorative ironwork on the roof. I stepped into the olfactory orbit of the L.A. Taqueria, which, even closed, filled my nostrils with the scent of refried beans and tortillas. I rounded the corner at the travel agent's and stepped to the curb, checking for traffic before I crossed the street.

I heard running. I felt a hard push; iron fingers dug into my upper arm and spun me around. A man in a hooded sweatshirt and ski mask stood about six inches away. Before I could catch my breath, he lifted a paper cup and threw cold liquid into my face.

I screamed. I shrieked like a banshee and clawed at my wet cheeks. I dropped my briefcase and sank to my knees on the concrete, my legs unable to support me. My eyes burned like fire.

Acid.

Just like Tobah.

The horrible screaming wouldn't stop, not even when a guy working late at the Italian bakery came out and lifted me from my kneeling position. By then, I was beginning to realize my face wasn't burning and my eyes were still functioning.

I cautiously extended my tongue and touched my lips.

Lemonade.

Some lunatic had rushed me on Court Street at four-thirty in the morning to throw a glass of lemonade in my face.

So much for my fear that Keith Jernigan would go back to Fran's fire escape. Instead, he'd done what his fax had promised: he'd met me outside the Bergen Street subway station with a little surprise.

I was sobbing with hysterical relief by the time the cops rolled up in their blue-and-white. Two uniforms stepped out and asked me what happened. I explained as best I could, but it was clear that throwing lemonade in people's faces wasn't really high on their list of priorities.

"I think this is part of a larger pattern," I said. "Let me get to my office and I'll show you."

They followed me across the street, while those few neighbors who were awake at this hour watched. The Korean lady at the fruit stand shook her head from side to side, as if she'd always known it would end like this.

I showed them my file with all the faxes, all the cards, I'd received. I told them about the hang-up phone calls and the feeling I'd had that someone was following me on the street. I explained about the double-exposed photograph and told them about the nightgown.

"So this guy your boyfriend or what?" The male cop's name was Riccio; he was young enough to be carded at the local tavern, a kid with acne scars on his chin and very new cop shoes on his feet, yet his tone carried all the world-weary cynicism of a man twice his age.

"No, he's a client."

"What kind of client, Ms. Jameson?"

"What do you mean, what kind of—"

"He come to you for a divorce, or what?"

I was beginning to get his drift. "Or what," I said tartly. "I represented Keith on a criminal matter. I won his appeal and now he faces trial in Supreme Court."

"So you represent this guy on criminal charges and now he's harassing you."

"I guess that's the size of it."

He shook his head. "Look, you represent those kind of people, you've got to expect some hassles, right?"

"Wrong. In the first place, I've represented 'those people' for over twenty years and nothing like this has ever happened to me before. And second, my profession isn't the problem here; Keith is the problem. You make it sound like I'm asking for it."

"I didn't say that."

"No, but you meant it."

"All's I'm saying is, you're gonna have this kind of thing from your criminal element, which you wouldn't necessarily have from your regular civil-type cases."

"Ha," I said, echoing Sylvia Franken, "you should see some of my regular civil-type cases."

At which point the thought crossed my mind: what if this was Grant Eddington's way of getting his precious *sagemono* back?

But how could throwing lemonade in my face help him do that?

While I considered the possibility, the doorbell rang. I was about to answer it when the older cop went to the door and admitted Detective Gallagher.

"I heard the sprint on the radio," he said to the uniforms. "I had a message from Ms. Jameson on an unrelated matter, so I thought I'd stop by and see what's going on."

I smiled at the cop jargon, which turned the execution of a search warrant in the apartment above mine into "an unrelated matter."

"Thanks for coming," I said. "I didn't know anyone else at the Eight-Four anymore. Not really. I mean, cross-examining someone does create a bond of sorts, but it's not the kind of thing you can use to extract a favor, is it?"

Gallagher's answering smile was warm but wary. "What kind of favor?"

"Look, I know there's nothing you can do at this point. I

have no proof that Keith Jernigan is behind any of this. I just want there to be a record somewhere that I think he's the one who's harassing me, so that if and when something he does amounts to a crime, the police are ready to step in."

Gallagher sent the uniforms on their way and said he'd take care of everything. They thanked him and went away; I offered my guest something to drink. Pretty soon we were in my office, cups of coffee beside us.

"You need to keep a record of every time something like this happens," the detective said. "Record all your phone calls. You got a tape recorder?"

I nodded, the irony not lost on me. The reason I had a tape recorder was that Keith Jernigan had given me one. It looked as if its main use was going to be the recording of his harassing phone calls.

"Keep everything that comes in to the house, all cards, faxes, other messages. Make a file. Take down the time of every encounter in a notebook. Make a record, as you lawyers say."

I nodded. None of this was new to me; I'd given similar advice to clients who'd been threatened by angry spouses, and I'd already begun keeping a file. But it felt good to have my own actions validated, my own suspicions taken seriously.

"You might want to change the locks in here," he said, gazing around the office. "Put in a security system."

"Let's cut to the chase," I said. "The reason you're telling me all this is that you can't make an arrest, right?"

"Right. We've got no proof he's the one who did this stuff. And even if we did, sending a greeting card isn't a crime. Now, the phone calls, that could be a crime, but only if we can show it was him."

"I do know the law," I said.

"Then you know we can't do anything until there's an overt criminal act."

I knew he was right. I also knew it wasn't good enough,

even if it would have to do. I thanked him and sent him on his way, exhausted and sticky with lemonade and sick of dealing with the fallout from my winning appellate argument.

Maybe I couldn't have Keith arrested, but I sure as hell didn't have to remain his lawyer.

I didn't bother going to bed. Instead, I went into Marvella's office and uncovered the computer. It took four hours to draft an order to show cause in Supreme Court, Kings County, asking the trial judge assigned to the Jernigan case to relieve me as defense counsel. When Raul came in, I gave him a copy, told him how to get it signed, and instructed him to serve it on Keith by afternoon.

Judge Tolliver would hear the case tomorrow, and I'd walk out of court a free woman. No more Keith, no more block-printed greeting cards, no more fax attacks, no more trouble.

Now if I could just convince Marvella to come back.

CHAPTER
FIFTEEN

"**W**ell, if he hasn't de-cathected from Fran," Mickey said, "then it's obvious he—"

" 'Decathected'? What kind of social work jargon is that?" I was groggy and irritable from lack of sleep. The day had seemed interminable and now that I was back from court, I was exhausted and at the same time too wired to sleep.

"Oh, well, *res ipsa loquitur*," my friend replied with an I've-got-you-now grin. "I mean, lawyers never use words ordinary mortals don't—"

"Okay, okay. Just tell me what the hell it means."

"Hmm. Cathexis. It's an accumulation of mental energy focused on some particular thought, idea, or memory. It's— oh, it's like investing an object or a person with a lot of meaning and then bonding with it in a way that seems out of proportion unless you realize the person is really bonding with the idea."

"Sounds like Grant Eddington and his damn *netsuke*," I muttered.

Mickey leaned back in the red leather client chair and clasped her hands behind her head. To my surprise, she nodded and said, "Yes. I think you're right. It's obvious those carvings mean more to him than just 'things' and we're not sure exactly what. But he invests them with meaning far beyond their actual value."

"Considering that their actual value is about eighty thousand bucks, that's quite a trick."

"But what interests me," she went on, "is the fact that you've managed to shift the focus from Keith to Grant Eddington. Why?"

"Don't worry, I'm getting off the case. I filed a motion. By this time tomorrow, both of us will have seen the last of Keith Jernigan."

But it wasn't tomorrow yet. I went upstairs to my apartment at about eight and was dozing in front of the television when the doorbell rang. I lumbered out of the armchair and made my way down the steps to open the outside door.

It was Keith. But he wasn't alone. Detective Gallagher stood next to him, a grim expression on his freckled face.

"I caught this guy prowling around in the back of your building," the cop said. "After what happened last night, I thought you'd want to know."

I turned cold eyes on my client. "I'm glad to see you, in a way. I've got a few things to say to you, and I guess now's as good a time as any."

I invited them both inside, then said to Gallagher, "Listen, you don't have to stay. I just need to talk to him, lawyer to client."

"Are you sure? I was going to take him in. We got a call about a prowler. I recognized the address and told the sarge I'd take the squeal. When I got here, this mope was halfway up the fire escape behind the building."

"I really think I can handle it," I said.

"You still protecting him, Ms. Jameson?" His cocky grin held a touch of contempt. "You defense lawyers are all alike. Bleeding-heart do-gooders who can't see that some people aren't worth the trouble."

"Be that as it may," I said gently but firmly, leading him back toward the outside door. "I have to talk to Keith lawyer to client, and if you're here, I can't do that. I'm not pressing charges, so there's nothing more for you to do."

He grumbled his way down the stone steps; I turned my attention back to Keith.

"I was worried about you," he said, stepping toward me with a look of concern on his face. "The guy at the bakery across the street told me what happened last night."

"Oh, I'm sure he did." I didn't bother concealing my disbelief. "I'm sure you had to hear about it from a third party."

"You think I did it?" His voice rose and he took a step backwards. "You think I threw that lemonade in your face?"

"Come inside and I'll show you why I know you did it."

I took him into my office and pulled the file with the strange faxes and greeting cards inside. I showed him the fax that warned me to be careful coming from the Bergen Street subway station.

"First, you tell me you're going to do something," I said, "and then you do it. Not so hard to figure out, is it?"

"But I didn't. I didn't do it and I didn't send that fax."

"What about the cards?"

He ducked his head. "Yeah, I sent the cards. I just wanted you to know I was thinking about you."

"And the phone calls? The ones where I pick up the phone and someone hangs up, then calls back two minutes later and does the same thing?"

"I wanted to know you were home. I wanted to hear your voice."

Oh, boy. This was *cathexis*, all right. Mickey's social worker instincts were right on the money with this one.

"You know something," I said in an almost conversational tone. We were both standing, I because I was too pumped to sit, and Keith because I hadn't invited him to sit. "I could live with all the rest of it. I could live with being harassed and stalked and scared out of my fucking mind last night when that lemonade hit my face and I thought for one horrible moment it was acid."

"Oh, no," Keith murmured, stepping toward me. "I never thought of that."

"Like hell you didn't, and get away from me."

He jumped back with a stricken look on his face. "I didn't mean—"

"I don't give a flying fuck what you meant. What really burns my ass, what really makes it totally impossible for me to continue representing you, is that you got Oliver arrested. That kid's one and only chance in life is to keep a clean record, and you—you told him to go out and commit a crime he never in this world would have done if you'd left him alone."

My anger was in full flood, and I made no attempt to dam it. I stabbed the air with my hand and said, "That did it. When I saw that kid handcuffed to a table because the Dungeon Master told him he could become a Red Messenger by stalking your ex-girlfriend for you, I decided then and there that I was finished with you. Done. I've filed a motion to get off the case; it's on for tomorrow."

I handed him a copy of the motion papers and said, "Raul's been trying to serve you, but it seems the address you gave us is a phony. So—consider yourself served, and I'll see you in court."

"But you can't—I need you. I want you to represent me, and I—I'll fight this. I'll tell the court I won't accept any other lawyer. If you won't represent me, I'll—I'll represent myself."

"Good luck. Don't let the door hit you on the way out."

"You can't do this to me. You can't abandon me like this. Those cops who set me up will just—"

"Tell it to your next lawyer," I said.

"Don't make me do something I don't want to do," he said in a low tone that scared me more than all the bluster in the world. "Don't abandon me. I hate it when people do that, and I have a way of making them sorry."

"Like you did to Tobah." I was shaking; the memory of the lemonade returning in a wave of horror. What if it hadn't been lemonade, but the deadly acid mix he'd used on Tobah? I'd be in the hospital with skin grafts on my face, hoping the surgeons could save at least one eye.

"Get the fuck out of here before I call Detective Gallagher and have you taken away in handcuffs," I said. I pushed him out the door and slammed it shut behind him, then locked it and stood glaring at him.

He pounded on the door and demanded to be let back in. He had more to say to me, and he was saying it at the top of his lungs. Finally, I turned and left him there, trudging back up to my apartment with the sound of banging and shouting in my ears.

He kept it up for a good fifteen minutes. I decided to give him twenty, and if he hadn't stopped by then, to call the cops. But suddenly, there was silence. He was gone.

Or at least he was silent. I drifted to sleep with uneasy dreams of Keith Jernigan slipping into my bedroom and smothering me in my white lace nightgown.

Judge Lucius Tolliver was an old adversary of mine. One reason I'd exulted in my appellate victory, in fact, was the thought of his getting zinged by the appellate bench.

But the trouble with old enemies in black robes is that they've got long memories and a great deal of discretion. Tolliver, beneath his veneer of Waspy dignity, was enjoying himself thoroughly.

"Counselor," he said in his plummy voice, holding up the first of the fax messages I'd received about Keith, "are you telling me you want to be relieved on the basis of an anonymous tip? Aren't you the one who argued before me that the police were wrong to rely on an anonymous tip when they searched your client for a weapon?"

"It's different when the police use anonymous information to substitute for probable cause," I said. "My argument in the Perez case was that the police officer had no reason to rely upon that anonymous tip when he—"

"Oh, so it's wrong when police do it but it's right when you do it, is that correct?"

Before I could answer, he hit me again. "And what about due process, Ms. Jameson? Aren't you the one who always says a man is innocent until proven guilty? And here you are asking to be relieved as counsel because your client may have been involved in some prior incident he wasn't even arrested for, let alone convicted. So aren't you convicting him out of hand, without any kind of due process?"

"No, Your Honor," I said, feeling myself on firmer ground this time. "I would like to remind the court that I didn't bring this motion when I received the first fax, or even the second fax. I didn't bring it when I started getting cards from my client in direct violation of my request that he refrain from contacting me in a personal way. I waited until such time as I was attacked on the street."

"Ah, but Ms. Jameson, what evidence do you have that this man was the same person who threw the lemonade at you? Did you see his face? Did you hear his voice?"

"No, Your Honor, but—"

"Ms. Jameson, as you've said in my courtroom so many times, suspicion and prior bad acts are no substitute for direct evidence of guilt. It seems to me that you're rushing to judgment about this young man."

"It's not just a single incident," I pointed out. "There's a definite pattern here, Your Honor, and it adds up to the fact that I no longer feel I can defend this man to the best of my ability."

"I don't like seeing lawyers place their own emotions

above their duty, Ms. Jameson. The State of New York has appointed you as this man's lawyer, and he's stated on the record in no uncertain terms that he wants you as his lawyer. Do you really expect me to deprive this defendant of his Sixth Amendment right to counsel of his choice just because you *think* he *might* have sent you a few greeting cards and thrown a soft drink at you?"

I wasn't sure who I hated more at that moment: the judge or my own client.

Keith sat next to me at counsel table. It was where he belonged so long as I was his lawyer. But it felt very odd in view of the fact that I was using everything I could to get off his case. He smiled at me as the judge talked; a sweet smile of warm friendship and forgiveness.

Had Tobah seen this smile when Keith managed to convince the police that he wasn't really dangerous?

Had Fran seen this smile when Keith denied that he destroyed her thesis?

Right from the beginning, Tolliver had made it as hard as he could. First, he'd questioned Keith, who'd firmly denied sending any faxes or throwing lemonade or breaking into my apartment to put the nightgown on my bed.

He'd admitted sending the cards. He'd admitted making phone calls and trying to see me. He'd said he was sorry and he'd never do it again. He'd looked apologetic and said he was sorry for getting Oliver involved.

He'd hit all the right notes. So far, I was hitting all the wrong ones, at least as far as this judge was concerned.

"I have reason to believe he might hurt me or the people who work for me," I said, holding on to my temper with great difficulty. I knew damned well that if any other lawyer in Brooklyn—any other female lawyer—were making this motion, it would have been granted already. Tolliver just wanted to make me gag on my own medicine.

"And what makes you think that, Ms. Jameson? Has this man threatened you in any way? Has he given you any reason whatsoever to believe that he's a danger to you? Tell me one threat he's made and I'll relieve you."

He bought me roses. He bought me dinner. He wrote me letters with my name in Greek. And he said I'd be sorry— but he didn't say why or intimate that he'd actually make me sorry.

I considered lying. But I hesitated too long; Tolliver might be bone-headed, but he wasn't stupid. He'd know at once that I was exaggerating in order to get what I wanted.

"No, Counselor," the judge said with a theatrical sigh, "you're on the 18-b panel and this case has been assigned to you in due course. You will remain as counsel until such time as the case is concluded—unless, of course, there is some *legitimate* reason why you should not serve. Motion dismissed."

The motion was dismissed and so was I.

I grabbed my file and made for the door at a fast clip. I had nothing to say to Keith and plenty to say to the judge that I would never say.

But Keith moved quickly too, grabbing my arm as we reached the corridor outside the courtroom.

"Hey, wait, I want to talk to you."

"Well, I don't want to talk to you," I said. Childish but satisfying.

"Look, I'm really sorry. I didn't mean to get Oliver in trouble."

"It's a little late for that, Keith. He's out now, but as far as I know, the charges are still pending. But then," I went on, not bothering to conceal my anger, "I'm not exactly up on Oliver's case since his mother quit working for me and will probably never speak to me again. So your being 'sorry' just doesn't mean that much to me."

"I could talk to Fran and get her to drop the charges."

"You go near Fran and she'll have you arrested. Which wouldn't bother me one damn bit except that thanks to that banana-brain in there, I'm still your lawyer. So I'm giving you sound legal advice when I say, stay away from Fran, stay away from Tobah, and stay the fuck away from me!"

"I didn't throw that lemonade," he shouted as I strode toward the elevator. "I swear."

"Hey, Counselor, wait up," a voice behind me said. I turned and looked into the smiling face of Detective Gallagher.

"I had to come over on a suppression motion," he explained. "A robbery case. Judge Kramer—you know, Toothbrush Kramer."

I smiled. Toothbrush Kramer earned his nickname by telling defendants that if they didn't obey his orders, they'd better come to court with a toothbrush next time because they'd be going inside.

"So how'd it go with Jernigan?" Gallagher asked. "You off the case?"

I shook my head. "Unfortunately, I managed to piss off Judge Tolliver to the point where he'd rather see me murdered in my bed than give me a break. I'm still Keith's lawyer, like it or not. Which means, I suppose, that I shouldn't be discussing him with you."

"Especially not in the public elevator," a voice muttered. I shut my mouth; whoever was talking had a point. Elevators have ears, especially in courthouses.

A card slid itself into my hand. I looked down to see the shield emblem of the NYPD and the name William Gallagher, Detective, Brooklyn North PDU.

"Thanks," I murmured as I thrust the card into my bag. "I'll call if I need help."

It was good to know that at least one member of the law enforcement community was ready to take me seriously.

As I walked home along Court Street, I found myself getting angrier and angrier. I was a good lawyer, damn it. I was dedicated, committed, ready to do whatever it took for my clients, guilty or innocent. And if I told a judge I needed to get off a case, I damned well should have been listened to. I wasn't one to duck out when the work got hard or the case got messy. I made my court appearances, I did my job as well as anyone else in the system. Tolliver had treated me like a whining malingerer out to dump a case when it got the least bit iffy.

What the hell was it going to take to cut me loose from Keith? A face full of acid?

When I reached the office, there were three messages on my answering machine, all from Grant Eddington, asking if I'd given any more thought to the "little matter we discussed." Very circumspect; no one listening to the cultured voice would have a clue that what he was talking about was making a payoff for the return of stolen goods.

I called him back.

"I told you before," I said, once he came on the line, "this whole mess has nothing to do with me. I don't represent your ex-wife, and if I did, I wouldn't help you blackmail her. I thought I'd made myself clear, but in case I didn't—"

"And I thought I'd made myself clear," he said with polished smoothness. "I don't care. I'm no longer interested in anything Nellis might do or say in court. All I want is the return of my property. And since you are her landlady, with the right of access to her living quarters, I'm prepared to be very generous if my property should somehow find itself in your possession.

"But," he continued, steel entering his tone, "I'm equally prepared to substitute stick for carrot. It is, I believe, a precarious existence when a lawyer practices alone, without partners. I understand that my wife's former lawyer, Ms. Avelard, is undergoing difficulties. I'd hate to see you in the same position, Ms. Jameson."

"Is that a threat, Mr. Eddington?" My voice swelled with triumph as I added, "You might perhaps wish to know that I'm taping all my calls these days. I've been harassed and the police suggested I—"

The phone clicked. Eddington had hung up.

I sat at my desk, bemused and frightened.

Kate Avelard was facing disbarment. I'd blamed Nellis for that, but now I had to wonder whether Grant had a hand in her downfall. Was it possible that he'd set out to punish her for taking his wife's case?

And was he about to do the same to me, unless I found the antiques he was convinced Nellis had stolen from him?

Did I have more than one stalker on my tail?

As if in answer to my question, the fax machine rang. What slid onto the tray was a detailed list of the items Grant Eddington claimed Nellis had stolen from him.

One of the missing *netsuke* was a Lantern Ghost, representing the spirit of a woman who killed her unfaithful husband and was doomed to wander through eternity, without peace.

I was beginning to feel a little bit like that myself.

I heard footsteps on the stairs inside the house, someone coming down from above.

The next thing I knew, Nellis Cartwright was in my office, saying we needed to talk.

"I don't think I ought to—" I began, but Nellis wasn't listening.

"I know Grant got in touch with you," she began. Then the phone in her purse made its insistent sound.

"Damn," she said, and gave me a wry smile. "I'd better take this. I'll make it quick."

She snapped open the phone and walked into the waiting room.

I wanted to tell her to take all the time she needed, since I really didn't want to talk to her anyway.

The last thing in the world I needed right now was one more client I didn't want to represent.

Especially when that client was the Lantern Ghost.

Card Three: Death

❧❧

THE SETTING SUN WAS A HUGE COPPER DISK THAT SHONE STRAIGHT AT HIM AS HE GAZED INTO THE WINDOW FROM THE rooftop. Straight down Amity Street and across Court Street and into his eyes. He blinked and purple dots appeared in front of his face. He kept his eyes closed until they turned first red and then, gradually, faded to black.

When he opened his eyes again, he focused directly on the plate glass window across the street. The one with the gold letters that proclaimed, with unconscious arrogance, CASSANDRA JAMESON, COUNSELOR-AT-LAW.

Her name in Greek on the card; that was a nice touch.

χασανδρα.

He'd seen her go inside. Dashing in, as if she had to use the bathroom, or a phone call needed to be answered before the machine clicked on. Of course, she tended to do things quickly. She was one of those tough New York women who walked too fast, talked too fast, and swore too much.

Five minutes had passed since she'd walked through the door. It felt like more; he could hardly believe the hands on his watch moved so slowly. He closed his eyes again and calmed his breath.

You had to calm yourself when you were shooting.

You had to relax the arm muscles holding the gun. Tight muscles meant missed shots. Ragged, shallow breathing meant you couldn't aim the way you wanted to. You were at the mercy of your breathing; if it wasn't right, the shot could go anywhere. Control your breath; control the bullet.

He controlled his breath, counting slowly as it went in and out.

What if she never came near the window?

What if she stayed in her office in the back? What if she went upstairs to her apartment?

He raised his sights to the floor above the gold-lettered window. Two casement windows instead of a big double sheet of glass.

He could do it. It wouldn't be as easy; she'd have to stand right in front of the smaller window in order to make a good target. But he could do it.

It wouldn't be as fitting, as symbolic, as shooting her right through that plate glass window with her name on it. He loved the idea of her lying in a pool of blood with the gold letters of her own name all around her in little pieces. Kill her, kill her goddamn name.

A figure stepped into the line of fire on the parlor floor. A woman, bending down and picking something up. A shadow, a dark silhouette he could barely make out thanks to the blood-red sun in his eyes.

He let out his breath in a long, slow sigh and simultaneously squeezed the trigger. He steadied himself against the recoil and heard the deeply satisfying sound of a bullet striking plate glass.

Like that German thing. Crystal Night. *Kristallnacht.* When the Nazis broke all the windows and declared war on the Jews.

The shadow woman in the window fell like a nine-point buck.

CHAPTER SIXTEEN

It was the sound you hear in the movies all the time. The sound of a shot fired from a very powerful gun. The sound of a shot connecting with its human target.

At first it was just noise. A very loud noise, and the sound of my plate glass window shattering and the thud of a body hitting a wood floor straight on, without any effort to stop itself.

I had no earthly idea what was going on—some old memory of a near-riot after a jury verdict flashed into my head, but there hadn't been any angry citizens massed outside my building when I'd come home, and besides, what were they rioting about, anyway? There was no Crown Heights jury case going on, and I'd know because I just came from Supreme Court, where—

I was up and running to the waiting room, my thoughts bubbling in my head without logic.

Nellis lay on the floor, sprawled on her back, her arms

and legs splayed, her long skirt up over her knees. One hand twitched; the fingers tried and failed to clench. A low, animal moan came from her mouth.

I ran over and knelt beside the body. Now I saw that there were little red blood bubbles forming on her lips. Now I saw that her head was only half there. The top of her head was—

No, don't look.

There's nothing you can do about it, so don't look.

She needs you to stay calm, so DON'T LOOK.

The cell phone lay next to her right hand. I picked it up and fixed my eyes firmly on my shattered window. Long shards hung in place like stalactites in a cave; as I severed the connection and dialed 911, one of them crashed to the ground with a sound that made me jump even though I knew it was coming.

I was less than coherent when the 911 operator came on.

"She's been shot. I think. I'm not sure, but there's all this blood and—"

"Miss, get hold of yourself. Who did you say has been shot?"

"Nellis. Nellis Cartwright. Oh, God, her hand stopped moving. I think she's—"

"Please, miss, give me your name and address in a calm, slow voice."

I swallowed hard and did as she asked, my voice wobbling. People had stopped on the sidewalk to look at the broken window. One or two pointed inside and someone yelled, "Hey, you okay in there?"

I held up my free hand and pointed to the phone, so they could see I was taking action. The 911 operator promised cops and an ambulance very shortly.

I put the phone on the table. When I set it down, I realized for the first time that I'd touched blood; red fingerprints stood out on the ivory phone handle.

The cops were going to love that.

I lowered my head and gave way to a long, low sound I hardly recognized as my own.

Grief?

Not exactly.

Shock?

Partly.

It was more a general sense of being overwhelmed by events over which I had no control. A sense of bad things happening to a lot of people including me, and a profound sense of my own inability to do a damned thing about it.

A hand touched my shoulder. I jumped, then relaxed when I saw Dorinda in her apron with the hand-appliquéd morning glories.

"How did you—" I began, then answered my own question. "Oh, right, key."

"What happened?"

"I don't know. She came out here to answer her phone and then there was this crash and I—oh, God, I knew something, but I—"

Dorinda put her arms around me like a giant mother; I relaxed into her embrace, trying to forget the sight of Nellis's head bleeding all over my Rya rug.

The cops came in like a swarm of bees. Suddenly the room was filled with blue uniforms and shiny black shoes and loud male voices and orders to be obeyed and opened notebooks in which people were writing.

One cop took me back into my office and settled me in one of the client chairs while he took the other. He walked to the water cooler and brought me a tiny cardboard cup of my own water. I took it gratefully, swallowed it down and held out the empty glass for a refill, like a child at a day care center asking for more juice.

"Is she dead?"

"We're waiting for the ME's office, ma'am."

"I thought so. She looked dead."

"I didn't say she was—"

"Look, I'm a criminal lawyer. I'm not stupid. She's still lying out there on the floor. If any one of you had the slightest reason to think she was alive, she'd be in an ambulance. So why can't you just admit that—"

I broke off. The cop was just doing his cop duty, and if I knew she was dead, why did it matter whether I heard it from him?

Maybe because she'd been alive such a very short time ago. Alive and obstreperous and demanding and more than a little crazy, but breathing and thinking and feeling and maybe even loving. Yes, in some part of my mind I was certain that if Grant Eddington had ever asked her to come back, she'd have dropped all her resentments and proudly taken her place at his side.

Now that would never happen.

"What was your relationship to the deceased, Ms. Jameson?"

Hearing Nellis described as "the deceased" almost brought me to tears again. Tears that really weren't about grief so much as shock.

"She was my tenant," I said, then amended the words. "Well, my subtenant, to be exact. She paid rent to Jerry Laboda, the prime tenant. He's in Indiana teaching law. He left—"

The cop held up a hand. "Ma'am," he said. "Please try to make your answers as brief as possible."

"Oh. Right. Yeah."

"Was the deceased consulting you on a matter of law?"

"She wasn't my client, if that's what you mean. But I did discuss her divorce with her before I realized there was a conflict of interest."

"And what was she doing in your office?"

That was a good question.

She was in my office because her husband thought I could get his netsuke *back and she wanted me to know that wasn't going to happen. Or she wanted me to tell him how much it would cost for her to return his precious objects.*

She was in my office because she wanted to embroil me in her domestic squabble.

She was in my office to make my life hell.

Not good answers.

"The truth is, I'm not quite sure why she came to see me," I said. "I'd just come back from court, and I was starting to return phone calls when she rang the bell and came in. She was only here a minute or two when her cell phone rang and she stepped into the waiting room to answer it. And you can see for yourself what happened next."

"You're saying Ms. Cartwright didn't have an appointment?"

I nodded, then added my own deduction. "You mean who might have known she'd be here at that exact moment? Nobody, that's who. It was a totally spur-of-the-moment thing as far as I was concerned."

"Do you have a legal secretary?"

"Not anymore," I said curtly. "She gave notice. And my investigator was out in the field, so there was nobody else here. Just me."

"Did Ms. Cartwright have any enemies that you knew about?"

"Only her ex-husband," I said. "In fact, he sent cops here to search her apartment. He accused her of stealing from him. But they did a thorough search and came up empty."

I had no compunction about turning Grant over to the tender mercies of Brooklyn North Homicide; the image of him standing on the rooftop of the building across the street and shooting into my plate glass window was all too easy to visualize.

Of course, Grant had just been on the phone with me moments before the shooting, so it was unlikely that he'd—

Except, of course, that phones were extremely portable these days, as Nellis had demonstrated with her cell phone.

Who was to say Grant hadn't pulled his phone out of a pocket, called me in hopes of establishing an alibi, and then substituted phone for gun, taking aim at his former wife?

The only question was: how did Grant intend to get his *sagemono* back with Nellis out of the way?

The phone rang. I gave the cop a raised-eyebrow inquiry. He nodded, so I picked up the receiver. The voice of Herb Radich, my most demanding and certainly my loudest client, filled my ear.

"What the fuck you mean sending me a fucking bill like this?" I held the receiver four inches away from my ear and tried to reply, but the flow was unstoppable.

"You think I'm fucking paying for every fucking cup of coffee you drink on Court Street, or what? Don't screw with me, Cass, I'm warning you. You better cancel these fucking charges or I'm out of there. You're not the only lawyer in the book, you know."

I'd been trying to break in with no success. Finally, I gave up any pretense of politeness and yelled, "Herb, what the hell are you talking about?"

"This fucking bill!" His shout topped mine by a good twenty decibels. "This shit-ass bill you had the fucking nerve to send me after we already agreed on a fee. We did agree, right?"

I ignored the heavy sarcasm of the last remark and said calmly, "Yes, we did. Which is why I didn't send you any bill. I don't know what you're talking about."

"Well, I've got a bill here for five thousand dollars, which is downright robbery, and if you think for one fucking minute that I'm going to pay it—"

"Herb," I said, loudly but firmly, "listen carefully. I didn't send you a bill."

The cop was looking far too interested in all this for my taste, but I didn't dare take my attention from Herb to ask him to leave the room.

"Then what the fuck am I holding in my fucking hand?"

It was one hell of a straight line, and in calmer moments Herb would be the first to appreciate a good comeback. But this wasn't the time to play games.

"Look, Herb, do me a favor. Fax it to me. Right now. And then give me five minutes to fax you a statement saying you're all paid up. This is some kind of office glitch, believe me."

I considered telling him I'd lost my secretary, but decided that sounded whiny.

Herb was an ex–Merchant Marine who would respect nothing except "No excuses, sir."

"Hey, one more glitch like this and I'm gonna be calling you from ICU. My blood pressure can't stand it. You do this again, I'll find a lawyer gives me less *agita*. Got it?"

"Got it," I said, but I was talking to a dial tone. I took heart from the fact that the last remarks were curse-free; that was the closest I'd ever come to an apology from Herb.

The fax machine rang; I stood over it as the paper slid oh-so-slowly onto the tray.

It was what I feared most: a genuine bill on my genuine preprinted bill forms with my genuine initials on the bottom.

Or at least a damned good forgery of my initials.

On a bill form that must have been stolen.

But then I checked the file number in the corner with the one on the manila folder that held Herb's partnership materials. Someone had also used the correct case number, and that was something no one outside the office should have had access to.

Herb Radich was the first and the most agitated, but as the evening wore on, he was definitely not the only client to call and complain about bogus bills. Some were over-charged, some had outrageous expense claims annexed, and one or two had "paid in full" scrawled across the bill even though they were in arrears. They had called to thank me; I hadn't the heart to tell them it wasn't generosity of spirit but a mistake.

Four clients asked for their papers; they were going to get new lawyers. Of those, three owed me in excess of seven thousand dollars.

Big bucks were walking out the door.

No bucks were walking in the door.

Was this what Grant Eddington meant when he said my practice might take a downward turn? Was this what Kate Avelard went through after she dared to represent Nellis in the ground war between husband and wife?

The phone rang. I'd been fending off irate clients too angry to wait until tomorrow to tell me exactly how they felt about their bills, so I considered letting the machine pick up, then dismissed the idea as sheer cowardice.

"Cass? It's Connie Hamilton, remember me?"

"Of course," I said warmly. I told myself I would have been just as warm if Connie's father hadn't left her a nice chunk of change in the will I was probating for her.

I steeled myself against the inevitable. Another bogus bill—or had I missed an appointment with her? Something relatively minor, yet just sloppy enough to drive a cold wedge of fear into the heart of a client already worried about her own problems and needing an entirely problem-free lawyer upon whom to rely.

I was wrong. It wasn't a phony bill and it wasn't a missed appointment. It was a letter, on my letterhead, to various banks and brokers indicating that the probate of Theodore Hamilton's estate would move considerably faster if I were named paid trustee in various matters under their control. It was a flat-out unethical, illegal, and immoral grab for money, using my client as hostage.

It was a crime. And it was exactly the same situation contained in one of the warning faxes I'd been receiving, the ones that featured every gory detail of some lawyer's disbarment proceeding.

"Please, Connie, fax me the letter. Right now." My voice held steady, even though I felt as if I sat at the edge of a volcano, ready to drop over the side. "I didn't send it and I don't know who did. I'm going to walk out of here as soon as I get the letter and take it to the D.A.'s office."

There was a pregnant pause on the other end of the line. "You don't have to," she said in a tiny voice, "they're right here. Look, don't be mad," she begged, "I didn't know what to—"

"This is being taped, isn't it?" My voice held no resonance; the words came out sounding as if I were on a respirator.

Hell, why shouldn't it? My entire career was on a respirator.

"Yes, it is, Ms. Jameson," a man's voice replied. It was smooth and with a slight Spanish accent. "How astute of you. I wonder," he went on, "if that is what accounts for your well-executed show of indignation. I wonder what you'd have said to Ms. Hamilton if you hadn't realized you were being recorded."

"You sound like Grant Eddington," I said. "You sound just like a man who threatened to destroy my practice, and since that's exactly what's happening to me, I can't help but wonder if he's behind all this."

"Behind all what, Ms. Jameson?" The voice was superior, calm, infuriating. "I'm sitting here with one letter Ms. Hamilton received in the mail."

"Let me guess, from an anonymous source."

"Precisely. Although the letter does mention banks that Ms. Hamilton agrees are the very ones in which her late father had accounts."

Nice syntax, I thought, but then he had the advantage of being able to think clearly. I was in the process of overdosing on carbon dioxide, breathing having been a low priority all day.

"Did you contact those banks? Have they actually received those letters? Because," I went on, determined to make my case as thoroughly as I could under the circumstances, "I'm telling you I never sent any such letters, and

I'm also telling you that someone's been tampering with my billing system. I've been getting calls all day from clients who got bogus bills. So there's someone out there using my name, my letterhead, my client base."

"Ms. Jameson, you're trying very hard to sound like an aggrieved citizen, but from where I sit, Ms. Hamilton is the aggrieved citizen and you're the suspect."

By the time I dragged myself upstairs to bed, I'd almost forgotten about Nellis Cartwright Eddington dying in my waiting room.

Almost.

But not quite. Because I couldn't forget the stench of blood and urine, the irrational sense that Nellis would be so embarrassed when she realized she'd lost control. She was so dignified, so careful of her image, so much a woman who'd hate being seen sprawled on a floor in a pool of blood. I really hoped she was thoroughly dead and not hovering over the crime scene like a revenant in a Peter Straub novel.

What a horrible thought. Dead and ashamed at the same time.

Or was I projecting my own deepest fears onto Nellis?

Just as I drifted into a fitful sleep, the phone rang.

"I'm not a threat to you. Honest."

"Keith? You're calling me at what the hell hour of the night to tell me you're not a threat?"

"I don't want you to worry about me. I won't do anything to you. I didn't mean all that stuff I said at the courthouse. And I didn't shoot Ms. Cartwright."

I sat up in bed and pulled the phone closer. Given my earlier speculations about cell phones, I wondered where Keith was. For all I knew, he was on the fire escape looking straight at me even as we spoke.

"You know about that?"

"It was on the news," he said in a small voice, then added with a rush of words, "plus I was there, but I don't want you to get the wrong idea because I didn't do it. I was standing on the street when it happened. I saw—oh, God, I saw the window break and that woman fell down and I thought it was you, so I ran across the street, and—"

"You should tell this to the police," I said, keeping my voice steady in spite of the surge of adrenaline that shot through me. Keith was there. Keith was across the street.

"They'll think I did it," he replied.

"If you were on the street, I mean at street level, then someone must have seen you. And if they saw you on the street, then you weren't on the roof, where the shooter must have been. It can only help you to go to the police, if you're innocent."

And if you're guilty, will Lucius Tolliver make me defend you on a murder charge?

"That Detective Gallagher's out to get me," Keith said in a sullen tone. "I don't know why, but he is."

"You don't have to talk to him," I replied. "There are other cops in the precinct detective unit."

"I'll think about it," he said.

It was the best I was going to do. As I moved the phone away from my ear, I heard a whisper. "I really like that white nightgown better."

CHAPTER SEVENTEEN

I rolled into Judge Coolidge's courtroom the next day at precisely two o'clock, ready to take on the entire Probation Department. I'd cleared my calendar, as the judge had requested the last time I'd been before him. It was only a week earlier, but it felt as if a lifetime had passed. Back when I'd last stood up on DeShawn Ripley's case, Nellis Cartwright had been alive, Marvella Jackman still worked for me, and I had a practice that wasn't on the verge of falling apart.

I had my paperwork in a large accordion file and my witnesses trailing behind me like baby ducks following their mother. I was more than ready to conduct the hearing that would decide whether or not DeShawn was in violation of his probation and ought to be sent back upstate to finish his felony sentence.

The courtroom was empty. No judge on the bench, no clerk at the desk, no court officers escorting prisoners. I sat my witnesses in the second row of pews and said, "Wait here. I'll go to the judge's chambers and find out what's happening."

I stepped into the labyrinth of corridors behind the courtroom and looked around. The last time I'd been before Judge Coolidge, his chambers were down the hall and to the right. I started walking, my mind churning with possibilities. Had the judge been stricken with a heart attack? Had he moved to a different courtroom since Thursday?

Had something happened to DeShawn in jail? I'd had three clients over the years who'd committed suicide in custody. Was this going to be the fourth?

I started walking faster. Whatever was going on, it wasn't good. Last week, the judge had ripped me in open court and ordered me upon penalty of contempt to be present and ready for a hearing. So where was he?

By the time I reached his chambers, I was breathing heavily. I stopped and took a deep breath, then knocked on the closed door. It was opened by a uniformed court officer, who said with a nasty grin, "Nice of you to put in an appearance, Counselor. Now turn around."

I gave him a quizzical look, then did what he asked. A split second later, I realized the implication. I realized it just as the handcuffs clicked on my wrists. They were cold and tight.

The officer spun me around so that I faced the clerk's desk. "In here," he said, giving me a shove that sent me stumbling in the direction of the judge's room.

"Here she is, Judge," he called out, his voice swelled with triumph.

I'd known for a long time that this particular court officer, whom I privately called Eric the Nazi, disliked me. I hadn't realized that his dislike had progressed to active hatred.

I was torn between outrage and puzzled confusion. I was on time, damn it. I'd done exactly what the judge had ordered me to do, so why all this?

I said as much to the angry man behind the big mahogany desk. I barely got the words "Your Honor" out of my mouth when he slammed the desk with a meaty fist and shouted, "Don't you 'Your Honor' me, Counselor. You have no respect for me or for these robes, and it's too late to start pretending you do. If you had any respect, you'd have been here when you were supposed to be and not make this court wait on your convenience. I put off two trials to deal with this matter, and you have the nerve to waltz in here five hours late and—"

Interrupting a judge is bad form. Interrupting a judge in full rant is plain crazy. But I was so shocked, the words just tumbled out.

"Late? This hearing was set for two o'clock. That's what you said last Thursday." I added a belated "Your Honor," hoping he'd overlook the interruption.

"And then I received a message indicating that you needed to change the time to nine-thirty this morning. I accommodated you, and this is how you repay me."

"Excuse me, Your Honor," I said, my mind racing, "but I didn't send any message. I was operating on the assumption that this hearing was set for two o'clock, and I have all my witnesses ready."

"Well, you can send them home, Ms. Jameson." His tone was sour. "I sent your client back to Riker's Island, and the probation officer goes on vacation tomorrow. So this hearing will be postponed for another three weeks at least. Which was why I was so insistent on getting this over with."

"I didn't send any message," I repeated. The handcuffs were cutting off my circulation. I was acutely aware of my vulnerability. If Coolidge actually cited me for contempt, I could spend the night in jail.

Why was this happening? Why was it that every time I stepped into a courtroom or called a client these days, I had to prepare myself for a disaster?

I bit down on my lower lip and drew air in through my nostrils. A long, slow breath. It came out ragged. The one sure way to avoid being held in contempt by this madman was to burst into tears—and I'd rather go to jail than do it.

The judge inclined his head toward Eric the Nazi. "Uncuff her," he said, his tone gruff.

The blood rushed into my hands with a tingle. I rubbed them; there were red welts where the cuffs had cut into my wrists.

"Ms. Jameson, you've always had a good reputation in this courthouse," Judge Coolidge said. "You're known as a good lawyer who fights hard for her clients and doesn't play games with the system. But I've been hearing things about you I don't like. It isn't just this hearing, it's other things. You've been making mistakes, and some of those mistakes are hurting your own clients. Now, I don't know who sent this message if you didn't, but I do know that my clerk called your office and your beeper number at least thirty times this morning, and we got no answer. I don't know where you were, but you should have been reachable by someone in your office."

He was right. I had a cellular phone now as well as a beeper, for just that reason. But had I given his clerk the cellular number? Apparently not. And why hadn't my beeper worked?

I looked down. It was clamped to the waistband of my skirt. I lifted it off and pushed the button. It showed one call, not from the courthouse exchange.

"Your Honor," I said, "I didn't get any calls on my beeper from the court. I don't know what's happening here, but may I ask what number you were calling?"

It was off by one digit. Whoever had been getting the clerk's increasingly frantic calls, it wasn't me. But how had the court gotten the wrong beeper number in the first place?

At one time, Keith had access to the office machines. He'd done things to the computer I still had no way to undo, and he'd been around enough to commit all my phone numbers to memory.

As to Grant Eddington, it was hard to see how he could have obtained the inside knowledge to screw up my practice, but he'd warned me it could happen and now it was happening, and that had to mean something.

None of this mattered to Judge Coolidge. I made a handsome and extravagant apology and was cut loose with a warning.

When I walked out of chambers, I felt like a felon on probation. One more false step, and I could lose everything.

One thing I lost right away was the confidence of DeShawn's family. I tried explaining that the mistake wasn't my fault, but they didn't buy it.

"Don't be telling me none of that shit now, you understand me?" His brother DeWayne poked a finger into my chest. "I ain't payin' no lawyer to make my man DeShawn lay up there in no jail for something he ain't did in the first damn place."

DeWayne's words were punctuated with amens from his mother and sister as well as DeShawn's girlfriend, Keziah. We were at a prayer service—and I was the devil.

By the time I left the courtroom, I was one more client shy. I'd agreed to refund the retainer, in spite of the fact that I'd already earned every penny of it with research and preparation. But the last thing I needed was another dissatisfied client taking his grievance to the bar committee.

I wondered if this was how Kate Avelard felt when her practice began slipping away and a host of grievances took the place of paying clients. And I didn't even have a dying husband to blame it on.

I didn't know who to blame it on.

But I was damn sure going to find out.

That night, I lay in bed, fully and horribly awake even though it was after two a.m. I'd get to the verge of sleep and the fear that Keith might be staring at me through the window would startle me awake. I even got up to check a few times, feeling more and more like a fool each time I came back having seen nothing but an empty fire escape.

When I wasn't thinking about Keith, I was obsessing about

my diminishing practice and the prospect that the next day would bring even more humiliation.

My professional life was over. They were going to disbar me, and if they didn't do that, they'd at least censure me and strike me from the rolls for a year. A year without an income. A year in which all my clients would find other lawyers. A year after which I'd always be tainted, always be whispered about as I walked by. " Isn't that the lawyer who—" And the person being asked would nod, either with a smirk if they hadn't liked me, or a mournful, pitying smile if they had.

It struck me: I'd be just like Tobah, only with a whole face. Everywhere I went, people would stare and know my story. Know my deepest secret that I hadn't been good enough, honest enough, to keep my license.

I turned over, the sheets tangling in my bare legs. I was cold on the bottom and hot on top. I was restless and unable to turn off my relentless mind, which never ceased reminding me how bad things were and how much worse they were going to get.

I reached for the alarm clock. Three-forty. I had a court appearance at nine-thirty—unless, of course, I'd screwed up and was really supposed to be there at eight. Not that anyone ever appeared in criminal court at eight a.m., but the way my life was going, I'd be the first.

Okay, so I'd be on time. What else could go wrong?

The client could dump me, having somehow heard through the Brooklyn House of Detention grapevine that I was no longer to be entrusted with his precious liberty.

The judge could hold me in contempt for failing to do something he'd told me to do by today or else. Motions? I'd made them. Reciprocal discovery? Turned over to the prosecution. Suppression hearing? Ready, Your Honor—and it wasn't my job to bring in the witnesses, or to produce my client.

So what could go wrong? Because I couldn't dismiss the idea that something was going to.

What if someone pretending to be me called BHD and told them the case was adjourned? They wouldn't bring him over to court, and the hearing would be delayed and the judge would consider it my doing.

Note: call the Brooklyn House of Detention first thing in the morning.

The D.A. could come in with a plea offer and tell the court I'd agreed to it. My client would go ballistic, thinking I'd sold him out, and the judge would accuse me of jerking everyone around.

Note: call A.D.A. McGill and make sure he doesn't think we have a plea bargain.

It was five minutes to four. I was bone-weary and had absolutely no confidence in my ability to get any sleep before I had to be in court.

I decided one way to lull myself into drowsiness was to review everything I now knew about Japanese antiques.

The *inro* is a tobacco container; it comes in two, three, or four compartments and is often lacquered. It is held in place by a cord secured by a carved bead called the *ojime*. The other end of the cord is slipped under the *obi* and held in place by a *netsuke*.

Tansu are Japanese chests. There are little ones and big ones, chests shaped like steps and special ones for the tea ceremony implements. There are sea chests and merchants' chests, some of which have secret compartments in them to—

I sat bolt upright. My eyes felt like pickled onions, but I was fully awake. Hadn't Nellis said her chest was a *choba dansu*—a merchant's chest? And weren't those the ones with the secret compartments?

But I'd watched her open every cubbyhole and drawer, even the tiny box behind the short drawer, and there hadn't been any—

But that's why they're called *secret* compartments, silly.

I jumped out of bed and groped my way toward the light. I stumbled into the living room, where my keys hung on a

carved wooden key rack. I pulled down the ones for the upstairs apartment.

If I couldn't sleep, I might as well see for myself whether
there was some other place in the *choba dansu* where Nellis
might have concealed her stolen treasures.

When I stepped into the dead woman's living room, the
first thing I noticed was a new photograph, one I hadn't seen
before. It was grainy, but deliberately so. The resulting image
of twisted trees above a rocky coast seemed vaguely menacing. I moved in and squinted. There was something else,
something nagging at me.

Then I stood back four paces and it jumped out at me. Hidden in the gnarled tree was the image of a Japanese Lantern
Ghost, a wraith of a woman with a howling mouth and a bleak
expression on her ivory face. Trapped inside the grasping tree,
she screamed for vengeance; the flames that licked her feet
rose up from the gnarled trunk of the dead tree.

It was the spitting image of the carving Grant had reported
stolen. And Nellis had no Lantern Ghost among her *netsuke*
on the cherrywood shelves.

But these were new photos. Nellis had said so. Unless
she'd exposed the image of the ghost a long time ago, before
she and Grant broke up. But no, the paper would have gone
bad. It didn't last forever.

She had Grant's *netsuke* after all. And she deliberately used
one of them as the basis for a new photograph, to be shown in
a major gallery, where Grant was bound to see it. She was
taunting him, dangling the *netsuke* in front of his face while
brazenly denying she had it. She was playing with his head
the way he'd played with hers.

But where had she hidden it? I'd seen the police search
with my own eyes. They'd gone through every purse in her
closet, opened every single box in the house, checked the refrigerator and the window sills and the toilet tank and any
other place I could have thought of.

They'd made her take out every drawer of the *choba dansu*

and they'd even uncovered the secret compartment. Nothing. So where was the elusive Lantern Ghost whose face stared balefully at me from the tree in the photograph?

One option was to get her stuff out of the apartment. It was part of her estate now, and therefore someone else's responsibility. I wanted it gone before anyone else figured out that it contained stolen property. I wanted it gone before the cops found the missing *netsuke* and decided I'd abetted a felony.

I didn't want to see any more pictures. I didn't want to know more than I already knew.

But that wasn't the truth. The truth was that I had to know. I had to know now.

I opened the door to the bedroom. The *choba dansu* shone in the low light from the living room, beckoning like a magic box in a fairy tale.

Pandora's box. If I opened it and succeeded in finding the secret compartment, would all the evils of the world fly out?

I felt as if I'd already opened such a box; the evils of the world were on my case already.

I knelt in front of the chest and slid the nearest panel to one side. An empty cavern yawned at me. I put my hand inside and felt my way around each wall, each corner. I tapped the ceiling and heard a hollow sound. I slid that panel closed and did the same thing in the next empty space.

Every drawer, every panel, told the same story. There was nothing inside. And no obvious hiding place. No lock without a key, no cubbyhole, no shallow drawer.

But there must be one somewhere. There had to be. Because I knew Nellis had the Lantern Ghost, and I knew she hadn't put it in a safe deposit box. Not only had she used it in the photograph, but I remembered her face when she said she loved this *tansu* because Grant missed it so much. No, she wanted those stolen *netsuke* close at hand. She wanted to look at them, hold them in her hands, and gloat.

It would satisfy her sense of irony to keep them in the *choba dansu*.

My knees ached and my thighs cramped as I squatted in front of the chest, poking and turning and twisting and prodding and knocking and sliding every single movable part. Nothing. No secrets.

Sweat beaded my forehead. I was obsessed. The clock on the bedside table told me it was five-thirty a.m., but I didn't believe it. Surely I'd been here a mere ten minutes. Except for the incredible stiffness in my legs.

I stood up and walked around, getting the kinks out. I poured a glass of water, drank half, and rinsed my face with the other half. Then I went back to work.

I took it inch by inch. I didn't leave one section until I was certain I'd done everything I could. I measured with my hands, comparing the empty space on one side of the chest with the equivalent space on the other. These chests, I'd learned, were perfectly balanced on either side, even though one side might be a drawer and the other a shelf.

If this didn't work, I'd come back with a tape measure.

Hell, if this didn't work, I'd come back with a crowbar.

Who was I kidding? The more I touched this wood, with its lovely patina, the more I played with the intricate ironwork, the more I let myself get to know this *tansu* inside and out, the more I loved it. I was beginning to feel just a hint of the obsessive fascination that had captured Grant Eddington.

But where in hell was that secret cubbyhole?

The top section had four drawers along the right side. I'd opened each one, but I hadn't removed them. Now I did. I took out the long drawers as well, and slid back the panel at the left side.

All the drawers were out, even the ones that contained what Nellis had called "toys." I tried not to look at them, feeling like a voyeur even though I'd already seen them once.

Two drawers with little button handles on them lay to the side. They were the empty ones Nellis had said she had nothing to put into. But wasn't there the slightest ghost of a smile on her lips as she made that statement?

I hadn't thought so at the time, but now—

Now I'd grasp at any straw dangled in front of me.

There was no wasted space in a *tansu*, except that between these two long, pencil-box drawers there was a tiny square panel about the same size as the drawer face, but without a metal button handle.

Wasted space?

Or the second secret compartment?

I stood up on stiff legs and went back to the kitchen. I retrieved a table knife from the drawer under the counter and came back. Gently prying away the slat between the two long drawers, I lifted it out and caught it with my other hand.

There was another box, a long pencil box just like the drawers, behind the slat. My heart beat faster as I took it out of the cubbyhole.

Whatever was inside was tightly wrapped in bubble plastic. I used the knife to cut the tape and unwrapped the first ball of bubble wrap.

I was unsurprised to find myself looking at a *netsuke* of a one-eyed ogre. I fully expected the other items to be the rest of his missing *sagemono*.

But what on God's green earth was I going to do with them?

If I told Grant I'd found them, it would only serve to confirm his suspicion that I'd been helping Nellis conceal her theft. If I turned them over to the police, they'd jump to the conclusion that I'd abetted a felony. If I kept them, I *would* be abetting a felony.

If I put them back and pretended I'd never come up to Nellis's apartment? Let the *choba dansu* pass through the estate to whoever was the beneficiary under the will?

There was a knock on the door.

Not the outside door, two flights down.

The door to the apartment.

CHAPTER
EIGHTEEN

My heart jumped into my throat. The cops? Grant Eddington, who just happened to be driving by at four o'clock in the morning? Dorinda, come to make muffins for the morning breakfast crowd?

"Who is it?" I called in a voice that sounded quavery and scared.

God, I hate fear. Especially when it's my own. I'd spent all of my childhood and most of my adult life refusing to give in to fear.

Afraid to leave home and go to law school in the biggest city in the world, where I knew no one?

Not me.

Afraid to leave the professional womb of the Legal Aid Society to start my own practice?

Not me.

Afraid to take the F train to Brooklyn at two in the morning? Afraid to take tough cases on behalf of tough clients? Afraid to do any damned thing I thought needed doing?

Hell no.

So I stood up and walked to the door with my head held high and my chin thrust out. I peered through the peephole—I may have decided to be fearless, but I hadn't taken leave of my senses—and swung the door open with an expletive.

"You."

"I saw the light. I thought you might be in trouble." He had a hard time catching his breath. "I was so worried about you. Especially after what happened to Nellis."

"Jesus, Keith, what the fuck were you doing outside my house at four in the fucking morning?"

Herb Radich could have taken cursing lessons from me. The aftermath of totally unwarranted fear is often anger, since I hate like hell having been humiliated into showing vulnerability. The fact that Keith hadn't actually seen my fear didn't matter in the least. I'd seen it, and I was the one who counted.

"I-I was worried about you. I was afraid whoever killed Nellis might come back for you."

"That is the stupidest thing I ever heard. Who the fuck gave you permission to spy on me? Who told you to skulk outside my door and watch every fucking thing I do?"

"I-I just wanted to protect you."

"Keith, the only person I need protection from is you."

His face fell. And as the words left my mouth, I realized how untrue they were. Now that Keith was standing here, shifting from one foot to the other, looking pathetically grateful for the fact that I was talking to him at all, it seemed impossible that he could actually hurt me.

Of course, that was probably Tobah's last thought before he threw acid on her.

"Tell me again where you were when Nellis was shot."

"Like I said, I was on Court Street." He ducked his head in a boyish gesture I used to think cute and now found nauseating. "I guess I was kind of hiding."

"Kind of hiding where?"

"You know that vacant lot on the corner across the street?"

"The one with the morning glories on the fence?" I'd told Dorinda she ought to go over there one night with a shovel, dig up the prolific vine, and move it to her window box. The sky-blue trumpet flowers would have been a perfect advertisement for the Morning Glory luncheonette. As it was, she made do with painted morning glories on the window, which had the advantage of being visible all year round.

"I guess. I don't know much about flowers."

"Did anyone see you?"

"I don't think so. Besides," he went on, trying for an ingratiating smile, "why would I shoot her? I hardly knew her."

"To know her is to shoot her," I murmured. The aftermath of fear is often silliness, and I was positively giddy as I once again realized how easy it was for someone to snuff out my former tenant's life.

It occurred to me that standing in the drafty doorway with a very expensive *netsuke* in my hand, talking to my stalker-client at an ungodly hour of the morning wasn't the sanest thing I could be doing.

At least, I could add coffee to the mix.

"Let's go downstairs," I said. "I'll just lock up and—"

I would lock up, but first, I'd put the precious objects back into the pencil-box drawer I'd found in the *tansu*. Later, I'd decide what to do about my find, but for the moment, I preferred not to have them in my direct possession.

I led Keith downstairs, unlocked the office door, and made straight for the coffeepot. Something hot and full of caffeine would help me see the whole mess in some kind of perspective. Keith made his way warily to one of the client chairs and sat down.

"I didn't kill her," he said again.

I didn't answer. Instead, I took two mugs off the wooden tree on the counter and set a sugar bowl and two spoons next to them. Then I walked to the mini refrigerator and brought out a pint carton of milk. I didn't answer until I had a cup of the healing brew in front of me.

Keith took his black. He wasn't drinking it, though, just cupped his hands around the warmth of the mug as if he was freezing. I was reminded of my very earliest coffee-drinking days, when I'd buy the vile, oily stuff at Kent State football games for the sole purpose of warming my cold hands.

Wearing gloves, of course, would have been terminally uncool, for reasons I'd now wholly forgotten. All I remembered was the heat of the coffee and the fact that over the years it grew to taste less and less vile.

Right now, hung over from lack of sleep and too many confused thoughts, cold to the bone from the unheated apartment and from the tenor of my thoughts, coffee seemed like the drink of the gods.

"I'm still your lawyer, thanks to Judge Tolliver," I said. "And as your lawyer, I have to warn you that the cops will definitely want to talk to you about the murder of Nellis Cartwright. As your lawyer, I must also advise you that you have no obligation to talk to them, and if you do decide to talk to them, I have to be there. Are you with me so far?"

"I don't know anything about it," Keith said. His earlier indignant denial had settled into a sullen unresponsiveness, perhaps because I'd retreated into lawyer-mode and was no longer talking to him person-to-person.

"Well, you admit you were on the street when it happened. At the least, you're a witness to something. You could help them pin down the time of the shooting and identify the people you saw at the scene."

"I was—" He swallowed hard; his Adam's apple bounced in his throat. "I was afraid it was you. I ran across the street and some guy in a white car nearly killed me. He yelled out his window—he must not have realized there was a shooting—and then he peeled on out of there. I was outside; I saw you bending over the body, and I nearly fainted with relief. I didn't know what was going on, just that you were still alive, thank God. I wanted to come in and be with you, but I was afraid you'd be mad."

He ducked his head again, but not before I saw the eyes fill and the lip tremble. "I mean, you're mad now, aren't you? You're mad that I was outside watching you, but I really only wanted to make sure you were all right. I just wanted to protect you."

"Protect me from—"

Oh, no.

"I was afraid it was you."

It could have been me.

Maybe it should *have been me.*

Did Nellis Cartwright die in my waiting room, shot through my plate glass window, because the shooter thought he was aiming at me?

But why?

Why would anyone want me dead?

And what the hell was the shooter going to do now that he'd managed to kill Nellis Cartwright Eddington while leaving me walking around?

Sleep was out of the question. I sent Keith home with the final instruction to say nothing to police; to call me if they wanted to talk to him. He gave me a phone number where he could be reached; it was, he said, a friend's number. There was no phone where he lived.

As the sun rose over the building across the street, I reluctantly turned to the work that needed to be done, work made all the harder by the absence of Marvella.

I was getting to the point where every day's mail delivery brought me to tears. Who wanted money I didn't have? Who was asking for their file to be sent along to their new lawyer? Who was threatening me with legal proceedings? Who'd made a complaint with the character and fitness committee?

I riffled through the envelopes and put them in piles on the desk. Bills to the right; others to the left. I sat for a moment and looked at them. What if I tossed them all into the circular file and let the Department of Sanitation carry them away unopened? What if I lit a fire and burned them, one by one, in a ceremonial purification rite? What if I ripped them up and flung the pieces out of the window like confetti?

The answer to the last was easy: given my current luck, I'd be locked up for littering.

It was Murphy's Law with a vengeance. Anything that could go wrong was going wrong. Any client who could make a complaint was making it; anyone who thought I owed them money wanted it—all of it, not just a token payment. Anyone who owed me money had discovered an ironclad reason why they didn't have to pay.

It couldn't all be coincidence. One or two implacable creditors, okay. A few disgruntled clients, well, it happens. You can't keep them gruntled all the time. An occasional dunning letter is par for the course in any business. Cash flow happens. But this was orchestrated, this was on purpose, this was outright sabotage.

I felt like Job with a law degree.

The only bright spot in the day was a call from Lissa Birnbaum.

"I wanted to thank you for what you said the other night," she began in her tentative, little-girl voice. "I really needed to hear it, even though it was hard at the time."

I searched my memory for whatever it was I'd said, and when it came back to me, I blushed over the wires. I'd essentially gotten fed up with the little whiner, and told her so in no uncertain terms. So what was there to be thankful about?

"I mean, when you said he didn't love me anymore, you were right. I have to face the facts, even if it hurts. So thank you for making me face the facts."

"Don't mention it," I said, then shifted the subject to her children, about whom she can talk for days. I heard more than I ever wanted to know about St. Ann's middle school.

I hung up feeling that maybe my bedside manner wasn't as bad as some social worker types thought it was.

I reached for my carved African letter opener—a present

from Marvella in happier times—and ripped open the last envelope, the latest bad news.

It was the worst yet: my mortgage holder had discovered my other troubles, and had decided to exercise its option to demand a balloon payment.

Balloons expand. So do balloon payments. It's a way for the creditor to get more security when it's feeling insecure. If I couldn't come up with twenty thousand dollars in ten days, I'd lose the building that housed my law office, my home, and my source of rental income.

But how? Where was that money going to come from? And what was the next disaster going to look like?

Whoever sabotaged my practice didn't just have access to my billing records; yesterday's botched court appearance meant they also knew my schedule. Someone hadn't just grabbed billing forms and stationery, they'd ransacked my private diary, hacked into my computer.

Keith had worked on the computer. Keith could have broken through the password-protection in order to get into my secrets.

But why would he? He claimed to want to protect me, not ruin my life.

But then he'd claimed he wanted to protect Tobah, too, and look what happened to her.

It was more than the computer. It was as if whoever was doing this was a fly on the wall, with access to what I was thinking and doing on a daily basis.

A fly on the wall or a bug on the wall?

I picked up the phone and called Raul. "I think I need an exterminator," I told him.

When you live in New York City, you aren't surprised to find bugs. But the bugs Raul's sweep uncovered weren't the six-legged kind; they were the kind that fit neatly into a telephone receiver. The one that lay in the palm of his brown hand was the size of a pencil eraser.

"Baby like this costs about sixty bucks," he said. "Wear it

in your tie tack or stick it behind your lapel, you got the whole conversation, no worries."

"Sixty bucks," I echoed. "Somebody compromised my entire professional life for sixty bucks. And it's illegal to tap someone's phone, so whoever sold this little piece of garbage is an accessory before the fact."

"Hey, this won't be the only one. I expect to find mikes all over this office. You want me to sweep upstairs, too?"

Upstairs meaning my apartment. Upstairs meaning my bedroom—the bedroom where Keith had laid the white lace nightgown on my bed.

"Damn right I do. I'm going to collect them all and show them to that asinine judge. He'll have to let me off this case after this."

But I knew better. The bugs might—but only might—help me convince the Committee on Character and Fitness that I wasn't incompetent, just the victim of illegal wiretaps. They wouldn't really care who'd planted the bugs; all they wanted to know was that I hadn't failed my clients out of negligence or stupidity. But to convince Judge Tolliver to relieve me as Keith Jernigan's lawyer, I'd have to prove that Keith was the one who placed the little microphone in my telephone.

I took William Gallagher's card from my file and called the Eight-Four. He was out, so I left a message. Two hours later, he vouchered the mikes as evidence.

"I'll send them to the fingerprint lab downtown," he said. "See if they can get a print and make a comparison. If Keith did this, we'll nail him."

We'll nail him—not words I usually enjoy hearing from a cop when the person being nailed is my own client.

I'd given the matter some thought before calling Gallagher. Was I violating my oath as an attorney by turning my client over to the police?

No, because I honestly didn't know who'd planted the bugs. For all I knew, Grant Eddington had somehow gained access to my office and made good his threat to ruin me if I helped Nellis in any way. For all I knew, some other client or ex-client thought it was payback time for something I'd done or failed to do.

I wasn't violating the attorney-client privilege, because this wasn't a matter of revealing something Keith had said to me in the course of my representation of him. This was an act—a criminal act, prohibited by federal law—and I had more than the right to reveal it to the authorities, I had a positive duty to cooperate with law enforcement.

I called the work phone number Keith had given me. I decided he had the right to know what was going on; he was still my client until such time as the judge listened to reason and let me off the case.

The guy who answered the phone said cheerfully, "Counter-spy."

"What did you say?"

"That's the name of our store. Counter-spy. Is there something I can help you with?"

Dazed, I asked if Keith Jernigan was there. The voice replied that he wasn't due until six, but I could leave a message. I declined and hung up.

Spy stores are a relatively new phenomenon, selling all kinds of listening and watching equipment, from hidden video cameras for catching the nanny napping to phone recorders to hand-held scanners. They skirt the bounds of legality, but they offer something people want, so they exist and profit from the growing paranoia of our society.

This was the "electronics store" where Keith worked; it might as well be called Stalkers R Us. It was in the business of selling precisely the kind of tiny bugging equipment Raul had turned up.

I began drafting my second motion to be relieved in the case of People v. Jernigan.

This time the judge had to listen.

CHAPTER NINETEEN

I had the *sagemono*.

Grant Eddington wanted the *sagemono*.

That had to be good for something. But what? If Grant was behind my professional troubles, then by doing him a favor, I might get a favor in return. If he wasn't, he'd thank me for my good deed and my professional life would still be in ruins.

But at least I wouldn't be in danger of being charged with possession of stolen property on top of all my other problems.

And besides, if I talked to Grant Eddington in person, I had half a chance of finding out where he'd been when his ex-wife was killed. So I retrieved the items I'd found in the *tansu* and headed to upper Fifth Avenue.

But a sense of unreality surrounded me like the aura of otherwordliness you feel when you're coming down with something and you're not yet aware that you're sick. You know things aren't quite right, but you honestly don't know why until you suddenly fall into bed and sleep fourteen hours and wake up with full-blown symptoms and then you understand why the last two days were so weird.

Was I really riding underneath midtown Manhattan on a shiny new F train with a hundred thousand dollars' worth of Japanese antiques in my leather backpack, on my way to see a possibly murderous drama critic?

I'd adjourned the rest of the day's cases by telephone; for once, the court clerks gave me no argument. They probably figured I was just this side of disbarred and was hustling to find my clients a new lawyer before everything hit the fan. Which wasn't as far from the truth as I'd have liked. I owed my clients better representation than that, but I couldn't deliver it unless and until I dispelled the black cloud hanging over my entire practice. And perhaps, just perhaps, returning Grant Eddington's property to him might accomplish that end.

It was a slender hope, but it was the only one I had at the moment.

I changed to the Lexington Avenue local and got out at 77th Street, then walked due west toward Fifth Avenue. Central Park got closer and closer as I walked, beckoning me with its golden-leaved ginkgoes and rust-red maples and dull gold oaks. What I wouldn't have given to be able to forget all my troubles and take a walk through the park, kicking leaves and tossing acorns and breathing the crisp, decay-scented air.

But I had work to do. I gave my name to the doorman at the apartment building where Grant lived. He used an in-house telephone to notify Grant that I was downstairs. After giving my name, he turned to me and said, "Mr. Eddington wishes to know the nature of your business with him, madam. He's working on his review at the moment and doesn't wish to be disturbed."

"Fine," I said, loudly enough to be heard through the phone. "I'll just take these things to the police, where they'll be held in the Property Room for the next decade or so while Mrs. Eddington's estate goes through probate."

I turned and walked away, quickly and decisively, forcing the poor doorman to chase me, panting and begging me to come back, as Mr. Eddington most definitely wanted to see me. I felt bad making the doorman pay for Grant's mistake, but I also wanted to make the point that I wasn't coming here on my knees, begging for anything.

I went up the same silent elevator and entered the same austere foyer; this time the single bloom in the *ikebana* vase was a pink-white orchid. Its sweetness softened the air, adding a distinctly feminine sensibility to the otherwise stark room.

As before, Grant met me at the door and ushered me inside. This time I was prepared for the overwhelming feeling I got walking into his treasure house of antiques and fine workmanship.

"You 'found' them, I take it." No hello, no offer of a drink. Just a preemptive strike not unlike the one he'd hit Nellis with when he closed out all their accounts the day before he told her their marriage was over.

"I'd rethink that emphasis if I were you," I said, going for a cold contempt that wasn't at all phony. "I found them. No little quotation marks around the verb. No sly hints that I always knew where they were or that I helped Nellis conceal them. I found them fair and square and the only way you're going to get them is through the proper channels so let's not—"

"What do you mean by proper channels?"

"I mean that as soon as you and I have a little talk, we're both going to call the police and tell them everything and let them decide exactly what to do with these things. I'm not going to be responsible for them, and I can't just give them to you. I have a license to protect, for one thing, and for another—"

I shook my head. "After watching you and Nellis, I have

no idea what's really in this bag. They could be your missing items or they could be cheap copies she picked up somewhere to torture you. I thought it would be nice to find out which before we involved the police."

He invited me to sit on the nearest chair. I did. He offered me something to drink; I asked for Perrier, knowing Grant Eddington wasn't a club soda kind of guy. He opened a little green bottle and poured the contents into a cut-glass goblet, then added ice and a lime quarter.

I took it and thanked him, then waited while he fixed his own drink and took a seat on the chair opposite mine, an exact duplicate. Very civilized. Very Fifth Avenue.

"Before we open this bag," I said, after taking a sip and putting the glass on a cork coaster on the table next to the chair, "I have a few questions I'd like to ask."

"I didn't kill my ex-wife," he said. "If that's one of your questions. I rather thought it might be."

"I wasn't going to ask it quite that bluntly," I replied, "but, yes, that was on the agenda."

"The police *have* questioned me, Ms. Jameson," he went on. "They're not quite as incompetent as you seem to believe. They asked me where I was when the fatal shot was fired, and I was able to tell them I was watching a rehearsal of the new musical *War and Peace* that's about to open at the Winter Garden."

A musical *War and Peace*?

Hell, if they could make a musical out of *Les Misérables*, what couldn't they make a musical out of?

"Do you usually go to rehearsals? Isn't that a breach of critics' ethics, seeing a play before the first night?"

His laugh sounded genuinely amused. "Most of my critics would say there are no such things as ethics among reviewers. But to answer your question, no, I have no doubt that I can review the play objectively when and if it opens, and my judgment regarding its merits can only be strengthened by understanding the evolutionary process that brought it to fruition."

That sounded like a grade-A crock, but I wasn't here to discuss the theory and practice of drama criticism. What did intrigue me was the "when and if it opened."

"You mean there's a chance a play like that, with all the money they must have invested so far, might not open?"

"There have been cases," Grant replied with a tiny inclination of his head, "in which the producers felt that opening the play would simply be throwing good money after bad."

"And a potential negative review by one Grant Eddington would be the kiss of death, to coin a phrase," I said. "So if the producer got the impression that a bad review might be written, he might decide to pull the plug—or—"

A thought was forming in the back of my mind, a thought that was perfectly consistent with the character of Grant Eddington as it was being revealed to me. "Or the producer might get the idea that the review would be a stinker unless he sweetened the reviewer with a gift. Maybe a nice piece of Japanese art for the reviewer's collection. Something small but valuable. Something he could easily hand over during the rehearsal the critic decided to attend in order to see that 'evolutionary process' you mentioned. Yeah, I'm beginning to see how this collection of yours grew so quickly."

"That is neither here nor there," Eddington replied. "The only important fact is that I was in the company of four producers, one director, one choreographer, and seventeen Broadway performers at the time the fatal shot was fired. Not to mention assorted stagehands and other minions of the theater."

How many times had this guy seen *Laura*? He was doing a perfect Clifton Webb, playing the part of a world-weary drama critic to the hilt.

But that didn't matter if his story checked out, and I had no doubt that it would. With the fate of the entire play resting on his review, no one in the theater was likely to forget the Great Man's visit to their rehearsal.

Which brought me back to the other reason for my visit. I reached down and pulled the drawstrings on my backpack.

He leaned forward in the lacquered chair, an expression of almost boyish eagerness on his smooth face.

I opened the top and pulled out the square wooden pencil-box drawer I'd found in the *choba dansu*.

Grant nodded appreciatively. "I see," he said. "I see where she hid them. Very nice. I suspected as much, that the police had no idea how to take apart a chest. I wanted to accompany them when they executed the search warrant, but they said that would be against policy. So they went alone and they bungled the search. But you, I take it, were shrewder than the police."

"I guess so," I said. "I just figured the Japanese had to be smarter than that. The hiding place Nellis revealed was too easy; anyone could have found it. And it didn't make sense that a Japanese carpenter wouldn't know that and compensate by making a second hidden compartment."

He reached for the slender box, his manicured hands trembling slightly.

I gave it to him and watched as he slid the top off the box, sliding it along the grooves and revealing colorfully wrapped objects inside. Underneath the bubble wrap, Nellis had used Japanese silk fragments to cushion the carvings; it looked as if doll kimonos were wadded up inside the box.

He picked up the nearest silk ball and began to unwind it. It was one I'd already opened, the Lantern Ghost I'd seen in Nellis's photograph. Grant smiled when it was fully unwrapped. He held it up to his eye and squinted at it, then reached into a round table and took out a magnifying glass.

From where I sat, the glass seemed to magnify his eye, like a Sherlock Holmes drawing. He gave a nod and a sigh of pure satisfaction and said, "Yes, Sukeyuki. Sheer perfection. Note the tiny hands, the expression on the face."

"I thought Sukeyuki was food," I muttered, although I knew better. I was reacting, I supposed, to the fact that this cold man melted at the sight of a piece of carved ivory, whereas he'd shown absolutely no emotion when he talked about his dead wife. And the Lantern Ghost brought Nellis to mind, not only because she'd used the image in a powerful photograph, but also because she herself seemed a Lantern Ghost, forever haunted by her lost marriage, never quite the same after her husband's betrayal.

And here was the betrayer, back in possession of his true love, his *netsuke*, while his ex-wife's body lay on a slab in the morgue.

He unwrapped each of the brightly colored balls and set them, one by one, on the table next to his chair. He greeted them as old friends, and fondled them with his fingers in a way that seemed almost obscene in its sensuous delight, like something one ought to do only behind closed doors and alone.

George Carlin had this terrific routine about "stuff." How we accumulate "stuff" and then have to buy containers to hold our "stuff" and spend money moving our "stuff" from here to there, and even sometimes pay good money to get rid of our "stuff."

It was a hilarious comic monologue.

But would you kill for your "stuff"?

I suspected Grant Eddington would.

I wondered just how carefully the police checked that alibi of his.

When he had the last of his treasures unwrapped, he sighed with postcoital pleasure and said, "Thank you, Ms. Jameson. I was afraid I'd never see these beauties again. It's enough for me to know they're safe and sound; I'll be happy to notify the police that they've been restored."

"Let's do that right now," I said with a forced cheerfulness that put Grant on edge, as I'd intended. "Now that we know these are the real thing, let's bring the cops up to date."

He dialed the phone with bad grace and we both waited in awkward silence.

"So," I said to break the tension, "what do you think of *War and Peace*? Is it another *Les Miz* or a miserable example of the Lloyd-Webberization of the Broadway stage?"

"Please don't attempt to parody my style, Ms. Jameson," the eminent critic replied, closing his eyes in mock pain. Or perhaps real pain; it was hard to tell. "Many others have tried, with varying degrees of success."

"Well, then how about telling me whether you had anything to do with certain little problems I've been having in my practice?"

His bland expression told me nothing. I pressed on. "Little things like clients getting phony bills and bogus letters going out on my letterhead and calls to court clerks that I never made. Things like spying on me with bugged phones and—"

"I'm a drama critic, Ms. Jameson. I'm not a spy. I have neither the expertise nor the motivation to do any of the things you've mentioned."

"It might be your way of putting pressure on me so I'd come up with those," I said, inclining my head toward the carved items on the table. "Or of punishing me for taking Nellis's case, the way you punished Kate Avelard."

"I? Punish Kate Avelard?" He threw his head back and I heard the first genuine laugh I'd ever gotten out of Grant Eddington. It wasn't a pleasant sound, but it had the ring of truth. I'd said something funny, not something threatening.

"You misunderstand my relationship with Ms. Avelard," he went on, his tone taking on a gloating quality that sickened me. "She and I understood one another very well," he went on. "I knew what she needed, and she knew what I needed, and we managed to reach a mutually satisfactory arrangement."

"In what way?" I didn't want to know, didn't want to hear that paranoid, hysterical, angry Nellis had been right all along. The lawyer she'd hired to protect her interests in the divorce had really been working for the enemy. Selling her out.

For money?

Money to keep Marc in the best doctors. Money to keep the children in their private schools. Money to keep up the expensive, tasteful Brooklyn Heights lifestyle that with Marc terminally ill and Kate preoccupied with his illness could no longer be paid for by their combined salaries.

It made a horrible kind of sense.

It also meant that Kate's troubles hadn't been visited upon her by Grant, who had no reason to punish her, but were entirely her own fault.

So whose fault were my troubles? If Grant hadn't pulled those strings to screw up my practice, who had?

Now that I'd solved one tiny portion of the puzzle, it was time to find out.

When I opened my downstairs door, I almost stepped on a pale blue envelope. I reached down and picked it up, noting the block lettering and lack of a postage stamp.

I was no longer naive enough to think a colored envelope meant an invitation or a card congratulating me or anything at all pleasant.

But this one—this one was different.

Not the card itself, which showed two impossibly cute mice, with bright eyes and big smiles and little red hearts circling them, even though they were standing apart.

I opened the card; something fell out onto the foyer floor. I left it there while I read the inside of the card.

DEAREST ΧΑΣΑΝΔΡΑ,
I THOUGHT ABOUT YOU THE WHOLE TIME I
WAS IN PRISON.

I STILL THINK ABOUT YOU ALL THE TIME.
PLEASE FORGIVE ME AND LET ME LOVE YOU.

I grimaced, but nothing in the message constituted a threat. More along the lines of an annoyance, a distraction, a messy little crush I ought to be able to nip in the bud.

Then I bent down to pick up the photograph that had fallen out of the card.

It was Keith.

Naked. Naked and erect, with one hand gripping his erection and apparently pumping away. His face was contorted in what could have been agony but was probably its opposite.

I looked more closely at the photograph—not at the image itself, but at the angle from which it was taken. Keith must, I decided, have placed a camera on his windowsill and aimed it at his torso.

Sick. Disgusting. Disturbing. Wacko.

And ultimately very, very satisfying.

Even Lucius Tolliver wouldn't force me to continue representing a client who sent me dirty pictures of himself.

CHAPTER TWENTY

I picked up the phone and called the Eight-Four precinct. I asked for Detective Gallagher and was surprised when the cop on the phone yelled out, "Liam, phone call."

I'd known his first name was William, but I guess I'd seen him as a Bill.

I felt like a total sucker. Keith had convinced me that he'd really intended to apologize to Tobah and that even the bizarre act of sending Oliver to spy on Fran hadn't been done to harm her. But this—if this wasn't the act of an obsessed wacko, what was?

Liam Gallagher agreed. He took the photo and said he'd have it tested for prints and would also check into possible obscenity charges. I also got Gallagher to sign an affidavit for use with my second set of motion papers asking to be relieved as counsel.

"You really ought to have better security in here," the young detective said, cocking a disapproving eye on the windows, naked of any silver wire indicating an alarm system.

"So my investigator keeps telling me," I replied, then added with a laugh, "and, in fact, Keith said the same thing. It turns out he works for one of those spy store places that sell both the security devices and the means to circumvent them."

"By the way," he said, gesturing toward the card, which lay open on my desk, "what's with the foreign language? What is that, Russian or something?"

"Greek. It's my name. It was kind of a joke. Keith gave me this, too." I pointed to the mug he'd given me the day I first learned about Tobah.

Liam looked startled when he saw the mug, then shook his head. "Weird."

"I suppose," I replied half-heartedly. Before all the craziness started, I'd liked the fact that Keith knew the origin of my name; I'd liked being his Trojan princess. But that didn't mean I wanted to see him without pants. I hardened my heart against the memories and let Gallagher bag the card as evidence.

The phone rang. "God, I miss Marvella," I said as I reached for it. I dealt with the angry client on the other end, who was unhappy that his case had been put off for yet another court date. All my clients, the ones I had left, were angry.

"Your secretary," Gallagher asked, "why'd she leave? Too much pressure?"

I explained about Oliver's arrest and Keith's part in it.

I also explained that I'd tried unsuccessfully to convince the complaining witness to let Oliver off the hook. I still felt bad about that, as if I truly was responsible for Keith's outrageous action in bringing Oliver into his sick fantasy life.

"I still have this feeling," I went on, "that if I could just talk to this Fran one more time, I could make her see that prosecuting Oliver isn't the answer. He's just a kid. He bought Keith's crazy story about live role-playing games, and he was just doing what his Dungeon Master told him to do."

"Sounds pretty far-fetched to me," Gallagher said with a shake of his head.

"He's a kid," I repeated. "He looked up to Keith. He didn't think Keith would send him out to do something illegal."

"Maybe I could help you talk to this Fran," the cop said. He gave a shrug. "For one thing," he continued, "she might know something about where Keith is now."

"Man, you're really taking this stalking thing seriously. I mean, I was afraid the police would think I was blowing this out of proportion, but you—"

"It's more than that," Gallagher said. "If you're right and Grant Eddington has an alibi for his ex-wife's murder, that kind of confirms my theory."

"And what is your theory?"

"You haven't thought of this yourself? I mean, you really don't know what I'm going to say here?"

"No, of course I don't know what you're going to say. So just say it."

"What if the shooter was Keith? And he wasn't trying to kill Nellis Cartwright. He was aiming at you."

I'd already had that thought, but further reasoning had refuted it. So I tried my reasoning on Detective Gallagher.

"But he knew me, and he'd met Nellis. He would have seen that she wasn't me."

"With the setting sun glaring into his eyes? From a rooftop across the street? Think about it. Just think about it for a minute."

How could I not think about it?

I'd just come home. I'd gone into my office and Nellis came down to see me two minutes later. Someone outside looking in wouldn't have seen her come down the inside stairs, wouldn't have realized there were two people on the parlor floor. Then her phone rang, and she went to the waiting room for a private talk. Someone outside would see a woman on a telephone. Thinking there was only one woman inside—me—the person took aim and fired.

It was all too chillingly plausible.

But why?

Why would anyone, even a certified wacko like Keith Jernigan, want me dead?

Hate is the other side of love, and all that?

You don't want me, so you have to die?

It felt too extreme, even for the man who'd sent me a naked photo of himself.

But the fact was that Nellis lay dead and her ex-husband, the only person with a motive, seemed to be in the clear.

But was he the only person with a motive?

What about Kate Avelard? She was facing disbarment and Nellis was the one pulling the plug on her career. And if Grant was telling the truth, Nellis was right about Kate; she'd taken money from the enemy, and she deserved to be disbarred. But with Nellis dead, that portion of the charges against her might well die too. She'd have other angry clients making claims, but Nellis's was the one that was truly dangerous, the one that might even put Kate behind bars for fraud.

Now I knew I was going around the bend. Kate Avelard, in her designer scarves and Old Maine Trotters standing on a rooftop with an assault rifle, taking aim into my window. It was crazy. Unthinkable.

But I had to like it better than the idea that I was the intended victim.

Going to see Fran required that we know her last name and her exact address, neither of which I had. But Gallagher made a phone call to the Manhattan Family Court and within minutes, he had both.

"Are you sure you should be doing this?" I asked as we

headed toward the Brooklyn Bridge in his unmarked car. "I mean, I don't want you to get in trouble or anything."

"Hey, I wouldn't be doing this if I didn't think it was a logical part of the Nellis Cartwright case. And you said yourself that the guy who arrested this kid wanted to go easy on him, so it's not like I'm stepping on any toes over here by talking to this lady."

"Well, thanks again," I said. "I haven't had this much co-operation from the Brooklyn police since Detective Button retired."

"Oh, yeah," Gallagher replied with a grin, "I remember now. Roy used to talk about you sometimes. Said you were okay for a total pain in the ass."

"That's pretty much what I said about him," I countered, "so I guess we were even." I felt a nice glow thinking that Gallagher had known Button; maybe my old comrade's retirement didn't mean I was all out of friends in the Department.

Fran Winslow lived in a very secure building on East 10th Street. It was what New Yorkers call a pre-war elevator building, meaning it was an elegant fortress with a big lobby and a doorman and rooms in which you could actually swing a cat.

When Gallagher knocked on the door, a high-pitched female voice asked, "Who is it?"

"Detective Gallagher, ma'am, NYPD."

There was a sound of metal scraping metal, of locks clicking in the door. Then the door cracked open, a brass chain still in place at eye level.

"Show me your identification," the voice said.

Gallagher opened his badge case and held it up just below the chain. There was a pause and then a hand lifted the chain from its hook and opened the door wider.

She almost closed it again when she saw me.

"I think you know Ms. Jameson," Gallagher said, motioning me inside along with him.

"You didn't tell me she was with you," Fran said, hugging herself tight and staring with accusing eyes at the two of us. I noted that she had four locks on the door, one of which was a police lock, a long metal pole in the floor that fitted into a slot on the door itself and could have kept out a battering ram.

Raul Maldonado, the security maven of Brooklyn, would have loved it.

This was not a way I wished to live—but then, Fran probably hadn't lived this way before she met Keith Jernigan.

"I asked Ms. Jameson to come with me for a reason," Gallagher said. "May we sit down, please?"

Fran unfolded her arms and led us, with bad grace, into the living room. Gallagher took the single upholstered chair, leaving Fran and me the love seat. We sat as far apart as we could, but it was still too close for her comfort.

"You still want me to drop the charges, don't you?"

I was about to start pleading Oliver's case, but Gallagher got in first. "There's been a new development we thought you should know about."

"I knew it! That boy got out on bail and—"

"No, ma'am, it's nothing to do with the boy," Gallagher replied. "Keith Jernigan is wanted for questioning in connection with another matter entirely. We merely thought you might have some idea where we could find him."

"How on earth would I know a thing like that? Do you think I visit him? Send him postcards?" Her voice was rising into a second level of hysteria—and that isn't a word I use lightly.

"We thought perhaps you knew something you didn't know you knew," Gallagher went on, a reassuring smile on his face. "Like maybe you received a card or a letter with a return address or a postmark, something that could help us find Jernigan."

"I showed everything to that Detective Palmieri," Fran said. "As if he cared. He was too busy," she said, glaring at me, "trying to give that boy a break. He didn't care what I'd been through. All he wanted was for me to drop the charges. Everyone's on that boy's side, and nobody cares about me. Nobody!"

Gallagher was good. In a soothing tone that a priest would have envied, he said, "Ma'am, I'm not here to take anybody's side. All I want is to talk to Jernigan about this murder, and—"

"Murder?" Fran jumped from her seat and put her hands over her face. "My God! Who did he kill? That poor Jewish girl with the acid? Oh, my God, I always knew he'd kill somebody some day. I just prayed it wouldn't be me, and now—"

She broke into sobs. Gallagher waited until they subsided, then handed her a box of tissues from an end table. She blew her nose and said, "I'm sorry. I just—oh, God, you don't know how it's been. I've spent years in therapy, trying to get over this nightmare. Because I knew." She looked at both of us, but her eyes lingered on me, as if willing me to understand.

"I knew he'd kill someone someday. I really, truly did. But every time I said that, to police or to my friends, they looked at me as if I was crazy. And I'm not."

"Nobody here thinks you're crazy," I said. She seemed to want to hear that, from me in particular.

"Oh, that's what you say now," Fran countered. "But I've lost friends over this. Boyfriends and regular friends. They think I'm paranoid."

She gave a bitter laugh and pointed to the hardware on her door. "They think I've taken security to an extreme. But they should see the garbage Keith sent me from jail."

My surprise must have shown in my face.

"Oh, yes," she went on, a hint of triumph in her smile. "From jail. He was incarcerated, so I wasn't really afraid he'd come after me, not physically, but he still played his sick little games."

She turned abruptly and walked to her bedroom, then returned seconds later with a huge manila envelope crammed with paper. One by one she pulled out greeting cards, very much like the one I'd turned over to Gallagher that very morning, with block-printed envelopes and cheery little messages and cutesy animals and handwritten obscenities.

"Jesus," I whispered. "I never knew."

"I suppose you didn't," Fran said. "I suppose the cards he sent you were all sweetness and light, weren't they?"

I nodded.

"That's the kind he used to send to me, when we were dating. And even when we lived together in Ithaca, he'd buy cards like this and leave them on the kitchen counter or slip them into my books so I'd find them later in the library. I thought it was so sweet, so thoughtful. Now I feel physically ill when I pass a Hallmark store. I can't see cards like this without thinking of Keith and how he perverted their messages into his own private language of stalking."

I saw a tiny opening and I took it.

"*He* did the stalking," I repeated. "*Keith* sent the cards. He's the one who wanted to get your attention, not Oliver. Oliver really thought he was playing some kind of live-action role-playing game; he was just doing what Keith told him to do. I swear to you, he's a good kid who never got into any trouble before, and believe me, from his neighborhood, that's a miracle. I'm asking you, please, to give Oliver a break on this."

"You can rest assured, ma'am," Gallagher chimed in, "that the Department will pursue any charges it might have against Keith Jernigan with the utmost vigor. This case of yours isn't the only way we have of bringing him to justice."

"You want me to drop the charges?" Fran repeated.

I hastened to clarify. "No. It would be highly unethical for either of us to ask for that. This is an ongoing prosecution and we have no desire to get in its way, but the corporation counsel will listen to you on the matter of leniency. As the complaining witness, you have a lot to say about what happens in court. All we ask is that you remember who's really behind the trespass and that you don't punish the wrong person."

"All right," she said. "I'll talk to Ms. Petroniak."

"Thank you," I said, with very real relief and gratitude.

"Now, about those cards, ma'am," Gallagher said.

"The last card I got—four days ago, by the way—was postmarked Brooklyn," she said in a weary voice. She handed the card to Gallagher, who smiled and put it into a plastic bag he pulled from his jacket pocket.

"Isn't it amazing," she said as she watched him, "how the police attitude has changed? When I told the Ithaca cops what was going on, they said, 'It takes two to tango,' as if I had to be equally complicit in order to be stalked. And here in Manhattan, the police said things like, 'It's a free country, ma'am; we can't stop him from standing across the street and watching your apartment for eight solid hours if that's what he wants to do.'"

I glanced at Liam, whose face wore an expression of mingled shame and pride. Pride, I supposed, because he was part of the new breed of cops who took women like Fran seriously, and shame on behalf of the cops who hadn't.

Fran's bitter laugh echoed in the tasteful, lonely room. "Only it wasn't a free country, not for me. Because I was afraid to go out at night, afraid to open my curtains even in broad daylight for fear he'd be looking through binoculars and see everything I did. And you know what the worst part was?"

Again she addressed her question to me. I was a woman, she seemed to be thinking, so why wasn't I as acutely conscious of vulnerability as she was?

I shook my head.

"After a while," she went on in a dreamy tone of voice, "I

started wondering what it was about me that caused all this to happen. Why was it that I, Frances Laura Winslow from Delphi, New York, attracted a world-class nut case while my sisters and my friends met and married normal men? What was I doing to encourage him? Was there part of me that wanted his sick attentions?"

I felt sick. Physically sick. I looked at the teak coffee table with the manila envelope overflowing with pastel envelopes, and I wanted to throw up.

Because she was right. It hadn't actually floated to the forefront of my brain yet, but way in the back somewhere was the same thought: had I gotten too friendly with this client? Had I invited his attentions because they made me feel good? Had I even encouraged what seemed to be a minor crush so I could enjoy the feeling of being wanted by a man?

Hell, yes. I had treated Keith differently from my other clients, as Mickey was the first to point out. I'd let him treat me to dinner and bring me roses and I'd enjoyed his company.

Had I invited a nude photograph with a suggestive message?

I didn't think so, but that wasn't really the important thing.

The important thing was that Keith was making me doubt myself, my own instincts, my ability to tell the difference between a friendly relationship and a full-blown tease.

The satisfied smile on Fran Winslow's face told me she was pleased to have struck a nerve at last. She ushered Gallagher and me to the door with a much calmer demeanor than she'd had when we first entered the room.

"Who did he kill, anyway?" she asked as she unlocked the chain.

"A woman named Nellis Cartwright," Gallagher replied. "But we think maybe the bullet was meant for Ms. Jameson here."

Fran gave me a look made up of one part sympathy and two parts triumph. "Then maybe you'll finally understand the way I've had to live for the past six years," she said. "Feeling like a hunted animal, when the only thing I did wrong was to let Keith Jernigan into my life."

We rode in silence across the Manhattan Bridge. It was nice being on this bridge for a change, since it afforded a fantastic view of the real beauty, the Brooklyn Bridge, with its arches and its spiderweb cables. The river sparkled below, a ribbon of silver separating two great cities.

I expected Gallagher to go straight to the precinct and leave me to walk home, or at least to drop me off and then head for the Eight-Four, but to my surprise, he accompanied me into the Morning Glory for a cup of coffee.

Dorinda was on the phone. She gave me a wave and tucked the receiver under her chin as she reached for my mug and the fresh pot of coffee. She poured as she talked, giving Gallagher a raised-eyebrow query to which he replied with a nod. She took a second mug from the overhead hook and poured coffee into it.

"Well, at least Vinegar Hill sounds like a place where people actually live," she said in her softly intransigent voice. "DUMBO is the stupidest name I ever heard. It makes me think of that wooden elephant in Margate."

She paused, then said, "You know, on the Jersey shore. Well, trust me; there's an elephant and people used to sleep in it. Yeah, like a bed and breakfast. In an elephant."

I smiled; I'd seen pictures of the Margate elephant, which had been a landmark on the Jersey shore. And what she was saying did, in its own odd way, make perfect sense. DUMBO was an acronym, coined in imitation of Manhattan's SoHo, which meant Down Under the Manhattan-Brooklyn Overpass; it was a warehouse neighborhood on the Brooklyn side of the two bridges, and it was an up-and-coming artists' colony.

She was talking on an old-fashioned phone with an actual cord that she'd absentmindedly twisted around her arm. I had no idea who she was talking to or what DUMBO had to do with—

The implication took a minute to sink in. But then I felt the warm glow of a clue well-deciphered.

Tobah had said Keith's friend with the loft lived in a place whose name was made out of initials. And DUMBO was an acronym. It was also a place that had lofts where artists lived and worked. Like SoHo, only a lot cheaper and in Brooklyn. Warehouse buildings no longer used in industry, but valued by artists for the vast spaces and huge light-grabbing windows crowded the area between the two bridges.

It was right next to the former whorehouse where Dorinda lived. It was cheek-by-jowl with the River Café, where Keith had wanted to take me to dinner only two weeks earlier.

I consulted my mental Brooklyn bus map. Two buses, Tobah had said, changing on Flatbush Avenue. I thought that would work, but I'd have to check to be sure. The St. John's bus ran along Flatbush, and he'd catch something from the Fulton Ferry section to reach it.

I was excited. I had a line on where Keith might be living, which meant I could stop waiting for him to send me obscene cards, I could go after him and force him to tell me what the hell was going on here.

If Keith Jernigan was hiding out in DUMBO, he wouldn't be hard to find. It wasn't a densely populated neighborhood; loft dwellers walked more than ten blocks to buy groceries on Henry Street. There weren't many people on the streets, and newcomers would be noticed by those who lived and worked there.

When I proposed that we look for Keith in DUMBO, Gallagher said, "Are you nuts? You," he reminded me in a firm cop voice I hadn't heard him use before, "are a civilian. This means you don't canvass, you don't go on a manhunt against a perp who may have killed someone. You stay here and I'll go back to the house, notify my sergeant, and we'll put out a squeal for the guy."

"No way." I stood up from the stool, ready to head straight to the warehouse neighborhood and start ringing doorbells.

The only way on God's earth I was going to avoid becoming Fran Winslow, living in her quadruple-locked apartment behind closed curtains, was to refuse to be passive. I was tired of reacting. I was sick to death of feeling helpless. Even if I trudged the entire length and breadth of Brooklyn to no avail, I'd feel better than if I just sat on my ass and waited for someone else to do something.

"Counselor, I'm warning you not to interfere in police business." Gallagher was standing too, and suddenly he looked tall and bulky and slightly menacing as he blocked my way to the door.

I sought refuge in the mantra Fran Winslow had used, in a very different context. "It's a free country, Detective. I just thought I'd take a long, healthy walk along the Promenade and maybe I'd end up between the bridges. It's a nice night for a walk, isn't it?"

It was, in fact, getting raw and damp and windy outside, but that wasn't the point.

Gallagher shook his head and said, "All right. Let's go."

He turned and said, "You got a picture of this mope somewhere, or should I get one from the precinct?"

I had a picture, all right. I had the old mugshot, which made him look like a seventeen-year-old hacker, and I also had a Polaroid someone had taken at the celebration party. He was smiling and clearly a little drunk, and he looked just like a guy who'd been let out of jail after serving time for something he hadn't done. He looked innocent in a way I could hardly remember now.

I handed the picture to Gallagher without a word and we set off into the chill afternoon.

I felt a surge of elation. I was going straight into the neighborhood where Keith apparently lived and I was stalking him.

Card Four:
The Tower Struck by Lightning

HE SHIVERED IN HIS LIGHT JACKET, WISHING HE'D WORN THE DOWN VEST UNDERNEATH IT, OR MAYBE A HOODED SWEATSHIRT even. You couldn't overprepare when it came to being outdoors for a long time in the fall. It got colder sooner than you expected, leaving you with stiff fingers and a deep bone chill that wouldn't go away.

And where in hell were his fingerless gloves, the ones he always used when he brought his long lens and camera with him?

He could write a book. *Dress for Stalking Success.* Sell a million copies to all the poor losers like him who just didn't know when to let go.

Oh, the shrinks at Dannemora had told him all about himself. How he wasn't even unique in his passionate connections to the women he'd loved. How he was a perfect textbook case and what to do if the "old feelings" rose up inside him again. He'd begun at last to understand that Fran and Tobie really had meant "no" even when they kept saying "maybe" because women are taught that "no" is hurtful and sometimes they say "maybe" but they really mean "no." Especially when they've already said "no" a hundred times and the only reason you got them back to "maybe" was by threatening to kill yourself in the lobby of their apartment building.

Or to kill them.

But you didn't mean it, not really; it was the obsession talking. You felt you couldn't live without them, so you told them that because that was always what the hero said in the movie and it always melted his lover's heart, so why wouldn't it melt hers? And if it didn't, well, then maybe you were both meant to die together. Because what good was life without love, and if the woman who was meant for you didn't love you, then you might as well be dead.

Well, that was his old self, the one he'd left behind back in the joint.

He was a new man, a born-again nonstalker, someone who would never again in this world make a woman's life a misery. A man who would take "no" for an answer, no matter how much his own heart said that "yes" was the right answer. A man who had learned from his terrible mistake.

So what was he doing on a rooftop, peering down at two people trudging wearily between warehouse buildings?

He'd promised never to stalk another woman.

But nothing in that promise precluded his protecting one with his vigilance.

CHAPTER
TWENTY-ONE

The sun was low in the sky and a cool wind was blowing off the harbor as Gallagher and I stepped out of his car at Fulton Ferry Landing. You could see the warehouses just past the Brooklyn Bridge, behind the Watchtower building owned by the Jehovah's Witnesses. We walked in silence; not much to say.

What we'd say to Keith if and when we found him was another matter entirely.

I'd have to remind him that the police wanted to talk to him about Nellis Cartwright, and I'd have to serve him with the latest motion to be relieved as his lawyer. But after that—would I tell him I'd received his card in the mail, or save that bit for the court appearance?

Or should I just stay quiet and let the policeman do the talking?

As the huge red ball lowered itself to the level of the Statue of Liberty, the thought occurred that I might not be able to say anything to him. We had nothing more than a hunch and a neighborhood; he could be in any one of a hundred warehouses, and his name wouldn't be on the bell if there was a bell, which a lot of these lofts didn't have because they were illegal as living quarters.

We started with six or seven names of people Dorinda knew. The first three said they knew nothing; the next two weren't home. Finally we hit someone who was present and willing to help.

Fazil thought maybe Henri would know. He pronounced the name the French way, so I was expecting a guy with a beret and an accent. Instead, the door was opened by a small, slim woman with about a half-inch of hair on her head and black footless tights under a huge white T-shirt that asked the question, DO WOMEN HAVE TO BE NAKED TO GET INTO THE METROPOLITAN MUSEUM?

She explained that her name was Henriette, also pronounced the French way. Her loft was filled with canvases and reeked of paint and turpentine. She walked on the concrete floor with her bare feet, the bottoms of which were coated with black dirt. She stood in the doorway, her face contorted with the effort of remembering.

"There was a guy, I can almost see his face. *Alors*, what was his name? What was his silly name? Ah, I am such a ninny with these American names. A name like Fazil, this I can remember." She smiled at my companion, her large dark eyes flirting with him even as her no-nonsense haircut denied any female wiles.

"But all you Americans are Bob or Bill or something equally bourgeois and therefore easily forgotten."

"This guy's name was Keith," I said dryly.

"Keeeth," she repeated, exaggerating the vowel sound. "This is not a name we have in France," she said. "What is his art? I can perhaps recall him if you tell me what art he makes."

"He's not an artist."

"Then what would he be doing here, in this place? This is

a place for artists, no? I do not know anyone here who is not an artist of some sort."

She moved to close the door; I noted with approval that Liam's shoe had already found a place firmly between door and jamb.

"He's staying at someone else's place," I explained. "Like a house-sitter, or maybe he's someone's guest."

"Ah, a guest," she repeated, satisfied that Keith's presence in her universe had some justification after all. "Who has had a guest recently?"

More thought. "I believe I met someone at the tae kwon do studio. There was a party there to celebrate Vicki's getting a show at Montague Street." She gave the name such a French twist that it took me a minute to translate.

"At the Summa Gallery?" I asked, my voice rising with interest. "That's quite a coup."

"No, not the Summa," Henri said with a lip curl. "That place is no gallery. It's a bourgeois extension of the artistic establishment. It sells mere decoration."

I should have known. No one who painted anything like the messy-looking oversized canvases I could see behind Henri was ever going to show at the Summa Gallery, which was devoted to a delicate, beautiful, and, yes, decorative style. The truth was that Vicki's show was "only a little ways from Montague Street itself, mere steps, you know, but to use the Montague Street name is to bring a bit of *cachet* and so—"

"Back to the man you met at this party," I said firmly. "What did he look like?"

"Like *un type très ordinaire*," she replied with disdain. "Brown hair, brown eyes, a brown shirt with plaids, brown trousers of that heavy cloth men wear here. In France, such a cloth is only for the little boys, but here, the grown men wear it."

"Corduroy," I guessed. She nodded.

"And the *souliers*," she went on, putting my high school

French to the test. "Such ugly shoes are never worn in Paris. Big, heavy, shapeless things that cushion the feet. Always you Americans want to be cushioned."

If the man she'd met wasn't Keith, he was Keith's double.

Henri gave us directions. It was getting late; the sun was low in the sky and the wind off the river was cold and damp. I was tired and my feet stumbled as I tried to keep pace with Gallagher on the slippery cobblestone streets.

I still had the eerie feeling of being watched and followed. Several times I turned quickly on my heel and took a wide-angle look behind me, hoping to catch a glimpse of shadow that would tell me I wasn't crazy, that there really was someone there. But each time all I saw was empty street.

Maybe my nerves were caused by the fact that empty streets simply don't exist in New York City, so it was impossible for me to believe I'd actually found one.

Then I saw it. This time when I wheeled around, hoping I'd moved fast enough so that the follower wouldn't have time to disappear, I saw the sleeve of a leather jacket.

I heard footsteps. I shouted and pointed. Gallagher ran in the direction I indicated, and I followed, knowing I couldn't keep up but determined to try.

We ran for three blocks. Liam turned once, suddenly, and then stopped in mid-block. "I don't know, Cass," he said as he gasped for breath. "If this guy was here at all, I don't know where he went to. He could have turned any of a dozen ways."

"But you did see him?"

He shook his head. "No, but if you say you did, that's good enough for me."

It wasn't good enough for me, though. I desperately wanted some confirmation that we were really being followed, that I wasn't following Fran Winslow into the nether reaches of paranoia. I trailed behind the detective with a heavy heart as we retraced our steps.

The tae kwon do studio was four long, lonely blocks away, on the ground floor of another huge warehouse building. The plate glass storefront had a large drawing of two martial artists circling one another warily. The martial artists wore white; one was a large Asian with a fat belly and the other was a blond young woman half his size. In the corner of the window, a hand-lettered sign proclaimed the class session hours.

I pounded on the metal door for several minutes. It wasn't a class time, according to the sign, so I didn't expect to be interrupting anything. When no answer was forthcoming, I turned and said, "Guess we'll have to come back later."

I was four steps away from the door when it creaked open and a deep voice asked, "Are you here about classes?"

The man in the drawing stood before me, wearing not the white clothes of the master, but a loud Hawaiian shirt over drawstring pants. His bare brown feet were thrust into Japanese straw sandals, and he carried a tall can of beer.

"No, we need to ask you a few questions about someone you might have met." I introduced myself and Gallagher and explained a little bit about our errand. The man raised an eyebrow but then stuck out a massive hand and said, "I'm Lyle Hinoluea. I'm the tae kwon do master. Come on in and have a seat."

Gallagher and I followed the big man into the cavernous loft area. There were three separate and very distinct areas: the martial arts classroom, which was painted a stark white and had paper globes over the light bulbs; other Asian accoutrements included a large fan open on one wall and a Japanese curved sword with a silk tassel hanging from it on the other. Neat shelves painted Chinese red held pairs of shoes and white jackets hung from a rod above the shelves.

The second area was the studio I took to be Vicki's. She was a weaver, and her loom took up a huge amount of floor space. Colored threads more complex than a spiderweb fed into the main part of the loom, where a piece was taking shape. It was made of bright colors, yet with an earthy undertone made up of moss greens and deep golds and midnight blues. On the wall behind the loom, a finished piece hung against the exposed brick. It was a nature scene, and yet it wasn't. There were no obvious references to trees or water or earth, and yet it was clear the artist was attempting to capture something of nature.

"Very interesting work," I said as we passed the two working areas. Lyle grunted; what, after all, can one say when accepting a compliment on someone else's behalf?

The third section of the loft was for living. The walls were painted a gentle aqua, and the furniture echoed the watery, tropical feel with chintzes in melon and mint green, yellow and orange. The dishes, displayed in an old kitchen cabinet, were Fiestaware and the table was covered with a gay, flower-printed cloth that could have been turned into Hawaiian shirts like the one Lyle wore.

"Are you from Hawaii?" I asked.

"Yes. Although I'm half-Samoan. Vicki likes to kid me, says I should have become a sumo wrestler. But tae kwon do is so—I don't know, subtle. I like being able to do something subtle even though I'm built like a Mack truck. So who is this person you're looking for, and what makes you think I can help?"

"We just came from talking to Henri," I said. "She told me she might have met this guy at a party you and Vicki gave."

"That was about a week ago," he said. He walked to the refrigerator, which had been hand-painted with hibiscus flowers. "Want some juice? I was going to make some for myself anyway."

When Lyle Hinoluea said juice, he didn't mean he was going to open a can. He took out six different varieties of tropical fruit and set them on the sink counter next to a restaurant-sized juicer. Within minutes, I was sipping a pineapple-mango-melon combination I had to tell Dorinda about. Liam went for the straight guava and asked Lyle how much he thought a juicer would cost. When we all had juice, Lyle sat down to business.

"The party," he said reflectively, seating his bulk on a white wooden chair and tilting it back ever so slightly. It creaked in protest, but it didn't break or topple him to the cement floor. "Everyone brought a guest. Or at least it seemed that way. But then it always seems that way around here. This couple invites someone they know from somewhere, and someone else tells another couple of friends about the party, and a few people come up just because they're walking past on their way home and they know they'll be welcome, so they go home and grab a bottle and come on over. It's not like we send out a bunch of engraved invitations or anything."

"Henri described this guy as being all in brown. Not dressed like an artist. And we think he's either house-sitting in the neighborhood or he's someone's guest. So you might have seen him on the street as well as at the party."

"First," Lyle said, his white teeth flashing in his moon face, "I'm not quite sure what it means to dress like an artist. And as for seeing someone on the street, well, that might narrow it down. This isn't exactly a street-life kind of neighborhood."

"Do you have a car?"

"No. Why do you ask?"

"Because if you don't have a car," I said, my voice quickening with excitement, "then you must take the subway. Picture yourself on the platform at York Street, waiting for the F. Is there someone you've seen there in recent weeks that you never saw before? Someone with short brown hair and brown, straight-looking clothes?"

"You mean geeky clothes?"

"Exactly."

"The Hush Puppy. I called him the Hush Puppy. On account of he kind of looked like a puppy, like he was lost or something. And he wore these comfortable shoes, you know, the ones that look like hell but they feel great on your feet. I'd wear 'em myself only Vicki'd take 'em and give 'em to the Goodwill if I ever brought a pair in here. She puts up with the shirts 'cause she thinks it's cultural or something, but the truth is, I don't like to wear ties. So I buy all the tropical shirts I can get my hands on and she goes along with it 'cause I'm making an ethnic statement."

His big grin got mischievous and he said, "I ought to buy a grass skirt and wear that all over town, she wants to see an ethnic statement. I learned how to do Pacific Island dances when I was a kid in Honolulu, too. What do you think, would a spear be too much?"

"Not for me," I said, enchanted. If the absent Vicki ever got tired of this guy, I hoped she'd pass him on to me. I was willing to bet that in spite of the hundred or so extra pounds he carried around, he'd be a lot of fun where it counted most.

"Now," I prodded, "do you have any idea where he might be staying?"

He thought about it, naming a few names to himself and then promptly discarding them, like a man choosing what card to toss in a gin rummy game. This one was out of town, but she never let anyone stay at her place. That one had a guest last week, but the guest left for Ireland this week. And another friend with a guest still had said guest, who was someone Lyle had met before and who worked in acrylics.

"Are these all living lofts?" I asked, setting my now-empty juice glass on the table. "I mean, are there any spaces that are just working studios? Could someone be staying in one of those?"

"That's a good one," Lyle said. "Most of the artists live here, but there are a few of us who come in to work but live somewhere else. One guy I know has this cottage out on the Island, so he's out there till November and then he comes back here for the winter."

"Pishegoss, Mishegoss," I murmured, remembering Tobah's Aunt Sylvia. "Where on Long Island?"

"Patchogue, I think. Vicki and I went out there once, took the LIRR, but I forgot the name of the town. Way the hell out, though. Pretty, if you like that stuff."

"This is sounding really good. Where is this guy's studio and what's his name?"

"His name's Roger Hofsteader and he does installations. Don't ask me what an installation is," Lyle said, spreading his pineapple-sized hands in front of him, "all I know is that's what he'll tell you if you ask what he does. He's still out on the Island, but I think there is a guy staying in his loft."

Liam and I left with directions to the loft, which took us all the way back into Henri's part of the neighborhood, but to a different building. When we rang the bell, there was no answer, so we did exactly what I used to do when I was a kid looking to see if the friend I wanted to play with was really home and just playing some kind of game.

We walked to the big warehouse windows, cupped our hands around our eyes to shield them from the waning light, and peeked inside.

There was nobody there. But there were pictures on the walls, big blowups that stared at me like the head shots they use to decorate beauty parlors.

At first I thought it was part of Roger Hofsteader's installation art.

Then I realized with a jolt exactly whose pictures they were.

Mine.

I was staring into the heart of a stalker. Lines from a Conrad Aiken poem came back to me:

> *Music I heard with you was more than music.*
> *And bread I broke with you was more than bread.*

Poetry for a broken heart. A very young broken heart. The heart of a college girl and her Outsider, her leader of the intellectual pack, the first man to love her for her brain as well as her looks. The words came back to me as I gazed at Keith Jernigan's makeshift shrine.

It was a virtual compendium of my life. A flyer from the L.A. Taqueria on Bergen Street, with the black bean burrito circled in red. A napkin from the Japanese restaurant where we'd celebrated my appellate victory and his release from prison. A copy of the photograph with the double-exposed skull underneath the winter church scene.

So I'd been right. He was the one who exposed the photographic paper and put it back for me to find and print over. I still had no idea what it meant, except that he was showing me he could come and go at will, but the sight of the photograph sent a chill through me.

Or maybe it was just getting really cold.

The loft was a large single room with no improvements such as the one we'd seen at the tae kwon do studio. No living quarters neatly sectioned off and decorated; just a pure art space with a cot in one corner.

"This is really creepy."

I'd almost forgotten that Gallagher was with me.

The window was big and there was a light on inside the studio, which meant we could see every inch of the space as if watching a movie.

"You think it's creepy?" I countered, trying to keep it light. "Take a look at these."

I hugged myself and then remembered poor, paranoid Fran. Now I knew precisely how she felt.

On the wall, blown up to the largest size a copying machine could handle, was a photograph of me putting the white lace nightgown on over my head. My legs were bare; the gown covered my torso with strategic effectiveness, but the picture was pornographic in its clear admission that it had been taken through a window without the subject's permission.

"You still think he didn't try to kill you?" Liam stood so close behind me that I inched away, needing space to think.

"I don't know," I replied.

"Well, this shows he knows how to use a telephoto lens," the detective persisted.

"There's a big difference between taking a picture and shooting someone in the head."

"How much of a difference? Think about it. How much of a difference? You aim, you push the shutter button. You aim, you pull a trigger. Either way, you're doing it from a safe distance. You've got time to run away. I see this," he said, nodding at the photograph, "as a trial run for the shooting."

"How'd he get the light?" I said suddenly. "I mean, I put my nightgown on when I'm about to go to bed, right? And this is daylight. No flash. So when was it taken?"

"You could be taking it off instead of putting it on. That would make it morning."

"Yeah, I guess. Somehow it looks more like—"

I broke off and put my hand to my mouth. "I remember," I said. "I did put it back on one morning because there was a knock on the door. It was Nellis, asking me when the heat was going to come on. I told her it wasn't that cold, but—"

My voice trailed off. "The important thing is that, yes, I guess I was putting the gown on in daylight."

"If I could remember the exact day," I mused aloud, "we could ask Keith where he was that morning. Could he have done it, or does he have an alibi?"

"Can you seriously look at all this stuff and have any doubts about this guy, Counselor? If so," Liam went on, shaking his head, "then you're the stubbornest woman I've ever met. I mean, this place is like a great big confession."

"Is it? Where's the gun? Where's any evidence that he wanted to kill me? All this," I made a sweeping gesture that was intended to take in the whole room, "is sick in the extreme, but it isn't evidence of murder."

"Not yet. But once I get a search warrant and go through the place, who knows what we'll find?"

"I'm still his lawyer," I said in a small voice, as the implications began to sink in. I'd led the police to my own client, and now I was ethically bound to snap into defense mode, at least until another lawyer took over the case.

I looked around the room, cupping my hands around my eyes and wiping the glass clear of condensed breath. It was a big workshop, with unfinished wooden benches and various implements, from woodworking tools to brushes and knives, on the paint-splattered surfaces. I caught a glimpse of another photograph, this one taken through the now-shattered plate glass window of my office.

Underneath, in careful letters, was the name ΧΑΣΑΝ-ΔΡΑ.

That did it. Only Keith used Greek letters to spell out my classical name. He'd sent me a card and had a mug made with the name and then used it on the masturbation card. If this wasn't proof positive that he—

But then something struck me. I thought of Tobah. I saw her sitting in the booth in the Tel Aviv Pizza, the mushroom slice in her hand. She was saying something. Telling me—

But what?

No. It wasn't *what* she'd said.

It was the way she'd said it.

A Hebrew word. *Chasid* or *Chanukah* or *Chabad.*

That was it: *Chabad.*

Pronounced with a guttural sound that could have been written *kh.*

But what did that have to do with—

My name was Cassandra. With a *C.*

But in Greek it was Kasandra, which began with the letter *kappa.*

The mug Keith Jernigan had made for me was spelled Κασανδρα.

The name on the photograph in the loft, the name on the greeting card that contained the masturbation photo, was Χασανδρα. With a *chi*, which would result in a *kh* sound.

Wrong.

Keith Jernigan was a meticulous researcher, a man who prided himself on what he knew. Wrong wasn't something he'd allow himself to be. He'd used the correct Greek letter in his transliteration; the card and the photo were poorly executed copies.

Copies meant to convince the police that Keith was a crazed stalker who'd killed Nellis and had me in his sights.

But if he hadn't written "Khasandra" on that photograph, then who had?

Who had created that bizarre room?

Who wanted to blame Keith for the murder?

Who wanted to convince the police to arrest Keith?

I had no idea. All I knew for sure was that Keith, my innocent client, really was, against all odds, innocent.

CHAPTER
TWENTY-TWO

"It wasn't Keith." I was so excited I blurted the words to my companion without preamble.

Gallagher took one step backward and said, "What are you talking about? How can you look at this place and say—"

"Because of the name," I cut in. Then I pointed to the photograph I'd seen through the window. I explained that Keith had used a *kappa* instead of a *chi* in his transliteration.

"You really remember what those Greek letters looked like?" Gallagher's expression combined scorn and anger in equal parts. I was shooting his pet theory out from under him, on grounds he found flimsy at best, fanciful at worst.

"It's my name, Liam. You always remember things about your own name. Like you knowing that 'William' means 'guardian.'" I smiled, remembering when he'd confided this fact. We'd been talking about names, about Tobah meaning "gift of God" and he'd said that both his names had meanings that involved protecting and helping others. I'd said the names suited him to a T, and his parents must have had a crystal ball when they'd baptized him. He'd blushed like a kid and looked pleased.

Now he looked sullen as he replied, "I guess."

"This changes everything," I went on, bubbling with a strange happiness. It was a measure, I supposed, of how much I'd wanted to believe in Keith. Even after his stupidity with Tobah and Fran, I'd felt he wasn't a bad guy. He was obsessed and needed boundaries, but he wasn't a killer and he wasn't after me.

But who was?

"Maybe whoever shot Nellis really wanted to do just that," I suggested. "Maybe this whole idea that the bullet was aimed at me is just a—well, I don't know, but doesn't it depend on the idea that Keith's been stalking me? And if he hasn't, if this is all someone else's work, then don't we have to look somewhere else for the killer?"

I sincerely hoped we didn't have to look too closely at Kate Avelard, but I wasn't ready to say that. Not yet.

"Ah, shit," Gallagher replied, rubbing his face with a hand made red and raw by the chill damp air. "Maybe we need to rethink this whole damned thing."

I shivered as a river breeze licked my face. I pulled my jacket a little tighter and said, "It would be nice if we could do that sitting down."

"There's a coffee bar up the street," Liam said. "I could use something hot to drink myself."

"How do you know so much about this neighbor—" I broke off. "Oh, yeah, the Eight-Four is around here, right? On Gold Street?"

He nodded; he was already moving at a fast clip in the direction away from the river and toward a distant light in a window.

The sun was lowering itself behind the tall buildings on the Manhattan side of the Great Bridge; we walked along deserted streets in a dusky shadow-world until a neon sign spelling out CAFE beckoned us with orange promises of hot, strong coffee.

Inside, it was warm and cozy. We were the only customers and the kid behind the counter almost turned us away, but then he recognized Liam as a cop and reluctantly agreed to draw two more espresso drinks before closing up. I made mine a double latte with lowfat milk and sat in the corner warming my hands and waiting for Liam to bring the coffees from the counter.

The first sip was hot and welcome, but after it went down, I grimaced and said, "What's in this stuff? It tastes—"

"It ought to taste like chocolate mint," the detective replied. "At least that's what I asked for."

I bit my tongue to keep from making a sarcastic remark about people who try to turn coffee into a soft drink. I prefer my coffee to taste like coffee. But Liam obviously thought he was giving me a treat, so I took another sip and said, "It's fine."

It was, in truth, more than a little bitter and the mint made me feel I was brushing my teeth while drinking hot chocolate, but it was hot and had caffeine and after a while, that seemed like enough.

Liam had reconsidered his position. "You're too close to the case," he pronounced. "You believe what you want to believe."

"No," I said firmly. "The name is wrong, and if that's wrong, then the whole thing is suspect. What if the real killer created that scene to look like a wacko serial killer shrine? What if—now, here's a real insight—but what if whoever shot Nellis actually wanted Nellis dead and it had nothing to do with me?"

I was feeling extraordinarily good. Perhaps it was relief. Or perhaps it was sheer physical pleasure in the warmth of the coffee bar and the latte slipping through my system. But the glow of light in the darkness made me feel as if I were inside a candle.

I liked the idea. I gazed around the tiny space, taking in every detail: the sheen of wood, the gleam of silver fittings, the deep colors of the artwork on the walls, the—

I was high.

It had been a while, but the sensation was unmistakable.

I was high as an elephant's eye, and I hadn't taken anything.

I looked down at the empty latte glass.

I hadn't taken anything on purpose.

I stared into Liam Gallagher's open, freckled face, hoping for a clue to whatever it was he was thinking.

And then I knew.

I was looking at Liam and I was seeing him for the first time as he really was: a guy who'd made a lot of excuses to hang around me, a guy who'd been on hand a little too often, a little too conveniently. A guy who wanted me to believe the worst about Keith, and who'd created the bizarre shrine as the final nail in Keith's coffin of guilt.

Just as he'd done when he framed Keith for the liquor store robbery.

I'd have felt better about this insight if Liam's face hadn't been melting.

In fact, the whole coffee bar seemed quite pliable, like plastic left in the microwave. Silly putty. I could put my hand on the table and leave an impression, fingerprints deep into the clay surface of the wood, and what beautiful wood it was, too, all grainy and shiny and—

Oh, man. I was slipping away into some drug-induced fantasy and I had no idea what was causing it. I considered asking Liam, but his mouth had collapsed into his chin and I was afraid he wouldn't be able to talk.

But why?

What could he possibly gain from killing me? What had I ever in this world done to him?

I had a moment's fleeting hope that he hadn't seen the truth in my face, but that hope fled as he said, "I knew you'd get it sooner or later. I was just hoping I'd be there when you did. And now, here we both are."

He took me by the arm and gently lifted me up, then gave a cheerful wave to the kid behind the counter. "We'll be going now," he called, and moved toward the door.

"I don't want to—" I struggled, but my muscles seemed frozen. I felt as if my entire body had been pumped with Novocain.

"I know you don't," Liam said in a loud, cheerful voice, "I know it's cold out and you'd rather stay here, but the man wants to close up."

He overtalked me all the way out the door. When we were outside, a half-block away and out of shouting distance, he stopped talking long enough for me to ask, "What did either of us do to deserve this?"

"You don't think Jernigan deserves something for what he did to Tobie David?"

"He served two years and five months for something he didn't do," I retorted, then added, "but then I guess you know all about that, since you were the one who made it happen. But why?"

"You ever heard of a woman named Sorichetti?"

"It sounds familiar, but I'm not sure why."

"She sued the city."

"A lot of people sue the—" I broke off as the memory flooded through me. "Oh, my God. *That* Sorichetti."

The case had horrified New York, and quite probably the rest of the country as well. It was back in the bad old days when cops considered "domestic disputes" to be outside their jurisdiction, something they shouldn't really get involved with. So when Mrs. Sorichetti told the desk sergeant she was sure her estranged husband, who had just taken their four-year-old daughter for the weekend, was going to harm the girl, the desk sergeant had told her to get lost. She'd practically camped out at the precinct, begging the police to at least drive by the house and make sure her daughter was all right. The cops had not only refused, they'd given the woman a hard time for bothering them and accused her of making the whole thing up to get back at her ex.

When they finally decided to check on the situation, he'd already stuck a fork and a knife into his daughter's thigh and was busy trying to saw off her leg.

Mrs. Sorichetti collected a bundle from the city of New York on the child's behalf, and from then on, cops were instructed to take complaints about possible violence within the family a great deal more seriously.

"*That* Sorichetti," he echoed with a touch of irony. "I knew the desk sergeant. He was a friend of my uncle's."

"The uncle who was killed in the line of duty?" I was having trouble walking; Liam held me up and propelled me along the street, keeping my stumbling feet from dragging on the cobblestones. He'd told me about his hero uncle the same day he'd mentioned his names; it seemed a very, very long time ago.

He nodded. "I was a kid when both those things happened. I heard my uncle talking about the guy and how he blew his whole career in a single day over one stupid mistake. And then my uncle got shot. Another stupid mistake, really, but this one earned him an inspector's funeral with the mayor and the PC saluting his casket. So," he went on, his voice as even and steady as if he were discussing the world series, "here you have two cops. Two sergeants. One screws up and has to live the rest of his life knowing his mistake almost cost a little girl her life, and the other guy screws up and he's spending eternity underneath a big white stone that says what a hero he was."

"And you decided you'd rather have the gravestone and the glory." I was hanging on by a thread; as my mouth made lawyer noises, my drug-addled brain was finding it all too easy to dwell on the horrible picture of the Sorichetti kid with kitchen implements sticking out of her.

"I decided I was never, ever going to be the kind of cop that desk sergeant was," he said with so much force that spittle gathered at the edges of his lips. "My uncle tried to defend him, said everyone had bad days, and maybe Mrs. Sorichetti came on hysterical. But, hell, you thought your kid was about to get whacked, you'd be hysterical, too. I figured the guy was lazy, the guy was arrogant, the guy didn't really want to do the job the city was paying him for. I said to myself I'd never get that way, I'd always listen when somebody came to me with a problem."

"But you didn't. You didn't listen when Tobah came to you."

"That was 'different'." His mouth twisted; the sour bile in his tone could have eaten through plastic. "I thought it was different, because she wasn't a kid. Because he loved her, and I believed him when he said he'd never hurt her. It was like the movies, was what I figured. He loved her, and if he tried hard enough to show her that love, she'd love him back. That was what I thought."

He sighed. "And if she didn't love him, then he'd get the message and get her out of his system. I didn't think it was police business. I thought it was what we used to call a 'boy-girl thing.' He never said he'd hurt her; he sent flowers and notes and made phone calls, but they were never threatening."

"Liam, I've talked to Tobah. They were threatening."

"Don't you think I see that now? At the time, I thought it was just his way of showing his love. Tell you the truth, I thought she was making a mistake, dumping him. He treated her like a princess."

He had already drugged me to the gills and was going to kill me. So why hold back? Why not confront him with everything I knew, thought, felt? What more could he do to me?

"Tell the whole truth, Liam. You thought she was a Jewish princess, taking advantage of a nice guy, making him jump through hoops for her. You thought she was the one playing games."

The sound that came out of his throat was somewhere between a sob and a growl. "I screwed the fuck up!" He squeezed my arm tight; I knew I should feel pain, but I didn't.

"I bought Jernigan's act, okay? I believed everything he told me about how much he loved her, and how all this was just a lovers' quarrel and it was going to blow over and he and Tobie were going to have grandchildren together. I didn't like the way she blew hot and cold. One day she'd file a complaint about Keith and the next day, she'd call the precinct and take it back. Or she'd beg the sergeant to send a cop around and then she wouldn't answer the door when he came."

"That wouldn't have been on Saturday, would it?" I said dryly. "She did observe the Sabbath, even if she wasn't a Chasid anymore."

"God, I don't know. All I knew was that she wouldn't answer the door or pick up the phone, so I put the complaint back in the drawer and went out to do some real police work. And the next thing I knew, they were calling me from Beth Israel saying there was a woman in the emergency room with my card in her pocket. My card. Just like the Sorichetti case. Her face was ruined, and I was the cop who hadn't followed up on her last complaint. I was gonna get burned for not following up."

"You want to reconsider your choice of words? Tobah was burned; you were just—"

"It wasn't my fault! I didn't know he was going to do that! And neither did she, really, or she would have acted differently. She wouldn't have stayed in her apartment, where he could find her whenever he wanted to, for one thing. She would have answered the door, Sabbath or no

Sabbath, if she'd really thought she was in danger. She would have—"

"Liam, stop. You know what you're doing here. You're trying to take the heat off yourself by blaming Tobah, but the truth is, a lot of people made mistakes here. And you know you were one of them. But you couldn't forgive yourself, any more than you could forgive that desk sergeant who let the Sorichetti kid get hurt."

"Jernigan was gonna pay. I had to see that happen. I tried like hell to convict him for what he did to her, but she refused to identify him in the lineup. She was still covering up for that piece of shit after what he did to her."

"She says she really wasn't sure. She couldn't see his face, what with the ski mask."

"Oh, for the love of God! She knew it was him. All she had to do was say so. She still wanted to protect him, and that made me sick."

"So you decided to set him up on a different charge."

"Yeah. I'll tell it straight. I wanted that smug little asshole behind bars where he belonged. You didn't see the way he strutted and strolled out of the precinct after Tobie blew the lineup ID. He gave me a look like, 'You idiot. You know what I did and I know what I did and you'll never prove it.' He practically dared me to throw something at him and make it stick."

"So you did."

"It took a few months, but I did, yeah. I saw my chance when a robbery complaint came in with a description that sounded a lot like Jernigan. I didn't really think it was him, but I made sure that photo found its way into the detective's photo array, and I dropped a few hints that I thought he was a good suspect."

"It worked. You did a good job."

"Until you came along. And even then, I didn't care at first. Hell, so what if he won his appeal and got out of jail early? I still got two and a half years out of him, years where he could sit in the can and meditate on what he'd done to that girl."

"So what changed your—" I broke off when I realized, and then answered my own question. "It was that line in the *Law Journal* interview about suing the city, wasn't it? God, you don't know how ironic that is."

"Oh, let me hear this. Let me get the irony here. I wouldn't want to miss the fucking irony."

"It wasn't my idea. I never had a thought about suing the city and neither did Keith. Of course, now I know why he didn't want to bring suit; he knew the Tobah stuff would come out, and he was just as happy to leave that in the past. But the reporter wanted to goose up the story, so she hit me with the question, over the phone no preparation. What was I going to say? In a case like that, you always think about suing the city, so I said we might. That was exactly what I meant, too. We might. Not, we were going to, or we had the papers all ready. We might. And for this, you decided to stalk me and screw up my practice and finally kill me. Only you got Nellis instead."

"I thought she was you."

"So I gathered. And now that you have the real me, what's the plan?"

Murder in defense of the self, Mickey had called it during a long bull session we'd had regarding a particularly gruesome murder that had caught the imagination of the news-reading public.

I'd called that social work talk, designed to transform an act of killing into something that sounded almost positive, almost justified. But I knew better; I knew Mickey had no more tolerance for murder than I did, and that she was just trying to explain something most people preferred not to understand.

Or at least to pretend they didn't understand. We all did things we otherwise would condemn in defense of what we considered our deepest selves—we stopped sending Christmas cards to an old friend who'd wounded us rather than tell her how we really felt, or we said something denigrating behind another person's back because we thought they'd attacked us. We refused to accept criticism that might tarnish our own internal image of ourselves, and we hated those who leveled that kind of criticism with a passion that years couldn't diminish.

We didn't kill. But we could, if we dug deep into our own souls, understand those who did.

Keith had thrown acid at Tobah in defense of his "self"— the self that could only survive if their bond continued, the self that believed wholeheartedly in their predestined love.

Nellis hounded Grant in defense of her "self"—the good wife self who only existed in terms of how Grant felt about her, the self who felt worthless without her position as Grant Eddington's wife.

And William Gallagher, the man whose first and last names meant "protector"—Liam killed to protect his own image as the savior in blue, the cop who came to the rescue. He hadn't rescued Tobah, and his failure rankled because he'd set himself up as a different kind of cop, a cop who took care of people.

He took care of Keith instead, engineering the identification of Keith as the man who'd robbed the liquor store, handing Keith's photograph to the investigating detective and suggesting that this guy could be the one. He'd helped pile up evidence against Keith, working from behind the scenes, his name on none of the police reports but his influence pushing the case toward one resolution—the conviction of Keith Jernigan for something he hadn't done in order to punish him for the crime he'd committed against Tobah.

And against Liam. That was the key; Liam Gallagher hadn't really paid Keith back out of a desire to avenge Tobah, a girl he'd barely known and never saw again. He'd done it to avenge himself for having been duped into letting Keith off the hook. If Tobah hadn't gone back to her community, she might have sued the city and won, like Mrs. Sorichetti. And that would have meant the end of Liam's career.

For him, not being a cop meant disgrace, a meaningless life, an unendurable humiliation. Not being a cop meant not being a protector, and that in turn meant not being Liam Gallagher.

Who wouldn't kill in order to save himself?

God knew I would—if I got the chance.

CHAPTER
TWENTY-THREE

"**W**hat in hell did you put in that coffee?" We turned the corner, Liam holding my arm with firm strong fingers and me stumbling after him like a drunk. The sight of the bridges lit up against the backdrop of the Manhattan skyline brought tears of sheer pleasure to my eyes. I could have stood there all night in the biting wind, gazing at the twinkling stars the lights made. I could have happily frozen to death on the spot, watching the lights and the bridges and hearing the hum of cars and smelling the river. The river smelled like stars, or the stars smelled like river; I wasn't quite sure which.

"A little of this, a little of that," my captor replied. "When they do the autopsy, they can figure out exactly what was in those little white pills. Mostly PCP."

"You always walk around town with angel dust in your pockets?"

I felt like an angel. Light and winged and very, very spiritual. If only I could make my legs work.

"I brought it for Keith. I thought it would be easier to sell him as a killer if I found him stoned and dangerous. I might," he added with a maddening lack of affect, "have had to kill him in self-defense."

One pill makes you larger, and one pill makes you small.
And PCP makes you strong.

"Builds strong bodies," I mumbled, "eight ways."

I put all the strength I could imagine into pulling away from Liam. As I did, another body flew out of the shadows and brought the detective down hard in a flying tackle that sent two bodies sprawling to the street.

Batman! Batman saw the bat-sign and came out of his cave to rescue me. While Batman wrestled Liam Gallagher to the ground, I ran. I ran like the cold, damp wind, even after I heard a noise that sounded an awful lot like a gun going off.

But guns couldn't hurt Batman.

So I kept running, even after the screaming started. It was horrible and it wouldn't stop and the sound made the bridge turn soft and rubbery and bend in the wind, lights moving back and forth like dancers. And I ran and ran toward the steps, toward the bridge. I needed the bridge. The bridge meant safety. The bridge meant a way home, a way to reach the Emerald City across the River Styx.

I felt like throwing up. In fact, one part of my drug-soaked brain realized that throwing up would probably be a sound move. It would rid my system of at least some of the drug rampaging around in my stomach.

Instead, I ran. The screaming had stopped, and I didn't know why. I suspected someone was dead, and I hoped it wasn't Batman. I turned around when I reached the top of the stairs, expecting to see Liam chasing me. He'd killed Batman. I knew that now, and I knew Liam would be coming to get me, but so far no one followed me up the stone stairs.

A couple of joggers and a bicyclist swept past me. I held

onto the railing and made my way on shaky legs across the wooden walkway that spanned the Brooklyn Bridge. It was elevated, the walkway, and rose several feet above the two roadways on either side, one going to Manhattan, the other to Brooklyn.

It would have been beautiful if I hadn't felt so sick and so scared. All of a sudden, the gorgeous sight that I'd been so enamored of turned into a neon jungle wilderness of cold and fear and lights that hurt my eyes and yes, you had to be very scared of those lights, those lights could kill. I'd be dead on the bridge and they'd find my cold body and stand over me shaking their heads and say, "The lights killed her. The lights made holes in her brain and—"

No. This was crazy. Lights couldn't kill me. Only Liam Gallagher could kill me and he wasn't here. He wasn't on the bridge. Batman had killed him.

I was safe. I slid down and squatted on the wooden walkway, huddled into myself, and shook with relief. I was safe from the lights and from Liam.

Until the red siren blared. Red noise enveloped me; I sat hiding in my tiny hole like the ivory mouse in Nellis's *netsuke* photograph. If I stayed small and hid in the secret compartment, they wouldn't find me. I scrunched up tighter and closed my eyes so they wouldn't see me.

The red noise blared and shouted, louder and then softer, whooping and then screaming like a bloody seagull and then finally subsiding into a cacophony of shouted words. Men in blue uniforms with shiny badges jumped out of the screaming cars and climbed up over the metal girders from the roadbed onto the elevated wooden walkway.

I rose and ran, but I'd lost whatever speed I'd once possessed. I ran to the other side and started to clamber over the girders, intent on getting to the opposite roadway, but a man on a bicycle grabbed me around the waist and pulled and suddenly we were both down and so was the bike and I was tangled in wheel spokes and the man was yelling at me.

"Don't jump," he said, and then called to the cops, "I've got her. I've got the jumper."

And then all the men and women in blue surrounded me.

"There she is," Liam Gallagher shouted. He pointed at me, and a man with a trenchcoat and a clipboard came closer.

He peered down at me through bifocals. The bicycle man gave way to two very strong cops, who held me by one arm each and stood as far back as they could, so my kicks couldn't hurt them.

I flopped and kicked like a dying fish. I screamed obscenities, which some tiny part of me knew wasn't a good idea, but the rest of my brain liked it a lot, so I kept on doing it.

"Can you tell me your name?" The man with the bifocals came so close his face melted into a big round moon and his eyes were huge and I didn't see why he had to know my name since I didn't know his.

"Why should I? And what's he doing here?" I pointed at Gallagher, who stood to the side with his hands clasped behind him.

I leaned closer and told the trenchcoat, "He killed Batman and he wants to kill me."

"I see your point," the trenchcoat said, but he was talking to Gallagher. He murmured, "Paranoid ideation. Delusional. May be dangerous to self and others."

"He killed Batman. I heard the shot. Why don't you do something?"

I'd stopped kicking and huddled back into a mouse, but then I realized I had the strength of ten because I'd drunk the chocolate mint latte, so I leapt forward, shaking off the two cops, and grabbed Liam Gallagher's legs and pushed him down. I jumped onto his stomach and started pounding him with my fists of ice.

Strong arms pulled me away, dragging my legs along the wooden boards of the walkway. I kicked at the blue men, but they pulled anyway. One took handcuffs from the back of his belt and was about to cuff me when Liam stood up and said, "I don't think that will be necessary."

I could hear talking behind me. Someone was on a crackly radio talking about a five-eleven and asking for an ambulance.

"Good," I said, my knees buckling with relief. "That's right. Send an ambulance to help Batman."

Only it wasn't Batman. The image of the man who jumped out of the shadows and knocked Liam Gallagher to the ground came back to me in extra-sharp focus and I saw at once that it wore, not a bat-cape, but a black leather bomber jacket.

Keith. It wasn't Batman who'd tried to rescue me; it was Keith Jernigan, my innocent client. And now he lay bleeding to death on the cobblestone streets of a neighborhood with the name of an elephant and if anyone needed an ambulance, he did, so I began to cry with relief and delayed shock.

There were other people there besides the cops. Regular people who were walking or bicycling across the bridge and who stopped to find out what was going on. I didn't mind them staring at me until I heard a cop answer a question by saying, "She's a jumper. Would have been over the railing and into the river if Detective Gallagher here hadn't acted fast."

Jumper? They'd said that before, but I hadn't really understood they were talking about me.

I glanced up and took in the entire vast sweep of the bridge, spanning the dark black river, a long, long way down.

Jump?

They thought I was going to—

"Had some trouble with her practice, I hear. Yeah, she's a lawyer. Must have gotten herself down in the dumps, had too much to drink, and decided to end it all. Good thing Detective Gallagher knows her."

At last the truth dawned. The ambulance that screamed its way onto the roadbed below wasn't for Keith; it was for me.

The men in white coats were coming to take me away.

The elevated walkway was about fifteen feet above the roadbed below. I calculated the distance, and then made my move. I kicked the nearest cop in the knee, and while he was down, I chopped the second one in the throat and ran toward the edge of the walkway.

I hoisted myself over the railing and made my way down the girders like a kid on the monkey bars. I could stop a car and tell them to take me away from here. I could go back to Brooklyn and see about Keith.

He couldn't be dead. He couldn't be dead because he'd tried to help me get away from Gallagher. I gave an animal howl I hardly recognized as mine and jumped down, landing hard on my knees.

The roadway was cement studded with steel bits that did a number on the tires passing along it every day; it was also unfriendly to my knees. Blood and dirt covered them, but oddly enough, I felt no pain although I could see bloody scrapes on my hands and knees.

Then the truck hit me. It was a blue panel truck whose brakes screeched and whose driver cursed at me in gutter Spanish just before the metal hit my shoulder, pushing me down and buckling my leg underneath my body.

This didn't hurt either, not really. It looked very much like it ought to, but it didn't. On the other hand, I couldn't get up no matter how hard I tried. My legs simply refused to work.

"Get me out of here," I yelled at the truck driver.

He called me a *puta loca* and spat on the ground.

I understood just enough Spanish to resent the remark, which I let him know in no uncertain terms, then said again, "You have to take me away before they come to get me."

The driver got out and started explaining himself to the ambulance attendants, who had just arrived in a clamor of sirens. For the first time, I realized I'd made a very dumb choice; instead of jumping onto the roadway without an ambulance waiting to take me away, I'd jumped onto the side where the ambulance stood.

Down the monkey bars came cops in blue and Liam Gallagher. The trenchcoat peered over the top, clutching his clipboard, but the look on his face said he wouldn't be making the trip. For some reason, that pleased me. Maybe without the clipboard, the men in white would have to leave me here.

"No, no, don't let him take me," I begged the driver and anyone else who would listen. I was afraid to look at my leg. I was afraid I'd see it in two pieces.

"He's not going to take me to a hospital," I explained slowly, clearly, and rationally, "he's going to kill me."

The problem was that inside my head, I was speaking slowly, clearly, and rationally. The look on the faces above me told a different story. I knew my mouth wasn't forming the words exactly right, but surely these people would get the drift.

Blood dripped into my eye. I wiped it away with an impatient hand and tried again. "No. I don't want him in the ambulance with me. Take me to Long Island College Hospital."

To my intense annoyance, Liam Gallagher gave the ambulance attendant the rolled-eye salute that meant *Don't listen to her, she's crazy.*

What was more annoying was that the attendant gave a quick nod of complete understanding.

"He tried to throw me off the bridge," I said, turning my attention to a cabdriver who'd gotten out of his car to stand and stare. If I couldn't win over the official samaritan, maybe I'd have a shot with a civilian. "He tried to kill me. You saw it. Tell them."

The cabby shook his head and said in a mournful tone, "That's what you get for tryin' to help, Officer. She thinks you tried to kill her. I saw the whole thing," he went on, "and far as I'm concerned, buddy, you deserve a medal. Savin' a crazy broad and then listening to her call you names. Man, I wouldn't have your job. Not for a million bucks."

The blood on my cheeks was joined by tears of frustration and pain. "You've got to listen to me," I cried, raising my voice so loud it hurt my throat. "I didn't let this car hit me so you could give me back to him."

What I failed to grasp was that admitting I'd jumped in front of the car on purpose wasn't going to do me a lot of good with the assembled bystanders. In their eyes, I looked and sounded just as crazy as Liam Gallagher said I was.

"Bellevue," the big EMS guy said.

"Right," his tiny partner echoed.

"No," I screamed. I tried to move. I actually tried to crawl away, to slink over to a truck stopped in the next lane. "Not Bellevue. Please, no."

"Been there before, I suppose," the little guy in white said.

"Oh, yeah," Gallagher confirmed with a shake of his head. "I've stopped this one from jumping off this bridge three times already. It's always the same story. She didn't jump; I pushed her. Sad, really."

I was fighting them with all the strength I had in me. Unfortunately, that wasn't much. The little one grabbed my arms and held tight, with a grip I never expected from his thin, wiry arms. The big one hefted me up and set me on a low padded stretcher, then pulled a seat belt around my legs and then my waist and then my chest, which included my arms and—

And I realized it wasn't a seat belt. I was in restraints.

And on my way to Bellevue.

To the psycho ward.

I wasn't conscious all the time. It took me a while to realize this basic fact. All I knew was that one minute I was screaming at the top of my lungs and struggling against the restraints as they shoved me into the back of the ambulance the way soldiers in old movies loaded shells into cannons. The next thing I knew, I was inside the most horrible noise I'd ever heard, a noise that wouldn't stop, a noise that careened with lightning speed along a bumpy street.

How could a noise move?

I pondered this question. My mind was strangely detached, working at solving the problem of a noise that moved.

I sank into sleep again. This time when I came to, I was being wheeled down a long white corridor.

Oh, no. Not one of those near-death experiences.

I refuse. I will not have a near-death experience. I will not be near death.

I wasn't near death. I was near commitment. I was at Bellevue and the doctors fully intended to take care of my leg first and my poor, deluded mind second.

I felt really good when I realized at last that the noise that moved was the ambulance siren. Good. Now that I had that straightened out, it was time to try once again to convince someone in a white coat that the men in white coats shouldn't be taking me away.

I said as much to the orderly whose dark face loomed up at me behind my head.

"Don' worry now," he said in a deep, rich baritone that spoke of the islands, "we only takin' you to X-ray. You relax, now, sugar. You ain't got no worries with Thomas here takin' good care of you."

"Thomas," I repeated. The name brought tears to my eyes. It was such a beautiful name, and he had such a beautiful face, dark as ebony, black as night, shiny as anthracite coal, with eyes that spoke volumes. Thomas would understand. Thomas would save me. Thomas wouldn't let them take me to the psycho ward.

I fell into a feather-pillow sleep thinking good thoughts about Thomas.

When they tried to sever my leg with a huge rusty saw, I came to with a scream.

"Don't cut it off!" I grabbed at the first white sleeve I saw. The Indian woman with the red dot on her forehead took my arm and held it back.

I didn't see a saw, but I knew they were going to take my leg, like they did to that guy in the lifeboat movie with Tallulah Bankhead. The pain was so great that there had to be two pieces of leg. Maybe they were going to sew it back on. Maybe they'd brought the lower part of my leg, the part below the knee, in a giant baggie with ice and they were going to perform miracle surgery.

Did the lower half of my leg still have its shoe?

This seemed important. If I'd lost one shoe, I couldn't click my heels three times and go home.

The woman with the red dot on her forehead frowned as she put my leg on something hard and cold, then twisted it as if she was taking the top off a jar.

I was being tortured. I was in South Africa and they were going to put electrodes on my head and twist my leg until it came off in her hand.

But it was already off.

Oh, God, it hurt. It hurt so much I screamed louder and louder, shaking my head and moaning and hoping to God someone in this torture chamber had a human heart and would come and put an end to my agony.

What had I done to deserve torture?

I offered to tell them everything.

They didn't care. They went on sawing off my leg. I shuddered with pain and grabbed hold of the hard cold thing they had me lying on.

The woman had a red dot in her forehead.

It came to me with a deep horror that she was dead. She'd been shot in the head and that was why she had a red hole in her forehead.

If she was dead, I was dead.

I was in the house of the dead, being tortured by the dead.

From this there would be no salvation. Not even Thomas, dark, beautiful Thomas, who most assuredly wasn't dead, could save me now. Hot tears dripped down my cheeks as I remembered how nice it was to be alive.

The pain was bad, dull and aching and radiating up my leg into my brain, but it wasn't acute. A big thing came down and rested almost on top of my leg and they put a big square plate inside and zapped me.

Zapped me with death rays.

But I was already dead. I was in the zombie jamboree and I didn't give a damn because I was stone dead already, so why were they zapping me with death rays?

I decided to ask.

The woman with the red hole and the white coat just nodded that sad, sympathetic, slightly exasperated nod I'd learned to expect whenever I tried to find out what was really going on.

"Look, you don't have to pretend," I said in a tone of sweet reason. "I know you're dead. I know I'm dead. So just tell me, why are you doing this to me?"

Instead of replying, she twisted my leg in the other direction.

I fell back into the featherbed of sleep, moaning, "Please. Get Thomas. I want Thomas."

When I woke, the pain was gone. It was an amazing sensation. No pain. Just a marvelous floaty feeling and the tremendous comfort of clean, crisp white sheets and a soft bed underneath me and dim lights and something poking into my arm, but that was good because I was thirsty and this meant they were putting water into my body.

Oh, it felt good to be alive.

If I was alive.

Well, hell, if I was dead, then it felt good to be dead. It felt good to be out of pain and in this quiet place with no moving noises and no torturing women with holes in their foreheads. All I needed to feel even better was Thomas.

I didn't get Thomas. I got a skinny kid who looked as if he hadn't slept in three days. He carried a clipboard and he introduced himself as Dr. Berger.

"Can you tell me your name?"

"You sound English."

"New Zealand," he replied with a shake of his head. "I'm a Kiwi."

"Kiwis are fruits," I said, narrowing my eyes. This guy was trying to figure out if I was nuts. He thought he could trap me into saying he was a piece of fruit and then they'd bang me away as a crazy person. "You don't look like a fruit."

He made a note on the clipboard. *Knows the difference between people and fruit.*

Score one for the good guys.

"And what year is it, Ms. Jameson?"

"You know my name. How do you know my name? They tortured me, but I never told them my name."

"Detective Gallagher gave us your vital statistics when he brought you in."

The name Gallagher brought it all back in sharp clarity, in vivid color. The damp, cold stone of the warehouse, the rank smell of the cop car, the bridge, the truck, the ambulance, the lady with the red hole, the shot that killed Nellis, Keith Jernigan lying in a crumpled heap on the sidewalk and Oliver Jackman out on bail and Tobah Davidoff's ruined face—everything flooded back.

"He tried to kill me," I said. I was calm. I wasn't yelling. I just said the words clear and crisp and Dr. Berger wrote them down on his clipboard.

Good. Now we were getting somewhere. If he wrote it all

down, they'd have to believe him because he was a doctor and doctors were even more important than cops, which meant nobody would listen to Gallagher once Dr. Berger started talking.

I told him everything. I started with Keith and his appeal and then Tobah and her face and Nellis and the *netsuke* and Fran with her terrible fear and the shot breaking my plate glass window and wasn't it a crime how much glaziers charged these days, but that's another story, and I was going to be disbarred but it wasn't my fault, it was because Marvella quit and the computer turned on me and became my enemy and wanted me dead.

No, it wasn't the computer that wanted me dead. It was Liam Gallagher because he was the one who threw the acid at Tobah only she was called Tobie then and—

No, no, that was wrong. Keith threw the acid but Liam wouldn't listen so he sent Keith to jail only I won the case so now Keith was out and Liam was afraid of him.

"Why aren't you writing this down?"

"You want me to write this down, is that it?"

"Yes. No. I don't give a fuck. Write it or don't write it, just do something about it."

"What is it you think I should do?"

The man hadn't moved. He stood there, clipboard in hand, not writing anything.

I had a brainstorm. There was one man who could get me out of all this. My old friend. "You have to call Detective Button at the Eight-Four and tell him I'm here. He'll know what to do."

"Detective Button."

I didn't like the way he said that. It wasn't a question and he wasn't writing it down. I decided to make it easier for him. "You could call him Lee or you could call him Roy but don't ever call him Leroy. He doesn't like to be called Leroy."

The man who called himself a kiwi nodded solemnly.

"Will you for God's sake write this down. It's important. It's a lot more important than anything you're going to do with that fucking clipboard."

"There's no need for that kind of language, Ms. Jameson."

"Oh, yes, there fucking well is. He's a fucking killer and I'm lying here talking to a fucking idiot and—"

It dawned on me that I wasn't helping my case. I swallowed hard and said, "You're right. I apologize. But please listen to me. This is important."

"So is this," he said, turning his attention to the clipboard. "Can you tell me who the president is?"

"The president of what?"

"The United States of America."

"Oh, that president." My mind reached out into the darkness and came up at last with, "I think Carter was voted out."

I gave the matter more thought. It seemed incredibly stupid worrying about who the president was when there was a killer to be stopped, but Dr. Berger really seemed to want to know, and since he was a foreigner it made sense that he wouldn't.

"This is crazy," I said, more to myself than to him, "I always vote. I keep up. I watch CNN. Just give me a minute."

He made another note on the clipboard and asked a few more questions. I answered as truthfully as I could, telling the truth, the whole truth, and nothing but the truth and impressing upon him that I was doing just that. "The whole truth," I emphasized. "Write that down. Nothing but the truth. So help me God."

He thanked me. I thought that was a nice gesture, and I said so.

"Call Button," I repeated as drowsiness threatened to sweep me into never-never land.

"The call button is right there," he replied, pointing to a

white dot on the railing. "Just push that if you need anything."

I relaxed. As long as I could push that white dot and get Detective Lee or Roy but not Leroy Button to come and help me, I was all right. I fell into a deep, sweet sleep, letting myself surrender to the warm feeling that came from the certain knowledge that now Dr. Berger was on the case and would see to it that justice was done.

Card Five: Justice

❦

HE DIDN'T KNOW LATIN, ANY MORE THAN HE'D KNOWN GREEK, BUT HE KNEW WHAT THE WORDS OVER THE DOORWAY meant.

All cops did.

"This is the place where the dead delight to help the living."

The morgue.

He squared his shoulders and walked through the door into the house of the dead. He'd been here before, but not like this. He'd never had to identify the corpse of a man he'd killed.

It wasn't like the old days. They didn't pull back a sheet and make you smell and practically taste the dead guy. They had closed-circuit television now, so you could be in one room and check out the stiff without getting too close.

AIDS, he supposed.

"Yeah, it's him," he said to the white-coated technician. Another thing about the closed-circuit, you didn't have to wear blue paper clothes that made you look like a space case.

"That's Keith Jernigan," he clarified, spelling the name for the swarthy man with the clipboard.

"We're trying to notify his family," the attendant said, "but it looks as if he doesn't have much in the way of family. A great-aunt upstate, is what I hear."

Well, that was a blessing. At least he hadn't whacked a guy with a family.

His heart tended to be heavy whenever he left the morgue. All that death, all that waste. What did it all mean? And why couldn't he and his fellow cops do something to stop the horrific parade of living, breathing human beings to this house of death?

And now he'd personally sent them two more. Nellie Cartwright, dead by sheer accident, and Keith Jernigan, killed in self-defense.

He believed that. He killed Keith in a flash of recognition, a surge of anger that carried him away and made him pull that trigger, not once but three times. Right in the belly an agonizing death he'd stood and watched, the gun poised to shoot again if necessary.

It hadn't been necessary.

He'd raced toward the river, gleaming silver-black, and thrown the gun as far as he could, then raced to the precinct.

Only he hadn't mentioned the dead man; instead, he'd said there was a crazed jumper on her way to the bridge.

If he'd had his way, there would be three, not two corpses in the morgue with his name on them.

Perhaps that could still be arranged.

He turned and walked south along First Avenue, in the direction of Bellevue.

CHAPTER
TWENTY-FOUR

"I said *what?*"

"You started talkin' about a zombie jamboree and said Dr. Patel was a dead woman wit' a bullet hole in her head." Thomas opened his pink mouth and showed white teeth as he laughed appreciatively. "I always think the same thing myself, that her red mark is like a bullet hole, but I never had the nerve to say it to her face."

"Oh, my God. What else did I say?"

"You said she cuttin' off your leg and all she doin' is puttin' it down on the X-ray table like they got to do to take pictures."

I had the mother of all hangovers. My head throbbed and I'd thrown up into a bedpan twice. Every cell in my body had its own tiny little microscopic headache and I knew, at last and without a doubt, that I'd been drugged to the gills the night before.

Well, in a bizarre way, that ought to help. Crazy as I

might have sounded, they'd get the bloodwork report and see that I wasn't nuts, just stoned out of my gourd.

I knew who the president was.

I could hardly wait to enlighten Dr. Berger.

He didn't show up until four o'clock in the afternoon. I'd begged the nurses for a phone, but they said they'd have to check with the Doctor. I begged them to check with him, and they said they would as soon as he came on the floor. I said I had to be in court and they gave me that exasperated head-shake that said as far as they were concerned, I'd said I had to be on Mars.

Finally I had enough of trying to be polite. "Look, I know my leg's broken, but just give me a pair of crutches and let me out of here. I have a lot to do. Now that you know I'm not crazy, can't we just—"

"Honey," the middle-aged nurse with the light brown skin and freckles said, "if you're really a lawyer like you say, then you know what a 9.41 is. You're here pursuant to Section 9.41 of the Mental Hygiene Law, as this paper will explain. So you aren't going anywhere, crutches or no crutches. Just lay back and relax."

I glanced at the paper; I'd seen them before, but never as a patient. It said I had "exhibited behavior likely to result in serious harm to herself and others" and I was therefore admitted to Bellevue Hospital for observation. I had the right to counsel at any time, but because of pending criminal charges, I would be released into the custody of the New York City Police Department for transportation to court if I protested my current confinement.

So two doctors had decided I was a nut case.

And if I didn't like that diagnosis, I'd go directly to criminal court, if Liam Gallagher actually brought me there instead of "losing" me on the way.

What about my cases, my clients, my practice? While I was in this bed, more and more of them would walk away from me and file complaints with the bar association about neglect.

On the bright side, I supposed a complete mental breakdown might be a defense to the charges, but an insanity plea would hardly help me rebuild my destroyed professional life.

What about Liam Gallagher and the fact that he murdered Nellis Cartwright and would probably get away with framing Keith for the crime? What about the fact that he'd probably shot Keith Jernigan and left him to die on the cobblestones of Brooklyn?

What about the fact that he'd tried to kill me?

Unless I could convince someone to listen, none of that would matter. I'd walk out of here in thirty days and pick up the pieces of my dead career, but I'd never regain credibility. I'd always be "poor Cass, you remember, the one who tried to jump off the Brooklyn Bridge and got carted away to the loony bin."

A single tear slipped out of my eye and rolled down my cheek.

But once that tear had fallen, I refused to let any others follow it. I dragged my protesting body out of the raised bed. My right leg was bandaged, but there was no cast, so I set it gingerly on the floor. Shooting pains told me this wasn't a good idea.

So I raised it and hopped on my left leg all the way to the closet. If my clothes were in there, I'd dress before confronting anyone else about my liberty. In a hospital gown with no back, I was a patient, someone easily ignored, but with clothing covering me, I was a lawyer.

And even a crazy lawyer is still a lawyer.

But the closet didn't have clothes in it. It had a shapeless white garment made of very heavy cotton with extremely long arms.

They called it a "camisole" but it didn't come from Victoria's Secret. The tag sewn into the back said it was made by the Humane Restraint Company of Waunakee, Wisconsin.

What a mental picture. A whole roomful of women sewing on machines, just like you could see every day in Chinatown or SoHo, only instead of making toddler clothes or junior miss sizes, these women were cranking out straitjackets.

I had only a shadowy memory of having worn the thing, but then I remembered the feeling of being wrapped up in a shroud and realized that what I'd felt was the tight binding of the arms around my torso. I shuddered and caught a glimpse of myself in the bathroom mirror.

I had plenty of bruises, cuts, and bandages on my hands, arms, and face. I had an elastic bandage on my right knee and a gigantic gauze pad on the other. But none of my injuries seemed serious enough to require hospitalization, which meant the only reason I was still here was that they thought I was a nut job.

Or a drug addict. I stood for a moment, despite the protests of my left leg, which was doing all the work, and reviewed what I knew about the Mental Hygiene Law.

My leg finally told me I'd better sit down, so I hopped back over to the bed.

I scanned the paper the nurse had left. I had a right to a lawyer, any time I wanted one.

I wanted one now.

I hopped toward the door of my room, then turned the handle on the door, ready to take a hike to the nurses' station and tell them I was ready to consult with counsel.

The handle wouldn't turn.

I tried again, then realized I'd been locked in.

I turned and looked at the window, which faced the East River. Bars. But hell, everyone in New York puts bars on their windows to keep the burglars out, so I hadn't seen them as something special, designed to keep the lunatics from running loose.

I banged on the door. No response. I banged again, using the heels of my hands to make nice satisfying sounds. I added vocal accompaniment, pretty much along the lines of, "Hey, somebody let me out of here!"

I supposed it wasn't the woman's fault that she looked exactly like Nurse Ratched. Solid and Germanic-blond and disapproving of madwomen making noise on her floor.

Of course, my first job was to convince her I wasn't a madwoman.

Actually, that turned out to be the easy part. She was more than willing to admit that I wasn't psychotic.

But if I wasn't a wacko, then I was on drugs, and if that was the case, then Mental Hygiene Law Section 23.02 kicked in. And that meant I could be released into the custody of my friendly neighborhood peace officer—Liam Gallagher.

Which meant I found myself in the bizarre position of arguing my way *into* Bellevue instead of insisting on my right to get the hell out. If getting out meant being turned over to Gallagher, I was staying put.

Nurse Ratched wasn't buying it. "People like you," she said, "ought to know better than to use those designer drugs. You never know what you're going to get into your system, you come in here ranting and carrying on and running us ragged, and then the next day, you're all hung over and sorry about that, and when can I go home to my nice yuppie life and forget about all this. And then next weekend, you'll go out and party and wind up back here. Only someday, you won't be here, you'll be a few doors down at the—".

"At the morgue," I finished. "The difference between me and those designer drug yuppies you're talking about is that I didn't take this stuff on purpose. And you know who pumped me full of chemicals? Detective Gallagher, that's who. So maybe you can see why I don't want to go anywhere with him."

"Still exhibiting paranoid ideation," she murmured. "I'll have to report this to Dr. Berger."

"Please," I said, "report anything to anybody. Just don't give me to Gallagher."

She said nothing, so I played my next card. "I'd really like to talk to an attorney. As soon as possible."

Nurse Ratched rolled her eyes. "All you lawyers are alike," she said. "You think law solves everything. Well, you won't get better until you take the first step, admitting that your drug problem is out of control. We can't help you as long as you're in denial."

"Denial is my middle name," I said cheerfully.

It was strangely freeing to be a nut case. I felt as if I could say anything, do anything, and the consequences would be far less serious than if I were still in the world. I was in a private playground, a day care center for adults, and tweaking the authority figure was one of the many games it was okay to play. It was like being a fourth-grader again, only this time I had no fear of being sent to the principal's office.

I lay back against the pillows and waited for a legal bureaucrat to show up. I knew just enough mental health law to know that I could ask for judicial review of my status, which would mean I'd have a chance to explain the situation to a judge. It would take far too long, but it might very well be the best I could do.

When the lock clicked open, I gazed at the door with anticipation. At last, help. At last, someone with a law degree instead of a medical approach that began with the premise that I was *non compos mentis*.

But the man who walked in and closed the door behind him wasn't an overworked member of the mental hygiene bureaucracy. It was Detective William Gallagher.

"I'm not going with you," I said. My voice wasn't nearly as firm as I'd hoped.

"You don't have to," he said. There was a strange, fanatic's gleam in his eye as he strode toward the bed.

There was a hypodermic needle in his right hand.

"What have you got in there?"

I moved as quickly as I could to the other side of the bed. I yelled at the top of my lungs. I yelled the one word I knew would get someone's attention.

"Fire! Help! Fire!"

He lunged across the bed; the needle poised like a dagger, ready to sink into my all-too-vulnerable flesh. I pushed myself off the bed and dropped with a thud to the floor, my leg screaming in pain, my mouth still screaming about fire.

I slid toward the window, scarcely realizing the truth: that there was no way out. The door was locked, and Gallagher was between me and the door anyway. The window was barred, and I was on the fourteenth floor, so even if I could get the window open, it would do me no good.

Was there anything in this room I could use as a weapon?

This was crazy. He couldn't possibly hope to get away with this. Even if he managed to get the needle into me, how was he going to explain what had happened?

The madman's expression on his face said he didn't care. He wasn't much of a planner, just a man who reacted to the circumstances of the moment and then tried to figure out how to deal with the consequences later. He'd proved that when he shot Keith; I had no idea what he'd told his fellow cops about that, but I was willing to bet it wouldn't hold up for long under a real investigation.

The question was: would there be a real investigation, or would the cops buy the word of one of their own, one of their own who seemed to have no reason to lie?

But even if Gallagher didn't get away with this, I could still be dead or brain-damaged from whatever was in that hypodermic.

I crawled on the linoleum floor like a toddler, scooting across the shiny surface on my bare behind, the gown only getting in my way as it bunched up under me. I hastily began to untie the string that held it in place behind my head, my fingers fumbling. I finally pulled tight and one of the strings snapped off.

I lifted the gown off my body, hoisted it over my head, wadded it into a ball, and threw it at Gallagher. It impaled itself on the hypodermic. Gallagher swore and pulled the cloth away with a vicious motion.

I scrabbled, crablike, in the direction of the door, still yelling about fire.

Gallagher leapt from the bed and landed on the floor, one hand grasping my good leg, the other ready to strike with the deadly needle.

To my intense relief, the locked door swung open and there stood Nurse Ratched, with the very welcome figure of Detective Leroy Button standing behind her. They both pushed into the room, Button making his way to Gallagher and reading him the Miranda rights while pulling handcuffs from his pocket, and Ratched shaking her head at me as though my crawling naked on the floor only served to confirm her worst suspicions.

Gallagher grabbed at Button's legs, stabbing the air with the hypodermic, yelling about not going down without a fight. He succeeded in knocking the detective to the ground, and then raced off down the hallway. I could see blue suits following him in a stampede of cop shoes and shouted orders to stop.

"They'll catch up with him," Button said from the floor.

I became acutely aware of the fact that I wasn't wearing anything.

"Could you hand me that gown?"

He did, with only the slightest smile to indicate his enjoyment of my predicament.

"What brought you here? How did you know I was in here?"

"You remember that message you left with Smitty?"

I nodded. "He didn't strike me as a guy who'd carry a

message for me, though," I said, draping the gown over myself. "He didn't seem to like you very much, either."

"He doesn't," Button replied, "which is why he passed on the message. He wanted to screw up my life, so he thought he'd send me on a wild goose chase. Only it turned out there really was a wild goose. I started going through the police files on all the cases involved, and saw that Gallagher was the thread that connected them. He was on the David case, and the Jernigan case, and he transferred to the Eight-Four a month before you won the appeal. He was prepared to keep an eye on Keith Jernigan from the moment the decision came down."

"Is Keith dead?"

Button nodded. "The body's next door," he said, and I knew he meant the morgue even if it wasn't exactly next door to Bellevue.

"I want to see it," I said. "Him," I amended.

It took a couple of hours for all the paperwork to be completed, but I was finally released into the custody of one of the detectives who'd accompanied Button. He was retired, but his old colleagues had cooperated with him when he'd asked for their help.

Then we walked the two blocks to the morgue.

I looked at his face for what seemed like a long time, and then I opened his shirt. The blood had been washed away, but the internal organs were in plain view, looking like something in a butcher shop. I could see the remnants of scar tissue around the wound, just as Tobah had said. Keith had burned himself as a way of expiating his sin.

"Has anyone claimed the body?"

When the attendant in the white coat answered in the negative, I asked, "Can I claim it? Can I arrange for burial?"

He said he'd have to see his supervisor about that; I told him to let me know—but on no account was he to send the body to potters' field without notifying me first.

I had no idea what religion Keith was, or whether he'd have wanted a church burial.

But I couldn't let him spend eternity in a mass grave on an island in the Bronx.

"It's a Klingon thing, Ma," Oliver said with a white-toothed grin as he settled himself behind the computer and moused up a *Star Trek* Web site with the *Enterprise* zipping across the screen.

"Why you got to be a Klingon, boy?" Marvella asked with mock indignation. "Why you can't be a Vulcan like that nice Tuvok? Or why not go to the party as Captain Sisko? I could make you a red shirt, and that Avery Brooks is one handsome man, let me tell you."

Oliver brightened. "Can I shave my head?"

"Go as the Vulcan. Then you can keep your hair."

"I'd rather be Worf," her son said. "Me Klingon," he said, pounding his chest like Tarzan. "Me baaaad Klingon. Vulcans are *p'taks* without honor."

Things were back to normal around the office—more or less. Marvella was once again at her desk, banging out motion papers on the typewriter while Oliver checked out the latest *Star Trek* sites on the Web. The place smelled of hot curry Marvella had brought in for lunch; I sat sipping the last of my real Jamaican ginger beer as I drafted a motion to suppress physical evidence.

I still had work to do as far as rebuilding my practice was concerned, but I was able to show the committee on character and fitness that the mistakes weren't mine. Liam Gallagher had hacked into my computer and copied my bill forms and letterhead, hoping to distract me from pursuing Keith's case to the full.

Gallagher was under arrest. He'd been sent for psychiatric evaluation; word from Button was that he might not be found competent to stand trial. He'd begun muttering about voices telling him to kill.

I didn't believe it, but that didn't matter. It was someone else's problem, for a change. All I knew was that because he'd been unable to deal with the truth about himself, two people had died.

More than anything, I wished the door would open and Keith would walk in and sit down next to Oliver and start talking Dungeons and Dragons. He'd just begun to have a life, just begun to deal with his many problems, and now his life was over.

I lifted my κασανδρα mug to my lips and swallowed a mouthful of cold coffee to still the trembling of my lip.

CHAPTER
TWENTY-FIVE

"It looks different," I said as I made my way along Kingston Avenue toward the synagogue where Tobah Davidoff was about to marry Mordechai Rosenzweig and his children.

"It's the *succahs*," Sylvia remarked. "Last time you were here, the *succahs* were in place."

I nodded. "That's it. The neighborhood looks kind of barren without them."

It was still bustling with activity; men clustered in groups and talked volubly, while women wheeled strollers and baby carriages, toddlers in tow. But some of the color had gone away with the dismantling of the tabernacles.

This time I was dressed to fit the neighborhood, wearing a long skirt and boots. Since I was unmarried, my head could remain uncovered outside, but Sylvia had a black lace veil for me to wear inside the temple. She'd put a scarlet toque over her own short hair, which gave her a gamine quality in spite of her bulk.

"I haven't seen this many beards since the sixties," I murmured as we passed yet another group of arguing men.

"Zivyah?" One of the men stepped out of the group and came toward my companion. "Zivyah Davidoff, is that you?" He gave Sylvia's name a European pronunciation that made it sound entirely foreign.

"If that's you, Mendel Gluck, then I suppose this is me."

Ordinary people would have embraced, or at least shaken hands. But I'd learned enough by now to understand why Mendel Gluck would not extend his hand to a woman who might be *niddah*—untouchable by reason of having her monthly cycle. I wondered if the ban extended to women who must surely be beyond the age of menopause.

"You've come for Tobaleh's wedding, then?"

"I have. And you'll be there, I suppose."

"Of course," he said. He wasn't a tall man, yet he stood a head above Sylvia. His dark hair was balding in a particularly unlovely way, but his face radiated a kind of open joy you didn't see on many adult faces. He wore glasses which threatened to slide down his nose and his teeth were too big, but there was something about Mendel Gluck I liked very much. And it was clear Sylvia did too.

"Weddings are the delight of the community," he said in the local sing-song accent. "Such *berachot* cannot be found anywhere else but at the *chupah*."

"A wedding is a real *simchah*," Sylvia agreed.

I would have agreed too, but I had no idea what they were talking about, except that it appeared both thought weddings were a good thing. I had a vague memory of attending Jewish weddings that ended in dancing the *hora* at the Tavern on the Green, so I thought the *chupah* might be the canopy, but as to the rest—

What was I doing here? What was a white-bread Protestant from Ohio doing on Kingston Avenue, about to attend a very Orthodox wedding?

Tobah asked me to come.

It might, I supposed, have been her last act of rebellion against the life she'd chosen. Or the life that had chosen her in spite of herself. A tiny moment of individuality, like going to a West Indian fruit market to buy tropical fruit for her *succah* table.

Suddenly I'm a mango?

I had to admit, the idea that I was the exotic one in this community pleased me. I wasn't just an Outsider, I was a representative of the world Tobah had tried out for a brief time, an envoy from Out There, come to witness her choice and find it good.

Sylvia said her good-byes and then murmured, "So old he looks."

Then she gave me a wide smile and added, "But then, I suppose he's saying the same thing to his friends. 'Poor Zivyah, she's not a spring chicken anymore.' Ha."

"You've known him a long time?" I seemed to be falling into the local speech rhythms myself.

"Since I first came here as a girl," Sylvia said. "His family lived below ours in a duplex on Ralph Avenue. His sister Yael was in my class at school. At first," she went on, her voice softening as memory returned, "they didn't have much to do with us."

"Why not?"

"I told you my papa was *ba'al teshuva*. That's like a convert, and some people don't think we're quite as good as everyone else. Remember, I didn't come to live here until I was twelve.

"It must have been a shock," I said.

"I used to say, 'It could be worse. We could be Satmar.'" She laughed. "The Satmar are the ultra-ultra Orthodox."

Her face grew solemn, as if being here and seeing Mendel Gluck brought back a host of memories, both good and bad.

"They took away my stuffed dog," she said, "and made me wear horrible ugly clothes. No jeans, no shorts. Only skirts way below the knee—and all the regular girls were wearing minis in those days."

"Why the dog?"

"The dog is an unclean animal."

"You weren't eating it, you were just—"

She gave a shrug. Don't ask me. That's what the rebbe said, so that's what Papa did. He took away all our stuffed toys and our non-Jewish books and our shorts and pants. My brothers grew *payess*, and Mama put on a *sheitel*. I went from public school to Machan Chana. I didn't mind the school, but I missed things like going to the museum.

"But I've seen Orthodox families in the Botanic Garden, I pointed out. "You mean they don't go into the museum? Because there are nudes on the wall?"

"It's not that so much, it's just that it has nothing to do with Torah. Going to the Botanic Garden is admiring the work of Hashem, so that's all right. But art is man-made and so it's not considered worth looking at."

"So that's why you left? So you could go to the museum?"

"I guess that sums it up as well as anything else. So I could go and see all there was to see and do all the things I dreamed of doing. Believe me," she said, taking my arm as we crossed the street, "I didn't do even half the things I thought I'd do when I left home, but at least I had a choice to do or not to do. That's what I wanted and that's what I got. That and my Lou, who was such a husband—"

Her voice cracked and she finished, "I just hope Tobaleh has one-tenth the happiness with this Mordechai that I had with Lou. How that man could make me laugh!" She gave me a sly wink and added, "In and out of bed, he was the best."

Perhaps it was Sylvia's mention of bed that made me bold enough to ask. I whispered, "Tell me it isn't true about the hole in the sheet. I'd hate to think Tobah had to—"

"You *goyim*," Sylvia replied with a decisive shake of her

head. "I don't know where you get such ideas. No," she explained, not bothering to lower her own voice, "sex is a *mitzvah*, a blessing. A man must be married in order to be a good Jew, and he must please his wife in all possible ways. Don't worry about Tobah; she'll have her husband's best efforts along those lines, and that's more than she ever got from that Keith."

"He's dead."

"I heard." Sylvia heaved a sigh. "Don't ask me to grieve for him, but Hashem grant him forgiveness for what he did."

There seemed nothing more to say. As we approached the huge temple where the wedding would take place, the crowd grew thick. Men in groups, women in groups, families with lots of children, all made their way, loudly and joyously, toward the big doors with Hebrew blessings inscribed over them. The men wore blue and white prayer shawls over their black coats; the women and girls were in what I would have called Sunday best.

We fell in behind and made our way into the synagogue. I followed Sylvia up the stairs in the back. We were going to the *ezrat nashim*, the women's section, so we could be present at the ceremony without becoming a distraction to the men, who sat below in the nave. Sylvia handed me a scrap of black lace and a bobby pin. I put the veil on my head and felt completely exposed, revealed to all as a gentile in spite of my modest skirt. Everyone else had elaborate hats or toques or turbans or scarves shot with gold thread, something expensive and showy, meant to tell the world that they belonged here and that they wore their best to *shul* in order to honor Hashem.

"*Baruch haba-ah,*" the woman next to Sylvia said with a polite nod.

Sylvia whispered, "*Baruch hana'em'tzet.*"

"Are you with the *chatan* or the *kallah*?" The woman wore a very stylish auburn wig and a royal blue beret tipped to the side. It matched her silk blouse.

"The *kallah* is my niece," Sylvia said, and then added in a carefully neutral tone. "I'm her Aunt Zivyah, Mimmi's sister."

A quick indrawn breath said that the blue lady had most definitely heard about Tobah's Aunt Sylvia, the worldly apostate. Her face wore a comical expression made up of equal parts horror and intense curiosity.

"I'm not with either, actually," the woman confided. "Devorah was my sister. I came for the children's sake."

Sylvia impulsively reached out and grasped the woman's hand. *"Baruch Hashem,"* she said in a throaty voice. "Thank God you felt you could come on such a day."

She turned to explain to me what I'd already guessed, that Devorah was Mordechai's first wife, the mother of little Yakov and Miryam and Armin, the woman whose untimely death by ovarian cancer made this wedding possible.

Below us, the pews were filling with men and boys, a sea of black and white, blue and white, with tiny dots of color added by the yarmulkes of the youngest boys. Clarinets and trumpets played a lively tune I would have recognized as Jewish even if I weren't in a temple.

Sylvia nudged me and said, "You should see the beautiful *ketubah* Mordechai had made for her. Such intricate work, such rich colors."

"The *ketubah* is the marriage contract?"

My escort nodded and opened her mouth to explicate, but the music changed into what even I realized was a processional. I craned my neck to see what was happening below, but it wasn't what I expected. Instead of maids of honor wearing pastel dresses, a tall middle-aged man with a black beard stepped slowly down the aisle, flanked by an older couple carrying candles.

"The groom," Sylvia whispered. "And his parents."

As the trio passed, each row of men and boys rose and bowed, as if to a king. When they reached the canopy, attendants placed a plain white robe around him.

"The *kittle*," said Sylvia. "It symbolizes the shroud of death."

"Oh." I would have added something sardonic, but the look on Sylvia's face said that she was reliving many happy weddings of the past and didn't want to be reminded that outlanders might have thought the shroud reference a little odd.

The canopy itself wasn't the decorated, flower-laden ones I'd seen at Reform weddings. This one was a simple prayer shawl, with fringe dangling from the corners, suspended on four poles.

Now came the bride, also flanked by her parents. Again, the congregation rose, row by row, as she passed, giving her the honor due a queen. When Tobah reached the *chupah*, she walked around Mordechai, circling him over and over again.

I turned to Sylvia with a question in my eyes.

"Seven circles," she replied. "This means he will be the center of her life from now on. Then there will be nine blessings. The rabbi will read the *ketubah* and the groom will put the ring on her finger."

"And then they break the glass?"

"And then *he* breaks the glass," she corrected. "In memory of the destruction of the Temple."

It was all in Hebrew. I understood only the opening words of each blessing: *Baruch Atah Adonai*. I also understood that a ring was inspected and placed on Tobah's finger and that a cloth-covered glass was stepped on, and finally the entire congregation called out *Mazel tov* as the *tallis* was removed from the four poles and placed around both Tobah and Mordechai.

I didn't need Sylvia to tell me that this meant they were bound together spiritually and physically for the rest of time. As they walked down the aisle, arm in arm, Tobah's good eye glanced up to embrace the women in the balcony. She smiled at Sylvia, who was by now weeping openly into a huge man's handkerchief.

"Now," Sylvia said, after blowing her nose in a determined manner, "we eat a wedding feast like you've never seen before in your life."

"I followed her down the steps and into the wedding hall next door, which was already jammed with people. We sat at a table near the door, for which I was grateful, since the heat in the room was already overpowering and there were more people streaming in by the minute.

Tobah sat on a bridal chair, her face flushed, a glass of wine in her hand. She wore an ivory-colored dress with a bit of lace at the throat, but no other adornment or jewelry except for the golden wedding band on her left hand. I noted that the ring finger seemed to have suffered less damage than the others from the acid that ravaged her face.

The dinner began with yet another blessing, this one addressed to a large loaf of *challah*. Once that blessing was finished, people were free to eat or to enter the reception line to pay respects to the bride and groom. Several people did both at once, noshing on slices of brisket or potato pancakes as they made their way through the lines.

The *klezmorim* played a loud dance tune. Suddenly, a group of young men lifted Mordechai, chair and all, to shoulder height and began dancing. They were joined at once by almost every male in the room. The fringed prayer shawls swung and bounced, the men lifted arms to heaven and moved in wild, exuberant steps until the music stopped.

But no women joined the dance. When it was over, the men placed the wedding chair back in place. A man with a pure white beard stepped forward, carrying a branch. I recognized him as the new rabbi. The musicians struck up a slower tune, and he danced, alone, waving the branch, before Tobah's chair.

"The rebbe dances before the bride," Sylvia whispered. "With a myrtle branch. He sings about how beautiful she is."

During most of the ceremony, Tobah had been veiled.

Now her face was plain to all. And it was obvious to all, including the rebbe, that she was not beautiful. Not anymore.

I swallowed some of the wine I'd been served by passing waiters.

"He means the beauty of her soul," Sylvia explained.

But was that enough? Would Mordechai continue to see her soul and not regret, one day, his choice of a woman with a face people stared at?

If there was a Hashem looking down on this gathering, I prayed that he would.

When the rebbe was finished, another tune started. Sylvia set her plate on the nearest table and plucked the wine glass from my hand, putting it next to the plate. Other women were doing the same, stepping into the dance floor vacated by the men.

"This one is for us," she said, moving toward a group of women who had begun a slow, evocative dance. Tobah stepped from her throne and grasped the hand of the woman closest to her. We all swayed together, moving back and forth in a sinuous rhythm that built to a climax as it got faster and faster. We were out of breath when it concluded, and when it was over, I felt for the first time as if I actually belonged here.

There were more courses, more songs, more dances, more blessings. The chairs of both Mordechai and Tobah were hoisted into the air several more times. Once, Tobah pulled little Yakov to her and held him on her lap as the men danced with her on their shoulders. The little boy giggled with delight. Miryam took my hand and taught me one of the women's dances.

At one point, Sylvia took my arm and led me toward the wall at the rear of the reception room. "Look at this," she said, pointing to a gaily painted design on parchment, with Hebrew letters inside a Star of David. "This will answer the question I saw in your eyes when the rebbe danced before the bride."

"It's the *ketubah*," I said, proud of my new knowledge, "but since I can't read a word of it, I don't see—"

"Ah, I forgot. The words around the edge, on the outside there, it's a quote from the Song of Songs. It says, 'You are fair, my darling, you are fair, with your dovelike eyes.' "

My eyes filled with tears. Probably the effect of six glasses of wine, I told myself. But it was more than that. Tobah had somehow found the strength to forgive Keith, and the fact that she could and did forgive was what really made Mordechai able to see the light in her dovelike eyes even if one of them was made of glass.

I had some forgiving to do as well. Keith, for one. Especially Keith. I'd judged him harshly in part because I'd wanted so much to believe in his innocence that when he turned into just another partly innocent, partly guilty flawed human being, I'd been outraged.

And if and when I ever finally forgave Keith, I could begin the task of forgiving myself.